"S
KA
PRE

"I don
discovere
can." He
immense
When his
ment rose in her breast. His palm trailed along her silken
thigh and his knuckles felt warm and strong against her
skin. But she shouldn't want his hand there, she told
herself. She shouldn't want the thrill that went down her
spine and made her breath come in short, quick gasps,
and mostly she shouldn't want the feeling that she really
did want it . . . and more.

"No, St. Bride. I'll fight you." She tried to push his
hands away but already the hem of her nightsmock was
almost up to her bottom.

"Go ahead, fight me, Kayleigh," he said, nuzzling
her. "Abandon yourself to fury and soon you'll abandon
yourself to me."

" *My Wicked Enchantress* is impossible to put down
. . . a real page-turner. Powerful, poignant, and beautifully
written."

—Kathe Robin, *Romantic Times*

Also by Meagan McKinney

NO CHOICE BUT SURRENDER

WHEN ANGELS FALL

TILL DAWN TAMES THE NIGHT

LIONS AND LACE

FAIR IS THE ROSE

THE GROUND SHE WALKS UPON

A MAN TO SLAY DRAGONS

GENTLE FROM THE NIGHT

*For who she might have been
For Jo*

With great fondness and appreciation
I would like to thank
my agent, Pamela Gray Ahearn,
and fellow writer, Rexanne C. Becnel,
for their steadfast belief in this book.

Author's Note:

Although Belle Chasse Plantation did at one time exist, mine is a purely mythical Belle Chasse. . . .

PROLOGUE

I'll serve thee in such noble ways
Was never heard before;
I'll crown and deck thee all with bays,
And love thee more and more.

James Graham of Montrose

She was Kayleigh again.

In her dream, she was back at Mhor Castle. It was a year ago, 1745. Culloden had yet to become a battleground, and the Highland winds that swept her dear home still whispered an idyllic peace.

She was laughing.

The rooms that she shared with her twin sister were in the east wing and she was in the dressing room now, watching Morna try on gown after gown.

"No, no, Morna!" She giggled. "That green brocade is too daring! Whatever will Mrs. MacKinnon think? She'll never let us go!" She laughed again and brushed a lock of shiny black hair over her shoulder.

"Kayleigh, I'm sick of having a guardian, so I don't care what Mrs. MacKinnon thinks at all!" Morna looked at her sister in the mirror, a mischievous smile playing at the sweet curves of her lips. Kayleigh watched as Morna brazenly lowered the already low neckline of the green gown.

"Well, that certainly should impress Duncan," Kayleigh said dryly. "But what will he think of a young miss going out for a picnic dressed in a ball gown? Morna, he'll think you're positively daft!"

"Oh, no, he won't. He'll like it well enough, I daresay!"

"And they think I'm wicked!" Kayleigh shook her head and moved to stand beside her twin sister. "Wear the blue satin gown, Morna. It's ever so much more appropriate for a picnic. Besides, Mrs. MacKinnon agreed that I should accompany you this time, and if she finds out you wore that gown, she'll never let you go anywhere again without an army of chaperones."

"Are you sure you're my sister, Kayleigh, and not my mother?" Morna gave her a disapproving look, but still her eyes were alight with suppressed laughter.

"At times, no, I'm not sure at all!" Kayleigh lightly pinched her, then helped unfasten the laces. Soon the emerald gown was tucked back into the armoire.

The harebell blue satin was a much better choice. Morna looked like an angel—something she, Kayleigh, knew she could never hope to do. Though Morna possessed the same indigo eyes, the same arch to her brows, the same upturned nose, and the same lush lips now as red as crushed rose petals, Morna was the one who had been born with the halo of silver blond curls. In contrast, her own hair was as black as a raven's wing. Since she and Morna were children, whenever people were asked to give one of the mischievous twins the benefit of doubt, it was usually the angelic-looking Morna they gave it to, not the black-haired Kayleigh.

"Will you help me pin my hair, sister?" Morna sat at her dressing table and peered into an ancient looking-glass. Behind her, Kayleigh took up the silver brush and ran it through the long silvery blond tresses.

"Kayleigh," Morna said after a moment, "why aren't you wearing a prettier gown? I daresay, that old gray woolen is hardly going to find you any suitors."

"I plan to sketch this afternoon. What would you have me wear instead? My best Spitalfields silk?"

"No, but you could dress up a bit. Duncan may bring one of his brothers today, and if he does, you'll look a shambles!"

"Do I look so wretched, then?"

"No, no! You're the most gorgeous sister I have!" Morna giggled and took the hairbrush from Kayleigh's hand. "But at least let me fix your hair. I'll pin it up like mine. You'll look ever so much more fashionable."

"If it pleases you. But don't be horrified when I come back from sketching and Duncan says I look a fright because all the pins have fallen out!" Kayleigh sat at the dressing table after Morna got up. This time Morna began brushing out Kayleigh's black tresses.

"Have you any more pins?" Morna shook a small jewel-encrusted box from her dressing table. Two pins fell out.

"No. Just put the ribbon back on, Morna. That holds my hair best anyway."

"Give me your box, Kayleigh. You *must* have more pins."

"No. Morna, I haven't any—" Kayleigh abruptly closed her mouth. She watched Morna cross over to Kayleigh's dressing table and open Kayleigh's jewel-encrusted box.

"*Dhé,* Kayleigh! This is filled with charcoal!"

"Yes, I sketch with charcoal." Kayleigh rose from Morna's dressing table, swiftly tying back her glossy dark locks with a blue satin ribbon.

"You're hopeless, you know. Mother had these boxes made to bring us good fortune. And you use yours for carrying charcoal."

"But I treasure it and keep it with me always!"

"I think when Mother gave us our boxes she meant them for a less domestic use." Morna placed both boxes side by side on her dressing table. She stared at them and her hands went to her hips. "Look, there's a huge smudge of charcoal across your portrait." Morna took a handkerchief from the table and rubbed the lid clean.

The cobalt blue enamel boxes with tiny sprays of diamonds and sapphires along the filigreed edges were identical except for the portrait painted on each box's lid. Also, below each girl's name was a phrase that the witch who had sold the boxes to their superstitious Highland mother said applied to each girl.

The phrase *The Beloved* had been inscribed on Morna's box. No one ever superstitiously crossed themselves when Morna was around, for the phrase was simply the English translation of her Gaelic name. Kayleigh's box however, had the phrase *The Bewitched* inscribed on it. And much to her English father's dismay, many a Highland servant had left Mhor Castle after seeing what was written on Kayleigh's little box.

"Come now, Morna. You'll have to forgive my sacrilege—at least for today." Kayleigh placed the charcoal-filled box in a pocket hidden in the folds of her gray gown. "We're already so terribly late, Duncan has probably left Nairn and gone picnicking without us, so much baggage that we are!"

"You're right, but still hopeless, Kayleigh." Morna sat down and finished arranging her hair. "I swear you'll become an old maid, or worse, find yourself with no option other than marrying Cousin Straught."

"Well, never fear the latter. I meant to tell you at breakfast that Cousin Straught is no longer pursuing me." Kayleigh jammed a hairpin into the blond knot at the top of Morna's hair.

"But how so? I thought he'd never give up. He's always seemed so . . . desperate." Morna shivered and handed her sister her last hairpin. "How I wish Father hadn't left him Mhor's hunting lodge! Ever since Mother and Father died, it seems Cousin Straught's been skulking around and running after you. I suppose he wouldn't be terrible as a suitor, for he's certainly handsome, 'tis true. But those unnatural eyes! And so terribly old! Why, the man must be at least five and thirty!"

"Och, and such a contrast to Duncan's youthful twenty-eight!" Kayleigh teased.

Morna rested her head on her hands and stared dreamily into the mirror. "Yes, but Duncan is so . . . he's just so . . ."

"Angry."

"What?"

"I daresay he's angry." Kayleigh tilted her dark head. "Do you recall how late we are?"

"Of course!" Morna tumbled from her dressing stool. She filled her box with ladylike accessories: a small scissors, some thread, her last stray hairpin; then she appeared ready to go.

"Your hem!" she suddenly cried out as if in agony.

"My hem! Has it fallen?" Kayleigh looked down at her skirt for telltale signs. Sure enough, one side was dragging on the stone threshold.

"I shall change as quickly as I can! I promise! I won't hold us up—"

"No, Kayleigh, I'll go ahead. I'll fetch Duncan and meet you back at Forsyth Knoll. We'll picnic there instead."

"You would go alone? What would Mrs. MacKinnon say? She'd likely have us flayed for such impropriety!"

"Mrs. MacKinnon will never find out. She's off visiting her ill sister, and if you don't tell her . . ." Morna's eyes narrowed mischievously.

"I won't tell her, but—"

"I'll see you at Forsyth Knoll, Kayleigh." Morna breezed out of the apartments.

Kayleigh tripped after her. "But Morna, perhaps you should wait!" Her words fell on deaf ears. Morna had turned the corner.

It didn't take Kayleigh long to change, and soon she was atop Forsyth Knoll watching Morna's carriage make its way down Moray Firth Road. She had thoughts of running down the hill and still trying to accompany her sister, but the day was too warm and indolent, so she stayed on the knoll.

All around her the heather bloomed a tender shade of mauve. Fragrant, piney gorse covered the hillside. The air smelled of juniper, sheep's wool, and the sea. Life was delightful.

Letting her skirts billow around her, she sat down on a

soft bed of bracken. She decided to sketch Morna's coach as it moved ever so slowly down the incline. But before she had retrieved her charcoal from her box, she realized something was wrong.

Startled and panicked, Kayleigh remained frozen on the incline as she watched Morna's carriage tumble into the ravine near the loch. Not a minute had passed after that before there suddenly appeared on the road almost a dozen men on horseback. She couldn't fathom why the men were there, nor could she comprehend why they were allowing her sister's cries to go unheeded while they dismounted and searched the wreckage.

Horrified that her sister was hurt and that no one was helping her, Kayleigh ran frantically down the incline. She had to help Morna! Halfway down the knoll, she saw one of the men—unrecognizable in the distance—open the carriage door. Relief swept through her breast that someone was aiding her sister. But before she could take another step, she heard Morna let out a horrible scream.

Kayleigh stumbled to a halt, her whole body numb from shock and disbelief. Soon the man emerged from the carriage, and this time she recognized him: He was her handsome rejected suitor, Cousin Straught. Behind him she could make out her twin's lifeless body rolling forward in the carriage. With inexpressible horror, Kayleigh saw a stain as red as hollyberries spread on the innocent harebell blue of Morna's dress. She couldn't muffle her scream. Only afterward did she realize that she had probably tolled her own death knell.

As soon as they heard her cry, Straught's minions shouted and pointed to her on the knoll. Instinctively she drew back, but not before her gaze met her cousin's.

Never had she imagined that refusing her cousin's hand would provoke such violence and insanity. But there it was, spread out before her. In one short moment her view of the world changed. The path she'd expected her life to take had now come to a brutal, inescapable end.

"Just like the other one, chums. Do it just like you finished the other one," Straught ordered his men." Then bring her to me, and we'll put her next to her sister."

Kayleigh looked down. Already Straught's men were making their way up the knoll toward her. She fled, though tears blurred her vision and her cumbersome skirts tripped her up. She tried to disappear into the woods near the loch, but all around she could hear the men pursuing her. She smothered a sob and kept running, this time down toward the loch, hoping against hope that she would find a kind soul down there who would help her.

But she was caught. Once she was out of the forest, a hobgoblin of a man appeared before her and took her arm in a gnarled grip. Forcefully, he pulled her farther down the incline. As soon as they reached the loch's edge, her cousin's terrible cohort raised a knife. The intent burning in his eye was to drive it right through her heart.

PART ONE

La Nouvelle-Orléans

Fair lady, by your leave.
I come by note, to give and to receive.

The Merchant of Venice (act III, scene ii)

Chapter One

Gasping, she awoke from the nightmare.

Her hands went to her face, and they came back damp. But the streams of tears only relieved her cheeks of some of their grime. Her heart still felt heavy, and her shoulders stiff. And she still felt as if she were suffocating in the heavy, humid air around her.

She lay for a long time in the darkness thinking of Morna. Her ghost seemed to hover about her, and she longed for her sister to appear, to keep her company in the long Louisiana nights and to be a friend in the difficult, lonely life she now led.

But Morna did not appear. And her only comfort was to heave a small sigh of disappointment and do as she had done a thousand times before. She let her mind drift back to a happier life, the one she had lived in Scotland, the one she longed for still. But the night seemed doubly cursed, for even that small comfort was beyond her reach. Try as she might, she couldn't remember the feel of French satin sliding against her skin. Nor could she remember the welcome warmth of a birch fire on a chilly night. Tonight, even the picture of Mhor Castle beneath the lacy flakes of the first snowfall seemed beyond her ability to imagine. She was losing the details.

A year away from home is bound to dull one's memory, she told herself. But then, in despair of ever remembering again, she shut her eyes tightly and forced herself to think of every detail she could recall so that she wouldn't lose even one.

"The Kestrel's been having the dream again." The statement came from the far reaches of darkness in the cottage. The voice called her not Kayleigh, the name of the young Scottish lass in her dreams, but Kestrel, for the small Old World falcon that always held its head against the wind.

"Nay," she denied softly, trying to remember the seals engraved upon the cutlery of Mhor.

"Nay, lassie, ye canna fool me." The voice softly reassured her in the early morning darkness. There was a shuffling sound, then a long bony finger poked her in the ribs. "Ye deny all ye want. But that cursed day at Mhor will na be forgotten!"

"I have forgotten Mhor. Mhor is gone." The words held more truth than she had thought possible. Dejectedly, she sat up.

"Come, lass. Where's that spirit that dared me to kill ye on the knoll that day at Mhor? Dared me so much that I found I couldna do it and we had to run here?"

"Perhaps it's gone, Bardolph. This Louisiana heat has taken it all away." She shook the Spanish moss that made up her bed. "I cannot breathe here! Oh, why are there no cooling breezes!"

"I've no cooling winds, but this morning I've brought ye something else yer heart desires."

As Black Bardolph lit the candle-wood in the window, she saw him peer at her with dark, sunken eyes. Rising from her bed of gray-green moss, she shook her ragged petticoat. A wee black kitten clung sleepily to her skirts, but soon it was pouncing on the palmetto bugs, catching its breakfast.

"So what is your surprise, Bardie? My heavens, you're up early to bring it to me—or have you been out all night?"

She arched one eyebrow and looked at him. Bardolph was certainly a creature of the night. With his gnarled body and long gray hair, darkness was kinder to him than daylight ever would be. He wasn't much to look at, much less to love, but love him she did. He had saved her life, and in the last year he had tried to make life bearable for her.

"Looky this! I found it on a windowsill drying last evening. I woulda brought it sooner, only the old nag who owned it was after me like a hound out of hell!" Bardolph opened a little sack and produced a billowy lavender petticoat. Kestrel walked up to it and took delight in running her fingers over the silk.

"Oh, Bardie, you're bad to the bone," she whispered.

"Aye, but I was thinking of ye. What use would I have for such nonsense? Try it on, lassie! I'll bet ye've forgotten what it's like to wear fine clothes."

"Did the owner treasure it so much then?" Kestrel hesitated.

"She has one of every color, I've heard! Try it on!"

She took the petticoat in her hands. Turning her back on Bardolph, she stepped into the garment and tied it beneath her other raggedy skirts. The silk petticoat felt wonderful, even if it was almost six inches too short.

"You're too kind, sir." In thanks, Kestrel kissed the top of Bardolph's homely forehead.

"Aye, that I am," he agreed quite pleasantly. "Now, get yerself presentable, gel. It's almost dawn."

"And what wily scheme have you thought up?"

Instead of answering her, Bardolph pushed her toward the washbowl.

Her morning's toilet consisted of little more than wiping her face with her dampened hems and combing her hair with her fingers. There were no lilac-scented baths in which to linger, and no ladies' maids to dress her hair. But despite Bardolph's occasional mockery of her efforts, she still did the best she could to make herself presentable. She wouldn't look like a heathen, she told herself, no matter how hard her life had become.

And her life had indeed become hard. She looked up to meet Bardolph's eye, but even his hideous visage couldn't run shivers down her spine like the lingering images of her dream. It was indeed a blessing to come awake after such a nightmare. She began tightening the laces of her bodice in an effort to forget, yet no matter how she tried to push the dream from her memory, she couldn't force it entirely away. Something wretchedly similar to grief stabbed at her heart. She pulled her laces more tightly.

"*Dhé!*" she exclaimed softly in Gaelic, "I broke it!" She looked at the broken lace in her palm, then hastily tied up her bodice as best she could. Because she was so impoverished, her bodice was now fashioned without stays. Months ago she'd sold those long pieces of ivory to pay their keep.

"Now that I've got ye a new petticoat, ye'll be needing some new laces, eh? Mayhap even a whole new bodice?" Bardolph teased.

"And where do you think we'll find the money to buy such things?" Kestrel shook her head.

"The *Bonaventure* is docking today. I've heard tell it's full of wealthy passengers. Even old Thionville's daughter is on it, returning from Paris."

"And you want me to do down there and pick a few pockets."

"Oh, lassie, I would do such evil meself, only ye know how me joints ache! And it's hard to pick a pocket when ye canna keep yer hands from shaking!"

"Aye, it's that rum you drink. It's going to kill you, Bardie."

"I'm fighting the thirst. Truly I am. But it's got me by the throat. If ye just fleeced a passenger or two, we could get along well enough with that. Ye could get a few new things, and I could get me some rum—just enough to keep my hands from shaking, ye understand! What about it, gel? The *Bonaventure* could be quite a haul.''

"This petticoat was a bribe, wasn't it, Bardie?"

"Nay! Nay! Though I coulda sold it . . . but I didna, did I?"

"I know when I'm being bribed." Kestrel crossed her arms over her chest and scolded, "You're rotten to the core, Bardolph Ogilvie. There may not be enough of God's good Grace to save you." She watched him squirm before her, but when one of his trembling hands raked through his hair, her heart flooded with pity. The drink *was* going to kill him, but rum was all the old fool lived for. That was all he had to live for. He had no memories of anything better.

"I'll go, Bardie. If those passengers are as wealthy as you say, I suppose they ought not to miss a purse or two."

"Ah, ye're an angel, love." He clasped his hands together to keep them from shaking. "Ye won't be too long, will ye?" he asked like a child.

"No, I won't be too long." She hiked up her skirts and pulled a knife from one garter. She looked at the *sgian dhu,* the black Scots dagger, that glittered in her hand. It was her finest possession, given to her the year before on the ship from Glasgow. Its previous owner had been a young man who was dying, and he had told her in a not very pretty speech that she might need it in the New World. As he had prophesied, she had learned to use it well. She kept it with her always, tucked inside a garter that was otherwise useless, for she had no hose.

"I've schooled ye well!" Bardolph laughed, showing old, rotting teeth. "Ye're a quick one, Kestrel. I only hope ye never meet one who's quicker."

Kestrel only grinned. "The day the underworld freezes to its core—that will be the time." She replaced the knife in its resting place on her calf. "I'll be going to meet the ship now."

"That's right. Ye bring back some coins! If only Straught

could see us now! We're na dead yet, by God!'' He rubbed his hands in anticipation.

At the mention of the name *Straught,* Kestrel froze. There were not many things that could dampen her courage, but her cousin's name was one of them. He had murdered her twin sister and would have murdered her had Bardolph not behaved like some fairy-tale huntsman, in the end unable to perform his master's wish.

''Aye, I bet he never thought I would live to see nineteen,'' she whispered almost to herself.

Suddenly deflated, she looked around the tiny *poteaux* hovel. The influences of her privileged upbringing seemed to have worn off long ago. But still in her heart she ached to be once again the lady she had been.

''Ye'll get even someday, lass.'' Bardolph seemed to have read her thoughts.

''Not *'we'll'* get even someday'?''

''Nay, I'm just an old rummy from the nether reaches of Edinburgh. I've got no powers to take revenge on yer father's cousin.'' He laughed, then looked glum, the grime-filled lines on his face deepening.

''I'll go back someday, won't I, Bardie? When I turn up again at Mhor, the gallows will be all Erath Straught will have to look forward to.''

''Aye, lassie, that's right! What with the townfolk believing ye're dead and all, they'll know what really happened when ye show up at Mhor. They'll know what killed yer sister was na an accident, it was murder. Then think of the consequences! Aye, just! So remember, lass, ye're a ghost haunting Straught's every pleasure. I'll bet he hasna had a night's rest wondering what became of ye. He just canna be sure that ye're dead, that somehow ye went the way of—''

''Nay! Don't speak the name!'' Kestrel groaned and bit her soft lower lip. A vision of two colors, vivid red and softest blue, pained her at her temples. It was her weakest spot, these memories of Morna.

But grieving for her twin couldn't help her survive. It couldn't put food in her belly, nor could it protect her from the creatures of the night. Only stealing could do that, and no tears, wishes, or dreams could make it otherwise.

Recovering her youthful resilience, she remembered her own plans. Plans for passage back to Scotland. It was difficult to keep her funds hidden from Bardolph's sticky fingers, but she had saved some. If the purses were heavy today, then one more day might be all she needed. She would return to Mhor soon, Kestrel thought, exhilarated with renewed passion. Whatever the risk, it would be worth it.

"The *Bonaventure* awaits!" The Kestrel smiled wickedly as she left the dockside hut, letting her patched skirt sway gracefully about her ankles as if it were the finest Chinese satin.

The walk to the quay was never a pleasant one. Where Kestrel lived on the batture, old rummies even worse off than Bardolph crowded the doorways of the huts. As she walked by, one of them took great relish in bowing to her. When she refused to acknowledge the greeting, the other rummies began to snigger.

"Mademoiselle! How high you hold your head! Much higher than your position, I think!" the drunkard called in broken English. The others who crowded in the threshold began to laugh, but Kestrel walked on.

Soon a harlot walked up to her, jabbering meanly in German. It was obvious that the haggard woman wanted a coin, but Kestrel certainly had none to give her. Put off by Kestrel's ladylike self-containment, the harlot pulled at Kestrel's skirt like a beggar. Finally, pushed to the wall, Kestrel pulled out her *sgian dhu*. Very quickly, she was left alone.

Kestrel knew she was never accepted among the river people. Particularly the whores who worked along the quay didn't like her because of her quiet demeanor and also simply because she was not one of them.

The men who were not made useless by drink were the ones she wanted to stay farthest away from, however. They seemed to hover around Bardolph like relatives at the reading of a will. Kestrel knew they were just waiting for Bardolph to die, for the high and mighty Kestrel to be left completely alone and vulnerable. Hadn't they said as much?

Kestrel frowned as she finally made her way onto the docks. But she soon shrugged off her unpleasant thoughts for the *Bonaventure* anchored before her. Having arrived from Paris sometime during the early morning, the stevedores were just now unloading it. Kestrel looked on, surveying the scene and trying to judge how best to capture her quarry.

A cow lumbered stiffly down the plank, its starved skin swaying underneath its belly with each step. The onlookers at the docks seemed to follow its every painful movement with delighted anticipation. Mouths watered at the sight of the animal. No doubt everyone was reminded of home, whether it had been France, Germany, Scotland, or even the Illinois territory. Beef was rare in New Orleans, and the precious cow would have to be guarded like a martyr preparing for sainthood.

But Kestrel noted there was one onlooker who was not impressed by the sight of the animal. Moving forward from behind the huge hogsheads of Barbados rum, she watched the man. He observed the procession from the half-deck of the ship. There was a vaguely annoyed look on his face as if he weren't used to bringing up the rear of a bovine parade. And he seemed none too pleased by the sight of the muddy colonial township of New Orleans, either, as it spread below him in the kind bath of morning light.

Kestrel covertly watched him. He was a handsome man, she noted, no more than five and thirty years. He was tall and broad shouldered, fairly towering above the Italian shipmates who scuttled along the decks securing ropes as thick as a meaty man's thigh and three times as heavy. But it wasn't just the man's handsomeness that caught her attention. It was something far more seductive. Nestled inside the folds of his foamy white jabot twinkled a sapphire the size of her small, delicate nose.

The gem was unquestionably exquisite and costly. When she saw the jewel glisten in the morning sun, she was drawn to it like a moth to a flame. Given to the right captain, it would pay for her passage to anywhere in the world. Anywhere in the world, she thought, where there were blue lochs, craggy hills, and Gaelic plaidies.

She heaved a great sigh, and mild disgust showed on her beautiful face. The gent seemed as fair braw as a man could be. She would need her knife to get the jewel. And that would entail a hearty risk. She stole another glance at the man and took note of the strength of his jaw and the gleam in his blue—or were they green?—eyes. Perhaps the jewel was not worth the taking after all. The man looked as if he could turn her knife toward her own heart as easily as he could swat at a fly.

But she could get his purse well enough. That task was elementary. A bump to the man's right and a slice with her knife was all it would take to have his coins.

Kestrel anxiously eyed her target. He wouldn't catch her, she reassured herself. "The purse then," she whispered, and crept nearer the gangplank.

The passengers of the *Bonaventure* descended the gangplank one by one. There was a very fat Frenchwoman dressed in cerise satin who, in her descent, grasped at the handles on her hoops as if they were the very tiller of a ship. There was a younger woman alongside her dressed in glorious shades of lime brocade that Kestrel looked upon with envy as green as the gown itself. She longed to reach out a hand, to touch the rich material and remind herself what it felt like. She had been only ten years old when her parents had died of the fever, but still she could dimly recall the way her mother's gowns had swooshed along the stones of the Great Hall and the way her father's heavy satin topcoats had felt around her arms, as unwieldy and secure as armor.

Her attention returned to the quay when the young French-woman began to speak, somewhat nervously, to the gent with the sapphire, who was descending the gangplank with her.

"St. Bride, you will visit *maman* and me? We shall be so lonely in this faraway place without your company. We are used to Paris with all its splendor, and this primitive town will be so hard to endure." The young Frenchwoman pouted as her delicate slipper-clad feet touched the weathered dock.

"But Lady Catherine," the man named St. Bride replied, "your *maman* would soon have you married to a comte. What pleasure could you find in my company? I'm afraid you may find me as coarse and heathen as this very township." He smiled, and Kestrel finally saw that his eyes were actually a perfect turquoise, shining from his handsome face far more brilliantly than the blue stone pinned to his shirt. They were also very much like the sea, as changeable as the oceans were with the weather, ready to destroy or caress merely upon whim. Unwillingly, Kestrel shivered.

"But St. Bride"—the Frenchwoman's lashes swept her powdered cheeks—"your company is preferable to that of any other man."

"You must not plead so, Catherine," Kestrel heard the woman's mother say harshly. "To catch a man, one must be coy! Come along now!" The comtesse broke from the crowd. She then allowed herself to be hefted into a gilt carriage that was waiting for them at the docks. "Your father awaits" was her final command before she settled herself against the brocaded cushions of the interior.

A motley crowd of ragged townspeople, doxies, and sailors formed near the carriage. Kestrel knew it was not just the pretentious display of wealth that had the crowd gawking at the vehicle's foreign splendor. Awe and fear also attracted them to it. The coach was easily recognized as Thionville's, and she was suddenly very glad to have paused. Jean-Claude de Thionville, Comte de Cassell, was not a man she wanted to answer to. Nay, she thought to herself in bitter amusement, not when he controlled all the thieving around New Orleans. With all his riches and the blessing of his king, the comte had the town by the throat. The only difference between him and the likes of Bardolph was the quality of his clothes. No, she was sure the comte would not appreciate her competition.

"I must go, St. Bride. You will call? I'll look forward to nothing with greater anticipation than a visit from you." When Lady Catherine again spoke, Kestrel now realized she was the daughter of the powerful and infamous comte. Her lips curled in disdain, Kestrel watched as St. Bride bent over Lady Catherine's hand and brushed it with his lips.

"That remains to be seen, my lady. But let's not rule out the possibility." St. Bride smiled wolfishly. A cynicism appeared in his eyes and Kestrel knew instinctively that he was not a man to be trusted.

When the farewells were completed, Lady Catherine and her comtesse mother were finally hustled away with all the pomp and circumstance of a king's coronation.

In the ensuing pause, Kestrel looked to her target. The crowd had thinned in the wake of the carriage. St. Bride now stood with a few male passengers from the ship. All the men except for St. Bride had their backs to her. As he faced her, Kestrel noticed the hard expression on his face. Although she was reluctant to admit it, it almost made her take a step backward. Shaking off her fear, she crept forward once more, this time taking note of his queued hair, which was touched with premature silver along his temples. Instead of softening the man's face, the touches of silver served only to accentuate his lean, predatory features. Again, she was tempted to turn back.

Normally she was fearless. After all, she'd been lifting purses for almost a year now, and she was known as the Kestrel. It was easy for her to go against the wind. She had nothing to lose. But this time, as she paused to build up her courage, she was worried. This man St. Bride did not look easy. Worse, he did not look nice.

With hesitation she barely understood, Kestrel took the first step toward the gent.

She waited for a moment when St. Bride's head was slightly turned away, and then she acted. Darting up quickly, her dagger in hand, Kestrel lifted the man's expensive woolen jacket and slit the leather thong holding his pouch full of gold. She felt the heavy purse fall into her palm, and in a second she was on her way. Without the sapphire, of course. She had summed the man up and decided not to be so foolish as to take a knife to his throat, jewel or no.

"Why you little beggar, you've cut my purse!" Suddenly a large, firm hand caught the nape of her neck. As she scratched and swatted like a frightened kitten, she felt the warmth of the man's hand on her skin, and that shocked her more than his iron grasp. Panicked and scared, she suddenly went limp. As an animal plays dead, she thought to fool her captor into letting down his guard so she could free herself.

"Nay, the purse fell. 'Twas I returning it to you." Kestrel remained limp. She looked up at the large man who towered above her, her sapphire eyes filling with anxiety. If anything, the man St. Bride looked amused, but—unfortunately—not forgiving.

"Returning it, were you? And all the while running in the opposite direction." St. Bride grabbed the purse from her delicate hand and placed it in the waist of his breeches. Still holding her by the nape, he turned to one of his companions, a short, ordinary-looking man, and exclaimed, "I say, what is this hellish place we've been brought to? What is there to invest in? Beggars and thieves?"

But Kestrel did not take heed of his words. At her eye level sparkled the freedom that she desired. She looked squarely at St. Bride's huge, powerful chest. Scotland bore its rampant lion before her in the form of a great jewel as blue as her homeland's skies. It was too much for her to resist. As soon as St. Bride's attention was away from her, she took her dagger, still in her palm, and wrenched violently at the neck-cloth. In his surprise, St. Bride dropped his hold on her, and she was able to break free.

But once again she had misjudged her quarry. It took him only two strides to cover the distance between them, a distance that had seemed twenty paces for her. As she neared the hogsheads, he ended her escape, pulling her up by the waist. But both of them misjudged the slippery Louisiana soil. It wasn't long before they were sitting in the swampy mud below the banquettes.

St. Bride started to laugh as he appraised his mud-soaked boots and breeches. Kestrel wasn't sure that was a good sign, though. His laughter sounded angry, not mirthful. She didn't know if he was going to let her go or break her neck. He extracted the gem from her palm and deposited it in the pocket of his breeches.

"Reach for the sapphire now, wench. In fact, this time I dare you." His eyes met hers, and there was a certain gleam of anticipation in his that unnerved her more than she would have admitted. This time she struggled even harder to free herself, but as she squirmed, he captured her tiny waist and pulled her down upon him. Then he smiled a wicked and handsome smile.

"Nay, let me go!" she cried, pushing at his chest. With that route of escape closed to her, she appealed to the man's better nature—that is, if the man had a better nature, and of this, she was not at all sure. "I'm only a poor, wee lass who's looking for a bit o' coin. Would you but take pity on a *bairn,* I know the Lord in his goodness will favor you the rest of your revered life."

She looked at him, hoping against hope that he wouldn't take her to the jail near the cemetery. She had never been inside it, but Bardolph had. He'd said it was worse than the docks. Vermin crawled upon the walls, and the dead moaned restlessly in their coffins, which were held down under the wet soil only by means of ballasts. She shuddered.

"Bairn?" He mimicked her Gaelic, then pulled one side of her shift down past her shoulder and exposed the soft, full flesh of her upper breast. "On the contrary, you're no child. And somehow"—he grabbed her chin and made her look directly at him—"somehow you appear a bit too refined to be in the business you're in. Why is that, guttersnipe?"

"Let me go," she pleaded, ignoring his strangely perspicacious comment. "Please," she finally uttered. With that, her thick, sooty lashes raised toward him, and her eyes, blue and dark, conveyed unmistakably her desire to be free.

"Since when do cutpurses know the word *please?"* he asked quietly. There was a long moment of silence while he studied her. Her face colored beneath the man's appraisal, for his eyes seemed to miss nothing; not the fine texture of her skin, nor the soft curves of her figure, nor the scars that ran along her ankles—testimony of the life she led.

Then she knew she had persuaded him. He was a busy man who reeked of power. He wouldn't waste his time taking a thief to the magistrate. But before she was out of his grasp, a voice sounded behind them.

"Ferringer, have Malcolm take the chit to the jailhouse. She's a little cutpurse, and she's ruined your clothes to boot." A smaller man whose back was all Kestrel had viewed before raised his foot to kick her. Unable to see more of him than his expensive silver-buckled shoes, she slid neatly out of his way—but not out of St. Bride's grasp.

"A cutpurse she is, but still of the weaker sex!" St. Bride raised himself, his eyes flashing angrily at the gent who had tried to kick her.

"No harm intended, Ferringer. But we've got to punish the criminals. This place is not even as civilized as Savannah." As the smaller man spoke, Kestrel was able to look at his face. Her eyes widened, and she stared at the man in morbid fascination. She was used to angry victims, but this man fairly stopped her heart from beating.

He was short, and yet he possessed a pleasingly masculine stockiness. His facial features beneath the sandy, queued hair were as disarming as they were distinctive. His lips were thin and perhaps a bit cruel. But a ruddy aristocratic nose, almost too long, pleasantly bridged his face, and his nostrils flared back dramatically. The man's eyes were as gray and familiar as the North Atlantic seacoast.

Kestrel looked closer at the man's eyes. They were not all gray—she remembered—for inside one of the irises was the tiniest bit of red, like the mark of Satan.

Her mouth opened, and a chill swept down her spine like the cold fingers of death. It was Straught. She prayed there was no recognition of herself in the man's eyes. And why indeed would he recognize her? After all, she was no longer the pampered heiress of a Scottish estate; she was now hardly better than a beggar. No, Straught wouldn't recognize her.

To him, Kayleigh had mysteriously disappeared. He did not know that she had been taken away by Black Bardolph Ogilvie, one of his own gillies, as she called Straught's henchmen. Straught hadn't known that Bardolph's joints ached and that Bardolph had feared he would soon be useless to his master and that he would be disposed of. Straught hadn't known that Bardolph had needed another to move around for him—to steal for his rum and to help him survive in the New World.

No, this man did not know where Kayleigh had gone. Perhaps he even thought her dead.

Kestrel knew she didn't want to die a second time. Slowly she began to back away from Straught, despite the constraint of the larger man who held her.

"Let me go," she said, hiding her fear in the softness of her voice.

"In good time." St. Bride looked down at her, his eyes warming to the strange, beautiful creature in his hold.

"Let me go!" she cried out in panic. She could almost reach her dagger, which had been flung aside in the mud.

"If you're a good wench, I'll give you a coin for your troubles. But in the meantime, quit your struggling!" St. Bride demanded irritably.

She refused. The gray-red eyes of the devil named Erath Straught were upon her, and she could almost see the Angel of Death creeping closer by the second. By God, he did recognize her!

"I say, let me go!" she cried out, and writhed in the man's grasp. Her hand finally felt the hilt of the *sgian dhu*. St. Bride, unaware of her action, took the razor edge of the dagger in the web of flesh between his thumb and forefinger.

"You little bitch!" he snapped ferociously as his blood gushed onto her petticoat. In his pain he dropped his hold on her, and she wasted no time. She was gone in a flash, leaving him with only the memory of slim, mud-spattered ankles and a pair of midnight eyes that had swept over him like blue velvet.

Chapter Two

"It was Straught, to be sure," Kestrel stated, still breathless from her escape at the docks.

"But how can it be? How did he find us?" Bardolph took a deep gulp from his bottle. He'd hardly been able to still his shaking fingers long enough to remove the wax cork. "I tell ye, it's those eyes. Make ye believe of the devil, they do. If ye saw them, then the gent had to be Straught."

"I saw his eyes," she answered quietly. "So many things I've forgotten, but I cannot forget *them.*"

"Without a damned purse, we canna get away!" Bardolph cursed. "That Brit with the jewel—his soul be cast to Satan for the company he keeps!"

"I'll get a purse. There's other game to be had." Kestrel looked down at her bloodstained petticoat Absentmindedly she said, "Let me wash off the blood . . ."

"Kestrel." Bardolph grabbed her arm. "It's all up to ye. I saved yer life once, but I havna got it in me to do it again." She saw that Bardolph was as frightened as she herself was. He trembled before her. The old drunkard had probably pre-formed only one good deed in his entire life, but he would pay for that kindness dearly if Straught ever found them.

"I'll do it this time, Bardie. I'll be the one to save us.

Somehow I'll find a purse. We'll be gone from here, I promise.'' Nervously she poured water from a bucket onto the rag that was her petticoat. When the blood was yet another unremarkable stain on the fabric, she wrung out the water and left the hut.

The day was long and arduous. To make matters worse, Kestrel could not go back to the docks. After her struggle with St. Bride, everyone there would surely be looking for the bloodthirsty wench who'd sliced his hand. So she settled on the barracks and beyond, hoping that a stray militiaman would be off his guard long enough for her to lift a gold watch or medal.

But she had had no such luck this day. She despised the barracks, for they were worse than the docks. The men in their three-cornered hats and long-skirted blue jackets yelled obscenities to her from their posts. They gestured with their bayonets until she felt sick.

And there were always new French militia there, too. Those young men didn't know about the enchanting gypsy girl, the *caird* lass who lived beyond the quay. They naïvely tried to grab at her until she fair wanted to slit their throats. Only after they learned she meant business with her shining ebony knife did they leave her alone.

Now with her pockets bare and darkness descending on the barracks, she knew she would have to give up. Militiamen weren't to be tangled with at night. Evening settled early beneath the long colombage barracks. At dusk, the crumbling barracks surrounded the square like a sentry of skeletons. The Louisiana humidity had taken its toll on the grand Louis XV briquété entre poteaux, brick between posts construction. Already candlelight shone between the exposed, crumbling walls of the buildings. Though it was a sultry evening, Kestrel shivered. She was suddenly aware how alone she was.

''*Jeune fille! Jeune fille!*''

Kestrel spun around. Though she was sure her cousin

Straught did not know a word of French, she suddenly was beset by the fear that it was he calling her. She almost wanted to laugh with relief when she saw the drunken militia calling to her from a window of the barracks. His comrades cheered him on, but their prey quickly disappeared as she scurried to the end of their building.

"I hope the roof falls upon their very heads!" she cursed to herself, eyeing with satisfaction a particularly rotten, bug-eaten post. Though her ill will and hexing thoughts gave her some comfort, they were no protection in the dark. *Sgian dhu* or no, she had to return to Bardolph. In New Orleans, no one liked a thief, not when everything in town had to be imported from France at an exorbitant price. She only hoped that tomorrow would not be so poor.

Avoiding the docks, she crossed over the quay and then paused, looking down upon the many huts that stood near the Mississippi River. Their walls were made of posts driven deep into the sandy ground and the roofs were less than thatch, fashioned of dried palmetto leaves. Smoke rose from the center of most as the occupants made their meals over miserable little fires like so many Choctaw Indians.

It was a tenuous life they led by the river, she thought as she watched the twinkle and dance of light between the wall posts of the huts. Their homes lasted only so long as the wood that was pounded into the sopping soil, which was a short while indeed. When the river began to flood, they would be forced to move to higher ground and then rebuild. It was a constant process of rebuilding and loss. And in such contrast to the small stone sheiling huts that were scattered through the glens of Scotland. To her, those seemed to have been standing from the dawn of time. They seemed indestructible, much like the Highlands themselves.

Kestrel's mouth pulled at a smile as she remembered one sheiling hut in particular. The Robertsons who lived in the shadow of Mhor Castle had been sheep herders for the old laird. Their three boys had run about clothed only in red plaidles until the snows drove them indoors. When winter was closing upon them, she and Morna had always trekked to their hut to give the boys shoes to wear on their tough, bare feet.

Looking at the small huts below her now, Kestrel wondered about the Robertson boys. She had heard of the last great battle fought in Scotland. She knew it had been near Inverness and the stories had told of a greatly changed nation.

But it could not have changed, she doggedly reassured herself, her black brows knitting in a frown. In the Highlands there was no great, creeping river that greedily swallowed all that men held dear. There was no stench of death and decay to be found in so northern a climate. She took a deep breath of the heavy air around her. Scotland had not changed, she told herself again. She would return one day to make sure it had not. And when she did, she would find it as steadfast and noble still as the sheiling huts made of Gaelic stone and Highland history.

Avoiding the docks, Kestrel hurried down the quay, not even trying to sidestep the crayfish mounds in her path. She slowed her pace as she made her way through the maze of huts to her own.

She had to get away from Straught. They would have to run. But for that, she would need a purse. Vehemently, she cursed the man named St. Bride. She cursed his quickness. She remembered the wonderful weight of his purse when she had so briefly held it in her hands. All their troubles would be over now, she thought, if not for that Brit. She and Bardolph would be leaving this damp netherworld forever.

"I've had no luck at all," she said to Bardolph as she entered the hut. It was too dark to see him. When he made no reply. Kestrel continued to speak, assuming he had gotten too drunk even to light a pine knot. "But tomorrow will be different. I'll get a purse then. At least Straught has no idea where we are."

She felt soft fur rub around her ankles in greeting. "Mo

Chridhe, och, it's hungry you are to be sure!'' She picked up her black kitten and nuzzled her to her nose. Fumbling in the shadows, she found the crude table where the pine knots were kept and sought a flint to light one. When the odors of pitch and turpentine pervaded the hut, she turned to her pet in her arms once again.

''Have we no fish for your supper?'' For the moment she ignored Bardolph, who was lying passed out on the floor, to find the dried pompano she kept in an earthenware jar for the kitten. But then a gurgling noise made her stop and focus her large blue eyes on the corner.

''Kestrel,'' Bardolph murmured. Watching in horror, Kestrel saw a rip in his gut that seemed to run from side to side.

''My God, my God! What happened?'' Her palm went to her mouth, and she ran to his side.

''Kestrel, 'twas Straught.''

''No, it isn't true. He doesn't know where we live,'' she whispered. Her mind went numb at the sight of so much blood. She hugged Chridhe to her chest until the kitten mewed to be free.

''He found out . . . he found out. Kestrel . . . perhaps some water. Be a good lass.'' Bardolph spoke in the lowest of tones.

Her free hand shook so, she could barely lift the ladle to the bucket. Still clinging desperately to Chridhe, she brought it over to Bardolph and helped him sip the water. Immediately she heard the gurgling sound once more. It was only too apparent to both of them that he was almost dead.

''Do na let them bury me here. I'll na be moaning for all eternity to be at peace in the ground. Promise me, Kestrel.'' He reached out his hand in supplication.

''Bardolph, don't move. You're . . . too hurt,'' she stated dumbly, her voice trembling.

''I saved ye, lass. Do na forget that. When ye had no hope in this world, I gave ye some.'' He pulled at her petticoats and whispered to her; the effort took his last breaths. ''Perhaps ye can be the end of him, eh? Perhaps ye'll be the one to do it . . . Kayleigh.'' Still clutching at her, Bardolph closed his eyes and prepared to meet his maker.

"Bardolph!" She shook his still form. "Don't abandon me! You cannot die!" In shock, she clutched his limp hand to her chest. Chridhe mewed to be let go, but she couldn't release her precious kitten, not now when Chridhe was all she had left in the world. Tears ran down her cheeks. She wanted to throw herself on his deathbed and find solace in her grief, but her mind would not let her.

Eventually she calmed herself and faced her terrifying situation. They had been fools to believe that Straught, with his cold, unemotional eyes, hadn't recognized her on the docks today. He had come for them, and now he had found them. The township had been too small to hide in.

She rubbed her tearstained cheeks and sat back on her slim haunches. Chridhe's silken fur on her palm was some comfort, but she couldn't control the whirlwind of her thoughts. "What to do now?" she whispered, her heart pounding with panic. "What to do now?"

"Hush, Kayleigh. Do not be moving." A man's voice— familiar, schooled, and precise—whispered behind her. Its coaxing quality made the baby-fine hairs stand up on her neck. Because of her overwrought state, the man had been able to steal into her hut. Now a warm, smooth palm went around her neck. "Throw out the knife, Kayleigh, and I'll let you turn around."

Closing her frightened eyes, she placed the voice instantly. Then her instincts rushed into play. Her hand flew to her garter and reached for her knife. But her reaction time was dulled by the shock of Bardolph's death—and she hadn't counted on yet another pair of male hands to contend with. From behind the first man, a huge brute came up in front of her. Overpowered, she lost the *sgian dhu* as it was forced into her bed of Spanish moss. Breathing hard, the brute pinned her to his chest by her shoulders. He then allowed her to turn around and face her more refined assailant.

It was Straught, of course. Those eyes stared at her coldly. She released a shudder.

"You're here to kill me then, my sweet cousin Erath?" she murmured. She tossed her head. "You and your band of cutthroats! How I remember those strangers swarming around Mhor that last day! You coward! Using an army against two young girls!"

"But I did need an army, for still you got away."

"And I'll get away again!" she cried out.

"Ah, but this time you've been so easy to capture! My apologies for taking so long to find you. But had I known you'd be waiting for me at the docks, I wouldn't have let all my business at Mhor and in London delay me." Straught ran a warm finger down her fragile throat, then stepped back to wipe his soiled digit on a hankie.

She shrank from his touch, although the brute's chest was far from being a safe haven. Chridhe didn't like the circumstances any better than she. Still in her arms, the kitten hissed protectively.

"What can I do for you, Kayleigh? Or is it Kestrel now? That's what the little whores on the quay called you when I gave them your description and a bit of gold." He laughed. "They don't like you much! But how appropriately they've named you! Especially after all we've been through. If you hadn't been so headstrong, perhaps you and I—and Morna— would all be living quite happily at Mhor right now."

Kayleigh forced her eyes from him. She couldn't think of Morna now. She couldn't! But still, guilt began to chisel away at her insides. Och, how she wished she could go back in time. How differently she would do things!

Straught watched her reaction. He then became thoughtful and scratched his sandy head. "I must say, in spite of all that has happened, I do feel some familial obligation to help you out. I mean, after all, there was a time when I was going to make you . . . my wife.'' His voice trailed off and he stared at her, making every nerve in her body dance, as if on a tightrope.

"If I had known—" she began, but he cut her off.

"What? If you'd known I would have you and your sister murdered, you would have married me? Ha! How noble of you, Kayleigh! You must be terribly upset that I didn't explain things to you beforehand. Everything would be so different now!''

"Yes, everything would be!" she cried. "Because I underestimated you, I now have the blood of my sister on my hands. I could have saved her if I had known what you were going to do!''

Straught's next words were soft and caressing. ''No, you couldn't have, love. If you'd known what I was going to do, you would have done what I'd expect from you: you would have spit in my eye, then have me thrown in the gaol.'' He smiled grimly and added, ''But things can change. How do you feel about your cousin now, lass?'' He stepped forward, and instinctively she stepped back.

"I thought so," he replied dryly. Then he turned angry and grabbed her chin so that she would have to look at him. ''I say, beneath all that mud and stench, can you still afford to be so high and mighty?''

She didn't answer. Fear seemed to have lodged in her throat and taken grasp of all its functions.

"I could take you back to the Highlands with me, Kayleigh. Would you like that?'' Straught released her chin, then paced, toying with the frogs of his elaborate gold-embroidered jacket. His rich appearance contrasted sharply with the rough-hewn *poteaux* behind him. He turned to face her, and his eyes met hers. She was terrified.

Smiling, he continued, ''But of course, I'd have to cut out your tongue so you couldn't speak of those matters best left unsaid. However, you could return to your homeplace. It wouldn't be so bad. There'd be no tongues wagging about

Mhor Castle. Think how lovely that would be! No one would ever call you a fishwife then, eh, Kayleigh?''

Again, she said nothing. Chridhe swatted at a lock of hair against her breast. Oblivious to the human suffering going on about her, the kitten tried to show her mistress that she was hungry for her dinner. Suddenly, Straught found the situation amusing.

''Cat got your tongue, love?'' he said, and started to laugh, his teeth gleaming polished and white. When he calmed down, he continued, ''Ah well, perhaps cutting out your tongue wouldn't work so well after all. I remember that as a child you could write. We'd have to cut off your hands too.'' Violently he grabbed her muddied palm, and she jumped back at the touch into the chest of the brute holding her arms.

''Leave me alone! Leave me alone, I say!'' she cried out to him, hating herself for the fear and weakness in her voice.

''Reconsider, Kayleigh. I'll give you one more chance. I don't want to have to kill you. What a sin it would be to murder a creature as bewitching as yourself.'' Straught stepped forward, and she cringed back once more. Calmly he said, ''Love, why don't you think of your father? He would have wanted this. I'm his cousin, after all. He admired me, and he would have wanted me to take care of you rather than have you out in the world fending for yourself.''

''How can you lie like that! My father pitied you, Erath. You were the poor relation! He pitied your constant lack of funds and your poor choice of friends! That's why he left you Mhor's hunting lodge—to take care of you! But he never should have given you anything whatever, for look what it got him—the ultimate betrayal! He was your blood and kin, and you murdered his daughter! You filthy beast!'' She was glad to finally feel anger again rise in her breast. She stepped forward, but the brute who was still holding her arms pulled her violently back into his chest.

''You little whore, I am and always have been the rightful

heir to Mhor, not Morna's lad, hot to let his britches down for that silly girl!''

''Morna's betrothed was a good man. He would have made her happy . . . he would have made any girl happy,'' she defended Duncan.

''But I would have made *you* happy!'' Straught fought to control his anger. He studied her for a long moment. ''Morna was too easy, I'm afraid. I suppose when I came to the end of my rope and concocted this plan, I knew who would give me trouble. Wee, dark Kayleigh. Somehow when I saw you that last time, running up that knoll with your skirts tripping you up and your hair blowing wildly in the wind, I knew we'd meet again.''

A long silence passed before she asked the question she had wondered about for an entire year. ''The people of Mhor—what do they think happened to me? You didn't have my body to dump near the carriage. You had only one.'' Her lip trembled.

''When you and Bardolph disappeared, we claimed that your body had been flung into the loch after the accident. They've still not given up waiting for you to wash up on some bonny shore. I suppose they're as superstitious as I am.''

''And what have you to be superstitious about? You've gotten everything you've wanted. Not even the threat of hell plays a part in your schemes!''

''I've not gotten everything I've wanted. I've not gotten you. And seeing you now, Kayleigh, makes me know that my enchantment was not in my imagination.'' He attempted to stroke her cheek, but she quickly lashed out at his hand.

''You'll never have me,'' she whispered.

''I know that,'' he answered sadly. ''I think I always have.'' His eyes swept over the miserable interior of the hut. ''But if I can't have you, then no one shall. And because the task must be done, I shall personally see to it that it is done.'' Straught reached down to her moss bed and took her dagger into his hand. Slowly, he stropped it on the thighs of his rich amber-satin breeches. He stepped toward her.

"You're a captivator, love. You always have been, you always will be. From the day you were born and I first held Kerr's precious Kayleigh in my arms, you've fascinated me, you've bewitched me. You were always the one thing beyond my reach, and even now, with all the dirt and grime upon you, what I wouldn't give to finally bed you. But"—he paused and looked at the edge of the knife, allowing his lace cuffs to fall provocatively along his hands—"I don't bed cadavers. And as I see it, love, your death is long past due." He smiled again, yet this time it was sad—sad and final.

Her fear lent her a certain detachment, and she noticed how nice his smile was. But it just didn't reach his eyes, she thought. No emotion touched those eyes. Nothing probably could—except possibly death.

"Please!" she cried as Straught tossed the *sgian dhu* to the brute, who held her with one meaty arm across her shoulders. As Chridhe spat in indignation, Kestrel was turned around. The man who faced her was barrel-chested and dark. He smiled thickly. The knife's short blade glinted in the meager light. It came closer and closer until it almost sliced her throat.

When the brute stopped short, the surprise on his face mirrored hers exactly. She then watched as he dumbly stared down at the floor. She followed the direction of his eyes.

At their feet, Bardolph had reached out an arm. He clutched at the brute's ankle, tripping him up. Somehow, Bardolph had gathered what life was still in him to save her once again.

"But Bardie was dead!" the brute suddenly gasped aloud. Completely unnerved, he took a step backward.

Kestrel herself could hardly believe what Bardolph had done, but she wasted no time pondering it. The deadly blade wavered in the brute's grasp, and she gave a violent thrust to ward it off. That was all that was necessary to topple the man. He landed on his backside; then he let out a groan. Her knife had accidentally lodge in the burly creature's own gut.

"Erath . . . I'm hurt!" the big man gasped in pain. The cut was deep, but it was on the side of his great stomach. Kestrel was sure it had pierced more fat than flesh.

"Shut up, Malcolm. You blithering idiot!" Straught quickly reached for the knife, but Kestrel was quicker. Malcolm screamed in pain as she wrenched it back into her possession, but she closed her ears to the awful sound. Before Straught could touch the bloodstained handle, she had her *sgian dhu* back in her hand.

"Run, Kestrel . . . run . . ." At her feet Bardolph gasped his last breath, urging her away. But she couldn't leave him, not when there was a chance he still might live. Spent from saving her, Bardolph released a sharp wheeze from his lungs. A wet, gurgling noise suddenly silenced in his chest, and his eyes stared sightlessly at the palmetto-thatched ceiling. Then she knew Black Bardolph Ogilvie was truly dead.

She turned to Straught, gripping the warm, sticky dagger in her hand. He was stalking her in the hut. She edged to the doorway; then by instinct she bolted from the hut. Holding Chridhe close, she ran out into the night.

It's of no use, she said to herself when she heard footsteps in the mud behind her. Running harder and harder still, her bare feet put little distance between the fine-leather-clad ones that pursued her. Yet she had one advantage that he did not: She was no foreigner to the town.

So she ran past the quay and over the ditches along the Rue de Bienville. Prostitutes cursed her for splashing mud on their indigo petticoats, and trappers laughed, trying playfully to catch her. But she would not be caught. Soon she saw fewer pedestrians, and she knew she was nearing the edge of town. In the distance she saw the windmill that ground their flour, turning slowly against a full moon.

When she crossed the last muddy street at the end of town, she ran even farther west, toward the incomplete moat that the slaves had dug. It had been a futile attempt to prevent attack from outsiders, be they Indians or the English. Now the long ditch of green water was the only obstacle between her and freedom.

If I can hide in the swamps beyond, she thought, he'll never find me. Cringing at the cold, slimy water, she was positive that the moat smelled worse than Bayou St. John in the summertime. But enter it she did, for she could still hear running doggedly behind her the well-shod feet of her cousin, Erath Straught.

"You have nowhere to go, Kayleigh!" Straught stopped on the bank. As she guessed, he did not attempt to enter the water and ruin his clothes. Instead he merely called out to her, "You'll have to come back to town or die in the swamps, love! You can't survive out there! No man ever has, I'm told! And if you come back, I'll get you! I'll have my friend Thionville, the Comte de Cassell, post a sign that says you killed old Bardie! The authorities will find you for me! Thionville will see you hung as a murderess! I'll get you in the end!" He gave an ironic laugh. "Remember that, my beautiful Kestrel! Come or go! Either way, I win!"

Damning his soul to hell, Kestrel reached the other slimy bank. She crawled out of the moat, and clinging to Chridhe, she ran, triumphant, toward the blackness of the swamps beyond.

Chapter Three

The house was ablaze with many candles. Built in the modern style of Louis XV, it was a bit more provincial than those great homes of the Loire Valley; but for New Orleans it was a grand palace, comparable only to the Ursuline Convent in size and style. Undoubtedly de Pauger, the designer, would have been proud of the home. It had stood for almost thirty years with only the addition of cement plaster to the exterior to keep the house from rotting away.

But tonight there were no disgruntled Alsatian contractors maintaining the facade, nor were there architects studying the building in the hope of learning the secret of its longevity. Instead, there was a party going on in its interior, and from it a thousand candles released a warm glow to the outside.

"Where do you hail from, St. Bride? Catherine tells me you boarded the ship in London, along with Erath." The Comte de Cassell raised his champagne glass to his lips as he surveyed the gathering.

"Yes, I was in London selling cotton from my plantation. But my home is in Georgia. The Sea Islands, to be exact," St. Bride replied, looking about the room as if he were searching for someone.

"But come now, man, you hardly look like a . . . peasant.

Surely you're from a place more civilized than that?" The comte appraised the cut of St. Bride's steel gray-satin coat. Its London tailoring was evident in the snug fit and superb overembroidery of silver threads. The coat and the candlelight made St. Bride's eyes a stormy blue and highlighted the silver brush of hair along his temples. Yet instead of looking formal and stiff as any other man would in the expensive coat, St. Bride appeared comfortable as well as inexplicably fierce. His sheer size commanded respect. His uncommon height made every other man in the room stand self-consciously erect, but still St. Bride towered over them all. Only the sly comte seemed to find St. Bride's intelligence more threatening than his physical stature.

Noticing the comte's interest in his wardrobe, St. Bride commented, "Sea Island cotton brings a good price in England . . . *my lord.*" He put sardonic emphasis on the comte's title, then released a slow, indolent smile, one that made the shorter man visibly anxious.

"Do continue! I like to hear about our visitors." Under St. Bride's piercing gaze, the comte squeezed a Lyons lace hankie from his fat wrist and solemnly wiped his brow. "Have you always lived in Georgia?"

"Yes. Always."

The comte raised an eyebrow. "Surely a man with your bearing—"

"Savannah is a beautiful town. I see no reason to leave it."

"But you have come here." The comte's statement hung in the air like a question.

"I plan to be an absentee planation owner after I clear up my business here. Georgia will remain my home." Abruptly changing the subject, St. Bride asked, "Have you seen Erath? He informed me that he'd be here, but I've yet to see him."

"You and he hooked up on the *Bonaventure,* I understand. I imagine one can learn a lot about a man living within the confines of a ship."

"Yes." St. Bride looked casually around the room. The party he sought was still not to be seen. He turned to the comte and asked, "Tell me, ah—my lord. Erath seems well connected in New Orleans, yet he informs me this is his first trip here. How is that so?"

"Monsieur Straught and I have had a longtime business arrangement. I value Erath's judgment, for he is shrewd and clever—just the kind of man I like to do business with. But unfortunately our business relationship is dwindling, for certain opportunities have dried up." He smiled unpleasantly. "Straught told me a bit about you, St. Bride. But tell me yourself—what business has brought you to our charmingly primitive little town?"

"I've bought a plantation west of here. Belle Chasse is its name. Have you heard of it?"

"Belle Chasse! *Mais non!* The indigo crops there have failed miserably. In fact, it is said that the former owner, Launier, killed himself after losing so much money. I heard they had to cut him down in his own bedroom. And the house! Why, it was never completed!" The comte let out a little laugh. "I am much afraid, monsieur, that you have been duped. I hope you were able to get the plantation for nothing."

"On the contrary, purchasing Belle Chasse and its slaves cost me a small fortune." St. Bride calmly sipped from his silver goblet. "And yet it will prove its worth ten times over. While I was visiting Paris, I found out from Launier's solicitor that Belle Chasse had made Monsieur Launier a very rich man. He killed himself from loneliness, I suppose, for he had no family, but most definitely not from lack of funds."

"I cannot believe this! Is it true? Why, I would have taken the plantation myself if not for the rumors—"

"I shall be a very wealthy man then," St. Bride interrupted, "because of the rumors. Already I've planned a fabulous new crop. I seek now a few men wealthy enough to contribute to it. In exchange, I promise they will be richer by year's end."

"And what is this fabulous new crop, *mon ami?* I would be very interested to hear!"

"Poppies," St. Bride uttered.

"Poppies!" the comte repeated in surprise.

"Yes, they're quite profitable, I've heard tell." Casually, St. Bride sipped from his goblet. "Straught is quite interested in my plans for Belle Chasse. I spoke to him at great length on the *Bonaventure*."

"And what a great coincidence! I would be most interested in this crop too! I am always anxious to invest my gold where it will be fruitful and multiply." The comte's green eyes lit up. "You know, of course, that Erath and I are great friends. We've done much business together. Could I persuade you to let me in on this venture? To tell you the truth, Monsieur Ferringer, I have dealt with laudanum before. If you plan to grow poppies, you will have a very special crop indeed."

"Yes. Very special." St. Bride smiled. "But I'm reluctant to include you in it, my lord. Perhaps in time you will understand."

"Nonsense! I can persuade you. I shall speak with Erath about my idea tonight. If we can all agree, I think you will find me an outstanding partner."

"If you don't mind, I shall reserve my opinion until I know Straught's."

"Fine! In the meantime, I insist that you accept the Thionville hospitality during your stay."

"Thank you, my lord, but Laban, my traveling companion, and I are leaving for Belle Chasse tonight."

"Ah, *mais non!* Catherine will be so disappointed." The comte spied his daughter sitting among a circle of admirers. Catching her father's beckoning eye, she stood from her gilt *pliant* and walked toward the men.

Wearing canary yellow satin and hoops larger than any door in the house, Lady Catherine was a splendid sight. But St. Bride seemed not to notice. Once again, his gaze wandered toward the doors.

"Looking for someone?" St. Bride turned his head, surprised by the voice. Having entered through a pair of side doors, Erath Straught now stood before him, just in time to greet Lady Catherine as she walked over to the group.

"*Mon cher* St. Bride, how do you like our island of civilization among *les sauvages?*" Catherine smiled and gestured around the finely appointed room. Meissen cornucopia adorned the wraparound mantel, and green velvet-cushioned *pliants* stood before tables inlaid with Boulle marquetry. Lady Catherine's eyes sparkled at the sight, but she was disappointed by St. Bride's reaction, for he did not seem to hold the same appreciation.

"I concede to that—an island it is. As for the savages . . ." St. Bride sipped his champagne and feigned nonchalance as he studied every aspect of Straught's appearance. His shoes and hose were spattered with mud, and there was a small dark stain at the bottom of his amber breeches. "As for the savages," he continued. "I met one of them today. Although she was hardly an Indian." He tightened his bandaged fist, thinking of the velvet-eyed Scottish girl who had wrought the damage.

"Yes, that little cutpurse was a wild thing, I admit." Straught calmly took a glass of champagne. "The people by the river are a bad breed. They've been cast off from their own countries. They're the dregs from the prisons of Ireland and Scotland. At least you may console yourself, Ferringer, that the little wench will come to an early end."

"I've hardly seen a beggar so undone. Not even in London. It's a sad thing to see a young woman meet with such misfortune." St. Bride's eyes flashed, and he seemed to be trying to control his annoyance. Changing the subject, he asked Straught, "Late business?"

"Yes. How did you know?" Straught's gray eyes slitted.

"Just a guess. What else could make you tardy for a magnificent gathering such as this?" St. Bride swept his arm across the room to indicate the rainbow of colored silks and precious jewels that surrounded them. In the background ladies whispered, fans snapped, and men laughed. It was an opulent scene, made more so by contrast with the squalid streets just beyond the gallery.

"It was unavoidable." Straught calmly took a pinch of snuff in his long nose. "However unfortunate, a man must deprive himself sometimes in order to achieve his goals. Don't you agree?"

"Most definitely." St. Bride's mouth turned up in a twisted sardonic smile. "But this particular deprivation agreed with you immensely. You appear more jovial than you were on the ship."

"I was merely anxious to get to port. The sea has always bothered me."

A feminine hand was placed on St. Bride's sleeve. Before he could continue his conversation with Straught, hot and breathless words were whispered in his ear. "Come, St. Bride, let me give you a tour of my lovely home. There is none finer in Louisiana." Lady Catherine took a well-buffed nail and circled the sapphire that was jabbed into the stock of his pristine shirt.

"I'm afraid I cannot, my lady. Laban and I must leave for the plantation tonight. I make profound apologies." St. Bride smiled and bowed. Lady Catherine pouted, but it had no effect on him, for he abruptly bade them all good night.

"When shall we see your Belle Chasse?" Straught asked. "I'm anxious to visit this fabulous plantation, considering our conversation on the *Bonaventure*." He held out his hand in farewell, but St. Bride waved it away, showing his bandaged right hand.

"Soon, I expect. You're certainly welcome at any time, be it for pleasure or business" St. Bride studied the parquet floor. "My lord comte, take time to think on what you wish for," he said enigmatically.

"You are greedy, St. Bride!" The comte laughed and

slapped him on the back. "But I believe I shall convince you to let in me on this plan, for I'm as greedy as you are."

"Then so be it," St. Bride said, clipping his words.

"Yes, I insist we begin our business soon." The comte turned slyly to Straught. "Erath, do you think we can convince St. Bride to let me in on his mysterious business?"

"For the right price, my lord, any man can be bought." Erath smiled his pretty smile, and St. Bride's eyes narrowed.

"Or sold," St. Bride bowed, artfully hiding the sarcasm in his harsh voice. "Good night, my lord, my lady."

"That damned comte wants in on Belle Chasse," St. Bride said, turning to Laban. Before they left the Thionvilles' and New Orleans for the long ride out to Belle Chasse, St. Bride had changed into doeskin breeches and jackboots. He had left his elaborate clothing behind, to be brought to the plantation later. Now the two men were riding along the narrow bit of road through the swamps that edged the Mississippi. They made only slow progress, and what little they did make was because the moon was full, lighting their way more effectively than a torch.

"Ah, what a mess! What did you do?" Laban's deep Jamaican baritone contrasted sharply with the shrill drone of the cicadas in the swamp. His horse broke into a trot, despite the mud that sucked at its hooves.

Catching up to him on a far less weighty mount, St. Bride answered, "I had to pacify him. What else could I have done? Refuse him outright and make Straught suspicious? He still doesn't trust me."

"No! No! But this plot gets thicker every time we turn around!"

"Yes, I know."

"But that doesn't matter, my friend. All that does matter is the end result. And you'll get him, I know, for if the great Duke of Lansdowne cannot, who can?"

"Yes, if the powers of Lansdowne don't haunt Erath Straught like a ghoul at his backside, nothing will."

"And in the end it will feel good, will it not?"

"Yes. It will feel very good," St. Bride said tightly, apparently still on edge from the party. "Straught is taking my bait. For a time on the *Bonaventure* he seemed reluctant. But since he left Scotland with hardly the clothes on his back, he is anxious to make money. Perhaps with the comte so eager, he'll let down his guard a bit."

"You'll get him, my friend. Inch by inch, you'll get him. Then perhaps when you have all that Erath Straught values, it will be better than merely slitting his throat."

"But have I done enough to get him?" St. Bride laughed bitterly.

"You've done more than most. There are not many men who go to such great lengths for justice."

"What else could I do? Sit back at Scion House and stare at that window seat where Mary waited for her 'true love'? Stare through those velvet curtains as she did, all the while thinking about what I could have done to change what happened—until remorse drove me mad?" St. Bride shut his eyes as if some kind of pain had suddenly lodged in his gut. When he opened them again, his eyes were cold and emotionless. "I should have stayed by Mary's side. I should never have gone to Georgia and left her unattended."

"There was no way you could have known what would happen, my friend."

"Perhaps not. Nonetheless, Straught's a blight on his own land. He's squandered the riches of his own family's castle, and the British have closed down his laudanum trade. It's time he was made to account for his actions. Not just for what happened to Mary, nor for the sapphires he stole from me. He's taken advantage of his own people, selling those defeated Highlanders enough laudanum to kill an army. He needs to be cut out like a cancer." St. Bride vowed, "And I'm the one to do it. As the Devil feeds upon sin, Erath Kerr

Straught feeds upon gold and the weaknesses of mankind. If there's one thing I know about Straught, it's that his greed is insatiable.''

A long silence followed St. Bride's speech. The men negotiated the poor road until St. Bride demanded. ''What is that strange sound?''

''A ghost of the bayou, perhaps. Truly, it sounds like a cat. But there can't be a cat way out here.'' Laban wiped the sweat off his smooth shaved head. ''Perhaps it's our imaginations?''

There was an eerie pause. For a short while the quiet reigned, and his words appeared to be true. But as they silently rode on, a small sound once again reverberated from the river willows to their left.

''What is that sound? Mewling? If it isn't some stray— what? Whoa, Canis!'' The Thoroughbred stallion reared up. St. Bride tried to calm the high-strung animal's nerves by patting it roughly along its sleek black neck. When the animal returned all four hooves to the ground once more, St. Bride asked Laban, ''What just crossed our path?''

''A black cat. Can you believe it? Ah, a bad sign! And all the way out here!'' Laban patted his own animal's hefty neck and peered into the forest on his right. Moonlight washed through the magnolias to a small clearing in the grove. In there both men could hear the constant mewing of a kitten as it sat in the clearing.

''No doubt the neglected plantation house is overrun by mice.'' St. Bride leaned toward his friend.

''Aye, a cat would keep them at bay.'' Laban returned St. Bride's stare.

''Let's do it then. If we can't catch the thing right away, we'll forget it. But methinks a cat would be handy in this wretched land, eh?'' St. Bride dismounted, and Laban followed after he tied the horses to a spindly cypress.

The two men walked into the clearing, listening for the telltale meow of the frightened kitten. Horning in on the sound, St. Bride walked over to a patch of wax myrtle and stooped very slowly.

"Do you see it?" Laban whispered to him.

"My God! It's a girl," St. Bride choked out. He frowned as he touched the small, wet form in the wax-myrtle branches.

"A girl? What? Is she dead?" Laban came closer for a better look.

"No, I can feel her shivering." St. Bride rolled the girl toward him. In the moonlight her face was revealed. St. Bride took a sharp breath. "It's her! The damned little wench who attacked me!"

"How can you be sure?" Laban peered closer.

"See the bewitching slant to her brows? And the way she's dressed? It's her, all right." St. Bride lifted her petticoat. Beneath it were two shapely legs, one holding the telltale dagger by a sodden garter. Scowling, he said, "As I told you, it's her." He ripped the knife from the girl's silken calf.

"What should we do with her?"

"Do with her? My God, this is all we need!" St. Bride dropped the petticoat. Abruptly, he stood and flung the offending weapon far into the swamps.

"Then we leave her," Laban stated.

"What do you think she is doing out here? She can't possibly live in this swamp. Erath spoke of her as one of the river people who live in the huts by the quay." His arms crossed, St. Bride stood over the girl and studied her quiet form.

"I don't know why she is out here, but I know what happened to her. See this?" Laban bent and held out the girl's palm. Two black fang marks were easily visible.

"A snake, no doubt."

"Yes. She's doomed." Resignedly, Laban stood. "Do you think anyone will miss her?"

St. Bride didn't answer. He didn't drag his eyes from the girl. He bent down one last time and swept a dark, wet lock off her forehead. Then, as if sensing his touch, the girl let out a soft moan of pain.

"What is she saying?" Laban asked.

" 'Morning,' I think. Or is it 'mourning'?" St. Bride shook his head. "Damn the inconvenience of this!"

"You're thinking of taking her?" Laban asked, sounding surprised.

"Should we leave her here, kick her out of our path like Straught?"

"I don't trust her, my friend. She reminds me of that wizened charm-hawker in Edinburgh. Do you remember the one?"

"They said she had the power to cast the Evil Eye. Yes, I remember her. She was an old hag, a witch. You can hardly compare her with this one." St. Bride appraised the girl. Her head was swung backward, displaying a vulnerable throat, a delicate collarbone, and a generous bosom. His eyes moved to her face, and he studied her refined features—the seductive arch to her brows, the slim bridge of her nose, the sweet, pliant curves of her lips.

"No, but perhaps she has the same ability." Laban pulled back superstitiously. "She did cut your hand, or have you already forgotten?"

"No," St. Bride uttered ominously, tightening the bandaged fist. "And if she dies, she dies. But if she lives, already I can think of retribution for that."

Laban scowled and watched as St. Bride picked up the unconscious girl, then moved to the horses. Eventually Laban followed him with the wicked black cat they had been chasing to begin with.

"Good." St. Bride acknowledged the kitten. "Perhaps we'll get some use out of the animal."

"Aye, it's easy enough for you!" Laban held out the hissing animal by its scruff, but his own huge body was cowed by the tiny razor-sharp claws that fought in his direction.

St. Bride mounted his horse and held the limp girl on his

lap. Turning to Laban, he said with some amusement, "Put the damned cat in your bag if you must. Think of me. At any minute the girl could awaken and try to slit my throat. Would you trade?"

"No. No, indeed!" Laban answered, unceremoniously stuffing the prickly kitten into his leather saddle pouch. He mounted and the two men started for Belle Chasse, each with his own cargo and his own thoughts.

Chapter Four

"What a miserable place," St. Bride remarked to Laban later that night as they peered into a bedchamber. They had arrived at Belle Chasse after the long ride through the swamps. Touring the house at Belle Chasse, they found it was built in the typical French West Indian colonial plan: three huge rooms to the front and three to the back. At the very back of the house there was a loggia painted to resemble marble and two cabinet rooms for bathing and *le nécessaire*. A gallery ran the perimeter of the house, and beneath all this, a raised bricked basement kept the wine cool and the servants respectfully apart from the family. There were no hallways; rather, each room connected to another and to the gallery. Because of this, even in the dead of August the faintest of breezes would waft through the house.

But St. Bride seemed unable to appreciate the ingenuity of the design. Beneath him, the varied-width cypress floorboards remained unvarnished and dusty. The roof would surely leak if many of the flat tiles weren't replaced soon. As he walked into his own bedchamber to the right of the salon, the *bousillage*—the filling of Spanish moss and mud between the posts in the wall—was exposed in so many places that the room smelled at once of mildew and fresh-cut lumber. The final insult was the huge hook that Launier, the former owner, had left in the exposed beam above the bed. It was just big enough to hold a man and a noose.

Despite these oddities, however, the thing in the bed-chamber that held both men's attention was the bedstead itself. A provincial walnut four-post bed stood directly in the middle of the room. It was obviously French-made, and it lacked a headboard of any kind. But the mellow, worm-eaten posts gleamed with wax, and the lustrous bedhangings of vivid rain-forest green satin gleamed brighter still. A brocaded counterpane of poppy red and gold threads covered the bedding. Crowning the entire structure was the softest and sheerest of silk gauzes. Despite its look of sensual innocence, it also efficiently kept away the bloodthirsty Louisiana mosquitoes.

"The old owner was a fool—no wonder he took his life! Launier could hardly put a decent roof over his head, yet look where he slept! These Louisianians are daft." St. Bride laughed at his incongruous surroundings. "They can import the finest of satins, yet they are handicapped to make even the meanest of fustian for themselves. What are we in for, man?"

"I couldn't tell you," Laban muttered. "Everything here is turned backward. Black cats in the swamps. Satin in the same room with river mud." Ominously he said, "I believe nothing is as it seems."

St. Bride only nodded, then sauntered to the salon and poured himself and Laban a brandy. The men drank in silence. A few moments later, St. Bride stated, "Speaking of nothing being as it seems, I wonder why was Straught so hell-bound to come here. Did he come here for the comte? Or is there some other reason? Their laudanum business has soured since the Brits shut down Erath's ships to Canton."

Laban didn't reply, as if he knew St. Bride was not finished with his musings.

"And tell me, Laban. What was Straught's business about

this evening? I swear to you he had blood on his breeches when he appeared at the party. Some might have thought it was mud, but I know it was not.''

"Was he fighting with someone, you think?" Laban crossed his legs in front of him and enjoyed his brandy.

"I don't know," St. Bride answered. "If only there were a way to find out!"

"In my opinion, we should have put a ball through his head when we discovered him in London. 'Twould have saved the world untold misery.''

"Ah, but you've got to learn patience, man. As I have. That way when you finally do take revenge, it is much sweeter." St. Bride swirled the amber liquid in his beaker.

"But look at the price you've paid to learn it." Laban's eyes darkened to jet.

"Yes, look at me and hold me to example." St. Bride became sarcastic. "The very picture of the patient young man. Why, if I hadn't been so young and impetuous, I never would have made that foolish purchase on the hangman's block ten years ago. What was it that you tried to do to your old owner in Jamaica, man? Geld him?" He let out a low whistle.

"He was a cruel and vicious taskmaster. I've the lash scars on my back to prove it." Laban scowled, then his voice rose to falsetto. "Besides, old Bridlington had no flesh to take.''

Both men laughed.

"That may be true," St. Bride finally choked out, "but you must admit, 'twas a stupid move for me to buy someone so mean and ugly and dangerous. What things we must attribute to the callowness of youth!"

"I've proven my worth."

"Yes," St. Bride answered dryly. "Though every morning I find myself checking the octave of my voice, lest some oversight has occurred and I've unwittingly offended you."

Again they laughed, and they didn't stop until they heard the crash.

"She's already making trouble," Laban announced quietly. St. Bride stiffened in his chair. Hearing a cry of fear, both men got up from their seats and found the bedchamber where they had left the girl. A small, raggedy slave girl, one of many purchased with the house, looked up from the bed where she was struggling to subdue her patient. A knocked-over candle threatened at any minute to ignite the nearby bedclothes.

Laban easily tamped out the fire with his jackboots, and St. Bride moved to the bed to help with the thrashing, half-dressed girl. Resolutely, he took the delirious girl's hands and held them against the mattress. The girl beneath him still struggled, but he was at least able to keep her from accidentally setting the house on fire.

"When did this begin?" he questioned the slave girl.

"Just now. The fever, it is terrible," the mulatto answered in a shaky voice. St. Bride returned his gaze to the petite figure that lay crumpled in the sheets.

Perspiration dampened the raven tendrils around her delicate face, and her cheeks flushed a fiery pink amid the unhealthy pallor of the rest of her face. Her eyes were open, but they stared off toward the far wall, their velvety blue depths unnaturally glazed. He touched the girl's smooth cheek. It burned like a fire iron. Perplexed, he ran his hand through his own tied-off mane.

"What do you think should be done for her?" St. Bride turned to the small mulatto girl.

"I am only Colette, the cook. I do not know," she said softly, looking more like a frightened doe than a French slave girl from Guadeloupe.

Another candle flickered halfheartedly on the commode. St. Bride looked down as the girl's pale, stricken face shone in the light. She had quieted a bit, but her lips moved with feverish venom-induced delusions. Her black kitten, comfortably disposed next to its mistress, hissed at both men ungratefully, then kneaded the moss-stuffed mattress and settled down once more. St. Bride nodded to Colette, who was holding strips of cloth and a pan of cool water brought from downstairs.

"If you're the cook, have you any herbs that could help the girl? Alleviate some of her pain?" St. Bride swept his bandaged hand over the unconscious girl's dirty, tormented brow.

"I may be able to help her." Colette put down the pan and fished for a remedy in her patched pair of pockets tied to her waist. St. Bride watched the mulatto move with a slight limp to the commode. His eyes softened as he saw for the first time the slave girl's club foot.

"Colette, do what you can for her. I know you can make her well," he encouraged in a gentle voice.

The mulatto nodded nervously. She dropped some yellowing herbs into the cup and held it over the heat of the candle.

There seemed little more that could be done for the girl, so St. Bride moved to the door. But then a cry of anguish held him back. The water pan that Colette was using to cool the girl's fever crashed to the floor as the girl began thrashing once more.

"Enough . . . enough!" St. Bride recaptured her flailing arms. Then, because there seemed no alternative, he nodded his head to the strips of rags that Colette had been using on the girl's forehead. Laban made use of them, and the girl was unable to thrash anymore.

"Enough," St. Bride whispered when the girl had finally quieted. She stared up at him with absolutely no recognition in her eyes, yet when St. Bride made a move to leave, she moaned to him, "Please . . . sir . . ."

"What?" St. Bride looked bewildered.

"Please, sir . . . help me," she implored him. She tried to move her arms, but the restraints held fast. Frustrated, she let out a terrified moan and begged, "Oh, please help me! Can't you understand? I don't want to die! Not when I'm

Kayleigh. Not when I'm Kayleigh!'' She released a tearless sob.

St. Bride's face turned grim as he watched her struggle with the bandages. He tried to quiet her, but it was a long time before she drifted back into a feverish stupor.

''I should not get too attached, St. Bride.'' Laban's voice broke the silence at long last.

St. Bride's head jerked up and he looked at Laban. Gruffly he said, ''Never fear that!'' He released the black-haired girl and abruptly left the room.

Chapter Five

Kayleigh opened her eyes.

She was not back at Mhor, her beloved castle, nor was she was in the hut she'd shared with Bardolph. Her surroundings were completely foreign to her. White linen sheets soothed her boiling flesh, and a cool morning breeze drifted in from double doors that led out to a gallery. Through the windows on those gallery doors, she could see two spindly rows of pecan trees. But having learned to survive on instinct alone, she turned her head sharply to see if anyone kept her company. On the other side of the room was another set of doors.

She was alone. Weakly, she sank back into the pillows. Suddenly, she remembered the snake. She looked down at her hand and saw two telltale marks on the palm of her hand that looked a bit swollen. A frown marred her pretty brow. She recalled the viper and the swamp and her cousin Straught, but after that there was nothing. No memories at all. Her eyes scanned the room once more. Where was she? Who had brought her here and cared for her? How long had she been here? No answers came. It seemed that between the night the snake bit her and the present there lurked a shadowy void.

Something swatted at her toes. She sat up in the bed and found Chridhe stretched lazily at the foot. She smiled weakly and reached out to touch the comforting black fur of her kitten.

"Where are we, Mo Chridhe? Who's been keeping us here?" she whispered. Kayleigh touched the soft cotton of the strange night smock she was wearing, then threw back the light cover-sheet and scanned the room for her clothes.

But not even the simplest of tasks was easy. She had to force herself not to look down at the floorboards, which seemed to be shifting. She had to keep her hands at her temples in order to keep her head from reeling. Yet she was determined to leave the bed. When she did, Chridhe remained on the sheet.

Irreverently, Kayleigh tossed the sheet over the kitten, whispering, "You traitor, you should be coming with me."

But the kitten only squirmed from beneath the sheet, turned over on its back, and closed its eyes.

As she slowly put one foot in front of another, Kayleigh peeked at her feet. She was startled by their condition. Scarred and rough they were, to be sure. But they had been scrubbed pink—no doubt by whoever had cared for her. She could hardly tear her eyes from them. She hadn't seen them this clean in over a year.

Shaking her head, she once more tried to seek out her clothes. But the room held nothing familiar. There was a wild cherrywood press in the pier, but its open doors revealed only a dusty, empty interior. There was a walnut chair near her bedside, but the rushed seat and provincial rococo chairback held nothing but toweling.

Where are my clothes? she asked herself. She looked down at the night smock she was wearing. Though she reveled in the fine smell and texture of the fabric, she knew it would not be enough to run away in. But then she noticed that the garment wasn't a night smock at all; rather, it was a man's shirt, so large that it fell past her knees. The sleeves were rolled up neatly to her elbows, but the top ties remained undone. The neckline was indecently low.

She tied up the front as best she could with her shaky fingers. How she ached to return to the soft bed with its cool, rumpled sheets! But she knew she had to find out where she was and who had taken care of her. She couldn't afford to stay in one place if Straught might find out where she was.

Throwing open the second set of doors, she looked about at a salon, but no one was there. The salon smelled of linseed oil and turpentine. She wondered if the floors had been newly varnished. Stepping out on her bare feet, the boards felt silky smooth.

What was it like to have such fine things around again? She tried to recall as she dizzily wandered through the salon. She looked around her and was reminded of the grandeur of her past life. The gilt marble-topped pier tables were so new that the horsehair packing was as yet still scattered near their crates. Two matching red baywood armoires towered over each end of the salon. Pie-shaped paterae edged their cornices, and each was speckled with dove gray paint. One of the massive pieces had its doors wide open; copper pegs twinkled back at her like orange stars from the shadowed depths of the interior.

With a heavy heart, she recalled the huge kas that stood in Mhor Castle's great hall. When they were children, she used to tell Morna that an evil Danish troll lived inside of it. Kayleigh smiled at the reminiscence but then she felt a tightness in her breast. Every day she vowed not to think of her sister. It only caused herself more pain. Yet it seemed every day she did think of her, despite herself and her efforts.

She decided that it was likely she would find something to wear inside the armoire. Feeling unbelievably light-headed, she made her way over to it. The salon was quiet and breezy as the magnolia-scented wind made its way through the louvers of the adjoining loggia. But she spent no more time appreciating the serene room—it took all her concentration to reach the armoire.

At long last her hands slid up the doors and she heard the

creak of the long iron *fiche* hinges. But she could hardly hide her disappointment, for the armoire held only stacks of musty linens and several bolts of *barzin*—no clothing at all. In frustration, she leaned on the door and stared into the cabinet's interior, wondering where she was going to find clothes.

"Looking for something to steal?" A man's voice shot out from behind her. A deep, rich voice which could have belonged only to a nobleman. In the back of her muddled mind, Kayleigh knew she'd heard it before. Suddenly a chill ran down her spine, and she stumbled back into the side of the armoire. She turned her head to the man who had spoken. When she saw him, her heart seemed to freeze in her chest.

She'd encountered this man before. He'd been on the docks the other day, and his blood had spilled on her petticoat. It was too awful to be true. Standing in the entrance to the loggia was Erath Straught's friend and traveling companion, St. Bride.

Kayleigh stared at him in mute horror. Fleetingly, she wondered if she was mistaken, but there seemed no doubt about it. The man before her possessed the same rough turquoise gaze that demanded subservience, and the same handsome face that would have made even a dock whore pine for romance. His unusual silver-touched black hair was neatly queued onto his neck with a leather thong. He stood before her, his face an unyielding mask of disapproval. She was terrified.

"You!" she whispered.

"Ah, you remember me," he uttered dryly as he walked up to her. "I certainly remember you. In fact, every time I look at my hand, the nostalgia almost makes me weep." He smiled then.

"I—I'm sorry about your hand." She looked behind him, sure her cousin would be there. But the loggia entrance remained empty.

"But why be sorry? I'm sure you've attacked people before." He closed the gap between them. "Haven't you?"

"My—my cousin, where is he?" she asked, unable to bear her dread any longer.

"Your cousin?" He seemed surprised at her question. "And who might that be?"

Kayleigh paused. This man didn't seem to know who she was. With sudden clarity, she knew she had remained alive because the man before her didn't know of her relation to Erath Straught. The relief made her even dizzier, and she had to hang on to the armoire door for support.

As if noticing her weakened condition for the first time, St. Bride reached out to steady her, but she drew back.

"No, stay away!" she gasped. She didn't want him to touch her. She didn't want anyone acquainted with her cousin to touch her.

"I suggest you go back to bed. I've work to do in here, and I cannot spend my time waiting for you to faint." With his strong arms bound across his massive chest, he waited for her to go.

"I just want my clothes—then I'll be off," she assured him.

"You needn't any clothes to go back to bed." He stepped closer.

"No, no! Please, I would like to leave now!" She tried to slide past him, but his hands caught her. Gently, he forced her back against the armoire.

"Stop this foolishness. I have work to do. We can talk about that later. Go back to bed, Kayleigh."

"Kayleigh? Kayleigh . . . ?" she whispered incredulously. With dark, frightened eyes she looked up at the man and suddenly felt sure he had lied to her. He could have found out her name only from Straught or Bardolph, and Bardolph was dead. That left only one possibility.

She tried to bolt, and had her physical strength been better, she was almost sure she would have made it. But as it was, she had hardly taken more than two wobbly steps before St. Bride pulled her up short. The force of his arm against her chest sent her backward, and then her head exploded with pain. She grabbed her throbbing temples between her palms, but this only unbalanced her further. It was barely a second before she saw the sharp edges of a table rushing up to her.

The crack to her head never came. Instead, she felt two strong hands capture her from the fall. From behind, she heard a low, muttered curse: "You damned little fool." Then two strong arms lifted her up and carried her back to her room.

"Please let me go . . ." She felt him place her back on the mattress, but the comfort of the bed couldn't calm the terror in her heart.

"Ah, there's that word again, *please.*" He looked down at her. He shook her as if that would bring the truth out of her. "Where did you learn such manners, Kayleigh?"

"My name is Kestrel!" she cried, unsuccessfully trying to pull from his grasp. In the end, weak and breathless, the only thing she could do was stare up at him. Meeting his hard, unflinching gaze, she summoned the courage to ask, "Who told you I was Kayleigh?"

"You told me your name was Kayleigh. You were delirious from the snakebite, and I've come to the conclusion that you must be still." He let go of her arms. "Stay in your bed, wild thing, until you have my permission to leave it."

"I just want to go. Please let me go!"

"You've no place to go now. You're out on a plantation, and there's nothing but swampland between here and civilization." As if that would placate her, he made to leave.

"No, please—let me go anyway!" She stopped him by grabbing the linen of his shirt.

There was a long pause while he studied her face. Then eventually his gaze drifted downward to rest where her shirt had come undone in her struggles. The pale rose half-moon of her nipple showed above the filmy batiste. She stared at it in horror; he stared at it judiciously. Mortified, she held on to him, afraid that any further movement would only decrease her modesty. His eyes met hers, and they softened for a moment.

''You of all people should know that that won't coax me into letting you go.'' He smiled; his teeth gleamed like stolen pearls. But then he refused to hear her pleas any longer. Reluctantly, he pried her small hands from his massive chest, stepped from the bed, and wasted no more time in her room. The last thing she heard before he walked away was the bolt shooting home in the lock on her door.

What was to become of her? she thought wretchedly when he had gone. She was at a strange plantation house, being kept by a man who was her cousin's comrade. But how much time did she have before Erath found her here? Who was this man St. Bride, anyway? She moaned. How on earth could she think with a smithy's hammer clammering through her head? Grimacing in pain, she gave in to her fears. She would die if she remained at this man's wretched plantation. She knew without a doubt that Straught would find her eventually and that all the agony she'd suffered before then would be for naught.

Looking up at the looked door, she knew she needn't even try to get up out of bed again. She sighed heavily. In exhaustion, she let her head fall back into the pillows. How could it have happened? Bardolph had been dead less than a few days, and already here was another man to control her.

Chapter Six

"Do we let her go today?" Laban entered the salon several days later and tossed his cock hat onto the settee. Outside, the sun blazed.

"I've been thinking about those jewels," St. Bride said as if he hadn't heard Laban. He leaned against the railing of the gallery and stared speculatively into the cool depths of the salon.

"Does the girl go back to the quay today? The slave Colette needs supplies, and I told her she could accompany me to town. I can always take the black-haired wench too. Get her off our backs."

"Laban, do you believe in an eye for an eye, a tooth for a tooth?"

"In some cases, my friend. What are you thinking of?"

St. Bride traced the thin red scar that ran between his thumb and forefinger. Then his eyes moved to the bedchamber door where his assailant was kept. "I think I've a use for Kayleigh. I'd like her to do something for me before we let her go."

"And what is that?"

"It's those jewels. Straught came so close to unloading them on the *Bonaventure*. Remember that wealthy American who disembarked at Bermuda? He had been willing to pay a fine penny for them, if I heard correctly. I want to make sure Straught still has them before we go any further.''

"That would be ideal—but what does the wench have to do with that? You can't possibly want her to spy for you. She's not trustworthy.''

"Not spy, exactly. I'm thinking of just one evening. Give Straught a few drinks, a beautiful woman, and the right questions, and I think we could get the answers we need. Then we could proceed without any worries.''

"And what makes you think Kayleigh's the one to do that for us?''

"Because Straught is ripe for a really beautiful woman,'' St. Bride answered thoughtfully. "That's all he talked about on the *Bonaventure*. He said rather enigmatically one time that he wanted the most bewitching female in New Orleans. And if I know only one thing about that young woman in yonder bedchamber, it is that she is truly bewitching.'' His eyes darkened as if he were thinking of the encounter of the day before. "I'm sure I've never seen a woman so utterly exquisite.''

"But wouldn't Lady Catherine be a better choice? After all, she would do anything for you, my friend.'' Laban looked at St. Bride pointedly. "Anything,'' he added.

"I don't want to indebt myself to Lady Catherine.'' St. Bride lifted one dark eyebrow. "I'd have myself a wife so fast, my head would spin.'' Both men laughed. When they sobered at last, St. Bride continued, saying, "Then it's settled. The wench we've been saddled with is the perfect choice. She owes me for not taking her to the magistrate, and better than that, she owes me her life.''

"Her station, though. Won't that be a problem?'' Laban suddenly shook his head. "After all, from what I gather, Straught is rather particular. I don't see him cavorting with just any whore.''

"The girl is oddly well-spoken. If we're explicit when we give her instructions, I think she can fool Straught well enough. Besides, Straught may be a bit homesick after all this time away from Mhor. And Kayleigh is, after all, Scottish. That's obvious enough from her slight brogue. No, she's just what Straught ordered on the *Bonaventure*. The more I think about it, the more I'm convinced."

"If that's what you want, my friend. Shall I go get the wench?"

"Yes, that's what I want. Fine. Go get her." St. Bride rubbed his jaw, deep in thought.

She was caught between Scylla and Charybdis. If she made one foolish move, she would be devoured, either by her cousin or by the enigmatic man before her now.

Kayleigh stood in the salon, squarely facing St. Bride. She'd been given an indigo-dyed osnaburg dress to wear, and her hair had been washed. It was now as it hadn't been in a year, clean, and shiny, falling in a silky, springy mass around her head. After waiting a full day in the prison of her room, she had been abruptly summoned. And she found the circumstances all very strange. There was only one thing of which she was sure. She was as frightened as she had been the day she and Black Bardolph had fled Mhor Castle.

"Are you feeling better then?" St. Bride asked her.

Slowly Kayleigh nodded her head. She swallowed hard and tried to be alert though her head pounded miserably and her body had been left weak, ravaged from fever. Crossing her sore, shaking arms in front of her bosom, she looked up, unable to avoid meeting the turbulent jade stare before her.

"I . . . I should like to leave," she began.

"And you shall! But first, I would like some restitution for the damage you've wrought." He waved his scarred hand before her. Then he rose from his seat, leaned against the pier table, and perused her. "Kayleigh, what would you say if I told you I have decided not to take you to the magistrate for attacking me on the docks? What would you say if I told you that I want give you a sweet bag of gold and let you go, free as a bird?''

''I would wonder if you were crazed,'' she replied uneasily.

His eyes seemed to smile, but his mouth didn't. He was making her uncomfortable, and he knew it. What did he have planned for her? ''Crazed? Do I look it?''

''I think you do by half.'' She averted her eyes. ''What do you want of me?''

''I want you to give company to a friend of mine.''

''Give company?'' Suddenly, she stopped. She felt the color rising in her cheeks. *Dhé!* Did he mean what she thought he meant?

''I'm sure a woman of your fabric should find him quite amenable. He takes regular baths, although considering the state in which I found you, I won't be surprised if that is not one of your particulars.''

''I don't care if you bathe regularly or not!'' she cried out.

''No, no! *Not* me!'' He seemed to be laughing at her, and his ridicule stung her to the quick.

''Not you?'' How could this be happening? The man was actually asking her to bed down with one of his cronies!

''Come now, you see, this friend of mine is a rather closed-mouth sort,'' he explained. ''And what I want is to find out some information he has. These things are delicate, you understand. I think he would tell a tempting little wench like yourself certain things that he would never tell me.''

''I—am—not—in the business of—''

''You needn't let him bed you.'' He was nonchalant. ''All I really want to know is if he has some jewels he has promised me. You can understand my predicament now, can't you? I really can't ask the fellow myself without implying that he's been lying to me. That's where you come in, Kayleigh. We'll simply give you a go at him for an evening, and after that, you'll be free and clear of any reprisals from me.''

"If I say no, what are these reprisals you speak of?" She looked into those damnable eyes.

"Far worse than what I'm offering you." He frowned, and brushed her creamy cheek with his thumb. "Come now, love. You've surely done more vile things for a bit of gold."

"I can't think of any at the moment!" Indignant, she swatted at his hand. Her anger and frustration were peaking. She had no idea what she was going to do to get out of this impossible situation, but she was going to have to think quickly if she were going to flee this plantation before she fell into bigger trouble.

"You'll like this gent, Kayleigh. He's a Scot like yourself. Has a castle near Inverness—you're familiar with Inverness, no?"

The blood suddenly drained from her face. "I am very familiar with Inverness." She stared at St. Bride in disbelief. He couldn't mean her cousin. What cruel irony was this?

"Good!" he exclaimed. "That will give you something to converse about. I know you'll like Erath Straught, Kayleigh. I hear the women find him quite appealing. And I promise you a healthy reward if you discreetly obtain the information I desire."

If he'd brushed her with a feather, she would have fallen to the floor, so great was her shock. How could this be happening? How could she have ended up in such a situation? She stared at St. Bride in horror. Did he have any idea what he was asking her to do? She would prefer to return to New Orleans where she was no doubt wanted for the murder of Bardolph than to do what St. Bride was asking of her.

"I said I would give you a reward, Kayleigh," he prompted her. "What say you now?"

"No reward is necessary," she stated huskily.

"What?"

"I'll not need a reward, for I won't be getting that information for you."

St. Bride's head tilted back. His eyes narrowed. "Are you attempting to refuse?"

"I will not do your bidding."

As if her refusal were as unexpected as snow in July, St. Bride appeared not to know what to make of it. He began to pace, circling her and studying her. "Come now," he began calmly. "I promise you a pretty new gown for the occasion and as much gold as you've probably seen in a year. Can you refuse that, little cutpurse?"

"I can," she answered nervously. She couldn't keep her eyes on him while he walked around her. At any minute she expected him to pounce.

"How about if I promise you a cottage—or better yet a shop—in that rubble and ruin you call New Orleans? Wouldn't you like that? Wouldn't that be just what you've always dreamed about?"

She closed her eyes to gather the courage to speak. "I will not do what you are asking of me at any price."

"No one defies me, you little Highland baggage! Do you know that?"

Her eyes flew open. Suddenly St. Bride assumed the imperious air of a man far more important than a colonial planter, someone—as he'd said—who was definitely not used to being defied.

"But I will defy you! For I'm not a doxy for you to be casting upon your friends! I will not be used like that!"

"How proud you are, my beauty! I wonder if you will be quite so haughty when the magistrate has you upon the whipping post!"

"I'll take the magistrate's hand over yours!"

There was a pause while St. Bride searched for a new tack. "How did you end up in the swamps?" he pressed her. "Were you running from someone? Was someone after you, someone you stole from? Were they about to catch you, and you ran into the swamps to hide? Would you like me to take you back to New Orleans?"

"I don't know."

"You don't know like the night won't fall," he said tersely. Then he softened. "You needn't be frightened of me, you know. You can stay here and rest as long as you need to. I'll get you clothing and you'll have some decent food in that belly of yours."

How she wanted to accept his offer! How delightful it would be not to be hunted like a vixen in the forest, not to be frightened or hungry. To have a soft bed to sleep upon and clothes that were clean and mended. Her eyes clouded a bit as she thought of the simple comforts that she had done without for months. How she wanted to accept—if only his offer did not involve Straught!

"But what else in this belly of mine?" she finally murmured when she thought of her *sgian dhu* which had almost found Straught's mark in the hut by the river. But he misinterpreted her.

"You needn't fear getting with child. I don't ask that you bed the man. I'll let that be your choice." He extended his finger and used it to raise her jaw. He then forced her to meet his eye. "I'll let you take your pleasure where you find it."

"My pleasure will be found when I'm set free." She stared at him balefully.

"Then you'll do it?"

She shook her head and tightened her lips.

"Shall I take measures to convince you?" St. Bride's voice was low and ominous.

"Nay, for I shall never be convinced."

It was obvious that the man had rarely been crossed. Fury shot from his gaze, and he suddenly shouted for his man. "Laban! Laban!"

Soon a big black man appeared through the loggia.

"Laban," St. Bride said, this time uttering words that drove terror into her soul, "take this bloodthirsty wench to town and deliver her personally to the magistrate."

The man came forward, and she retreated back several

steps. "Wait!" She beat away Laban's hold, suddenly regret-
ting her decision. "Is there not another alternative?"

"Laban, take her." St. Bride calmly motioned to his man.

"No! No!" she pleaded. "Don't be taking me there!
Why did you save my life if you meant for me to end up
in jail?"

"Laban, take her," St. Bride repeated, watching her face
closely.

"*No!*" She pushed away at the black man's hands, then
turned and made for the loggia.

She made it down the loggia steps and through the courtyard, but even so Laban easily strode behind her, almost as
if he were letting her wear herself out. And wear her out he
did, for when she was just past the stables, the game ended.
Releasing a cry, she felt her captor catch her by the arm and
force her about.

But it wasn't Laban who caught her; it was St. Bride. She
fought to be free, yet so soon after her illness, she fell like
a limp kitten into his arms, all the fight temporarily sapped
from her body.

St. Bride tilted her chin up, and her glaring eyes met his
amused ones. "Come along. I hear the magistrate's got a
particular appetite for cutpurses. I don't know if he'll hang
you but then one can never tell. He might have a frightful
spell of indigestion today and just be downright disagree-
able."

"Don't wreak your vengeance through the magistrate,"
she panted. She struggled against his chest, but it was of no
use. She was too weak, and he was too strong.

"I don't want to take you there. Don't make me." St.
Bride's breath was warm on her cheek.

"I will not do what you ask!"

"Do you think I want to send you to jail? Do you think I
want vengeance for this?" His cut hand brushed along the
cream of her throat. "You asked me why I saved your life—

well, it definitely wasn't so that I could see you hung by that slender neck of yours. But if you refuse—"

"Oh please, just let me go. Let me go, and I shall never bother you again!" She struggled in vain against the forged muscle of his arms.

"Let you go? You spurn my offers of a better life in exchange for one evening's work and cry to be set free, to go back to that damned wharf where I found you. Tell me this, little thief—is stealing and whoring so much more preferable?"

Stunned by his aspersion, Kayleigh could only look up with horror in her eyes. Embarrassment and anger flamed in her cheeks. She tried very hard to remain undaunted, but finally she could stand it no longer. Imperiously she spat, "You ignoble wretch! I am no whore! And I curse you for saying so!"

"Ah, forgive me, my snow queen!" He shook her. "Of course, your virtue is unquestionable!"

"It *is* unquestionable, and don't ever forget that!" She pulled her arm free of his grasp.

"Yes, yes! The quintessential virgin. You were out on the docks just to take the air." His gaze lit upon the vulnerable pink of her lips. His eyes studied every generous curve until finally they lingered at the moist parting. Suddenly she found his lips upon her own. But his was a swift and angry kiss, for she was quickly shoved aside. "Yes, you taste just like a virgin." St. Bride spoke softly, but the sarcasm of his words dug into her heart.

"You vile oaf!" She tried to run from him one last time, but he was prepared for this. He let out a laugh and captured her easily, lifting her clear off the ground.

"I see our little Gaelic witch has a sore spot." His face drew closer, and she noted the angry spark in St. Bride's turquoise eyes.

"Let me down," she commanded. With her feet swinging free and ungrounded, and her body pressed hard against the length of his, she was becoming increasingly aware of their differences. Her soft chest was jammed against the hardness of his, and she truly believed his one arm would have been much more suitably placed around her waist than wrapped intimately around her buttocks.

"No kicking," he warned, apparently amused by her discomfort. "I won't have a chit like you rendering me useless."

"Let me down." She caught her breath and swallowed her hysteria. She didn't want to be held, she didn't want to be touched. Not by this man. He had already gone too far.

Noting her disdain, St. Bride slid her to the ground. But the trip was painfully slow, and she was sure it afforded him intimate knowledge of her body. She, in turn, felt the intimate geography of his as well. When her feet touched the soft soil once more, she was more than ready to end their contact, but he seemed unwilling. He still held her within his arms, his eyes sparkling with amusement—and something else, something she couldn't quite define yet knew she didn't like.

"What a prize you are, Kayleigh," he said for no apparent reason.

She instinctively shoved at his chest. "Nay! You're like the men at the barracks! You'll see only what you want, won't you? And no doubt not like it one wee bit if my mind gets in the way and protests. Well, don't you be touching me like that again!"

Laban walked up and said, "The carriage is ready, St. Bride."

"No!" he snapped. "Let this bloodthirsty little wench cool her heels in the wine room for a while. Then we'll put the proposition to her again."

Laban came up and took her by the arm. He pulled her across the bricked courtyard, ignoring her protests. Before she disappeared through the arched doors of the basement, she turned to level St. Bride with her stare, but he seemed to be laughing at her. His eyes sparkled like the Atlantic, and he called to her, "You owe me, Kayleigh! So think hard on what your life is worth. Think hard on the small cost of compliance.''

She fair wanted to shriek with frustration. But she had already been shoved into the dark little room where they bottled their wine.

Chapter Seven

The wine room was really the plantation's equivalent of a jail. It was certainly as dark. But once Kayleigh had adjusted her eyes, she was able to make out what was around her. Mounted on one wall were eight barrels containing a sweet-smelling port. Along the opposite wall, rack after rack of empty bottles lay waiting to be filled. The third wall was taken up by a large table where the wine was bottled. The fourth wall, however, was nothing but a set of wrought iron bars. This and an iron door kept the servants well locked out of the master's store of spirits—and kept Kayleigh well locked in.

It was cool in the bricked first floor of the plantation, but that was the only thing she found good about it. She spent several hours pacing the little room, pausing now and then to shake the iron door, as if to make sure it was truly locked tight. It was. In the end, spent and exhausted, she slid down to the floor and put her head on her knees. *Dhé,* she was tired. How much fight did she have left?

A noise made her lift her head. The battened shutters of the door nearest the wine room were being opened. Light cascaded into the room beyond, and the dust motes flew like clouds of silver.

St. Bride walked in and stood in front of the wine room, casting a shadow where she sat. He paused, and his stare became thoughtful before he pulled up a stool from a far corner. He sat down and easily placed his long jackbooted legs on the crosspiece between the bars.

"Have you thought on my offer? Or would spending the night here encourage you to make a decision?"

"I've come to a decision already," she countered warily.

"Ah, but not the right one."

"It's the right one for me." She rose from the floor and stood in the shadows of the wine racks.

"But what's a little seduction, Kayleigh? Seduction is easy. Surely you know that, for look how artlessly you do it." He grinned and lifted something to his lips. In the half darkness of the basement, she made it out to be a small piece of sassafras root.

She studied him, desperate to figure him out. She noted he hadn't bothered to shave that evening, but the dark growth on his face only accentuated the brilliance of his teeth when he smiled. He nonchalantly stared back at her, all the while chewing on the sassafras root. It was rather a provincial habit, yet this man seemed hardly of the lower classes. With his soft batiste shirts, so fine that they possessed a better hand than silk, and his shiny black jackboots, obviously of German design and custom made just for him, St. Bride was no peasant.

But he was definitely a heathen. Her thoughts grew darker as she watched him take great pleasure in biting the root and rotating it in his mouth. There was the tiniest smile on his lips while his tongue licked its edges. Before she could even articulate the reasons why, she found the entire display abhorrent. Abhorrent . . . and yet fascinating. St. Bride's hard mouth was mesmerizing her beyond explanation.

She caught her lower lip with her teeth and turned her head. "I've made my decision, so take your wretched self and be gone from here."

"But I'm here to make you understand, love, that what I'm asking you to do is terribly easy."

"No, not easy!" she exclaimed while walking to the bars. She then put both her hands on them and added, "What you ask is impossible!"

St. Bride's gaze never flinched from her own as he stood and threw the sassafras root to the bricks. He then walked over to her. When he got there, all he uttered was, "Impossible?" before his hands clasped around her own that were clasped to the bars. She wanted to pull back, but she told herself there was no need to fear. What could the man do with several rails of iron between them?

She couldn't have been more wrong.

The briefest of seconds passed as her gaze locked with his. Under his scrutiny, all her senses seemed to blossom until she was nearly overwhelmed with sensation. The iron between her palms turned to ice, the hands on her own turned to fire. The pungent scents of steel, wine, and dirt assaulted her nostrils, and the corvine cries of the jays outside in the pecans became deafening, surpassed only by the resounding thump of her heart.

Quietly he came closer, and as if by magic she felt herself drawn to him. Her lips seemed to move, against her will, toward those harder, more forceful ones above her. She didn't want him to kiss her. In fact, she couldn't think of anything she wanted less. But as his head lowered ever so slowly, she found herself accommodating by tilting her head back and presenting her lips to his.

Their mouths touched; the contact was shocking, exhilarating, dangerous. With a flutter of lashes her eyes closed, and deep within her she released a moan. His lips tasted bittersweet with sassafras, and they moved with the utmost gentle persuasion. They possessed her until her feelings rioted in tumultuous anarchy. Summoning the will to free herself became a monumental task. Though fear made her want to draw back, something else made her pause—something that tingled in her belly and made her legs grow weak as she felt the rough velvet of St. Bride's tongue along her lips. Was the man some kind of warlock? What was this power he was wielding? He was making her do things she never dreamed she would comply with.

She wanted to pull away, and she made one weak move. But before she could break away entirely, his hand left hers and ran up the back of her neck, forcing her to stay right where she was, forcing her to take and return his kiss with all the furor of a wanton. The bars pressed against her cheeks, and soon she was cursing them for being in the way. By some strange magic, she wanted to feel the scratchiness of his jaw and the breadth of his chest, not the unyielding iron that was between them.

"You see how easy it is?"

Her eyes flew open. Was St. Bride speaking? Had the kiss ended? Her free hand went to her lips as if she needed proof that it had. Her lips felt tender, yet deliciously sated. Confused, her eyes met his and she stuttered, "What—is—so—easy?"

"Seduction," he answered darkly. "Many fall prey to it. You should see to it that you don't."

"It has no effect on me!" she retorted.

He just smiled. "Well then, that's good, is it not? It makes me think you're the perfect companion for my friend Straught. You can get the best of him without letting him get the best of you." Then he added slowly, "As I just did."

"What makes you think it wasn't I who got the best of you?" she asked defiantly.

"Perhaps I'm not so sure." As if he spoke the truth, his face sobered. But in their embrace she was close enough to see the twinkle in his eye as he asked, "Shall we try again to make up our minds?" His hand tightened on her nape.

"Nay, that's not necessary whatever!" She hastily shrugged off his hold and backed away from the bars. She wanted no more of his spells, for he was a canny sort if she ever saw one. He was the only man who had ever received a kiss from the Kestrel, and if she didn't watch him, she might find herself in the same situation again.

"I can see you're a rather obstinate young woman, Kayleigh. What more shall I do to convince you? It's such a simple task I'm asking you to do." He frowned and watched her retreat.

"Who are you that you think you can be so devious and controlling? I won't do your bidding, I tell you, and I shall not tell you so again!" After her final refusal, she watched anger flare in his eyes.

"We'll see if you're so inflexible in the morning. I daresay a night spent down here will make you sing a different tune."

"I daresay it will not." She crossed her arms over her bosom.

"Fine. Have it your way," he said sternly. "I'll just play jailer for a few days—until you come to your senses and realize what's good for you." He exited through the battened shutters, and then she was alone in utter darkness.

Several hours passed. This time her imagination took flight in the dark. The dampness of the ground permeated her skirt, and unbidden she had a sudden, awful idea that perhaps the wine room held a snake . . . or two.

She pictured them wrapped around the wine caskets or hiding in the black crevices of the rack. It was all she could do not to clamor to be free, not to give in to St. Bride's deadly plan for her. Afraid to sit down, afraid even to walk for fear of arousing any sleeping serpents, she just hung on to the bars as if for dear life. Every now and then she glanced over her shoulder to the racks and prayed that she would see no shadowy movement there.

With a gasp of relief, she saw the battened shutters open again. But it wasn't St. Bride this time. Rather, it was Colette, the mulatto slave who had tended her while she recovered. Colette walked with her usual stiff, slow steps carrying a faience trencher filled with food. As she drew closer, Kayleigh made out that the plate contained a heaping pile of rice and beans. Steam rose from the fragrant meal, and Kayleigh's stomach rumbled belligerently, demanding that she eat. But she couldn't eat. As the little woman drew forth the key to unlock the door, Kayleigh knew this might be her only chance to escape. She couldn't outrun St. Bride or his gillie Laban. But she could outrun Colette.

In nervous anticipation, Kayleigh watched Colette put down the heavy trencher, then unlock the door. After she limped inside, Colette held out the plate to Kayleigh.

"Would you put it over on the bottling table? I'm afraid my arm is aching. That's looking much too heavy for just one hand." For effect, Kayleigh held her arm to her side and rubbed her wounded hand as if it were truly sore.

Warily, Colette obliged. But first she pulled the iron door to, as if to discourage Kayleigh from attempting an escape.

It wasn't discouraging enough, however, for as soon as Colette set the trencher on the table, Kayleigh made for the door. She was on the other side before Colette could release a cry of disbelief.

"*Non, non,* mademoiselle! Please do not do this!"

Kayleigh saw Colette struggle to reach the door. The slave looked terrified, and Kayleigh's heart went out to her.

"I'm sorry," Kayleigh whispered to her before fleeing to the battened doors. She would gladly have traded places with Colette. If all she faced from St. Bride was a beating, she would have taken it and been done with it, but the consequences she faced were much more grave than that. She gave one last pleading look at Colette, then, given no other choice, made her final escape.

"What do you make of her?" Laban asked St. Bride as he solemnly ate his dinner from a faience plate.

"I think Kayleigh'll come around. After all, what does she have to lose?" St. Bride laughed softly and pierced a shrimp with his knife.

"Not her virtue, 'tis for sure!" With a scowl of disapproval, Laban gulped his wine.

Suddenly Colette burst into the salon and interrupted the men's dinner. "Please, master! Please, Monsieur St. Bride! Please do not punish me! I don't know how it happened! I was just helping her with her sore arm! I thought she might be sick! I didn't want her to strain herself!"

"What is this? My God, woman, stop cringing as if we're going to string you up and flog you!" St. Bride stood up and gently shook Colette.

"I want to believe you—but you may change your mind when you find out that she has escaped!" Colette hung her head.

"Escaped?" St. Bride echoed.

"Gone?" Laban followed.

"*Oui,*" Colette admitted in defeat. "And I know she is very far away by now, for it took me forever to get to the top of those steps." She turned her eyes to the loggia stairs. "But I thought her arm—"

"It's all right, Colette," St. Bride interrupted. "It could have happened to any of us. That Kayleigh is a crafty wench. You're not to blame." He walked to the gallery and viewed the sunset. A twilight glow was setting upon the pecans, but in the distance a black gathering of clouds just tipped the horizon.

"St. Bride, do you want me to go after her?" Laban asked from behind him.

St. Bride shook his head. "No. This is between me and her. I'll find the wench myself."

She had hardly been gone an hour before she heard the hoofbeats. During her brave attempt at flight, she'd traversed several fields of dead, uncut indigo, but St. Bride's description of his plantation had proved correct. It was surrounded by swampland. She couldn't take the road, for that would be the first path her pursuer would take. So she instead took to the fields, only to be turned back time and again by encroaching wetlands.

Then it began to rain.

The sky released pail fulls of water and the black, windy storm blew branches from the live oaks that were scattered over the plantation's fields. Soaked to the skin, she walked aimlessly through the old indigo patches, hoping to find a route away from Belle Chasse that was neither swampland nor road. But that possibility seemed to become more and more distant. She hoped to go north. It was quite a distance to Fort Maurepas, but there at least she would be free of the magistrate and Belle Chasse's indomitable master.

But her hems grew heavy with mud, and with every passing minute it took a greater effort to go on. Finally, exhausted beyond endurance, she turned her eyes to the faraway lights of the plantation house. That was when she heard the hoofbeats.

They were quiet at first, muffled by distance and rain. But soon they grew loud and thrashing as the rider forged his way into the uncut field. She began to run, but it was as if she were being pursued by the devil himself. Everywhere she ran, the horse seemed right behind her. She was still too weak to go very far, and although she tried with all her might to get away, the horse and rider finally descended upon her.

"How did you find me!" she cried out in the pouring rain. The stallion reared directly in front of her, then came to a halt, its master wet and furious. Without a sound, St. Bride reached down and took her by the waist. Before she knew it, she had been laid across the pommel and was on her way back to Belle Chasse.

Too quickly they reached the misty, candlelit silhouette of the plantation house. Released to the ground, she trudged up to the forbidding structure and took shelter beneath the upper-story gallery. Once against the wall, she sank down against the bricks. Spent and exhausted, she was convinced she couldn't have taken even one more step. She wondered how long St. Bride would take to put up his horse; then, as if thinking of such demons made them appear, her eyes found St. Bride striding up to her, his face rigid with anger.

"The final sin." He wiped the rain from his eyes.

"How did you find me?" she demanded.

"You left a trail. The indigo has never been cut," he answered in a low voice.

"So what is your punishment to be this time? Will you flog me until I faint, or will you just put me to the wall and shoot?"

"I should cast you back out into that furious storm!" He took one step closer.

"Yes, why don't you?" she dared, her eyes suddenly glittering with suppressed fury.

"Oh, but I'm not going to. And do you know why?" He took another step closer.

"No." She looked up at him. He was almost upon her now, and she hadn't the vaguest idea how she would gather the strength to fend him off.

"Because I would rather do the punishing!" Angrily, he forced her to her feet.

"Take your hands from me, you cad!" She pushed against him and thought of their kiss in the wine jail. He was not going to control her any longer, not if she could help it.

"Goddamn it! There you go again! Putting on that ladylike demeanor, as if this were some kind of social and you did not want my dance!" He clenched his teeth. "Do you know what you've done this time? I had go out there and look for you. I, a great man of the realm, had to go out into the rain for over an hour to look for a cutpurse! If I hadn't seen the trail you made in the indigo, I'd still be out there! And for what? You! A little thief who has already sliced my hand, run away from my good graces, and then forced me time and time again to rescue her! Well this is it, I tell you!"

"What are you going to do?" she hissed.

"I'm going to teach you a lesson. Perhaps a good thrashing is what you need!"

"Let me go! Let me go, I tell you!" But he had already taken her to the stairs. He pulled her to his lap and seemed just on the verge of spanking her like a spoiled child when he stilled. Sitting on his lap, she looked up at him. His eyes locked with hers, and all at once she seemed to be back in the wine room under the spell he had worked that afternoon. His lips drew closer. Like a magnet, they attracted her own. Expecting to be beaten, she found herself on the very brink of kissing him!

She abruptly turned her head.

"Don't," he whispered.

But she would not comply. She would not kiss him. He seemed to realize this, and his hold on her slackened.

"You were stupid to run away. Don't you remember you almost died in the swamps out there?" His voice was oddly concerned.

"I've been more stupid," she answered with true regret.

"Look at me." When she refused, he cupped her jaw and forced her to turn her head. "Listen, love, I'll give you a choice." He continued, "If you want to return to New Orleans, Laban will take you there tomorrow. But if you don't want to return to the gutter, you may stay here. I've need of another servant."

Her brow grew troubled. She couldn't let Laban take her back to New Orleans. She knew that a hangman's noose was probably the best thing waiting for her there. And fleeing Belle Chasse by herself was proving no alternative at all. He was right—she had been stupid to leave. The next time she would truly die in the swamps, she had little doubt of that. So what was left her? To remain at Belle Chasse for a little while longer as a servant. If her cousin ever did visit St. Bride, she had some faith that she would be able to dodge him. At St. Bride's plantation she would be safe for a while. And perhaps in the meantime she would be able to figure out

St. Bride's connection to Straught. That could prove useful. But it was still so very dangerous!

"What's it to be, Kayleigh?" he pressed her.

"I don't know." She looked at him, but this time his gaze was cool and dispassionate. He unceremoniously dumped her from his lap and walked to the loggia stairs.

"I am going to retire for the night, and I suggest you do the same. Tomorrow, if you so choose, Laban will take you back to town and redeposit you into the gutter." His eyes flickered over her wet, disheveled appearance as she knelt upon the floor. "I invite you to sleep in the house, but if you prefer, you may sleep here on the bricks."

She shot him a scathing look, but he countered it, saying, "Don't cross me, wild thing. I'm in no mood to tangle with you again tonight." With that, he turned and ascended the steps.

It didn't take long for Kayleigh to make up her mind to sleep in the house. She had no penchant for sleeping on the floor and she needed a nice soft bed so she could sort out her tangled thoughts and make a decision on her future.

She followed St. Bride, all the while fuming at his arrogance. Och, how she wished she could show him! She was tired of being called a thief and looked upon as lower than a snake's belly. She was no pauper, not really. If she could get back to Scotland or exact revenge on her cousin, she would show this pompous Brit! Why, she would show all of them!

With her thoughts on her troubles, she stumbled on the stairs and barely caught herself on the banister. When she looked up, St. Bride was at the top of the stairs studying her with a frown.

"You needn't be concerned about my condition," she told him sarcastically. "I'll be an able servant, should I choose to stay."

"Ah, but you should be concerned, love," he answered ominously, his eyes trailing down her figure. "Because if

I'm forced to carry you to bed again, this time I'll be joining you there.''

"Nathrach!" she cursed furiously in Gaelic. Then she scurried up the rest of the steps, rushed past him, and locked herself securely in her bedchamber.

Chapter Eight

The visit was bound to occur, but not in her worst nightmare had she dreamed it would come so soon. Kayleigh was standing in the loggia the next morning waiting for Laban to ready his cart when she saw the rider and coach. She didn't have to look hard to know who the visitors were. It was Malcolm Quinn on the steed, to be sure. She'd have known him anywhere—the Irish-bred gillie, Erath Straught's skewed version of a nobleman's vassal.

With a quick intake of breath, she watched the rider approach the rear courtyard. Quinn was ambling along the allée of pecan trees in no great hurry. But his casual attitude didn't keep her heart from doing a flip-flop in her chest, nor did it stop her hands from trembling in her pockets. For following Quinn with great fanfare was a black hired coach that had to be carrying her deadly cousin. In panic, she lost several precious seconds wondering if they'd come to Belle Chasse for her.

Kayleigh swallowed the horror rising up from her throat, and took in every awful aspect of Quinn's appearance. He was thinner than when she had last seen him. His pudgy face had taken on a pallor seen in those who'd been ill or lost blood. She, of course, suspected it had been the latter.

Suddenly Malcolm looked up to the loggia as if by premonition, and Kayleigh leaned back from the shutters, praying he hadn't seen her. But she knew she was trapped. Since there was only one way up to the house and that was through the loggia, there was only one way down too.

"Laban is ready, Kayleigh."

Startled, she turned to face St. Bride.

"Go on. Down to the courtyard. He is ready to take you back to New Orleans."

"To town?"

"Yes, woman, you're free to leave if you so choose."

"No, no," she stuttered, and backed away from the loggia stairs. Good God, she couldn't go down to the courtyard now! Any minute her cousin was going to alight from that black carriage. What was she to do?

"What are you waiting for?" he demanded.

"I ..." She stopped. She had to find a way to avoid walking down those steps to the courtyard, and the only way to do that was to refuse Laban's ride. "I've had a change of heart," she said suddenly.

St. Bride studied her, then moved into the loggia. "What are you talking about?"

"I don't really want to go back to town. In fact, I want to stay here." She stole a look through the loggia slats, and her heart leaped to her throat. As she had feared, her sweet cousin Erath was emerging from the coach. She murmured desperately to St. Bride, "I've lied to you. I don't want to leave here. You see, I have no better place to go at all."

"I find that hard to believe in light of your past behavior." He looked truly suspicious now. She didn't know how she would convince him of her new-found desire to be his servant. But then a terrible idea came to her mind, and as a last resort, she closed her eyes and said the words she thought would convince him.

"All along I've had no desire to seduce your friends."

The air around them stilled; then, like a death knell, she heard footsteps on the loggia stairs.

"What are you saying, Kayleigh? That all along you've wanted to seduce *me?*" St. Bride's voice was hushed. His eyes had narrowed so that she could barely make out the turquoise of his irises.

"I should like to stay. Perhaps I could be a house servant. Oh, please, let me stay," she begged futilely, evading his stare. But why was she even trying? she thought, with resignation. Her cousin must be upon them by now.

"You have visitors, St. Bride. Shall I still take the wench to town?" Laban appeared at the top of the stairs. Kayleigh nearly gasped with relief at the sight of his disapproving face.

"Visitors?" St. Bride smiled then, but it was not a smile that made his handsome face boyish. It was a smile that turned his eyes a deep, stormy blue. There was desire in them, Kayleigh thought. But this desire seemed to have nothing to do with physical lust; rather, it resembled blood-lust more closely. She wondered why that was, but Laban interrupted her thoughts.

"Shall I go to town?"

Rubbing his jaw, St. Bride debated within himself, letting his eyes flick up and down Kayleigh. Finally, as if making the only decision he could in such a short time, he said, "No, I don't think Kayleigh will be going to town just yet, Laban. Of all things, she has told me she wants employment here. So why don't you tell Straught and Quinn to come up, and we'll have refreshments."

In disbelief, Laban's eyes opened wide, but with an uneasy nod he cast Kayleigh a black look and trod back down the stairs.

"If you want to be useful, go to the kitchens and tell Colette to prepare some food and wine. Then bring it up here."

St. Bride's order was clear, but she already knew how to dodge it. "Yes, yes. But I have to fetch something from my room. May I go there first?"

"Be quick." He walked to the slats to observe his guests' progress. "Oh, and Kayleigh," he added with great emphasis. "If I were truly looking for a *house servant,* I would want one much more capable at domestic duties than you are and . . . less attractive. Do you understand?"

She nodded, but the meaning of his words were lost. All she could think of was to get to her bedchamber and hide before Straught showed his terrible face in the loggia.

"All right then. I'm glad you've decided to stay. I think you'll find me very easy to please."

With a nod, St. Bride dismissed her. She smiled weakly and left. When the door to her room was shut, she fell to her knees with relief.

It was several moments before Kayleigh could gather her wits and decide what to do. She listened for heavy steps upon the loggia stairs, and when she heard the telltale shuffle through the loggia, she went through the French doors onto the gallery and stood just behind the shutters that opened into the salon. It was a big chance, but if she couldn't flee, she should at least hide. And as long as she was going to hide, she felt she should take the risk of finding out what business these men had between them and if they were going, perchance, to bring her into the discussion. If they were, she would be better off on the gallery than trapped in her bedchamber when Straught came to call. Hearing their business begin, she moved forward to listen.

"Are you interested?" She saw St. Bride hand Straught and Quinn each a glass of brandy. Erath dabbled at his, but Quinn took his own in two gulps and then paused to belch.

"Interested? Naturally I'm interested. But I don't want to make any mistakes. I've checked you out thoroughly, Ferringer. I know all about your little plantation on Wolf Island in Georgia colony." Straught stared at St. Bride, but instead of being intimidated, St. Bride merely returned an equally piercing stare. Then St. Bride smiled maddeningly. Quinn tried to look nonchalant as he pawed the scruff of his beard.

"And?" St. Bride dropped his gaze.

"And I think you know what you're doing." Straught was tight-lipped. "But I must see the seeds. I know good seed when I see it, and I won't go any further until I'm convinced this thing will be a success."

"I'll show you the seeds." St. Bride kicked aside several rush-seated chairs near the mantel and revealed a huge leather-bound trunk against one wall. Using a brass key he opened it, revealing several rice-paper bags.

"Open them," Straught commanded Quinn. Obeying, Quinn went down heavily upon his knees. He opened first one bag, then another. From the gallery, Kayleigh risked a glimpse of them. She thought they could almost have been gunpowder, for the seeds were iron gray and very small.

"Very good," Straught said after he inspected the bags. He then turned to St. Bride and said, "These seeds are of the best quality. They must have cost dearly. How did you pay for them?"

"I haven't. I've been given them on credit. That's why I must have your answer soon."

"And what if that answer is no?"

St. Bride snapped down the lid on the trunk. "Then I daresay we have nothing more to talk about. And I shall have to find a partner elsewhere."

"Have you any gold?" Straught quizzed. "After all, my share and Thionville's share will hardly cover the cost of the seeds." He tossed his head in the direction of the trunk.

St. Bride walked to the mantel. He removed several heavy silk purses from it and threw them down to Quinn. Eagerly, Quinn tore at them.

"You keep all this gold out here at the plantation?" Quinn practically salivated over the loot. Pure gold was a rare and valuable currency indeed, far more useful than jewels or paper notes. "Are you a fool then, man?" he asked St. Bride.

"Have you forgotten this is a primitive land? A man would cut your throat for one of these coins, let alone these many thousands!"

"Yes, we do have a problem with thieves, even here at Belle Chasse." St. Bride smiled almost to himself. "But I think between the two of us, we can handle any situation that might arise."

As St. Bride spoke, Laban came up behind Quinn. From his vantage point at the base of the trunk, the pudgy Scot looked up at both men. Both Laban and St. Bride were uncommonly large and fierce. Soon he nodded his head in compliance. "I see what you mean," Quinn muttered.

"Good." St. Bride smiled, replaced the purses on the mantel, and turned to the business at hand. "Straught, now that you've had time to check me out, I must tell you that I'd like some time to do the same. I've decided that it would be to my advantage to take on investors after all, but I want to make sure I have the right ones. I'm not a man who enjoys making mistakes."

"I've found out that your plantation on Wolf Island doesn't make nearly enough income to support this kind of place. I'm surprised that you would be so particular." Straught rubbed the rim of his beaker with a finger.

"Although I do need more gold than I first predicted, I will not make a hasty decision."

"What if Thionville and I don't want to wait?" Straught snapped. Seeing his master's agitation, Quinn raised himself from the floor and hitched up his breeches.

"Belle Chasse has the acreage to amass a fortune. Not even Louis XV would be able to resist the opportunity. I've put together figures showing the profits I expect to make. I must confess the figures are quite dazzling." St. Bride raised a vaguely satanic eyebrow. "You and the comte will wait."

Kayleigh peeked through a slat and saw the pleased look on St. Bride's face. He was fingering the back of a chair as if he were trying to control a pent-up impulse, yet his every gesture and every polite smile belied this. Was the Straught's friend or his foe? She couldn't decide. But the fact that St. Bride wanted to be in with Straught at all was enough to make her distrust him completely.

How she wanted to leave! she thought as she pulled back from the shutters. But she couldn't. There were no bars keeping her here, but she was still a prisoner. She was trapped by circumstance. Her only consolation for the present was that she had been left out of the men's conversation entirely. That was a good sign.

Turning back to the conversation in the salon, she suddenly froze in place. A huge man was standing at the opposite end of the gallery watching her. The black disapproval on his face was nothing she hadn't experienced before, but she had yet to find it so thoroughly hateful.

"Laban." She silently mouthed the name and backed away from the salon shutters. As he lumbered up to her with his huge twenty-stone frame, her terror nailed her feet to the boards. He'd caught her in the act of eavesdropping. Spying. She had brought trouble on now.

She forced her legs to move, but he grabbed her by the neck. She would have screamed, but she wanted the occupants of the salon not to venture forth onto the gallery.

Yet her desire was soon forgotten. Without words, Laban led her back along the gallery to her room. When they arrived, she heard muffled voices through the bedchamber doors that led to the salon. St. Bride and Erath Straught were continuing their discussion, unaware of the quiet struggle between her and the black man. Laban silently shut and locked the salon doors behind him.

He then forced her into the walnut fauteuil. He quickly tied her wrists to the arms of the chair with his bootstraps, all the while refusing to meet her imploring gaze. With a grim set to his mouth, he finished lashing her to the seat, squelching any rebellion as easily he would have a child's.

Laban exited through the gallery doors and locked the

shutters behind him. She heard his footsteps grow fainter and fainter as he walked first to the loggia, then down the stairs.

So he's left me for St. Bride to deal with, she murmured to herself. She felt miraculously relieved. But then another thought occurred to her. *Or he's left me for Straught.* She turned panicked eyes toward the locked doors.

Colette carried a tray of cold pigeon breast and figs up the loggia stairs to the salon. She entered the room and unobtrusively placed a cabriole-legged cypress table in front of St. Bride and the strangers. She silently put down the tray and began the preparations as if all she prayed for was a hasty retreat.

"Thionville can come by anytime and see the plantation. But I must know how much he plans to invest. I'd like to have your figures too." St. Bride watched Colette as she set out their food.

"I'll let him know what we've discussed. But I can give you only a couple of weeks. By then we must have an agreement." Straught watched Quinn take a yellow faience plate filled with the rich fowl and begin stuffing his mouth.

"Perhaps we will have an agreement then. But let me ask you—why have you had a change of heart? When I discussed some of this on the *Bonaventure*, Straught, you seemed ill at ease about it."

"I had other business to take care of. Now that that's off my mind, I can concentrate on other matters." Straught's eyes roved once again to his man Quinn. He seemed disgusted by Quinn's robust appetite, but when Malcolm saw his master staring at him, he merely smiled, showing the chunks of pigeon caught in his gapped teeth.

"I presume this other business was taken care of the night we all gathered at Thionville's house?"

Erath nodded his head.

"What other ventures are you involved in here?" St.

Bride's question was left hanging as Straught abruptly stood and shook his hand.

"I've got to get back, Ferringer. I wish I could stay and see more of Belle Chasse, but I must leave that for another time. Come along, Malcolm."

"Yes, sir, Mr. Straught." Quinn quickly put down his plate and stood also.

"Oh, Ferringer," Straught said before he descended the loggia stairs. "Give Malcolm the figures you've drawn up on Belle Chasse's expected profits. I know Thionville will want to see them."

"I'll dig it out and send Quinn on his way. He'll follow you shortly." St. Bride went to the armoire at the end of the room and rummaged through several stacks of papers.

"Malcolm, I expect to see you. No dawdling with the slaves today, understand me?" Straught shot an appreciative glance at Colette, who shrank back into the corner. He then waved a brusque farewell, and in less than a minute the borrowed coach rumbled out of the courtyard on its way back to New Orleans.

"Yes, sir, Mr. Straught," Malcolm grumbled under his breath. He picked up the pigeon breast again and gnawed on it, eyeing Colette, until St. Bride produced the necessary papers.

"Here you are." St. Bride handed him the figures. Seeing Quinn pause over the pigeon, he said, "By all means, take it with you. You're looking even paler than you did on the *Bonaventure,* Quinn. Doesn't Straught treat you well?" St. Bride smiled, but it was anything but hospitable.

As Quinn walked out, St. Bride turned to Colette.

"What happened to Kayleigh? I told Kayleigh to serve." The words were hardly out of St. Bride's mouth when Quinn, still in the loggia, began coughing and gasping for air. He fumbled for a brandy decanter on a small table nearby. After swallowing the piece of pigeon in his throat, he apologized.

"I've dawdled long enough, Mr. Ferringer. I must be going

now. My hearty thanks for the fowl." Quinn gave them an odd look.

"You've lingered here overlong," St. Bride answered with a frown.

"Yes, Mr. Straught will be wanting these figures. Good day to you, Mr. Ferringer." Strangely enough, as he descended the stairs, Quinn looked as if he wanted to clap his hands with glee. Soon St. Bride saw him heading through the pecans, giving Belle Chasse many backward glances.

"Now, what does that mean?" St. Bride muttered aloud, rubbing his forehead in agitation.

"You've got a bigger problem now, my friend." Laban's voice boomed from the loggia.

St. Bride demanded between clenched teeth, "So where *is* Kayleigh?"

"Ah, the enemy lurks within." St. Bride stood in the gallery doorway of Kayleigh's bedchamber looking straight at Kayleigh, who was bound to the chair.

"It's not what you think." She leaned forward, but the bootstraps held her back.

"What do I think?" He sauntered into the room, closing the louvers behind him with a heavy, clacking thud.

"You think I was eavesdropping on you. And you ask why I would do such a thing—" She stopped abruptly when St. Bride pulled a knife from the waist of his breeches, but she was relieved to realize that he was simply going to cut her free. She rubbed her wrists and looked at him.

"Have you a curiosity about me or my friends? Did you get a good look at Erath Straught? Are you perhaps thinking that he would not be such a bad chap to tumble with after all?" St. Bride's eyes locked with hers.

She jerked her head down and colored at the crude statement. "I am not going along with your plan whatever, no matter what Erath Straught looks like. I told you that."

"Good," St. Bride said evenly. "That's just as well,

because you see, he's got more enemies than friends these days.''

''Which''—she licked her dry lips—''which are you?''

''His friend! Friend! You remember that if ever you get to town and chance to see him.'' He stroked her sleek dark head.

She nodded, too frightened to speak.

''You've got a lot of bad habits, love, did you know that? I knew about the thieving and the lying. But I didn't know that I could add spying to your other admirable traits. Why were you out on the gallery and not serving, as I asked you to?''

Again she was silent.

''What did you think you could gain by spying on me? Is it my gold you're after?'' He shook her. ''Well?''

''No, no. I really don't—'' she pleaded, but he wouldn't let her finish.

''You can't have my gold, Kayleigh. Not unless I give it to you. And you must know, one catches more flies with honey than with vinegar.'' He brushed the flawless cream of her cheeks with his thumbs and muttered as if to himself, ''Ah, if only you were just one tenth less exquisite. My God, I don't need this.''

''That man, Erath Straught . . .'' she sputtered, and then trailed her words. What was she going to tell him? She had no easy explanation. Worse, St. Bride himself was as much an enigma as his relationship with Straught. Only now she'd just found out he was involved with her cousin up to his handsome forehead.

''What about him?'' he asked tersely.

The words slipped from her lips. ''It was him I was watching. Not you.''

Suddenly St. Bride paused. When he spoke again, his voice was low and harsh. ''He's quite a rake, I hear. Find him handsome, do you?

When she didn't answer, he demanded, ''Does Erath

Straught now hold a fascination for you? He can do that to females, I know. Believe me, I know. With his fine clothes and fair, boyish face, I'd hate to see you fall—''

"No, no, I never would," she told him, although she fair wanted to scream it.

"But he does. I can see it now in your eyes." St. Bride's voice became tight. "You just wanted to get a glimpse of my pretty-mannered friend, didn't you? Have you reconsidered my initial offer? Do you prefer Straught in your bed to me?''

"No!" She leaped up from her seat. His senseless words were making her furious, but she knew she couldn't let them get the better of her. She was in a dangerous situation, and she had to be careful. In an effort to be left in peace, she made for the gallery, thinking how crazy the conversation had become. It was almost laughable what St. Bride thought. She'd be laughing herself if they weren't talking about Erath Straught.

"I don't take this personally, you know." He followed her and grabbed her on the veranda. Abruptly, he pulled her face up to look at him. When he touched her, she felt his hard palm run over the smooth arch of her back. Suddenly he smiled, but his smile was harsh and somehow sad. "You beautiful, heartless creature. Only a creature with your past would bite the hand that feeds you if you thought it better that way.''

"You're wrong! I don't want him—nor you!" she gasped.

"But that's not what you implied earlier, you fickle little baggage! You wanted my favor then." St. Bride's eyes turned ominous and blue. "You know what I think? I think you need to be taught a lesson. You need to learn to be true to your word. And I'm just the man to teach you."

"Please, no," she whispered. Then her mouth was plundered as it had never been before. Once his lips had captured hers, his tongue sought out each recess, making her yield to its force and tenacity. Her resistance to his intimate touch only made him go deeper, so deep that soon she was moaning, her body turning to liquid silver, ready for him to do with as he pleased. Her sanity seemed so tenous that she couldn't quite grasp what it told her to do. But eventually his large hand moved up her unbound waist to cup her heaving breast. The shock of it made her come to her senses. He was touching her where she had never, ever been touched before. He was heartless and cruel. She knew without a doubt that to succumb to him now would be fatal.

Suddenly her teeth clamped down on his tongue. With a gasp of pain and surprise, he drew back from her.

"Savage!" She shuddered, putting her arms in front of her chest to shield herself from his touch. But her slim, creamy neck was still vulnerable, and his hand found it quickly. His smooth grasp sent shivers down her spine, and she saw the scar she had inflicted on him glisten in the fading sunlight.

"If I'm a savage"—he paused—"then I've certainly found my mate." He flung her aside and walked to the end of the gallery. Without a backward glance, he descended the loggia stairs until she could see him no more.

Chapter Nine

What a terrible fix she was in now. Wretchedly, Kayleigh paced the gallery later that afternoon and wondered what was to become of her. She leaned her head against a column and looked to the River Road. That was the way out. She would have to keep her eye on the road—at some point it would have to have travelers. She would beg them for a ride. Her only hope was that a traveler would come along soon.

"Ici, I have some things for you." Colette came out onto the veranda and motioned for Kayleigh to return to the bed-chamber. Kayleigh was curious to see what she had, but then out of the corner of her eye she spied St. Bride and Laban riding away from Belle Chasse through the pecans.

"Colette, where are they going?" Kayleigh went to the railing and put her hand to her eyes to shield her vision from the blinding afternoon sun.

"Monsieur Ferringer and Laban have gone into town. There is a tavern there, and tonight I think they mean to seek it out. Tonight they want to celebrate."

"Celebrate what?" Kayleigh asked, wondering if it was the deal that her cousin and St. Bride had made earlier in the day.

"I don't know. They didn't tell me."

"I see," Kayleigh answered forlornly. She wished she had known they were going. Perhaps she could have thought up some way to accompany them. Then, once they got to New Orleans, she surely could have disappeared. Och, then her problems would be so much smaller.

"The master told me to bring you some more clothes. Since you will be staying." Ignoring Kayleigh's black mood, Colette returned to the bedchamber and laid out the bundle she had brought in from the salon.

Kayleigh followed her, then looked down at two blue osnaburg gowns. The heavy linen dresses were painfully unadorned, but still her begrudging heart wanted them. For the first time in a year she was actually going to have an extra change of clothing. She wouldn't have to wear the one dress they'd already given her until it was ragged.

Along with the gowns, Kayleigh also found a pair of shoes and stockings and several petticoats and kerchiefs. These bits of clothing were perhaps not much for a girl who had once been dressed in the finest silk, velvets and satins, but she was grateful for them.

"Are these yours? Am I taking your gowns?" Kayleigh gave Colette a guilty look.

"*Non,* these clothes are Babet's. The laundress. She is not so skinny." Colette smiled and brought a hand to her thin chest.

"But won't Babet miss them?"

"A seamstress was here from *Des Allemands,* the German Coast, a few days ago. She made us all many dresses. These can be spared." Colette turned to leave.

"Wait." Kayleigh touched her arm, feeling oddly anxious for company. "What—what has St. Bride said to you? I don't know what I'm to do here."

"All I was told was to give you your meals and these clothes. Monsieur Ferringer did not tell me anything else."

"But I'm to be a servant here. Didn't he say so? Didn't he give me something to do?"

"Non, mademoiselle." Colette cast her eyes to the floor.

Worriedly, Kayleigh bit her lower lip. This was not a good sign. This was not a good sign at all. If St. Bride didn't want her as a servant, he probably wanted her here as his *mistress.* She had put herself in a bad position, and now it looked as if she would have to pay the piper. That would probably be that evening, when St. Bride returned.

"If you will excuse me, I must return to the kitchens."

"Colette, wait—I wanted to ask you. Did St. Bride punish you when I went away? I mean, did he—?"

"Non, he was very kind. I'm sorry, but he was much more angry with you."

"You needn't be sorry," Kayleigh said with a rueful smile. "After all, I duped you. I'm just glad you didn't have to pay for my mistake."

"Oui, mademoiselle." Colette moved to the door, then paused. Tentatively she asked, "Would you like to come to the kitchens for some dinner?"

Kayleigh gave her a tremulous smile. "Yes, thank you, I would like that very much." Feeling a little more optimistic, Kayleigh followed her out the door.

Later that evening, Kayleigh paced the salon in agitation. Colette had refused to give her anything to do, and after she'd eaten, she'd felt she was in the way in the kitchens. So as darkness had settled upon Belle Chasse, she'd wandered back to the house, her footsteps echoing through the empty rooms making her wonder what would happen when its master returned.

Frustrated, she slumped into an armchair in her bedchamber and let her gaze move through the doors to the veranda. Sunset's last rosy hue was just rouging the tops of the pecan trees. Sounds of low, throaty singing came from the slave village behind the plantation. Babies' cries were hushed as field workers were led home after preparing the land for St. Bride's new crop. Colette had named the many nations that

made up the slaves in the village. There were Hibou, Man-
dingo, and Congo, but there were also second-and third-
generation slaves who could claim to be Louisiana natives.
In the twilight, Kayleigh wondered how many slaves Belle
Chasse boasted. From the evening hum of activity, she suspected there were hundreds.

Through the open verdigris-painted shutters, she saw the
river that ran black against the shore. Like a great oily serpent,
it wound its way toward New Orleans. Against her will, her
mind wandered to the *poteaux* hut by the river where Bardolph
lay. Sadly she thought of him. He'd saved her life twice, and
her only repayment had been unfulfilled promises. She hadn't
even been able to give him a decent burial. With a lump in
her throat, she hoped fervently that he had forgiven her for
that. A tear blurred her vision. Finally she turned from the
river, sick from its very presence.

She left the bedchamber and wandered into the salon. There
she began to pace, begging her mind to come up with a
solution to her troubles. As she paced, something on the
mantel caught her eye. It was bright and shiny, and when she
inspected it, she found it was a cobalt blue enameled thimble.
She picked it up, remembering the seamstress that Colette
had mentioned earlier, and she wondered if it belonged to
her.

She studied the pretty object, then frowned. For some
reason the little thimble tickled her memory. It took a moment
before she could recall, but then she knew what it was.

Her box.

The thimble was the exact same cobalt blue of her box.
And Morna's too, she mused. Her brow furrowed, and she
fingered the cobalt lip of the thimble. Where was her box
now? She'd still had it in her pocket when she and Bardolph
had left Mhor. They'd used it to pay for passage to New
Orleans. Was it in someone's possession in Glasgow? Or had
the captain of their ship, the *Deepwater,* sold it at some exotic
port of call? She turned the thimble over in her hands, wishing

that she held her box instead. She longed for some physical keepsake of her family, some remembrance of how much they had loved her and how much they had prayed for her happiness.

Slowly her palm closed over the thimble. She wanted it, not only because it reminded her of her box, but also because it might entice a traveler to take her back to New Orleans.

Suddenly her fingers trembled. *"Ladies would not, could not steal!"* She could almost hear her mother's plea from the heavens above. *Dhé*, but stealing was harder when things around her reminded her of who she really was. New dresses and a clean bed had brought back vivid memories of her more noble life. She turned her eyes toward the mantel and told herself to put the thimble back.

But soon she was wondering who would even miss the thing. The seamstress had probably acquired a brand-new thimble, and certainly St. Bride would never miss it. It was obvious that he had other things on his mind.

She turned and looked behind her. There was no one there. She returned her gaze to the thimble and reminded herself of her determination to return to Scotland. In the Highlands she would find people who remembered her and her family. She would receive justice for all the wrong done to her by Straught. But she couldn't do anything stuck in a backwater Louisiana plantation, like a lamb ready for spring slaughter.

With this new thought, Kayleigh made her decision. In the blink of an eye, she swept the thimble into her pocket. Then she gave an innocent shrug and found a flint to light a taper on the mantel.

The room was soon bathed in candlelight. She turned to the veranda and the road beyond. There would certainly be no travelers tonight. She would have to wait until morning. Resigning herself, she took a pewter candleholder and made to retire to her bedchamber and the soft bed it contained.

But she should have known the evening would not be so quickly over, for leaning against the salon entrance to the faux marble loggia stood St. Bride, watching her with a most intent gaze.

"So you're back," she whispered in a cautious voice. "I didn't hear you arrive." The thimble fairly burned in her pocket.

"Yes. Did you miss me?" The edge of his mouth turned in a wry grin. She noticed he twirled one of those bedamned roots between his fine lips. She noticed, too, that although his words were smooth and perfectly articulated, his eyes seemed slightly more brilliant than normal. And his gait as he sauntered into the salon was much less steady than it had been earlier that day.

"Drink?" He went to the pier table and unstopped a glass decanter. "I haven't any sherry," he said. His eyes flicked to her and he continued, "I hope brandy won't offend your . . . drawing-room sensibilities." Suddenly he tipped his head back and laughed. Kayleigh prickled with ire.

"I haven't any use for your brandy."

He put a glass in her hand. "You may" was all he said.

Her fingers began to tremble at the ominous words. She lifted her eyes to him, but he had swaggered over to the settee with the decanter and settled there, swinging one jackbooted leg over its arm.

"Sit down," he invited, but it was more of a command. Not ready for a confrontation, she took the nearest armchair and watched as he sucked on the tip of the sassafras root. Pensively, he outlined the scar on his hand with his forefinger, then his sea green eyes slid over to her. "You're one dangerous female, love."

His words didn't warrant a reply, yet in order to keep her nerves from stretching to the breaking point, she had to avoid answering him by taking a sip of the brandy. The liquid burned all the way down her throat, and she shuddered. But afterward she could face him more confidently.

"And what's to be made of it?" she finally said.

"Nothing"—he sat upright and perused her—"because

I'm dangerous too.'' With that, he reached over and took the brandy from her. He took a long draught from it, then placed it firmly back in her hand.

''It's obvious you've misunderstood what I said this morning,'' she began, feeling nervous again. ''Colette doesn't understand that I meant to be a servant here.''

Abruptly changing the subject, he asked, ''How did you get here, Kayleigh?''

''You—you brought me here.''

''No, how did you end up in New Orleans?''

She took another sip of the brandy. Had he seen Straught again? Was that why he asked such a question?

''I came here from Scotland.''

''Yes, yes.'' He turned to her. ''But for what crime were you sentenced to living here? Were you a prostitute in Edinburgh, perchance? Or if I looked for it, would I find the brand of a murderess on that fair flesh of yours?'' He tipped down one shoulder of her dress. Quickly she pulled it back beneath her kerchief, but not before he'd had a glimpse of the smooth skin of her shoulder.

''I've committed no crime. I'm an innocent. I was not sentenced to living here, I came of my own free will.''

''You came here alone?''

She paused. ''I came here with a friend.''

''Where is this friend?''

''He's dead.''

''He?'' St. Bride raised one black eyebrow. ''What was his name?''

''Bardolph Ogilvie,'' she snapped. Where were these questions leading?

''Was he the one who taught you to steal?''

''I didn't want to steal. I had no choice. Bardolph was getting too old, and he had to have his rum.'' She bit her lower lip. She had no idea why she was offering information to someone who could not be trusted. Perhaps that was what made St. Bride such a dangerous man.

"What did you do after he died?"

"Nothing. I came here." She didn't feel like talking anymore.

However, St. Bride did. "Where do you come from in Scotland?"

She stared at him. She didn't want to answer, but she didn't want him to continue to think she was some kind of criminal. She decided the truth—or at least part of it—would be best.

"I come from a castle. A great castle."

"You worked in a castle, eh? And who was your laird?"

"I had no laird. I didn't work there."

"You didn't? What did you do there?" Maddeningly, he lifted one jet eyebrow. His implication was clear.

"Your thoughts should be boiled in lye!" Affronted, she began to stand, but he reached over and shoved her back into the chair. Then he leaned back on the settee once more and removed the root from his mouth.

"You're right. After all, you're dominating my thoughts." He paused, then took a long swig straight from the decanter. "You know, Laban doesn't like you, love. He thinks I should be rid of you."

"Laban may be right." She had no fondness for Laban either, but at least the black man was straightforward about his feelings and didn't play these cat-and-mouse games like St. Bride did. Where was he leading her now?

"At the tavern, Laban and I had a good long talk about you." St. Bride looked at her. "We had gone out to talk about my great success with Erath Straught, and yet all we talked about was you."

"How odd," she murmured, inching back in her seat.

"Yes, how odd." He stood and leaned over her, bracing himself on the arms of her chair. "I have business here, Kayleigh. What am I doing getting entangled with the likes of you?" He leaned closer. Suddenly his face became very serious, almost like that of a little boy begging candy and being refused. "So what say you and I have a go at it and get out from under each other's skin?"

That was all she was going to take. Disgusted, she pulled his hands from her chair and stood up. "You are drunk," she proclaimed. "And not only that, you are the most befuddled lout I have ever set eyes upon. I would rather clean chamberpots than stay here and take this poor excuse for courtship."

"You can clean chamberpots here. After all, isn't that a servant's duty?"

She looked at him over her shoulder. "I expect it is, but I'll not be a servant for you!" She finished calmly, "It's clear I've made a mistake thinking I should stay here."

He laughed. "That again! Well, you're not leaving. Not now. You've got bats in your belfry if you think I'm going to let you trot out of this mess without paying me my due! No, you made your offer this morning, love. Now you're just going to have to stand by it."

"I offered to become your servant. Nothing more!"

"A servant, eh?" He towered over her, and her eyes grew wide. "Well, what would you say if I told you I only have need of a *personal* servant?"

"A personal servant? I'll do no such thing!" she retorted, taking a step back.

"Then be off!" His voice lowered to hardly a rumble. "But before you do, take off that dress."

"It's my dress!" Her hand flew to her bosom.

"No, it's *my* dress. I paid for it. It's not what I would pick to clothe you in, but it's still mine. You haven't earned it— all you've earned is a stay of execution. So give it back." He held out his hand.

"Then where are my clothes? Give those back to me, and you may have your cursed dress!" Her eyes blazed with anger. He was playing with her again, and she didn't like it. Not one wee bit.

"Can't, love. We had to burn your clothes. They were

covered with blood. My blood, I might add.'' He rubbed his chin, took another sip from the decanter, then grinned wickedly. "I said, give it over."

"No! Don't be ridiculous! I can't leave here with nothing to wear!"

"I said, give it over." Though he was unsteady, he was quick. He lunged for her, and she was forced to run. She ran in the wrong direction, however, for she ended up in St. Bride's bedchamber, facing him off on the opposite side of his bed.

"I'm not going to take off this dress, St. Bride Ferringer, so you might as well get that into your thick drunken head!" she cried out at him.

"Oh, you're not, eh? Well, I have the law on my side!" he stated dramatically.

"You and the law be damned!" she cried just as he rushed her. She tried to get out to the gallery, but he had her off her feet and tossed her onto the bed before she could even catch her breath. In order to hold her there, he threw himself on top of her, covering her entire body with his. She struggled like a wildcat against him, but this only served to burrow them deeper into the down of the mattress. After a moment, as she lay panting, he reached for her fichu. She grabbed his hand to stop him but he quickly pulled her off. He made several attempts to remove her kerchief but she was able to thwart them all. Losing all patience, St. Bride finally ended the game. He took control by pinning both her hands over her head with his own. In horror, Kayleigh watched him grab the knot of her kerchief with his teeth. Unwillingly she released a soft moan of defeat. An emotion swirled in her stomach that was surrender, excitement, and fury all wrapped in one. A prisoner of his strapping body and vise-like hold, she couldn't move an inch. Instead, she was forced to lie quietly and watch him loosen the knot with his strong white teeth. It was unbearable. But worse was the agonizing caress of his breath warm against her skin, and his lips, warmer still when they finally kissed the spot between her breasts where her kerchief used to lie.

"Quit," she whispered, almost drugged from his touch.

"Make me," he parried just as he began working on the hooks of her bodice. Before she even realized he'd released one of her hands, he had seven tiny steel hooks undone on her bodice. His finger was just about to slide beneath her shift and caress one of her nipples when she gasped her dismay and displeasure.

"I said quit, you animal!"

She tugged at the hand on her bodice, but St. Bride only laughed. He retreated a bit, however, and his hand moved down her body to rest intimately on her hip. Angrily, she pulled that from her too. Eventually his hand gave way but not before it took part of one of her pockets with it. Hearing a chilling clink, she knew the thimble had fallen to the floorboards.

"What have we here?" St. Bride placed one arm on her chest, then tipped his head over the mattress to retrieve the thimble. When he had it in his palm, he laid over her once more, holding the cobalt-blue piece up to her eyes. It looked positively insignificant in his large hand.

"It's—it's not what you think. Colette let me have it. She wanted me to sew something for her," she defended herself, her chest heaving up and down from her struggle.

"Liar. This thing doesn't belong to Colette. This was my sister's thimble. I carry it for good luck." His eyes darkened. "You were stealing this from me, weren't you?"

"Nay, why would I want the thing? I cannot sew whatever."

"Aye, that must be true. Sewing is a lady's craft. Not much for the likes of you."

"Ooh, *amadan!* Get off me!" she cried out, unable to take his abuse any further.

"I won't have you stealing from me," he said suddenly in a tone that was low and serious. "I won't abide it—you hear me, little thief?'' Heeding the growl of his voice, she quieted and looked straight at him. The words he whispered next were sobering. ''The hangman's shadow has already fallen on your path. You understand, Kayleigh?''

Reluctantly, she nodded.

''You owe it to your savior to be sweet and compliant. No more stealing.''

''I think you deign to be my keeper, not my savior,'' she said hotly.

''Perhaps. But how can you blame me when you're as fetching as you are wicked?'' He dropped a small kiss on the swell of her breast exposed by her partly unhooked bodice.

Her nipple tingled and hardened with his touch. It was almost more than she could stand. Never had she felt such eddying emotions. She wanted to run from St. Bride and succumb to him all at the same time. Her nerves felt singed and raw as she tried to hide the strange desire that surged in her body. Nonetheless, his kiss put a blush to her cheeks and her heart beat so fast, she was sure he could see it throb in her bosom.

But she was not going to let this dominating rogue best her! Not even at games she didn't quite know how to play. Refusing to surrender, she let her fingers itch for her *sgian dhu.* If a man at Broutin's barracks had dared even half of the intimacies St. Bride had, he'd have surely found her little black dagger holding him at bay. That had always worked in the past. But even if she had her *sgian dhu* back, she wondered if it wouldn't be an impotent weapon against St. Bride. He was so unlike any other man she'd ever come up against. With him, she found herself so easily overpowered, so willingly controlled, that before she even knew what he wanted, she found he had already taken it.

''You know what I think, Kayleigh?''

She glared at him balefully as he lifted his head.

''I think your laird must miss you—that is, if he's still

around to miss you.'' As if just struck by this thought, he asked solemnly, ''He is still around, isn't he?''

''Nay!'' she told him furiously. ''I killed him off in his own bed because he would not get off me!'' She shoved at him mercilessly and St. Bride seemed to drown in his own laughter. He rolled to one side and that was all she needed to scramble to the end of the bed. She stood and quickly retrieved her modesty by rehooking her bodice.

''Kayleigh, my sweet, dark angel, would you like this thimble?'' He held it out to her as bait, but she refused to move a muscle. She stood near the door, watching him as if he were a madman just let loose from Bedlam.

''You really should take it, dark love,'' he prompted. ''It matches your eyes. And besides,'' he added wickedly, ''you'll need something to wear when I take back that dress!'' He lunged for her, but this time she was ready. With her eyes wide, she artfully sidestepped his drunken clench and skittered to the door. She ran through the salon and pulled armchairs into his path to slow him down. But still he was quick to follow.

''You think I'm to be put off by this?'' He released a lusty grunt and shoved a chair aside.

''You besotted rogue! Stop this foolishness!'' she told him, backing behind a bergère. She knitted her slanted black brows in frustration, but this only seemed to make her more taunting and provocative to him.

''Where can you run, Kayleigh? Why not cooperate and hand over the gown?'' He laughed and watched her jump as he cleared another chair from his path.

''I'll go to Colette and stay with her. She'll protect me from you. She has no love for men!''

''She may not have a great love for white men, but I daresay she likes her own kind well enough. I don't think either she or Laban would appreciate your visit right about now.''

"You mean she—? And Laban—?" A frown marred her forehead.

"Yes. So you see, you have nowhere to go but to curl up in my bed."

"I'd rather curl up with an alligator!" She clambered over another chair, but St. Bride was approaching fast. As he neared, all her street instincts came into play. She grabbed a pewter candlestick and held it up, making it clear that she meant to use it if he made it necessary.

He stopped. His brow turned thunderous and he boomed, "I will not be robbed in my own house, nor will I be threatened!" With that, his arm struck out and easily hurled her poised candlestick to the floor. Defenseless, she backed into the loggia, finally stumbling to a halt when her feet met with a jardiniere planted with yellow tulips.

"St. Bride, you must not do this,' she pleaded.

"Come along—take off my dress," he said as he strode up to her.

"No!" she cried when she felt his hands upon her.

"Then you agree to be my personal servant?"

"No!" she cried out again.

St. Bride smiled. Moonlight and shadow fell upon his face from the louvers. The scent of sweet olive drifted through the slats, and the sultry evening breeze seemed to affect both of them. Kayleigh was a bit slower in her movements than usual; St. Bride was more persistent. His hand went to her bodice, and he began unhooking it once more.

"You can't have my dress," she protested as he leaned against her.

"Come along. You'll enjoy yourself. I promise." He kept unhooking.

"No, St. Bride." The hysteria was rising in her voice. She didn't know how she was going to stop him now. There seemed no way to stop him when he had that gleam in his eye, no way at all.

"Please—" A sob caught in her throat. She was utterly

terrified now, and without even knowing it, a tear had begun to fall down her cheek.

St. Bride quit unhooking. His thumb gently wiped the tear away. "What's this?" he asked.

"You must stop. You can't have my dress. I'll be your damned servant if I must. But you cannot have my clothes." She sniffed and wiped the rest of her tears with her hand.

"Have I so frightened you, then, with my play?"

Mutely, she nodded.

He put his disturbingly warm palms on either side of her cheeks. "God, I could stare at you for hours! You're very beautiful, Kayleigh. In fact, under the right circumstances, I might even call you exquisite." He looked at her face and his eyes missed nothing. Not the creamy tear-stained cheeks, nor the lips that seemed as moist and sweet as crushed berries. His turbulent gaze met her velvety one and he seemed to take particular notice of how her thick black lashes were spiked with tears. His thumb wiped away the moisture that clung there. Then his hand swept her hair that was now a mass of disarrayed locks. His voice became quite husky. "But what a puzzling creature you are. Every time I make up my mind about you, you prove me wrong."

Almost as if she were a child, he rehooked the front of her dress. Then, with an uneasy hand, he rubbed his jaw and took a step back.

"How old are you?"

"Nineteen."

He looked unspeakably relieved that she was no child.

"I don't understand any of this. . . ." He seemed to grope for the right words. "I didn't intend for you to get upset. Rather, just the opposite."

She turned from him.

"Kayleigh, why are you upset, love?" He took her arm.

"I've had no man before, and I dare say, I won't have you." Her eyes flashed.

"Are you saying—?"

"I'm untouched," she whispered. The situation was utterly humiliating, and only made more so by having to discuss her virginity with this particular man.

At her confession, St. Bride looked down at her with a sardonic grin. His fingers touched her lips.

"You've a brilliant disguise, virgin."

She should have slapped him, but she was tired of this battle of wills. All she wanted was to quit his company for the night and retire to her little room. Without another word she turned to go.

But he stopped her, saying, "A servant asks her lord to excuse her before she leaves a room."

His request made her tremble with barely restrained anger. "Would you be so kind as to allow me to leave, master?" she said sarcastically, her eyes blazing.

"That's much better; however, in the future, I think we'd best work on that tone."

She pulled her arm from his grasp. But before she stumbled from the loggia, she cried out to him. "I'll be your servant, Mr. Ferringer. I'll even be your *personal* servant if you wish. But you'll rue the day you made me the offer. I promise I'll turn you into a miserable wretch!"

Chapter Ten

In contrast to Kayleigh's thoughts, the next day was glorious
to behold. The sun tempered its heat behind fat cottonwool
clouds, and the sky was a perfect robin's egg blue. Watching
from the gallery doors, she took a deep breath of the clear
air that came through the slats.

She hardly slept all night. Around and around in her
thoughts, she'd wondered about St. Bride. Finally, she concluded that she would never know about him, for she was
determined that she would not be at Belle Chasse long enough
to find out.

Because of her restless night, she was up at dawn. Now
she turned her eyes toward the salon beyond her doors. She
heard St. Bride rise, and with great satisfaction she heard him
bang around the salon, obviously feeling the effects of his
overindulgence in spirits. She even had to stifle a giggle when
she heard him pulling on his jackboots, for he cursed at every
painful move he made.

Kayleigh ran her hand up and down the slats. She forced
the verdigris shutters to swing wide and stepped out onto the
veranda. It was a beautiful day, almost enough to make her
forget how beautiful Mhor was on a spring morn.

"Good, you're up." A wretchedly familiar voice called

out when she reached the veranda railing. Turning to face him, Kayleigh grimaced as St. Bride sauntered from his bedroom. Handsome as always, he walked toward her, clad only in jackboots, chamois breeches, and a French-seamed batiste shirt. In spite of his overindulgence the night before he appeared well rested and well groomed, while she stood before him barefoot, kerchiefless, and so very tired that she felt she would drop where she was standing. If his plan was to wear her out, he was succeeding.

"Excuse me. I promised Colette I would help her in the kitchens." She tried to move past him, but he took hold of her arm.

"I've a better way for you to earn your keep." He took hold of her arm. Through the loggia and into one of the cabinet rooms, he showed her a huge copper bathtub.

"I should like a bath before I begin the day. Tell Colette to heat the water, then ready it for me."

Shocked almost beyond words, she stood by, unable to believe what he was asking her to do. She knew he'd asked her to be his personal servant, but she'd had no idea it was to be *this* personal.

"What are you waiting for?" he dared. She met his gaze; then, determined not to let him see her rattled, she coolly nodded her head and departed for the kitchens.

It took the better part of an hour, but St. Bride's bath was eventually ready. Pail by pail, Kayleigh had trudged up the loggia stairs and filled the copper tub with hot water. She found an expensive block of castile soap and several snowy linen towels. She laid these on the stool next to the tub, then went to fetch her "master."

"Ready so soon?" St. Bride exclaimed from the salon, though even Kayleigh could see that his breakfast coffee had turned cold and his biscuits hard.

"I'm not used to such domestic tasks. If you will forgive me." She gave him an exaggerated bow.

"Yes, I forgot about the army of servants you're used to

having to do such trivial tasks for you.'' He rose and walked to the cabinet room. When she moved to the loggia stairs, he said, ''Don't go anywhere. I may need you still.'' He gave her a blinding, wicked grin, then disappeared into the cabinet room.

She didn't get far—hardly to the salon, in fact—before she heard him cursing and calling her name.

''Kayleigh! Goddamn it, Kayleigh! Get in here! Get in here, I say!''

She scurried to the closed cabinet-room door, then hesitated. With her hand on the doorknob, she debated whether she should enter. St. Bride might be undressed. Although this fact didn't seem to make him less adamant for her appearance, it did give her pause.

''Kayleigh, I'll not ask you again! Get in here!''

She turned the knob and entered the room. Relief flooded her when she saw St. Bride. Though he had indeed stripped, he had a towel wrapped around his hips.

''Is something wrong?'' she asked, genuinely curious to know what had him so angry.

''This water is scalding! What are you trying to do? Boil me like a crawfish?'' Furiously, he thrust forward his hand, the one with the scar. It looked as if it were sunburned.

''The water is that hot?'' Horrified, she looked at his burned hand. ''I had no idea, truly! Colette said the water was ready. I thought all I had to do was to carry it to the tub.''

''Don't you know you have to add cold water to this tub before a man can sit in it?''

''I've never drawn a bath before. My baths were always drawn for me. Truly, I didn't know.'' She furrowed her delicate brow. ''Shall I get Colette? Perhaps she can make a salve.''

''No, no. It's not that bad.'' He scrutinized her. ''You didn't do it on purpose?''

''I didn't. I wouldn't! Please believe me.'' She held out her hands in supplication.

He gave her one more distrustful look, then commanded, "Go, then. Get me some cold water."

She nodded nervously and immediately obeyed.

By the time she had carried the pailfuls of cold water to the cabinet room, the bath was almost cold anyway. She walked into the room with the last pail only to find that St. Bride was already in the tub. Mortified, she put the last pail by the door, then quietly tried to exit.

"Kayleigh, who drew your baths for you?" He stopped her at the door with a look.

"I told you, I lived in a castle. I'm used to servants, not servants' chores." She averted her eyes, but she found it hard not to stare at him. Sitting before her in the tub, his entire body seemed to beckon her gaze. His dark chest hair sparkled with enticing droplets of water. The supple muscles in his abdomen flexed with his every movement before they blurred beneath the waterline. When he began soaping his chest, for some odd reason the sight of his hand rubbing back and forth along his rock-hard pectorals made her a bit light-headed. The room seemed to close in around her, and she had to excuse herself.

But St. Bride wouldn't let her.

"Kayleigh, I would like you to scrub my back." He held out the soap.

"I won't do something so improper," she admonished. She didn't dare move closer to the tub. If she did, his lower half, beneath the water, would be all too easily viewed. She was, sure she couldn't handle that.

"Improper!" He laughed. "Is that also reminiscent of your castle days?" Playfully, he flicked some water at her. "All those servants drawing your baths and teaching you propriety—didn't they ever mention that it's quite improper to thieve?"

"Don't make fun of me," she said quietly.

"Ah, but you intrigue me so. What a tangle of contradictions you are!" He held out the soap again. "Come, scrub my back, then you can help Colette in the kitchens."

She paused, but she knew she had no choice. St. Bride was not going to let her go until he'd had his way.

Unnerved, she skirted the tub, walked up behind him, and grabbed the soap from his hand, not daring to look down into the all too clear bath water. She wet the sponge in the water behind him, adamantly telling herself that this was not the first time she had seen a man's buttocks, nor would it likely be the last. She squeezed a spongeful of water onto St. Bride's back, then soaped it as furiously as she could.

She ignored the feel of his slick skin beneath her fingers and the smooth ridges of muscle that ran the length of his spine. She was also able to overlook the fresh smell of the soap and the more provocative, clean smell of him beneath it. But her nerves got the best of her when she brushed away his wet, dark queue in order to better wash his shoulders.

Beneath her palms, his shoulders flexed and relaxed. With those movements, an odd tightening began in her belly. The feeling soon spread like flames, consuming her thoughts, her strength, her motivations. Feeling her pause, St. Bride turned his head. Anxious to hide whatever it was that she was feeling, she went back to scrubbing his back; but in her overwrought state, the soap slipped from her hand. In horror, she watched the soap disappear into the water beneath his waist.

"You've dropped the soap." He seemed to take great relish in stating the obvious.

"It's—it's of no account. I'm—I'm done. I'll rinse you." Nervously, she searched for the sponge and was appalled to find he held it in front of him.

"Looking for this?" he asked.

"No," she refused, all too quickly.

Reaching for a towel, she was about to use it to rinse his back when he said, "Kayleigh, I think you've missed a spot. I think you'd best retrieve the soap."

"Ooh, *amadan!* Your back be damned!" Terrified, she dropped the towel and scurried to the door.

"Why, Kayleigh, have I done something to upset you?" he asked with apparent genuine concern.

"I will not go searching for the soap in your bath water. I won't do it, I tell you!"

He looked up, and she knew he couldn't miss the red stain of embarrassment on her face. He didn't, and he started to laugh.

"Well, if you can't handle this simple chore . . ."

"If you will excuse me now?" she asked in a furious monotone.

"I'm not sure—you haven't finished your task." His brilliant turquoise eyes narrowed.

"Please, may I be excused?" she ground out, at once frightened and furious. The man was maddening!

"All right. Away with you, baggage. I'll rinse my own back." In his mirth he pretended to throw the sponge at her. She started, which only made his laughter grow. She left the cabinet room, her eyes sparkling with animosity.

When St. Bride found her nearly an hour later, she had just decided that the life of a thief was far easier than that of a servant. Colette had asked her to stir a custard on the *potager,* the ancient French-devised stove used for cooking sauces. But the task was not as easy as it looked. The fire beneath the *potager* was too hot. She stepped away from it for only a moment to stroke Chridhe and give her some breakfast. But then an ancient slave named Grand-Louis came to the kitchen door, adamantly asking in French for his dinner. When she returned, she discovered the egg mixture had begun to boil over. By the time St. Bride arrived, her hair was out of its pins, a huge black smudge was painted across her face, and the boiled-over custard had caught fire on the stove. Uttering several colorful curses, St. Bride threw a small sack of flour onto the custard and extinguished the flames. Then he turned to her.

"Are you hoping to get only me, or are you trying kill everyone on this plantation?"

"I know now why Bardolph chose to live on the streets. All these tasks are impossible!" Petulantly, she sat down on one of the kitchen chairs and looked at St. Bride through the smoke.

"I can see it's going to be even more impossible to get you to do them correctly." Holding out his hand, he added, "Come with me then. Colette can teach you these tasks some other day."

He grasped her hand and pulled her across the rear bricked courtyard.

"What are you doing?" she asked as a black stableboy, Mathias, beautifully attired in scarlet wool and gold bullion fringe, held out a saddled bay mare.

"I've got to tour the fields and have need of company. In short, we're leaving the house for a while. Isn't that what you would like?" St. Bride cocked his brow.

"Not with you!" She pulled back in dismay.

"I must ask, do you ride?"

"I am not going anywhere with you." She tried to pull back farther, but he blocked her way and took his mount from another festooned slave.

"Do you ride, Kayleigh? In between the lessons in stealing and cheating was there time for equitation?"

"Bastard," she murmured, hurt by the insult. Yet St. Bride heard her anyway.

"You've already proven your command of the English language. What I want to know is, can you ride?" He casually mounted the huge black stallion before him and calmed the animal, saying, "Easy, boy. Easy, Canis," as it pranced sideways on the cobblestones.

"Yes," she answered through clenched teeth.

"Yes?" he echoed in dismay. "Are you sure? I was positive you'd be forced to ride up here with me.' He halted the stallion right beside her.

"Well, now that you know that's not necessary, perhaps I can go to the kitchens."

"I don't think the kitchens could withstand yet another Armageddon today," he mocked dryly. Then he dared, "So the little lady can ride too! All right, get on the mare. Let me see how a street urchin handles a Thoroughbred."

She saw the challenge in his eye, and her resolve grew strong. He was laughing at her. He expected her to take up his gauntlet, get on the mare, and promptly fall off. He didn't know she really could ride. Why, she could probably outride him! It required more skill to stay on a temperamental Shetland through the craggy knolls of Mhor than it did to take his mare through a few flat fields!

Before she could stop herself, she snatched the mare's reins from Mathias, flung them over the animal's head, and mounted without even a leg up. Then she delicately positioned herself in the sidesaddle and began trotting toward the road.

She turned and saw a look of amazement on his face. It was obvious that he had had no idea she was an accomplished horsewoman. His expression quickly turned to puzzlement, however, for he then, no doubt, wondered where she had learned such skills. And as Kayleigh trotted the mare farther along the drive, St. Bride's face took on another look of dismay.

He legged Canis into a canter and was soon gaining on her, but she was not about to be outdone. She brought the mare into a full gallop and took to the fields. She hadn't counted on the power of the horse behind her, however, nor on the quiet manner of the mare beneath her. Soon the two horses were neck and neck. She had no intention of stopping, but St. Bride had his own plans. Without even telling her to slow down, he leaned over and unceremoniously jerked her off the saddle. Caught by the waist, she was suspended in midair until her bottom landed on his pommel. Her seat ached almost as much as her heart when she saw the riderless mare raise her tail and gallop freely back to the plantation.

"How dare you? That was not necessary whatever!" she accused him.

"Oh, no? To watch my best mare be stolen from right under my nose?" he gasped. "And that's just the kind of thing I want to talk to you about. Where did you learn that little trick?"

"It wasn't a trick!" she hurled at him. "You asked if I could ride, and I proved to you that I could! If only your mare hadn't been so sluggish—then you wouldn't have played such a trick on me!"

"Sluggish! I gave her to you so you wouldn't fall on your sweet little rump! How was I to even suspect you could ride like that?" Just as angry, his hand tightened around her waist, and he refused to let her even think of scrambling from the saddle. "Where did you learn to ride like that?" he demanded.

She fumed. Och, how she wanted to tell him the truth! How she wanted him to stand in awe of her breeding and wealth. But she knew that besides being dangerous, telling him those things wouldn't necessarily mean he'd believed them. He'd already laughed too many times when she'd told him about Mhor castle. And besides, the little she knew of St. Bride Ferringer told her he simply was not a man to stand in awe of anything.

She finally retorted sarcastically, *"Dhé!* How can one be an accomplished horse thief if one cannot ride?" Then she scooted over the pommel until she was almost on the stallion's neck, crossed her arms over her chest, and refused to give him even the satisfaction of meeting his eye.

All conversation put to an end, St. Bride held Canis to a walk as they made their way farther into the fields behind the plantation. Unable to lean back for fear of touching St. Bride's lightly clad chest and unable to relax for fear of the barely reined stallion beneath her, Kayleigh sat stiff and unyielding on the pommel.

Beasts, she thought ungraciously. *I'm surrounded by them.* They rode along what seemed like miles of swampland.

Brilliant white egrets flowered the area; their long elegant necks bobbed as they foraged for insects along the cattailed bayous. Even Kayleigh had to admit they gave a strange grace to the drooping, shrouded flora unique to Louisiana. But upon hearing the occasional call of a bull alligator, she shivered; her mind unexpectedly wandered to the terrible night when St. Bride had found her in the boughs of wax myrtle.

Guiltily, she peeked over her shoulder at her savior. Perhaps St. Bride wasn't such an awful man. Perhaps she should try to show more gratitude to him. After all, when she thought about it, his kindnesses had been numerous and surprising in light of the fact that she had cut his hand and tried to steal from him the very morning of the day he found her helpless in the swamps. There weren't many men who would have bothered—she knew that only too well.

But still, how infuriating she found him! And worse, how disappointed she was to find him involved with her cousin Straught.

Covertly she glanced at St. Bride as he studied the lay of the land, no doubt for his wicked poppies. How could a man so independent and sharp-witted get mixed up in one of her cousin's nefarious schemes? With an inexplicable sadness in her breast, she watched him scrutinize the soggier grounds, those fields preferred by black-eyed Susans and other such weeds.

"Would you like to go to Versailles, love?" he suddenly asked, interrupting her thoughts. They had stopped near a cluster of live oaks that stood like an oasis in the desert of flat, abandoned fields and desolate green swamp.

"Versailles? Did you say Versailles?" she questioned, wondering if madness ran in his family. That would at least account for his friendship with Straught.

"Yes, I said Versailles. Let's take a tour, shall we, and sit in the shade?"

She twisted around to face him. St. Bride was talking like a true madman now. Perhaps the heat was giving him delusions of Versailles, for in the middle of this desolate Louisiana plantation there was nothing that bore any resemblance to the Sun King's magnificent palace.

"Would you like to?" he asked again.

Did one tell a madman nay?

"I suppose," she answered, hesitating.

"Good." He suddenly pulled her to his chest and spoke with laughter in his voice. "I have a desire to impress you with my riches."

"You must know you don't have to impress me with your riches." She wanted to tell him just what he could do with what few riches he did have when a look of intensity in his eyes quieted her. They took in every aspect of her, from the way her hips swayed with Canis's languid gait to the way her raven locks, mussed and untended, graced her kerchiefless bosom. St. Bride looked like a starving man before a banquet, and she didn't know what to make of the fact that she seemed to be the main fare. When she met his gaze once more, she saw a slow, lazy smile touch his lips.

"Welcome to Le Petit Versailles, Kayleigh."

She sat upright and looked once again at the cluster of oaks that he had referred to as Versailles. St. Bride dismounted, taking his saddle pouch with him, and reached for her. She was still unnerved by the earlier look in his eye, but she allowed him to help her off Canis. She gave great thought to the way his strong, able hands seemed to linger at her tiny, unbound waist.

"Why are we here?" she asked slowly.

"Let's just say for a romp, shall we, Kayleigh?"

"What? Never!" She hastily moved out of the reach of his possessive hands.

"All right. We won't have a romp. Just sit with me, love." Ignoring her accusing looks, St. Bride sat nonchalantly and rested his head on a huge live oak trunk. His white shirt was loosened at the ties, and she could see a fine mist of perspiration covering his chest. The day had proved to be a hot one after all, and typically a storm that would dispel the heat could be seen brewing in the low distance. The spot in the shade was very appealing, especially when her heavy dress clung maddeningly to her skin and she could feel drops of perspiration running down the middle of her bodice. But she didn't want to sit with him, even if her only alternative was to stand in the brilliant June sun. She knew better.

"Pray tell, why is this place called Le Petit Versailles?" She stayed far away from the circle of his grasp. "I know little of France except what I've learned in this bastion of hell Louis XIV has made. But I do know that a mere cluster of trees cannot be compared to Versailles, *petit* or otherwise."

St. Bride studied her. "Kayleigh, your accent is flawless. Say again, Le Petit Versailles."

When she refused, he leaned back and peered at her through half-closed lids.

How had he been so astute as to pick up her knowledge of French? Her brow clouded. Morna and she had been given lessons in French, of course, along with drawing, needlework, and penmanship. But how could St. Bride tell she knew French when she had uttered but one phrase? Och, the man was maddening in his cleverness!

"Do you speak French, love?" he asked quietly. Again when she didn't answer, he prompted, "Of course you probably learned some of the language just being here in Louisiana. There are all kinds of Frenchmen here—trappers and that sort. Do you speak it, Kayleigh?"

"Not with much understanding," she lied.

"Je voudrais te séduire . . . ici!"

She paled. He had told her quite directly that he wanted to bed her. Here.

He whispered, *"Prends tes mains et me caresses—"*

But "Take your hands and fondle me" was all he could get in before she cried down at him, "You lecher! Stop this wicked talk!"

"My pet, you have an intimate knowledge of French!"
He seemed utterly delighted.

She was utterly bemused.

"What do you make of it? I learned from the trappers!"
she rationalized.

"No, I think not." He demanded, "Say, *'Je te désire.'*"

"I do not desire you!"

"Say it, just say it. After all," he added with great zest,
"what can words convey when your body speaks with an
infinitely larger vocabulary?" He chuckled, then moved
quickly. Before she could stumble from his reach, his hand
had the hem of her skirt.

"Let go!" She pulled on her dress, but he held fast.

"Say it, Kayleigh. Tell me what we both know to be true—
in French." He laughed. But the harder she pulled, the harder
he laughed. When her expression turned stormy, St. Bride
was fairly rolling on the ground trying to contain himself.
His pleasure in annoying her seemed to have no bounds. In
the end Kayleigh did tell him what she thought—and in
French.

"You!" she spat in a perfect, refined accent, "are a mindless, grunting savage whose only thoughts rattle around in
your breeches!"

Hearing this, St. Bride abruptly stopped laughing. But he
did not let go of her hem. Instead, he lifted his amused
turquoise eyes and exclaimed in English, "Rattle? I'll have
you know I fill out my breeches too well for any of that!"

She returned to English and said, "Ooh! You're contempt-
ible!" With that she snatched her skirts away and stomped
to a different part of the shade. Anger burned in her throat,
and knowing that he had gotten the best of her only made it
worse.

"Come back, little French maiden," St. Bride baited her,
lounging back on the trunk of the live oak.

"I am not French!" she snapped.

"Ah, but your understanding of the language is flawless.

And when you speak it, well . . ." He laughed. "Yes, that is flawless too. How so?"

His question, while innocently spoken, was dangerously probing. She wondered if she should tell him about M. Girard, the French tutor she had had back at Mhor. But of course she shouldn't. He would never believe her, and besides, it would only lead to more questions, some she could not answer. Because they could not continue in this vein, she quickly changed the subject, asking again, "Why do you call this miserable clump of trees Little Versailles?"

St. Bride's eyes narrowed and he paused. A glint in his eyes told her that he'd noted her reluctance to talk of herself. This made her nervous, and she wiped her heated cheeks with the back of her hand.

"Little Versailles is just another dream of Launier's." The glint was gone, and he seemed to accede to her wish. She was relieved—for the moment.

"Who is Launier?" She made no effort to hide her curiosity.

"He was the man who built Belle Chasse," he answered, and removed a silver flask from his pouch. "But he meant Belle Chasse to be only temporary. He was going to build a great empire out here beneath the live oaks and althaea. See over there?" He pointed to a ponderous oak with branches so old and heavy, they were weighted into the soft ground.

"Yes."

"There he was going to build a little red pagoda. And over there?" He pointed to a dip in the soil filled with stagnant water.

Kayleigh nodded.

"A waterfall. Launier was going to make his place a dream palace filled with all sorts of fanciful chinoiserie."

"How do you know this?"

"I have his drawings and plans. He was a bit crazed, that one. But perhaps I'm a bit crazed too." St. Bride grinned then, wickedly, beautifully.

"Perhaps?" Kayleigh quipped, looking away from the smile, which bedazzled her. "I think that must be a certainty. This place is filled with nothing but dreams."

She looked around her. Where she saw weeds, a man named Launier had seen cultivation and beauty. It reminded her of those times when she'd been most desperately home-sick and gone to the Mississippi's edge to imagine that it was a blue loch instead. But in the end it had been a river full of mud, and in the end Launier's Petit Versailles was nothing more impressive than a clump of shade trees in a barren field. Suddenly she almost felt like crying, both for herself and for Launier.

"I suspect Launier's dreams were as dark and wild as my own." St. Bride took a sip from the flask and watched her pace. "But then, unlike Launier, I like my dreams dark and wild—and I have the means to make my dreams come true. Others, alas, do not."

Kayleigh stopped pacing. How cruel he was to bring up her poverty, her forced indebtedness to him!

"I'll have the money for my dreams someday."

"I wasn't referring to you necessarily, dark love," he answered. Then in one swift, violent action, he claimed her and toppled her onto him.

"If I built this Little Versailles, Kayleigh, would you live here with me?" he asked as she struggled against him.

"I wouldn't live with you even in the *true* Versailles!" She pulled away from him and grew hot seeing that her bodice gaped below their locked hands. How she wished for a kerchief!

"What if I built you a great house full of Chinese servants with long black braids down their backs and even longer mustaches?"

"I would not stay!" She wanted to scratch his eyes out, but instead she pulled back to attain some modesty. *Dhé!* She had known he was up to this. Why did his taunts make her so impassioned?

"Well." St. Bride furrowed his brow playfully at her panting figure. Taking in her refusal, he said in a voice that grew huskier with every word, "Then let's forget the house. I'll go home and grind up all my gold. I'll throw the gold dust up into these trees and let it settle upon the spiders' webs and birds' nest. And we'll simply live beneath its glittering canopy, and every night I'll lay you down and kiss you and lick you and—"

"What befell Launier must be affecting you too," she retorted while he clasped and reclasped their hands. "You misguided—!" She suddenly ceased her movement, appalled by the prominence growing beneath her.

"That's right. Stay still." He stroked her hair, watching the highlights dance in her mane. She ached to be free of his touch, but embarrassment and dismay bade her comply with his wishes.

"Wine?" he asked, holding the flask up to her piquant face.

She shook her dark head.

"Drink. I know you haven't eaten, but it will do you good." He held the flask to her rose-hued lips and forced several swallows down her.

"No more," she coughed. Already the sweet, heady wine was working its magic. Her empty stomach and the lack of sleep the night before left her vulnerable to its effects. And she knew without a doubt that St. Bride was aware of this. Everything the man did seemed calculated and manipulative. He had a counterattack ready for her every move.

But the wine gave her bravery. She asked, "What are you about, St. Bride Ferringer? You don't care about pagodas and waterfalls. And I daresay you're not so foolish as to grind up all your gold for mere fancy."

"No, but perhaps just for you . . ." He smiled again and put his finger to her soft lips. Seeing her rigid features, he withdrew and became more sober. "What are your dreams, dark love? Will you tell them to me? Perhaps I may make them come true."

The question took her aback, but she answered, "I dream of leaving here."

"And if you left here, where would you go? Back to New Orleans? To Fort Biloxi? To some desolate entrepôt upriver?" St. Bride reached up and plucked a stem of low-hanging althaea. He tore off the hollyhock's lavender blooms and gently placed them along the crown of her hair.

"I would return to Scotland," she said breathlessly. She didn't know what a temptation she made with her eyes shining and her hair mussed and strewn with flowers, but she was soon to think it a curse.

"They've had a war in Scotland, Kayleigh. It's not the place for you. Besides, didn't you flee from there once already?"

Tentatively, she began again. "Scotland is my true home. It's a beautiful place, and I'm determined to see it again. I— I would do anything to return there. I would do anything to leave here."

"Anything?" He gave her a speculative gaze. Then, as if he didn't quite like the deal, he offered, "Would you like to go to Georgia?"

"Georgia? Is that where you're from?"

"That could be the place for you, Kayleigh. I anticipate my visit here will be a short one. If it's your desire to leave Louisiana, I could send you to my home on Wolf Island and meet you there when I conclude my business here."

"You misunderstand. I have no desire to live with you." She wet her lips and prepared for battle.

"What is so repulsive about me? Have I warts on my nose?" He stuck his handsome face close to hers. "You positively cringe when I come near you. I ask you, love, am I too old and too ugly for your taste?"

"N-n-no." She pulled back.

"Could it be I'm too poor? I agree that Belle Chasse lacks

splendor, so go to Georgia, Kayleigh. Wolf Island will dispel any doubts you have about my wealth.''

''I don't want to be any man's mistress. I want to return to Scotland.''

''You don't know what you've been offered, love.'' Suddenly, St. Bride showed the side of himself that refused to be crossed. ''Do you know who I am?'' he clipped.

''Who are you then?'' she countered, annoyed by this unexpected outburst. ''I know you speak fluent French and that you have vile friends and thousands of poppy seeds in your salon. But after that, I know nothing about you, not the slightest thing. I'm not even sure I want to.''

St. Bride appeared to curse himself inwardly. Shaking his head, he warned off further questions by stating, ''I speak French like any man in my position. Laban is not vile, though I do see the animosity between you two. And the poppy seeds are to be my crop here at Belle Chasse.''

''And a wonderful crop that should be indeed,'' she answered sarcastically. She struggled once more, then groaned with frustration when he didn't let her off his lap.

''Thank you for your opinion, madame. Once again you spurn me, but I advise you not to be foolish. You'll have no better prospects than with me. Believe that.'' With his forefinger, he gravely caressed the light and shadows that were playing across her face. Traces of her exhaustion showed in the violet crescents underneath her eyes. He became aware of her fatigue, and his voice and his touch grew even more gentle. ''Know that I don't want things to be this way, Kayleigh.''

''Give me the means to go to Scotland, and perhaps things will be different.'' She colored. Her offer was shameless. She wasn't even sure she would carry it out. But if that was the way she might go home . . .

''Back to seducing me now, are we?'' St. Bride whispered evenly. ''Well, your offer is generous, but I'm not sure I could fulfill my part of the bargain. You see, that's the one damnable thing about you, Kayleigh. The longer I'm with you, the longer I must have you stay.''

Resentfully, she burst out, ''I understand. If I were a man, things would be different. I would have been beaten for my stealing and then left alone. Why is it that a woman's fate must always be far worse?''

''If you were a man and had done what you did yesterday, you would be dead.'' The words hung in the air like smoke from a pistol.

Kayleigh trembled as he lightly kissed her earlobe. ''Nay . . . that's not so.''

''Laban would have tossed you over the gallery to your death on the cobblestones below. He knows what to do with eavesdroppers, all right. For him the task would have been as easy as getting rid of a ship's rat. Be glad for your womanhood, Kayleigh. It's saved your very life.''

She turned from him. Her voice dropped to a whisper, but she still couldn't hide her bitterness. ''So I could be your plaything . . .''

''You decide your fate. I can be your mentor who saved you from the swamps and from rotting in jail, or—'' He paused. ''Or I can be your enemy who has captured you and demands your subservience.''

''No,'' she said to him, unwilling to be given such a choice. ''No,'' she repeated, stunned by the harshness of his offer. Then in her anger, she said more than she wanted to. ''You cannot treat me this way. Do you understand that? There are men in Scotland who would die to make you take back those vile words.''

''Vile words? Mine? When you only soil your character further with your absurd little lies?'' He refused to look at her. His nostrils flared imperceptibly, only hinting at his anger. ''At least let us admit who you are, Kayleigh. You're a product of the quay, there's no need for pretense. You've proven yourself to have no honor, no loyalty, no morals.

While this does make you . . . difficult, it also makes you . . . desirable to one such as myself.''

She felt his arm tighten around her, and he continued, ''I'd like to forget about your past indiscretions, love. And I'd like you to help me forget by coming to my bed willingly. I promise to treat you gently. As my mistress, you'll be clothed in the best satins and brocades and bejeweled in finest diamonds and sapphires. My offer is not made lightly.''

''Why make such a bid for an unwilling girl?'' she asked bitterly. ''I know dozen of others who would jump to grant your every wish for what you offer.''

''But not you?''

She took a deep breath and looked him squarely in the eye. ''Not me.''

He took a pensive sip of wine and then gently placed the silver flask to her lips. She tasted the heavy Bordeaux and allowed him to think on what she'd said.

Finally he spoke. ''You're indebted to me. How do you propose I seek my payment?''

At her silence, he continued, ''Lie with me one time, dark love, and your debt will be canceled. You won't be sent to jail, and you won't be forced to stay on as a house servant. I may even see fit to find you passage to Edinburgh.''

She looked at him and saw the seriousness of his face. Gone was the boyish glimmer to his eyes, gone was the rakish cast to his mouth. Instead, a shadow lurked in his expression, a shadow that was not cast by the live oaks above, nor by the impending storm on the horizon. She knew he was a man of strong desires; a tingle went down her spine as she wondered how he would react if those desires were denied satisfaction.

''If I refuse, what then?'' she whispered as he lightly kissed her wine-reddened lip.

''Does this make you feel nothing?'' He nipped softly at her lower lip. He tugged on one petal-soft earlobe, then his fingers lifted her heavy black tresses and caressed her silky nape.

"Nothing," she murmured, though her cheeks burned and her palms perspired. She was quick to attribute this to the heat of the day.

"How does this feel?" he growled from deep in his chest. Pulling her down fully onto his hard chest, he positioned himself even closer to her, his knee parting her thighs as she half lay above him. She could feel his manhood, even though there were layers of clothes between them, and she could feel the dark fur of his half-naked chest that brushed against the swells of her bosom uncovered by the cut of her bodice. She squirmed and resisted, but against her every movement, he remained implacable. He had ceased his aggression and was now merely holding her, but he held her with arms of tempered steel. Now all he waited for was a response that would please him.

That was the way she would fob him off. Deep in her heart she knew he was no rapist, and if she truly showed no passion for him, she knew he would stop this insanity and allow her some peace. With this her only hope, she tried desperately to shut him out of her senses. She closed her eyes to the sight of him, lean and handsome below her. She closed her eyes to the masculine sinew of his neck and the tiny pulse in his throat that throbbed with emotion. She even had some success numbing her body to the feel of the long, hard length of his, to the feel of his torso as it writhed beneath her own, and to the feel of his legs, like long leather-wrapped cylinders of iron splayed beneath her loins.

But in the end, try as she did to shield herself, he still found a chink in her unsteady armor. The touch of his lips on her hot skin made her breath come deep and quick. And she realized that St. Bride's scent was earth, fire, and sky combined. *Dhé,* she couldn't remember ever experiencing anything like it—yet she knew it instantly. It was like a drug, one she thought she hadn't wanted but now did want desperately. The more she concentrated on keeping him out, the more his scent filled her empty senses until she was fairly giddy with it. It made her body turn traitor and her mind babble like a fool. She didn't want this. She didn't. But something deep within, something that had grasped that scent and would not let it go, told her she did. She moaned.

Opening her eyes to St. Bride, she felt as if she would explode from the war that raged inside her. But then he ended her internal struggle, as she somehow had known he would.

Whispering to her in their intimate embrace, he spoke the words that pushed her over the edge. ''Come along, prove your disdain for my lovemaking.''

At that moment she could not, so he rolled her onto the grass, and they kissed as they had never kissed before. St. Bride's lips drew on hers with an expertise to which she was not immune, and in only a few horrifying seconds she realized that, not only was he kissing her, but she was kissing him back.

Her mind groaned in frustration, but her body tingled with delight. The more she took of his mouth, the more pleasure she felt. His lips were not as she had imagined. They were not painful and abusive. They were merely hard and demanding.

Like he himself was, she thought disjointedly. Yet his hardness was being permitted—no, welcomed—by her sweetly curved lips, and his demands ever so slowly were being met.

When she could bear the struggle no longer, she opened her mouth and bade him enter. She felt his surprise at her offering in the slightest of pauses. But his own pleasure seemed to deepen when, to his questioning invasion, she moaned her delight from deep within her belly.

''That's right, Kayleigh, have me,'' he whispered over her. While she lay beneath him, feeling the spring of grass under her back, he brought the silver flask again to her lips. He seemed to be presenting her not with red wine but with an aphrodisiac elixir that would take her through the next steps with ease.

Before accepting more wine, Kayleigh's eyes met his for one sizzling moment. At that, all her resolve dissipated into the humid air around her. St. Bride's eyes flickered down her with pleased admiration as she drank from the flask. Wine dribbled down her chin in his enthusiasm to ply her, but he stanched the flow with his tongue just before the rivulet of Bordeaux ran beneath her bodice. Then, because he found the taste of her skin so pleasurable, he trickled more wine onto her from the flask and savored the treat once again.

As his mouth drank from the kerchiefless expanse of her chest, she moaned and arched back, her senses spiraling into the fiery holds of an unwilling passion. St. Bride trailed his tongue lower and lower, and she found herself inwardly cursing the resistance of her gown. When he began to slowly unhook her bodice, she choked with frenzied delight. She prayed only that he would be quick to release her from the hellish heat of her clothing so that she could feel the slick rigidity of his body instead.

"My beautiful girl, I will have you. I have the means and the desire."

The words, whispered to her in his uniquely harsh voice, forced her eyes to open. She looked into his warm turquoise eyes, and although she wanted to kick herself for such abandon, Scotland was this near. All that she wanted in the world was within her grasp if she would only comply with this man's one wish.

He bent to kiss her one more time, but now the magic was gone. This time the lady in her willed her to stop. She couldn't forfeit something as precious as her virginity to a man she didn't love. And from St. Bride she had had no promise that love would come. Suddenly this fact weighed upon her like a pile of bricks. She'd always imagined surrendering herself to a husband under the protection of a marriage bed, not to a strange man beneath the sparse shade of some live oaks. All at once the price of Scotland seemed too dear.

Her hands were caught in his hair. Somehow her fingers had woven through the strands of silver on his temples. In an attempt to stop his kiss, she hastily extracted them.

"What is it?" he whispered, seeing her fear-ridden glance.

"Don't," she uttered softly. "No more, I say."

He stared down at her for a very long time, his gaze penetrating clear to her soul. Whatever he found there bade him close his eyes and groan.

She felt as if she'd been doused with ice water on this, a sweltering day. Sobered from St. Bride's heady touch, she recaptured Kestrel's ingrained instinct for self-preservation. She pulled back from him, then slid from his tense frame and sat upright. She refused his touch and slumped her head back against the live oak trunk. She stared upward to watch the blackened clouds that promised rain. Anger at herself rumbled within her like the storm's distant thunder, and although she didn't know it, her eyes flashed like blue lightning.

"My body has betrayed me," she moaned.

St. Bride was silent throughout her rejection. He merely stared at her and fought to regain control over his body. His face was unreadable when he finally said, "Betray yourself, Kayleigh, for that's a far better thing than to betray me." He held out his hand for her to come to him again, but she adamantly refused it. Instead, she arose from the grass, clutched at her wine-soaked bodice, and ran all the way to Belle Chasse without giving him a backward glance.

Chapter Eleven

The afternoon storm arrived like clockwork, as predictable as the smells from the kitchens. Colette baked bread every day at three o'clock. And it was then that the heat from the day would boil up to the sky and make the clouds react in the form of rain. The ground would cool, and the baking could be done in a small amount of comfort.

Just escaping the first huge droplets of the storm, Kayleigh made her way to the kitchens to find shelter. She was pale, and her eyes appeared large and wary in her delicate face. Colette noticed at once.

"You are ill again?" The mulatto frowned as she looked at her. "The herbs—perhaps I didn't give you enough?"

Kayleigh grimaced at the very thought. Colette's herbal concoctions were as foul to the tongue as street sewerage was to the nose. Another bout with the mulatto's cures would surely finish her off more quickly than another snakebite. She answered with haste, "Nay, I feel fine. Perhaps I'm just hungry."

"Eat then. I have made some rice pudding." Colette motioned to a huge bowl on the cherry kitchen table.

"The custard!" Horrified, Kayleigh turned to her. "Was it completely ruined? Chridhe was hungry, then that old mad slave Grand-Louis interrupted me. It all got so out of control. I've never cooked before, you see.''

"Yes, the custard was quite hopeless. Particularly because of all the flour. Was there a fire, mademoiselle? The *potager* was completely black.''

"Truly I'm sorry! I hope it didn't cause you much grief. St. Bride put out the fire.''

"Laban told me St. Bride came in here, then dragged you out by your arm.'' Colette's eyes widened.

"Yes.'' Kayleigh added ruefully, "I think St. Bride was anxious for a ride.'' She furrowed her brow. And he almost got one too, she thought.

"You are ill! So white, you are! Come, take *les herbes.*''

Kayleigh looked up on hearing Colette's concerned voice. She watched as the mulatto limped over to the shelf that held an assortment of mysterious blown-glass bottles.

"No, no, Colette! Truly, I am just hungry!'' Quickly, she scurried over to the cherrywood table and served herself some pudding.

It was mild, sweet, and wonderfully chilled, having been buried in the ground in an earthenware *jarre de Provence.* She hadn't tasted food so perfectly prepared since she and Bardolph had stolen some puff pastries from the old La Direction. In a humiliating amount of time, the pudding disappeared. She sat back, sipping a thick *café* that Colette brought to her. She remained preoccupied with it until a swift knock came at the kitchen door.

Colette anxiously dusted the flour from her smooth hands, then limped to the cypress door. Flinging it open, she saw no one in the courtyard, but lying in the doorway was a bunch of gold and black wild flowers. Laughing, Colette scooped them into her arms and came back to the kitchen.

It was then Kayleigh noticed the pretty flush on her cheeks. Colette also were a new calico gown and a fresh linen apron, so white it compared to the blossoms of a wild magnolia. The change in Colette was subtle, but standing before her now Kayleigh saw no longer the drab, work-worn little slavey who had helped her get well. Colette was now a beautiful young woman.

Curious, she exclaimed, "What goes on about here?"

"It is something I thought would never happen." Colette smiled and hugged the homely black-eyed Susans to her breast.

"And what is that?" Kayleigh looked at her with doubt-ridden eyes.

"I am being courted," Colette answered in a hushed, breathless voice.

All Kayleigh could do was look at her incredulously, not understanding at all how a mere bunch of weeds could cause such a look in Colette's sweet mink eyes.

"His comings and goings make little difference to me," Kayleigh stated later that evening, still helping Colette in the kitchens. She had not seen St. Bride since her return from Le Petit Versailles. During dinner, Colette had mentioned that he had gone into town on some unnamed business. Later, when the pretty mulatto had offered information about his return, Kayleigh shrugged her shoulders and put her off.

She truly didn't want to know, Kayleigh told herself, ada-mantly returning her attention to polishing an already spotless beaker. Besides, under no circumstances did she want to remind herself of her wanton behavior under the live oaks—nor of something else that had happened that evening.

She rubbed her neck wearily. The day had been a long one, and as it progressed, it had grown only worse. Frustrated that her thoughts continued to wander to St. Bride time and again, she had offered to collect the linen from Babet. As she returned to the kitchens, through the dusky light of the courtyard she'd seen a note attached to a distant cabin door—Laban's door. Although she dreaded a chance meeting with him, her curiosity had gotten the better of her.

Sauntering up to the cabin, she had first looked for any

late stableboys or laundry slaves and seen none. Quickly she had walked to the door and more quickly still had read the note, drawn in bold masculine strokes.

Laban,
I have gone into New Orleans to see our dear friend Straught. It will keep Kayleigh in her place.

St. Bride

It will keep Kayleigh in her place? Kayleigh bit her lower lip and reread the note. It wasn't clear what that first word was: "*It* will keep Kayleigh in her place" or "*I* will keep Kayleigh in her place." She reread the words again, desperation slowing the beat of her heart. The *It* had to be an *I,* she told herself. There was a scrawl next to the capital, to be sure, but it was a slip of the quill—it had to be. She frowned. *It will keep Kayleigh in her place.* The words echoed through her thoughts, digging up spooks that would not be buried. Was she a bigger fool than she thought? St. Bride's acquaintance with Straught unnerved her. But was it more than an acquaintance? Did St. Bride know more about her than he was telling?

Stop this! she had told herself resolutely. She was a fool, all right, a fool to misread a simple note. She forced herself to see an *I* where an *It* had been. When she was finally convinced the word was as she hoped, she allowed her shoulders to relax, and her breath became regular once more.

Yes, she saw an *I,* she had told herself as she turned from the door. For she could never have kissed a man involved with hurting her family. Her body might betray her, but her soul never would. She would have known from the first touch if St. Bride was anything like Straught. There would have been a sign—marks in his iris or a chill to his voice. And there wasn't one, she reassured herself. St. Bride was nothing at all like Straught. She trembled a smile then. I must be daft, her thoughts twittered to her. Now I'm defending our kiss—

next I shall be defending him. With a laugh of relief, she had spun around, ready to return to Colette.

"You laugh, Miss Kayleigh. You think he cannot do it?" Laban's huge, meaty arm reached behind her to the door and tore the note off the square-headed nail. He had sneaked up behind her, apparently on his way from Colette's cabin to his own. Despite his cumbersome weight, Laban had the ability of his master to be swift and silent.

"Laban, I was just . . ." Her words dwindled as she realized how bad the situation must look. Once again Laban had found her in a compromising position.

"You were just spying again." His words, eloquently spoken in a deep West Indian dialect, shot ice through her heart.

"I'm not a spy," she defended.

"You didn't know this was my cabin?" He balled the note within his black fist and pointed to the kitchens. "Colette would have need of you, I think. Perhaps she can be a better influence." With that he lumbered past her, shutting his cabin door resolutely behind him.

Now as she sat in the kitchens helping Colette, Kayleigh couldn't help but feel guilt stab at her breast. Not that she had done anything to feel guilty about—quite the contrary. But knowing that Colette could hardly approve of her reading the note on Laban's door, she already felt the loss of their budding friendship. It was especially painful since she otherwise seemed completely surrounded by enemies at Belle Chasse. Laban had always distrusted her, and her actions to date had only reinforced that initial distrust. And St. Bride's attentions were unwelcome at best, completely unnerving her and her sense of self-possession. But Colette had always been a friendly face. Perhaps it was their common vulnerability that had led her to trust Colette, or perhaps it had been the young mulatto's unwavering honesty and calm dignity. Whatever the reason, Kayleigh was saddened when Colette turned doubtful eyes upon her.

"Are you very angry with me?" she blurted out.

"The master has been good to you. You have cheated him with your disloyalty. You should not have read his note to Laban." Colette frowned.

"He wants something of me. And I dare not trust him enough to give him what he wants. How else can I check on his motives without delving into business that may not be my own?" Kayleigh tried to answer in the most honest way she could. She did trust Colette—but she had to be canny nonetheless. She could not reveal too much, for she knew Colette's own loyalty stood firmly with the master of Belle Chasse.

"Monsieur Ferringer, above all, is innocent of any wrongdoing." Colette wiped down the cherrywood table.

"Innocent? St. Bride? If you only knew how uninnocent he is! St. Bride Ferringer hasn't a chaste thought in his head, nor an unproven part to his body!" She turned from Colette in embarrassment. "When he touches me—that's when he frightens me the most. He believes me to be other than what I am, Colette."

"And what are you, if not a *prostituée?*"

A shocked silence filled the kitchen. Even the coals at the hearth hissed more quietly than before. It was obvious that Colette was in an unusual fit of temper and had spoken the words before she realized what she said. Regret was profound and immediate in her face, but it was not enough to prevent a huge, silent tear from welling up in Kayleigh's stricken eyes. The tear threatened to slip down the planes of her cheekbone, but from staunch practice, she closed her lids. When Kayleigh opened them again, the tear was gone. Her eyes were clear and brilliant, and her back was stiff and straight.

"It's a terrible trick fate has played on me. I am just the opposite of what everyone here thinks. Because of this, my agony will be thrice what it would have been."

"I am sorry, Kayleigh, *vraiment.* My words were mean

and spiteful.'' Colette shook her madras-covered head and laughed. ''All these men! Why we put up with them—?''

''I don't put up with them.''

''Ah, but you must! It's our lot in life.''

''Nay, it is not mine. I've never been with a man, and I daresay I never shall.''

Colette responded with a sharp gasp. ''No, I cannot understand this! The life you've led, surely you've—?''

''Bardolph only made me steal. He knew he couldn't make me . . . bed men for coin.'' Kayleigh hated the way her voice shook. She wondered if she was making a mistake telling Colette this.

The little mulatto grew silent at this latest information, but she soon returned a broken reply. ''It will not be so very bad for you, Kayleigh. I know your fear well, but you must count yourself lucky that your first time will be with a man like St. Bride.'' There was sympathy in Colette's face, but underlying it was a calm acceptance of the very circumstances that Kayleigh found unnerving.

''I mean to be clear of Belle Chasse before anything of that sort takes place. In fact, when the time comes, I believe I shall go north, perhaps to Fort Rosalie or to Fort Maurepas.'' Kayleigh clung to her old resolve.

''I am afraid you will not.'' Though Colette squeezed her hand reassuringly, her words were anything but that. ''It is not easy to leave Belle Chasse. You know that better than anyone. There is swamp in every direction a man can ride, except for the River Road. And that has few travelers. Men go mostly by the river, not on the perilous road. Have you heard the stories of the Indian massacre at Fort Rosalie? Remember them again, mademoiselle, for even if you desire to travel north, you must not travel alone. I think you must have the master take you where you want to go, but more and more, I think, he will not want to take you.''

''He will take me! Why should he not?'' Futilely, Kayleigh

balled her hands into fists and ground them against the kitchen tabletop.

"Because you are very beautiful."

Kayleigh looked up. Colette's brow delicately furrowed as she continued, "Laban, he knows the master well, and perhaps this is why Laban cannot like you. Laban says that the master's mind has not been on what it should be. It is not always on *la belle chasse.* Whenever you are near, St. Bride looks upon you with such a desire, Laban has told me he has never seen it before. He has told me that you will prove to be the master's weakness. Just like the Lady Mary Greenling."

"Mary Greenling?" The unexpected name shocked Kayleigh out of her prepared denial. A vivid picture of a pretty young wife tending to her husband's needs in a faraway Georgia plantation came to her mind. The name was mild and docile, much like Morna's had been. Yet Kayleigh disliked it immediately. Her wanton behavior while in the company of St. Bride came back to haunt her. "Is he married then?" she asked bitterly. "He makes public his lusts for me, yet all the while he has a wife?"

"Non, a sister," Colette reassured her.

"Lady Mary is his sister?" Kayleigh frowned. Now, why did she sound so relieved?

"Oui, but Mary was his half sister. Laban told me she died a few months ago," Colette whispered, as if revealing a most intimate secret.

"How?" Kayleigh barely breathed the word. But before Colette could give her an answer, Laban appeared in the darkened courtyard. Through the crude batten doorway, they saw him walking toward the kitchens with an intent look upon his face.

Noting his approach, Colette murmured, "We will speak of this never again, Kayleigh. I will keep your secrets, and you will keep mine. I have told you more than I should have. But it was to ease your fears and for nothing else. St. Bride is a grieving man. If your virginity is the price to ease his sorrow, you will find no haven for your plight with me. He is greatly admired by those who served him. While I feel for you, I serve him too. My loyalty must be his completely.'' With that Colette limped to the hearth and doused the fires for the night.

Kayleigh watched her, stunned and bewildered. When Laban entered the kitchens with a thick, dark scowl on his face, Kayleigh seized the opportunity to excuse herself and escape to the house. At least there, she knew she could be alone and sort out her thoughts.

It was another sleepless night. As she lay in her bed, she heard St. Bride's late arrival. When he stomped through the loggia, the chill of the note she'd misread on Laban's door retraced its path down her spine. Again she was struck by the fact that he was a complete mystery to her. She was frightened of who St. Bride might be.

Yet in the wee hours of the morning, when her thoughts could not be tamed, the memory of his kiss beneath the live oaks was evoked, unbidden, time and time again. And with it the feelings were revitalized. But they could only coil within her, restless and dissatisfied, for she was unable to relive the moment fully without St. Bride's touch and St. Bride's scent. She rolled onto her side and bit her lower lip. She was not willing to hand St. Bride her virginity. That, she vowed, she would give only to a man of her choosing. The ghostly shreds of her fine upbringing still clung to her, and she knew that lying with a man must be for love only. Anything less than that would be sin.

So why did she now ache to see him? Disgusted with herself, she tried to turn a deaf ear to the noise in the next room as he readied for bed. But she heard two heavy thuds that had to be his heavy jackboots coming off, and then her ears fairly burned to discern which piece of clothing he was taking off next. She heard the scrape of a chair and wondered if he'd tossed his shirt onto it or . . . his breeches. Frustrated, she rolled onto her stomach and forced herself to sleep. But then she began to wonder what he was doing in his bedchamber. Was he fast asleep? Or was he lying on his bed staring at the canopy? Had his trip to town left him relaxed and pleasured, or was there that hardness about his mouth that she had seen other evenings when he was tired? At this thought, Kayleigh had the strangest urge to go to him. She wanted just to touch his lips, to ease the tensions that might be found there. Suddenly she wanted to see him smiling at her as he had on the docks when he had grabbed at her petticoats and they had both landed bottoms down in the mud.

Kayleigh shook her head and wondered for the last time what had gotten into her. Then she almost wanted to laugh. *Dhé!* She had to get away from Belle Chasse! It was making her as mad as the rest of its inhabitants.

The next day the summer sun beat a ferocious path on the land. Beneath it, clapboards buckled, paint peeled, and roof tiles cracked. The only relief was from the afternoon storm that fed the wild irises and the low Mississippi. But as the natives knew, during the Louisiana summer time would begin to stand still and the oppressive weather would remain until the first evening chills of October.

Late that morning, Kayleigh found herself with the tame chore of feeding the pigeons. She suspected that Colette was delighted to have her out of the kitchens, and though Kayleigh couldn't blame her after the mess she had made yesterday, she did long for her company.

She threw seed around the *pigeonnier,* a tall square dovecote with a steep four-sided roof. As tradition had it, it sat markedly on the front lawn of the plantation so that all passersby could judge the wealth of the owner. Belle Chasse's had just been filled with the pretty doves, and Kayleigh marveled at the pigeons' desire to stay near their home. When Joseph and Mathias had first allowed the doves free access, she had expected they would all fly away. But on the contrary, they seemed content to feed in their grand home, hardly taking note of the daily disappearances of their neighbors. Their rents were collected in flesh. Kayleigh found it hard not to draw a parallel between her own life and that of the birds.

"Miss Kayleigh, may we comb your hair?" A little voice brought her out of her reverie. Looking down, Kayleigh saw the little slave child named Valentine holding out her hand. In it was a silver comb. Behind Valentine her five-year-old twin, Venus, giggled.

"Why, you little snitches—you've taken St. Bride's comb! And what is this?" Kayleigh exclaimed in her softest brogue. Looking down at the twins, she added, "You have new dresses, I see. Come, turn around and let me look at you! Valentine, where did you get them?" Kayleigh watched as each girl spun, patting down their sugar-beet maroon petticoats as they whirled in the breeze.

"The white master, mademoiselle. He is so very kind!" Valentine answered, and both girls giggled.

"Och, is that so?" Kayleigh cocked a doubtful brow, but not wanting to dampen their pleasure, she kept her opinion of the master to herself. Again seeing the comb, she said, "You little girls have a streak of mischief in you that I certainly recognize. Do you still want to comb my hair?" Seeing their imploring eyes, Kayleigh couldn't help but laugh. She was fascinated by these two little girls. And from the moment they laid eyes upon her, the twins seemed to adore her as well. "Oh, I suppose it would be all right then. But we've got to be canny, *bairns*. I don't want St. Bride to find out what we're up to. For all I know, he'll think I put you up to snitching his comb."

She smiled and eased herself down into a crude cypress armchair under the shade of the gallery. Then she unpinned her shining dark tresses. Her hair cascaded down the back of the chair, and both the twins stroked the silken mass, enchanted by its beauty.

"Have a care now," she commented as first Venus, then Valentine ran the comb through her hair. Slumping her head back, Kayleigh felt slightly guilty about the twins' obvious admiration. A year ago she would have expected it—it was her very birthright as the spoiled daughter of a wealthy landowner to receive an underling's regard. But now their awe seemed undeserved, and it made her vaguely uncomfortable.

With heavy lids, she lolled her head, letting the comb's motion relax her. A hot wind cooled her warm forehead. Mo Chridhe found her empty lap, jumping onto it from under the eaves. Her hand stroked Chridhe's fur in rhythm with the twins' combing, and she stared up at the cypress beams and uneven floorboards of the gallery until her eyes could hardly stay open. The day was unbearably hot—this alone seemed to beckon her to nap.

Venus giggled in the background . . . or was it Valentine? her mind wondered, tottering between reality and slumber.

Almost imperceptibly, she felt the touch. It began on her hairline and wound its way along the soft, curling hairs of her temple, then over the pink satin of her cheek. It meandered beneath her delicate chin, and only when it began to tilt her head back farther did her eyes reluctantly open. This was not the touch of a child.

Looking upward, she found St. Bride staring down at her, his expression as inscrutable as granite, his eyes as unfathomable as the sea. Yet he himself missed nothing. Each fragile feature was caressed by his vision, from her smooth forehead and slim, slightly turned-up nose to the perfect oval of her face and the heat-induced blush of her skin. But it was her lips he finally sought. Moist and slightly parted, showing the inner dusky hue of rose petals, they were much like a rose themselves, yet not tight like a bud or overblown, but perfectly formed and in their prime of youth. It seemed he could not resist.

Bending down, his lips touched her own in a soft, chaste manner that neither frightened her nor overwhelmed her. Her nose came near to his throat and the scent that clung to him was intoxicating, a mixture of pungent soap and his own mysterious, unnamed essence that mocked his restraint, it being not nearly so pure as soap. She briefly mused on her own scent, wondering if hers was as heady and arousing to him. But the kiss didn't last long enough for her to find out. Two small giggles escaped in the background. Groaning, St. Bride lifted his lips, wickedly tilting a fine ebony eyebrow.

"Our cupids have seen enough." He straightened, and Kayleigh became aware of the length and power of his form. From her position in the chair, St. Bride towered above her, lean and predatory. Her own vulnerability loomed even larger. Snapping her head up, she quickly sat upright and whirled in her chair to face him.

"I took your comb, St. Bride. And—and I asked the lassies here to comb my hair." She handed him the silver comb and tried her best to look guilty. It wasn't hard, for she did feel guilty. She didn't want him even to speculate on the twins' mischief. Venus and Valentine were too dear to be punished.

"*You* took the comb? Then why haven't you deposited it beneath your bodice or tucked it safely under your mattress?" He leaned against the brickwork, and his eyes twinkled in amusement. "Really, love, it's not very smart of you to go and steal a man's personal effects, then parade them beneath his nose."

"I was just borrowing it. I meant to return it." It took all her will not to look at the twins. She hoped they weren't frightened.

"I say, Venus and Valentine have a penchant for black hair and white skin," he answered.

"They're just little girls, St. Bride." Becoming unnerved, she forced his attention away from the twins by taking up the heavy weight of her locks and desperately trying to pin them.

"Leave your hair. It seems I have a penchant too." His large bronzed hands took her fragile ones and bade her quit her tidying. "Besides, I've no desire to punish little girls. I've a present for you, Kayleigh. I meant to give it to you at

Little Versailles. However,'' he added dryly, ''things did not go as planned.''

Kayleigh raised her chin, remembering all too well why that was so. But she lowered it immediately, for it was impossible to ignore the package he dropped in her lap. ''What is it?'' she whispered.

''A gift'' was all he said.

Frowning, she turned the package over and over in her hands. He was bringing her gifts—just like her suitors back at Mhor. But now she wasn't a lady of the manor, she was a servant—and servants, she well knew, did not require courting. What was St. Bride up to?

''You needn't have done this,'' she said.

''Such a regal attitude, my lady—frowning upon us peasants,'' he taunted.

She prickled beneath his sarcasm, and he grinned.

''I confess the gift is meager. But I didn't want to give you anything too valuable out of fear you would hawk it to the next passerby on the River Road. I daresay you'd be gone within the hour.'' He laughed and demanded, ''Open it.''

''No, thank you,'' she refused.

''But, sweetling—'' he offered.

''Amadan!'' she cried.

''My pet!'' he coaxed, then paused to wink at Venus and Valentine, who burst into a fit of childish giggling. It was more than Kayleigh could take. Dropping her head, she bit her lip to keep from laughing too. *Dhé,* how could she feel like laughing and murdering in one single breath? St. Bride would drive her mad if she let him!

''Open the package, Kayleigh.''

Resigning herself, she pulled at the coarse wrappings, and amongst the appreciative sighs of the twins, she pulled forth a great handful of satin ribbons. Emerald, amethyst, and ruby ran through her hands like the tatters of a magician's coat. St. Bride picked up the sapphire ribbon, and its smooth satin glistened brilliantly in the sun.

"They're beautiful!" she exclaimed in a hushed voice. "They're the color of gemstones."

"But alas, even gemstones would dim in comparison to the radiance of your beauty," he answered, his voice caressing her like a lover's hand.

Startled by his tenderness, she raised confused eyes. She quite expected that St. Bride had spoken in jest, but when her gaze locked with his, he was quiet and sober. He brushed a curl from her cheek with the back of his hand and said, "Let me trust you, dark love, and the next time I'll fill your lap with the very jewels."

She turned away. His offer somehow tarnished her. If she were to gain his trust, the only payment she would want would be to trust him in turn. But how would she ever get him to understand that?

"Perhaps I'm not as greedy as you would have me be." With a sad little smile, she admired her ribbons.

"I make you a good offer, Kayleigh. Why be so hasty to turn it down?" He lifted her chin with his hand and forced her attention back to him.

"Thank you, St. Bride, but no." She met his stare. Hers was steady, yet melancholy.

"Someday you may change your mind . . . and have a change of heart."

"I'm afraid not. . . ." Her words dwindled away, and she shook her head. The silence that followed was heavy, falling upon them like a wet cloak.

Kayleigh's troubled gaze trailed over to the twins. They were eyeing her ribbons in awe and admiration as if they ached to touch them. Without aforethought, she handed several ribbons to each girl and helped them tie them to their stubby braids. Then she impulsively handed them more to take to their Mandingan mother, Babet, the laundress. Afterward Kayleigh watched Venus and Valentine run off, their valuable treasure held out in their hands like a satin pillow laden with jewels.

"For a little cutpurse, you're unusually generous with your meager possessions," St. Bride remarked stonily.

"I've had many ribbons before, but the twins never have."

"Was it the ribbons you didn't care for, or the fact that they were from me?"

If there was hurt in his eyes, he hid it brilliantly. But his words demanded apology, and she immediately stumbled to give him one. "That was thoughtless of me, St. Bride. The ribbons are truly beautiful, and I know you wanted me to have them. I should have been more considerate."

He ran his hand through his hair in exasperation. The hardness was apparent around his mouth, and she felt an urge to touch him there. But she didn't. He became even more distant, and she regretted her actions more with each passing moment. His gift had been kind, and she had been thoughtless. She should have tied the ribbons to her hair and flirted brazenly with him. That would have made the hardness go away. Now she wondered if it ever would.

She looked up and found St. Bride studying her. Then, as if in retaliation, he invaded her privacy with his eyes. His gaze traveled down her skirts and bodice and lingered in the most inappropriate places.

Uncomfortable, Kayleigh crossed her arms over her chest and dared him to continue. But there was no need. He looked as if he were judging her worth, as if she were a slave on the block; yet all the while he scowled, too, as if trying to talk himself out of purchasing her. Also in his eyes was that terrifying blue desire, and she knew protest would be useless. He had made up his mind.

He would pay her price.

She watched him walk away. His back presented him as an unyielding adversary that she was not sure she could best. She clenched her hands, and had she anything other than Chridhe in her grasp, she would surely have flung it at him and accepted the consequences of her act regardless of their severity.

Dropping Chridhe to the ground, Kayleigh rose angrily from her seat. She stormed past the rear courtyard and looked to the newly sown fields beyond. In the haze she could see Little Versailles, that lush shadowed haven. Like a balm for her raging emotions, their cool blue shade beckoned her forth. She kept it within her sight as she walked past the stable. She pondered how far she could go before someone might take it upon himself to force her back to the house. Running her finger along a weathered clapboard of the stable, she looked to see if anyone was watching her.

In the stable young Mathias and the old, shriveled slave Grand-Louis were busy cleaning the harnesses by rubbing amber glycerine into the leather straps. Grand-Louis was uttering a soft chant. Mathias had his eyes not only on the martingale he was rubbing but also on a laundry slave named Lise. Satisfied that she could retreat to the shady haven for a while without detection, Kayleigh turned the corner that lead to the rear of the building, out of sight of the slaves.

"Damn you, gel! After three days I thought I'd never get you!" She felt the length of her hair, still unbound, grabbed violently. Tears of pain stung her eyes as she tried to make out who her assailant was.

Quinn! Her mind cried silently. There was no mistaking his pudgy gut and his muddy, unintelligent gaze.

"Have a care! Do not speak above a whisper, or I'll be dragging you back to Mr. Straught myself." Quinn watched for her compliance, twisting his hands further through her hair.

"How—how did you find me?" Her teeth chattered despite the day's heat.

"Why, lovely, Mr. Ferringer told me." He leaned his head back and laughed. "It was my own grand opportunity."

"St. Bride told you I was here?" she asked in stunned amazement.

"You cannot trust that mean son of a whore, now can you? I've been trying to tell Mr. Straught that all along, but still he likes the chap. Not me, though—I'm no fool." He pulled her close. "Nor you, eh, Kayleigh? I saw him kiss you beneath the gallery. I think I'm understanding the situation better all the time. But still, you don't trust that graying stallion completely, do you? His friendship with a certain gent from Mhor, your sweet cousin Erath, makes your handsome young Ferringer almost an enemy, don't it?"

"What do you want, Quinn?" she spat at him. She'd always thought him dull-witted, but now she could see that Malcolm Quinn possessed a peasant cunning that she shouldn't underestimate. Taking a bold initiative, she began her defense. "Are you planning to take me back to Straught? Needless to say, I'll die right here to avoid that." She wrenched herself from his odious grasp.

His very presence sickened her, but his words were even harder to stomach. She couldn't believe that St. Bride hated her enough to write her death sentence by telling Quinn she was here. She'd hardly suspected that St. Bride even knew who she was, but now, the words *"It will keep Kayleigh in her place"* came back to haunt her.

"Tame yourself, lassie. I've my own plans for you."

"St. Bride sent you here then?" Her heart turned to stone.

"That one? I don't do his bidding! I found out using my own wits! Ferringer mentioned your name to one of the servants after Mr. Straught had left to return to town. I was waiting for some papers when I heard it. I knew it couldn't be anyone else but you. Mr. Straught told me you were dead. My, but you're a hard one to kill, lassie!"

"I am, so don't think you'll be succeeding where Erath has failed." She backed away from him, feeling ill and yet strangely relieved. St. Bride hadn't told him. He hadn't!

"I'm not here to kill you, Kayleigh. Mr. Straught's the one who wants you dead."

"Yes, of course," she exclaimed sarcastically. Then changing tack, she asked, "Tell me, Quinn, I've wanted to know.

How did sweet Erath know we were in New Orleans? Bardolph thought we were safe."

"He found a trinket of yours, Kayleigh. A box."

"My box!" she exclaimed.

"Mr. Straught spent many a night walking the floor, let me tell you, waiting for you to show up and expose his little deed. He sent some men looking for you and old Bardie after you disappeared. Can you imagine his relief when his blokes told him they'd found your box in the possession of a ship's captain out of Glasgow? Mr. Straught talked to this captain—his ship was the *Deepwater,* I believe—and he found out you'd come here."

She was sickened at the thought that her box, the very box her parents had given her for good fortune, had brought her so much trouble instead. "And why did Straught take so long to find me? I sold that box over a year ago."

"He's broke, gel. Mr. Straught's been living pretty high off Mhor's riches, but they ain't been enough for him. He went looking for more money. He got himself in a fine mess with a gent from London. It seems Mr. Straught had a quick tumble with the gent's relation while the gent was out of the county. Things went awry, and since then, this old blighter's been plaguing Mr. Straught like the devil, though Mr. Straught ain't even seen the whoreson's face!"

With morbid delight, she listened to Quinn's account of Straught's woes. She pictured the man after Straught as some old gentleman, a squire perhaps—one with a daughter Straught had taken too many liberties with. She hoped the squire would be merciless when he found Straught. She hoped he would have him hung. "I pray this gent finds Cousin Erath . . . and—and soon," she said with vengeance.

"Maybe he will, maybe he won't. But I've found you, haven't I now?" Quinn grinned. "Fate has such a big role in our lives, now don't it? But you should know all about that, fey Kayleigh. Mr. Straught believes in it with all his heart. Finding you here, I'm thinking he's right."

"What do you want, Quinn? I know you aren't here for my cousin because I'd be dead by now. So if not to murder me, then what?"

"I've come to be taking some of the gent's riches." Quinn leered.

Fear and indignation swept over her as she saw his intentions, but they turned to gales of fury when his hand clamped down on her untouched bosom.

She hissed at him through clenched teeth, her eyes spewing blue fire, "You saw the gent's kiss. If you hurt me, don't doubt he'll blow your hide right off your filthy rump!"

She was pleased by the frightened look on his face as he released her. Everyone thought Malcolm Quinn was slower than an idiot, but she was at least heartened that Quinn's murky intelligence knew better than to lock horns with St. Bride. She was not St. Bride's mistress, of course, and her value to St. Bride was speculative at best. But Malcolm could not know that.

"Don't be raising your voice for the darkies to hear." Malcolm seemed to wrestle with this news, but he soon brightened. "So you be his wench now, Kayleigh? All the better indeed!"

"What do you want, I say!" In agitation, she looked around her for eavesdroppers. She would never be able to explain why she was clandestinely meeting with a man St. Bride obviously disliked and distrusted.

"You meet me regular, Kayleigh. You bring me silver, gold—anything worth having from yonder house. Me in my turn won't be informing the honorable Mr. Straught that you're alive and well and bedding the master of Belle Chasse."

"I cannot, you fool! The things would be missed!"

"Then wheedle them out of him. You've the charm to do that. I don't care the means you use. But I'm warning you, wench. If'n you don't comply, I'll have Mr. Straught here at dawn with your blood running down your back like your sister's.'' He pulled on her arm to draw her near. His grasp was like a manacle, and she knew she would be sorely bruised for a fortnight. ''Have a care, Kayleigh. You're in a mess now, and you've no one to trust. Though you've escaped the knife twice, there is no third time.''

''Get out!''

''You bring me some baubles tomorrow and every day hence. Don't get yourself caught. 'Cause if Ferringer don't wring your pretty neck, you've got two others who will.'' Quinn pushed her aside. Giving her a warning look, he lumbered off toward the eastern swamps where, no doubt, he had a horse tied up in a wild magnolia clearing.

Chapter Twelve

"Again a visitor?" Kayleigh murmured later that afternoon as she stepped from the hot kitchens.

"Again? We've had no visitors today." Colette gave Kayleigh a curious glance as she mopped her neck with a linen towel.

"We haven't? It seems so recent that Mr. Straught and Mr. Quinn were here," Kayleigh covered up hastily, adding to herself, yes, only too recent. Her breast ached, and the roots of her hair still stung from Quinn's viciousness. She had not dared to tell Colette what had happened earlier with Quinn, so she had remained somber and silent.

Both women watched the gilt coach make its way to the rear courtyard. It was the one Lady Catherine de Thionville and her mother had used that day on the docks.

Kayleigh hung out of sight in the kitchen doorway and eyed the newcomers with unveiled distrust. She watched as first the bejeweled comte and then his porcelainlike daughter descended from the rocking vehicle. After they had disembarked and she was reassured that her cousin was not among them, Kayleigh retreated into the kitchens to hide.

"Who are they? Do you know?" Colette asked.

"Lady Catherine, I suspect. And the gent is Thionville the

Terror,'' Kayleigh stated uneasily, watching from the safety of a small window.

"Why do you call him that?" Colette asked from the door, admiring the heavily gilded and crested coach.

"Everyone in New Orleans calls the Comte de Cassell so. He's notorious." Kayleigh smirked while she helped with the tea tray.

"And why is that?" Colette asked.

"He's like the old Church—for certain monies he will sell you forgiveness. Och, but don't we live in a corrupt little place?" Kayleigh released a black little laugh.

"You make no sense! The Church only forgives sin. What does the comte forgive?" Colette frowned.

"For a bit of gold—on a regular basis, mind—the Comte de Cassell will forgive you for not allowing him to break your arms."

"Kayleigh, you're not right!" Colette gasped.

"No? I'm quite sure." Kayleigh arched one eyebrow for emphasis. "Bardolph used to talk of him constantly. Of course, we were hardly worth the bother of Thionville the Terror, Bardolph and I. We didn't own the clothes on our backs, let alone have money to buy the comte's 'Indulgences.' But buy them we did, nonetheless. Bardolph made sure we had enough to give to him so we wouldn't awaken one day to find our legs snapped beneath us. With Louis XV behind him, Thionville is too powerful for anyone to ignore, even a mere cutpurse. Why, I think the governor must pay him too."

"What—what does the comte want here? Monsieur Ferringer, is he in danger?" Colette limped back to the door, looking at the coach. Her face was drawn and apprehensive.

"St. Bride's in no danger. At least he has the funds to pay the comte. I expect the comte's here to collect." Kayleigh smiled suddenly, mischief aglow in her eyes. "I believe I'll be taking the tray to them." Yes, she thought to herself, I want to see how St. Bride bristles when he hears the comte's bit of news!

Almost joyfully, Kayleigh picked up the large silver tray. She had little worry that the comte would recognize her and betray her to her cousin. In the past the comte had always dealt with Black Bardolph, and now she doubted that he would think her anything but the serving girl that she was. With her hips artlessly swaying, she carried the tray to the house.

"You're looking well, St. Bride." Lady Catherine was just lowering her kissed hand when Kayleigh entered the salon with their refreshments. Keeping her eyes demurely on the floor, Kayleigh set the tray down on the gilt pier table and pulled a crudely carved, skirted cypress table to the salon's center. All the while, she listened to the conversation. If St. Bride sent her a scorching look, she merely returned it with a smile—soft, secretive, and ever so sincere. Och, he would be getting his, she thought with blithe pleasure as she poured out the tea into wafer-thin Export teacups. Thionville would extract his payment. And the exquisite joy of it was that she would be here to see it all.

"Would you like to view the plantation from the gallery, Lady Catherine, Comte?" St. Bride crooked his arm and allowed Lady Catherine to take hold of it. Leveling Kayleigh with a quelling stare, he turned to Thionville.

"It's too hot for me, St. Bride," said the comte. "Take Catherine out there if you must, but I shall remain here, taking refreshment." The comte turned his eyes to Kayleigh. She expected him to inspect Colette's pastries, but Kayleigh got the feeling that he was inspecting her too.

Setting up tea, she ignored the comte as he fanned himself with a hankie. His rotund carriage overwhelmed the delicate settee. Kayleigh wanted desperately not to be interested in the couple on the gallery, but she watched them nonetheless. Through the many gallery doors, Lady Catherine, resplendent in peach satin, listened attentively to every word St. Bride uttered about his wonderful plantation. And as they wandered down the colonnade, Kayleigh was struck by the couple's handsomeness.

A strange knot formed in her throat the more she looked at them. And it was then that she felt it. It had crept upon her like a stealthy vine, having been fed on the injustice and humiliation of her past. She denied its existence, but still it persisted, twining around her heart like rampant honey-suckle. She was jealous.

Kayleigh watched as Lady Catherine studied St. Bride's appearance. He wore only the simplest and finest of satin waistcoats and breeches and was attired in gray right down to his stockings. The deep slate color was relieved only by the brilliance of his white shirt and the sparkle of his smile. His hair was neatly queued to his neck by black bullion cording. The silver at his temples looked remarkably youthful against his handsome, unlined, laughing face.

She thinks him a prize, Kayleigh thought, turning her attention to Lady Catherine. The beautiful Frenchwoman moved closer to him, giving him a better view of her bosom, artfully framed by her low neckline and the frilly dog collar of ruffled Venetian lace. A brooch of pearls and emeralds caught the collar provocatively. Kayleigh noticed that strands of these same jewels were woven intricately into the woman's powdered hair. Catherine was beautiful, wealthy, and a lady. And no matter how dearly Kayleigh wanted to doubt the latter, she knew Lady Catherine's position alone would bid any gentleman to defend her virtue to the death.

Turning to the task at hand, Kayleigh tried not to listen to their conversation, but the temptation was too great. She wanted to know what they were saying, although she could have kicked herself for being so interested.

She tipped her head toward the open gallery doors and heard St. Bride say, "The slaves have already begun planting the poppies."

Next to him, she saw Lady Catherine leaning against the

railing while one doll-like hand swept down a chamfered
column.

"My daughter will have St. Bride's hand in marriage yet."
Spinning around, Kayleigh faced the comte, who was still
seated on the settee.

"Forgive me, my lord. Is there something you need?"
Nervously she took a step back.

"Nothing. I was telling you that my daughter will have
St. Bride yet. St. Bride is a man worthy of her hand, not
like those other dogs that have come courting her in this
chamberpot of Nature we call Louisiana. Though St. Bride
is a commoner, he will prove his worth." Thionville nodded
to the distant sowed fields through the gallery doors.

Kayleigh looked through the doors, too, not at the poppy
fields but at the couple. St. Bride was smiling tightly at
something Lady Catherine was saying to him; then, with a
firm nod, he bade Lady Catherine walk with him around the
corner, where their talk was out of earshot.

In mute dismay, Kayleigh watched them go. She was
shocked by the stab of jealousy, although she had utterly
convinced herself it was something else. With a vengeance,
she poured out the tea.

"As I said, she will have him yet." The comte smiled at
her, and Kayleigh lowered her eyes.

"That is none of my concern, my lord."

"I would have thought so, but I see otherwise." Thionville's green eyes narrowed. "You look familiar, *jeune fille*.
What is your name?"

"My name?" She frowned. She couldn't tell Thionville
her real name because of the comte's wagging tongue; she
couldn't call herself Kestrel, for the comte might connect
her with Bardolph and demand overdue "Indulgences." She
certainly couldn't afford any more of those, she thought wryly,
thinking of her meeting with Quinn. She wondered if even
St. Bride had enough money and goods at Belle Chasse for
all her debts.

"Colette," she lied brightly as she poured out the tea. She handed Thionville a cup with lemon, as the French preferred it, and reminded herself to give St. Bride his with cream.

"Colette, you are? A pretty, coquettish name. But you do not look French, mademoiselle." The comte accepted the tea, and his eyes lingered on her woolen dress, where her bosom was held by her shift.

"Puff pastry, my lord?" Kayleigh tried to ignore his questions by offering him a selection from her tray. Truly wishing she had some stays to make her feel less naked under his stare, she retreated to the tea table, unable to ignore his probing looks any longer.

"Tell me, child, how long have you worked for St. Bride?"

Stumped by this question, Kayleigh found herself at a loss for words.

"She has worked for me a long time," St. Bride interjected, entering the room with Lady Catherine, who clung ever so helplessly to his strong arm.

"Colette doesn't seem to be English, nor is she French— am I correct?"

"Colette?" St. Bride questioned, raising one infuriating eyebrow. Panic coupled with embarrassment crept slowly up Kayleigh's chest until even her ears turned shell pink.

"I . . . ah . . ." She felt compelled to speak, but the comte interrupted her.

"I find Colette a most capable servant. St. Bride, she would not have a bond, would she? If she does, I will most assuredly take her off your hands—perhaps even give you a little for your trouble." Delicately, the comte lifted his cup.

Kayleigh was astounded. She didn't like the fact that Thionville seemed interested in her, not one bit. But Thionville the Terror could have anything he wanted without paying a single livre. Now, not only had the comte not demanded monies from St. Bride, he was actually asking St. Bride to take *his* money. Again the question arose in her mind: Who was St. Bride that even Thionville kept to his bounds?

"How much are you thinking of?" St. Bride casually took a sip of tea. Kayleigh's back stiffened.

"Name your price!" The comte patted his forehead excitedly.

With fury in her eyes, Kayleigh looked at St. Bride. They were speaking of her as if she were not even in the room. It was as if she were some sort of pet, and they were bantering over her pedigree. Looking up, her eyes wandered over to where Lady Catherine sat on a squab-cushioned bergère. The women's eyes locked, and velvety midnight blue met icy spring green. Lady Catherine was not the least perturbed by her father's interest in the servants. It was as if she were accustomed to her father's dalliances. However, there was an anger within the woman's cold eyes and it seemed for Kayleigh alone.

She doesn't want me around here, Kayleigh thought in amazement. She'd rather I lived with her father than here at Belle Chasse. Turning to St. Bride, she began to wonder if Lady Catherine's wish would be fulfilled. St. Bride was taking a long time to make up his mind. While he did, Kayleigh could only fume behind the tea table.

Eventually St. Bride turned to her, amusement sparkling in his turquoise eyes. Kayleigh watched a slow, wry grin turn up one corner of his mouth. "I think, after all, I shall have to pass on your offer, my lord."

Lady Catherine's mouth tightened, but her father seemed the most disappointed. Deflated, the comte stared at St. Bride and Kayleigh. Soon his face puckered, and his eyes slitted. "I understand. I haven't enough *livres,* have I, St. Bride?"

"I'm afraid not." St. Bride turned from Kayleigh. "Besides, we have other business to attend. Have you brought the money? Greater than nine thousand pounds—wasn't that your share?"

"That was the amount we discussed. I've also brought you Erath's share."

"Did Straught find some gold then? When we were on the

Bonaventure, he talked of paying with some jewels he had come by." St. Bride drummed his fingers lightly on the armrest of the walnut settee. He looked quite nonchalant, but Kayleigh noticed the slight hardness around his mouth. She wondered if these were the jewels he had wanted her to find out about.

"No, he was forced to pay in jewels. You will still accept them, won't you?"

"Of course."

"Then here it all is. I despise playing courier, but Erath said it was my turn to make this tedious trip. He said he would make the next visit to check up on Belle Chasse's crop." The comte rummaged through his large purse and tossed his share of gold onto the cypress table. Then with a flourish he dropped an exquisite sapphire necklace and bracelet onto the table. Unable to contain herself, Kayleigh gasped at the sight of so many glittering jewels. Each piece was made *en suite* of triple strands of diamonds, clasped with a huge square sapphire in the middle.

Almost reverently, St. Bride picked up the necklace. The strands of diamonds cascaded down his bronzed hand. He touched them as if he were a Catholic fingering a rosary.

"Straught told me he had three pieces," St. Bride abruptly accused the comte.

"Three pieces? Why . . . are you sure?" The comte colored.

"Yes. Quite sure."

Nervously, the comte rummaged through his brocaded purse. Suddenly, he seemed to find the missing piece. "Ah, how could I have been so stupid! Of course, here it is!" He tossed out a matching brooch.

"Delightful." St. Bride smiled sardonically.

While this scenario was being played out, Kayleigh looked on from a corner, amazed that Thionville the Terror was paying off St. Bride instead of the other way around. The comte was obviously investing in the poppies that St. Bride was growing. But still she knew there had to be more to it than that. She wanted to know the reason behind the comte's rare respect for St. Bride. Was it just that the proud man commanded it?

Their business concluded, the comte rose to depart. "We should have a crop by August," St. Bride said. Lady Catherine allowed St. Bride to kiss her hand in farewell, but a glint in her eye spoke of unfinished business. St. Bride himself acknowledged this with a wry twist of his mouth.

"St. Bride, Papa and I are thinking of giving a ball. We expect to have it in less than a fortnight." Lady Catherine turned to Kayleigh, who was shocked at the venom that shot through the woman's celadon eyes. She turned back to St. Bride. "You wouldn't think of not coming, would you?"

"I'll come, certainly. What kind of ball is it to be?"

"Why, a *bal masqué, naturellement.*"

"Ah, my favorite kind." St. Bride seemed to find this particularly ironic, and Kayleigh noticed a decided menace about him that had not been present at the beginning of the visit. But neither of the Thionvilles seemed to notice this change. The comte departed in pleasure, and Lady Catherine departed in frustration.

When they were gone and their coach disappeared through the pecans, St. Bride unexpectedly tossed the necklace to Kayleigh. She caught the heavy bejeweled piece, then stared at St. Bride, bewildered. But he only slouched in his chair and burst into ironic laughter.

Dhé, what she had suspected was true. St. Bride was a madman. Carefully, she laid the glittering necklace on the cypress table once more, then picked up the tea tray, ready for a hasty exit. She should have known her troubles were not over, however, for St. Bride said to her retreating back, "Come back here, *Colette.*"

Kayleigh grimaced. No, she thought as she put the tea tray down once more, her troubles were not over yet.

"It's really quite remarkable, you know," St. Bride said to her from his chair.

"And what is that?" she asked, already annoyed at what was surely to come.

"Why, how pale you've grown since yesterday! I wouldn't have recognized you—*Colette*. I think you must be ill." He stretched his long legs before him and casually crossed his arms over his muscular chest.

"You cad." Rebelliously, she turned from his stare.

"Well, love. Let me hear it. Let me hear your artful confession. What's the story to be today? Oh, I do hope it's another fairy tale. With your love of Gaelic lore, you do those the best. Where are you going, little one? We aren't through by half." He effortlessly grabbed at her retreating petticoat, and she was caught in one neat bunch.

"I owe the comte 'Indulgences.' I didn't want him to know who I was." Her answer was as stiff as her body.

"Indulgences? What kind of place is this, I ask you! Who are you?" The question caught her off guard.

"I'm Kayleigh," she snapped.

"Yes, our Kayleigh, always hiding from someone." St. Bride shook his head and pulled forcibly on her petticoat.

"No, please!" Before she could stop him, he had pulled her to his lap.

"Shh. We can't have the servants hearing all this complaining. What a scandal!" His normally harsh voice was softened by amusement.

"You beast! *I'm* a servant!" From experience, she knew it was useless to struggle against his iron strength. She quieted, only to sit on his lap fuming with impatience.

"A servant? On the contrary, I would have you much more than that. Besides, we cannot have a young lady who reads resort to mere servitude, can we?"

More explanations, Kayleigh thought, doomed. "I cannot read." She tightened her lips.

"Ah, but Laban has told me otherwise. While I was in town, he caught you reading a note on his door."

"Laban lies."

"And what would be his reason?" St. Bride put his arms around her waist, and she could feel cords of muscle tighten around her. His forearms brushed beneath her tender breasts.

"He hates me," Kayleigh retorted.

"Not good enough, love." He smiled and breathed heavily of her jasmine-scented hair. "If Laban hates you, how would lying about your ability to read hurt you? No, I think *you* are lying. Now and always, it's you, Kayleigh, the perennial teller of tales, great and small."

"I was just standing near his door. I don't know what you wrote."

St. Bride nuzzled the baby-fine hairs on the back of her neck. "Then how did you know the note was from me?" he whispered huskily.

"I guessed," she answered weakly, wishing he would stop touching her. A tingling sensation was slinking down her back. When she felt his tongue, hot and smooth, upon her throat, she couldn't stop a betraying shudder from coursing through her body.

"Please . . ."

"Oh, Kayleigh, shall I force a revelation again? I warn you, if my French makes you blush, my penmanship will make you burn. Would you like me to leave you a note one night before you retire to your cold little bed?"

"No." She moaned.

He laughed and picked up the necklace.

"Look, Kayleigh! Look what I have!" He dangled the necklace before her. "Have you ever seen anything so beautiful?"

His enthusiasm was hard to resist. Suddenly, she smiled at him and shook her head.

"You like it, don't you?" He chuckled. "I'll have to keep it well locked up then!"

"You!" she spat, and tried to get off his lap.

"No! Wait! Kayleigh!" He held her tight. "Today all my

wishes have been fulfilled. Now all I have to do is wait for my precious crop to bloom.''

''Och, then you're a fortunate man,'' she said sarcastically.

''I am a fortunate man—and also an unfortunate man. For now that all my wishes have come true, I find I still have one more.''

''And what is that?'' Her eyes met his, and suddenly there was no need for him to answer. She felt his fingers entwine in the thick black knot of hair at her nape. St. Bride's fingers, unlike Quinn's, were gentle. Before she could stop him, his lips began their tantalizing descent to hers. With lazy expertise, he plundered her mouth, allowing her to slip down between his knees. He soon had her trapped completely. Her spinning head couldn't organize even the weakest rebellion, let alone command her body to carry it through.

Softly, she groaned her protest as his fingers went to the hooks of her dress. Soon only the sheer barrier of her shift was between his large, sun-bronzed hands and her full, straining breasts. With its large, open neckline, he easily slid one shoulder of the white undergarment down to her arm and abandoned it where the fabric tightened at her elbow. Looking down, Kayleigh saw her one unblemished breast peek from the folds of linen. It was tender and startlingly pale against the tanned, muscular hand that reached for it.

Despite her twisting emotions, she tried to turn away, fearful that St. Bride would discover the black and blue marks from Quinn's grabbing her other breast.

But she wasn't quick enough. As his hand moved ever nearer, Kayleigh realized that without a doubt she wanted his touch. She wanted it like the sun upon her back in a harsh, unfriendly winter, wanted it like a bonfire in the loneliness of snow. And yet she dreaded his touch, too, for it was like fire and she could be consumed by it. But in the end, she knew she would have it. She finally resorted to closing her eyes, as a coward would, before accepting it upon her.

She had no forewarning of the great hot surge that rose

within her as his skin melded with hers. Her breath came with dizzying quickness that only increased when his thumb played lightly over the rose-hued nipple. With studied intent, he brought it to a hard, aching crest, and she found that his touch only made her yearn for more.

Relief drummed in her veins when he lifted her to a higher place on his lap and then bent his head to capture the peak with his white, even teeth.

But her desire was never met. Through the open loggia, she heard the heavy sound of footsteps on the stairs. They were distinctly Laban's.

"Don't come further, Laban. I have no need for visitors now." St. Bride raised his head and fairly snarled in the direction of the loggia. This stopped Laban dead in his tracks. But there was no warding off the humiliation and embarrassment that Kayleigh felt as she fought to hide her nakedness in the wake of the intrusion. Her shift was hopelessly wound around her elbow, and she could hardly pull the material up enough to cover herself properly, let alone retain her dignity. Pulling from St. Bride, she was dismayed at his refusal to let her go, and soon tears of frustration welled up in her betrayed blue eyes.

"You savage, let me go before your wonderful Laban—" Her words were cut short as Laban, still unseen, shouted from the stairs.

"It's Canis, St. Bride. He's gone down in his stall. Looks to be the colic." Laban's words were slow and pointed.

"Get him to his feet and walk him. I'll be down shortly." St. Bride lifted his hand and rubbed his jaw in agitation. But his other was still damnably clasped to her waist.

"Yes, sir." They heard Laban descend the stairs.

"Your horse awaits." Kayleigh tried to keep her voice from shaking. St. Bride turned to her and he looked almost mad with a crazed glint in his eyes.

"My horse will survive. Come." He rose, taking her small hand and leading her toward his bedchamber.

"Tend to your horse." She pulled back, her sanity returning. She didn't want his touch—and she certainly didn't want him baring her further, only to ask her unanswerable questions about her bruised flesh.

"Would you prefer I sell you to Thionville?"

"You have no right. I've no bond."

"Easy enough to fix that." He changed his angle of attack and picked her up as though she weighed no more than Mo Chridhe and carried her to his room.

"You would force yourself upon me, then?" she cried. Her shift fell away when he scooped her up, and she grabbed at it with vengeance. Her tenuously clad bosom heaved against the hardness of his rippling chest while he carried her, and although the crisp hair that escaped from St. Bride's shirt was tantalizing, Kayleigh could not reconcile herself to what he wanted to do. It was lust, pure and simple, that drove him. No better motivation could be found, and she would have only heartache if she allowed his seduction to proceed. As she writhed to be free, he flung her onto his satin-dressed bed. She watched in mute dismay as he began to take off his shoes.

"You positively astound me, Kayleigh. Never was there a more reluctant woman." The first shoe met the floor with a dooming thud.

"No, I say! How many times do I have to say no!" she pleaded with him, crossing her arms to attain more modesty.

"I won't force myself upon you. Not now. You know I can use other means. You remember you weren't so contrary on the settee, my love." He jacked off his second shoe and tore off his shirt.

Panicked, she kneeled on the mattress and anxiously watched as he began unbuttoning his gray satin breeches. Already his half-naked splendor made the room seem much smaller than it actually was.

"I would have more than just a tumble, St. Bride," she

reprimanded. She then tried to climb off the mattress, but he easily walked to the edge of the bed and forced her back.

"Then I will give you more." With those words he grabbed her up in his arms and pulled her to the edge of the bed. His eyes glittered with heated emotion as he stared down at her. With his hands pulling her arms from her chest, she was thrown against him, then his lips came down on hers in a long, smoldering kiss. She surrendered one helpless shudder when she felt her bodice slide open, furthering the contact between them. But her hands quickly moved to his waist in an effort to push him away. She succeeded, however, only in making his unbuttoned breeches slide farther down his hips. Horrified, she ceased her struggles immediately.

When the kiss ended, she was furious. "I will not be your mistress," she said adamantly, wiping her kiss-bruised lips with the back of her hand.

"I've asked you before, what better life could a man offer you?" He looked down at her still in his arms.

"I would be married. But my choice for a husband is definitely not you."

"You jest." St. Bride seemed truly amazed.

"If I say nay, I lie. If I say yes, I lie. Which is it?" She trembled, her blue velvet stare accusing him through the dark veil of her tresses. He was stumped for an answer and she knew it. "Go to your horse now," she whispered. "He will give you a better ride than I."

"You truly expect me to offer for you?"

"I told you, you're not the man I would have for a husband. I expect to marry a man who is thoughtful and kind and who treats me like a lady, not like some willing tavern wench!"

"And I expect to marry a lady who doesn't steal and lie and who can hold her tongue better than a shrewish fish-wife!" He grabbed her arms and gently shook her.

Kayleigh looked down at the mattress. "Do you treat all your servants this way? Have you had Colette also?"

They were just the words to stop him. Suddenly, instead of wanting to bed her, he looked more bent on murder.

"You really are an impossible woman! But think on this: We're not through." He shoved her back on the bed and angrily began rebuttoning his breeches. "I'll control you yet, wench. That I swear," he uttered in a low, frustrated voice.

"You won't ever control me," she answered huskily, watching him scoop his shirt from the floor. "Not unless I want you to."

"Then I'll make you want me to."

With that ominous statement, St. Bride left for the stable.

Chapter Thirteen

He knew she was stealing—he had to know, Kayleigh mused darkly, staring at the conspicuously bare mantel in her room. Intently, she set her chin upon the heel of her palm. After all, St. Bride's uncanny blue-green eyes took in everything that was about his plantation.

Her silken brows slanted with a frown. So why wasn't he stopping her? Och, how that man puzzled her. Every time he touched her, he exerted more and more power over her body; every time he spoke to her, she found it more difficult to evade his questions. The silver was disappearing, yet he chose not even to address the obvious. Ever since that afternoon in his bedchamber several days before, he seemed to have drawn back from her—as if to study her and decide what move to make next.

Now he had her more terrified than ever before. What was he up to? Kayleigh gnawed on a thumbnail and then self-consciously stopped herself, remembering her mother's lectures on such behavior. Having nothing to ease her anxiety with, she frowned, scouring her mind for the evidence that St. Bride surely had against her.

She believed the first damning clue to her thieving had come the morning after her initial meeting with Malcolm Quinn. She had gone out to the veranda, as she was wont to do when she first awoke. In her billowing, pristine night smock, she had turned from the railing to find St. Bride on the veranda, too, his mouth forming an elusive smile.

"You startled me," she had said, her eyes caught by his.

"I've been here all along."

"Have you now." Her words dwindled as she watched St. Bride's detached amusement turn to something else. Without warning, his face darkened. Not quite understanding the reason for this, she had looked down and noted that her open night smock exposed a healthy portion of her breast. But more horrifying was the bruises from Malcolm Quinn's assault, exposed along the top of one breast. She knew that there was a thumbprint, too, underneath her tender bosom. Looking up, she saw that St. Bride knew it too. It was obvious what the marks were from—there was simply no mistaking them.

"What happened?" he had asked, a fierce protectiveness suddenly in his voice. He had walked up to her then and reached for the exposed tender skin of her bosom. With a featherlight touch, his thumb ran along the bruises, rubbing her flesh most gently. With anger in his eyes for her assailant, he looked to her to name him.

"It was forced upon me. I didn't want to be touched." She stumbled upon her words, darting a glance at him.

His face softened, and her heart applauded with relief. He questioned her with great understanding.

"Was that all he did? Just touch you?"

She nodded helplessly.

"I'll kill him anyway."

The words were as cold and terrifying as any she had ever heard. But St. Bride continued as if he had never said them. "Who was he, Kayleigh? One of the slaves? Laban assures me they are all to be trusted." He seemed to chastise himself. "Tell me who he is. Women will not be abused in my home."

Hating herself for what she knew she had to say, she closed her eyes, then spoke, knowing full well what his reaction would be, "I cannot tell you his name, St. Bride."

"You must. I have a right to know, as the master of this plantation. I must know which of my men—"

"He is not one of your men." She couldn't bear to look at his face.

"Then who is he? Name him," he demanded.

"I cannot," she pleaded, her voice husky with emotion.

"You would protect this man, though he's hurt you and bruised you?" With barely leashed fury, he asked, "Is he your lover then?"

"He is not my lover! God forbid that ever to be so!"

"Then let me help you, damn it! You have no one else!"

She ached to tell St. Bride. She wanted so badly to give him Quinn's name and to have him make sure Quinn never came back to Belle Chasse to blackmail her. But as always her cousin stood in the way, threatening her at every turn. How could she reveal Quinn's name without jeopardizing everything? How could she think that she was more important to the man in front of her than his entire plantation of poppies? She couldn't. So with a heavy heart she kept her mouth closed. St. Bride would have to think what he would of her. She had no other choice.

St. Bride finally broke the silence. In exasperation he threatened, "If you don't tell me, Kayleigh, you shall not leave this house without my escort again. I shall keep an eye on you until I know you can walk safely through Belle Chasse. I swear you'll never know a moment alone."

Pain glinted in her eyes as she answered, "I hardly know a moment alone now. What will be changed?"

"As it is, you have a room to yourself. Shall I make you share mine?"

Her first reaction was to slap him, but he was ready for her. Capturing her arm, he forced it to her side. "Don't sap your strength fighting me on this, love. Tell me the name, or I'll find it out myself. Your decision."

"Ooh," she groaned. "Let me go!"

"Surely." He released her wrist, and she wasted no more time. Taking refuge in her room, she locked the shutters behind her. She did not dare even to breathe until his retreating footsteps told her he was through with his rampage.

Now as she stared at the empty mantel, Kayleigh thought of the evidence that was mounting against her. She had been meeting Malcolm Quinn's demands, having no other feasible choice for the moment. Quinn, in turn, had been keeping his paws to himself and appeared to have kept his promise not to tell Straught about her. However, despite her enormous efforts to save herself, she seemed to be drowning in strife as the days passed. In less than five days, she had been forced to steal three silver goblets, a bronze doré snuff box, five gold buttons, and a small Meissen figurine of Harlequin kissing Columbine.

She squeezed her eyes shut, cringing at the thought of the figurine. It was the most obvious thing she had taken to date, for it had sat on the lozenge-adorned wraparound mantel in her own room. It would be her ruination yet.

The evening after she stole the figurine, St. Bride had entered her room unannounced. Colette was helping her bathe in the hip bath, and both women had jumped at St. Bride's intrusion. The bare hollows and soft ivory curves of Kayleigh's back were to him as he stood in the doorway. But Colette's nervousness more than hinted at St. Bride's belligerent mood.

Kayleigh was quickly handed a linen towel to cover her front, but she still presented St. Bride with an ample view of her lush backside. Not daring to stand because of the towel's inadequacy, she had been forced to sit in the cooling water, shivering and trying very hard not to look guilty. Finally, she'd twisted her head around and seen St. Bride's stare fixed on the empty spot on her mantel. Her heart plummeted.

"Excuse us, Colette," he suddenly demanded without even glancing at the mulatto. Colette nervously complied, skittering to the door of the salon. In seconds they were completely alone. Though she dreaded his gaze, Kayleigh saw him slowly turn to her. Her eyes darkened with worry.

"Babet was in here earlier, returning your linen," he stated blithely. "She seemed to think something was missing and she wanted to assure me it was not Venus or Valentine who was the culprit."

"Is something missing?" she choked out, clutching the meager linen towel even more closely to her chest.

"No, nothing at all," St. Bride answered, his smile laced with doom, his eyes telling Kayleigh more than she wanted to know. A shiver coursed through her when he stooped to pick up the sponge in her bathwater. She started when he squeezed water onto her back. He then reached for the damp towel that was around her. When she refused to relinquish it, this only made him release a black little chuckle. His hands then slid to her neck and formed a noose. For a moment she wondered if he was actually going to choke her. But instead, his thumb began to caress the throbbing pulse in her throat, then his mouth found the sensitive spot. His kiss sent chills of excitement and fear down her spine. When he was through, the spot on her throat was chaffed and red.

"Return to your toilet, madame." Abruptly, he stood. He stroked her damp tresses once, then he left, shutting the door with a disheartening thud.

"Whatever was that about? Do you know, Kayleigh?" Colette asked a minute later when she was able to return. Immediately, the little servant found the pink spot on Kayleigh's neck. When Kayleigh's hand flew to hide it, Colette briskly went about her business, taking the sodden linen towel from Kayleigh's grasp and again rinsing her from a copper-lined pail.

"I wish I knew," Kayleigh finally answered, desiring fervently that her guilt could be washed away in the waterfall from Colette's bucket.

Reliving the scene now, Kayleigh groaned. Her mind was going to snap from all the deceptions and lies. The pressure building inside the walls of Belle Chasse was unbearable. She was certain that St. Bride knew what she was doing. But still the question plagued her: Why wasn't he doing anything to stop her? She would have to extricate herself from this mess—she would have to! But how?

Her nerves stretched taut, she rose from her chair and resigned herself to meeting Quinn. She was late as it was. Reluctantly, she made her way to the stable to retrieve her prize. Her only chance to get the figurine out of the house had been yesterday morning. Although the figurine was light, it was awkward to hide, so she had placed it in some dirty sheeting and made to carry it out to the laundress. Once there, she had unwrapped it and hid it beneath some new straw in the stable.

Quickly retrieving it, she stole across the back buildings until she was out of sight of the house. She paused to catch her breath. Her stomach rebelled at the thought of another meeting with Quinn. He hadn't touched her since the day she'd implied that she was St. Bride's mistress, yet still she feared him greatly. Quinn was much too greedy. Rape was in his nature, and she felt it was only a matter of time before he would break the indefensible boundary she had set.

Kayleigh bit her lip in anxiety. She truly was a creature with nine lives. Every time she met with Quinn and placated him with stolen treasure, she felt she had escaped her fate once more. But as even Chridhe knew, a cat runs out of lives. How many lives did she have left? she wondered. With a shiver, she knew she had already used up more than her share.

Looking down at the lovely figurine, she traced the green

and gold diamonds that made up Harlequin's waistcoat. St. Bride had other figurines at the house. There was even one called Louisiana, portraying an Indian woman riding on the back of an alligator. But the one in her hands was like one that had been at Mhor.

It had portrayed a Highland lass and laddie in an embrace. She remembered that she had liked it, for it was of Scotland and ever so romantic. But her mother had not shared her feeling. Her father had bought it in London as a gift; his own heritage had not allowed him to understand that it would offend her mother's. For the Meissen manufacturer had casually placed a bloody broadsword alongside the hip of the man, and his brilliant green and blue plaidie was slightly tinged with red. Her mother was aware that the English insisted on portraying Highlanders as bloodthirsty heathens.

Yet it was not so! Kayleigh now determined painfully, thinking of her Lowlander cousin and his love of the English. He and his kind were the bloodthirsty ones. She and her kind were the . . .

Innocent? She frowned looking down at the stolen figurine. Nay. Though her virginity was still intact, she had become far from innocent. There were times when she almost didn't blame St. Bride for his blatant distrust of her, for perhaps she was not to be trusted.

Bitter thoughts came to mind with this realization. When she'd been surviving on the streets, perverse glee would overcome her when she took money she especially needed from a wealthy gent. Her soul be damned! It had been the joy of rebellion, beating the odds against her survival. She had done what she had to to remain on this earth another day. But with each new trinket she lifted, had her soul not become more and more unsalvageable? Sometimes she could almost feel her good parents' shame.

And stealing was different now. Thinking of Venus and

Valentine's adoring eyes, Kayleigh cringed. They would all hate her forever if she were found out—and perhaps she would deserve it after all.

Letting out a great sigh, she looked to the thicket where Malcolm Quinn waited for her. Hiding the gold, pink, and green Meissen in the folds of her petticoat, she walked across the clearing to meet him.

St. Bride watched the couple in the thicket meet with nary a word. Kayleigh, as usual, proved unsettling because of both her plainness and her beauty. Of those things plain, the first was her dress—a simple blue osnaburg gown commonly worn, not only by slaves, but also by bondswomen newly arrived from Ireland or Scotland. She possessed no jewels at all, not even the meanest of rings upon her small, work-worn hands. But then, it was obvious, she had no need of them. Kayleigh's jewels were her eyes, sparkling and blue like pear-shaped sapphires aglow in the morning sun. Her hair dressed her better than the richest satin brocade. Although it was shamefully bound by mere wooden pins, any man could look at it and ache to loosen her tresses, to lie upon them as on a rug, and to make love to their bearer until she moaned beneath him.

St. Bride scowled and turned his full attention to her partner, whom he recognized as Malcolm Quinn. The fat man was a strange mixture of rich and poor: his worn fustian waistcoat sported all-too-familiar gold buttons, and his thick, dirty fingers were beringed in silver and gold.

As he rubbed his unshaven jaw, St. Bride gave a start as Quinn raised his voice. Pointing angrily to a chipped spot on Columbine's porcelain gown, he twisted Kayleigh's raven hair until she gasped from the pain.

But she was a quick one. When Quinn let her go, she sidestepped his damaging slap, then laughed at his clumsiness, mocking her tormentor with perfect, brilliant white teeth.

"You need me, Kayleigh! Don't be forgetting that!" the fat Malcolm Quinn called to her as she left, but Kayleigh refused to answer. Instead, she made her way back to Belle Chasse without another word.

Watching her go, St. Bride's turquoise eyes narrowed speculatively. Then he slipped into the brush unseen once more.

Chapter Fourteen

Her soul was going to burn in hell forever for her sins, Kayleigh thought dismally. Her sins knew no boundaries at all, it seemed. Her eyes went reluctantly to an amboyna casket on top of the commode. She was actually running out of things to steal, and now several days later, she was in St. Bride's room stripping the bed linen, as promised. Babet had taken ill, and Venus and Valentine were being kept with their *maman* to tend to her needs.

Again against her will, her eyes wandered to the veneered bombé casket.

The temptation was too great. Before she had taken all the wrinkled sheets off the top mattress, she had walked over to the commode and opened the lid of the casket. It was not the first time she had peeked into its velvet-lined depths. Nay, she had done that twenty times if she had done it once. But never had she mustered the courage to take possession of its contents. Nestled like a mystical blue apple among boughs of white-linen handkerchiefs, St. Bride's own sapphire reflected its forbidden gleam in her eyes.

How she positively ached to take it! With it she knew she would have some power over Quinn. After all, the jewel was no small trinket. In truth, it was probably the most valuable

thing at the plantation. For the sapphire, Kayleigh knew Quinn
would bow to her demands. It would surely take her anywhere
she wanted to go. She could get away from Belle Chasse and
all its disturbing emotions.

She smiled at the thought, picking up the wicked jewel to
study it. She held it up to the looking glass, and behind her
the sheen of the emerald-satin bedcurtains gleamed a perfect
backdrop. She spun to face St. Bride's bed as it glimmered
with tropical delights. The curtains hung green and lush and
overwhelming like a thick jungle. Like some exotic rain forest,
its rumpled ruby and gold counterpane became like robust
blooms, and its silken gauze draped over the posts like an
early morning mist.

Though her imagination dressed the bed better than did
the satin drapes, still she was drawn to it. Taking the jewel
with her, she gingerly sat on the bed made only more decadent
by its plain surroundings of whitewashed walls and a muted
verdigris chair rail. Also, as Kayleigh soon found out, the
bedstead had more than the usual two mattresses. There was
not only one of corncobs and one of moss, but on its top
layer was a thick, fluffy cloud of the finest goose down,
specially brought from France.

The feel of down, like the jewel that she held tightly to
her bosom, was something Kayleigh could understand and
appreciate. Knowing that St. Bride was off somewhere with
Laban seeing to his precious poppies, she allowed herself to
fall back on the bed. She let the spring and softness of the
mattress remind her of earlier days and earlier luxuries.

It was almost as fine as her featherbed at Mhor, she thought
judiciously. Her satin drapes had been of brocaded pink, and
there had been no large, mysterious hook embedded in the
beams above. But still the similarities persisted.

And yet, there was the scent.

Kayleigh inhaled deeply. The fragrance was not of late-
night fables and laughter between sisters. This seemed to be

of something else, something intangible and difficult to picture. A bed emerged from the dark recesses of her imagination much like the one she was lying on. But on her imagined bed, she did not lie alone.

She was bare, though warm and ever so sleepy. Yet her companion would not let her sleep. A kiss made her senses come alive, and as the man beside her brushed back her heavy locks, she made out his face, intense and impassioned. His hair held the slightest hint of silver that tried to mock his youthfulness and boyish ways but it only succeeded in making him appear handsome and irresistibly masculine. So when he bent to kiss her, she didn't resist. On the contrary, she welcomed him, taking his large, muscular body into her arms.

He paused then so that she could see in his eyes something she had never seen before. It was there among all the other emotions he had spent upon her, and it glowed clear and pure like the reflections of a Caribbean sea.

"I love you," he said. And she laughed for the delight it brought her. "I love you," he repeated again and again and she only laughed more, for the sound of his words was joyful and natural. It was like the sound of turquoise waves that lapped over pink beaches, and she wanted them to go on forever.

But they would not go on forever.

Sitting upright, Kayleigh searched the room wild-eyed. Her sudden vulnerability, she was sure, could be seen by anyone there. Only when she was satisfied that she was still alone did her unwilling thoughts return to her daydream and what it revealed.

She fretted. Why had her mind betrayed her this way? Why had she imagined such a thing about St. Bride? Even when her body had proven itself weak and easily manipulated, her thoughts had always been her own!

Jumping off the mattress, she tried to rationalize her daydream as a result of the corrupting influence of the bed. Perhaps it was too soft, she thought, grasping at straws.

Vehemently returning to the task at hand, Kayleigh went to the pile of clean linens. A noise from the loggia made her jump, but it was just St. Bride returning and she thought nothing of it.

She carried the linens to the bed. But suddenly stricken, she discovered the sparkling sapphire still loose on top of the counterpane. Footsteps in the salon let her know it was too late to return it to the casket, so without giving thought to the consequences she grabbed the jewel, shoved it down the middle of her snug bodice, and once more took to changing the bed linen—but this time as if she were pursued by the hounds of hell.

"What a jewel you're proving to be, Kayleigh." St. Bride hung in his doorway watching her work.

Flinching at the word *jewel,* Kayleigh went back and forth several times, saying to herself "He knows" and "He doesn't" before she concluded that it had been simply an unfortunate choice of words. Ripping off the last of the used linen from his top mattress, she nervously changed the bedding, thinking it an unfortunate choice of tasks.

"I'm terribly busy with Babet ill and her girls unavailable. Is there something you need?" She looked up and could have bit her tongue at the jade amusement in his eyes. He did not take the hint, however. Instead, he walked farther into the room as if to afford himself a better view of her bending and stretching across his bed. He leaned back on his commode, and his elbow knocked the amboyna casket. In horror, she knew it would be only a matter of minutes before he would check its valuable contents.

But St. Bride never moved. His piercing gaze seemed to find an ungodly amount of diversion as she stooped to tuck a corner.

"I want you to know I'm going to town with Laban," he said easily.

"Are you now?" she commented, smoothing the heavy silk counterpane with her palm. Och, she didn't care where he went with Laban. If only he would be on his way and remove himself from the vicinity of that cursed amboyna casket.

"Will you miss me?"

She furrowed her brow and refused to look at him. How he unnerved her! As if his predation weren't bad enough, she still had that constant, terrible feeling that he knew much more than she thought he did. Sometimes she swore he knew everything—from the fact that she was stealing from him to her relationship with Quinn and Straught.

"Would you like to kiss me good-bye?" St. Bride baited her, ignoring her delicate scowl. "If you do, I've a trinket to give you."

"I have work to do, St. Bride."

"No, you must have it. I insist!"

"No, really, you must allow me to work. I've . . ." Her words faded away as he turned toward the amboyna casket.

"I believe it's in here," he mused. With one eye, he watched her horrified reflection in the glass over the commode.

"I've come!" She flew to his side. Hastily, she diverted him by rattling off reasons why she was undeserving of his kindnesses. "I don't need any more gifts. Truly, look how I've abused your generosity so far, tossing off your beautiful ribbons and the like. Anything further would be wasted, and I—" She stopped abruptly as his finger traced the delicate skin exposed above her fichu. Panicked, all she could think of was the old saying that if the sapphire had been a snake it would have bit him. Her breathing came more quickly, and her chest almost heaved beneath his feathery touch.

"But my present's right here, love. And it's no trouble to retrieve it." St. Bride indicated that it was in the amboyna casket. She wondered vaguely if his gift was the sapphire, but she was soon too startled to think further. Her eyes grew wide and she felt his fingers dip below her bodice and emerge triumphant, his sapphire within their grasp.

"How did you know!" she cried.

"I'm not as dull-witted as you would have me be."

"You're not dull-witted whatever. But you be the spawn of the devil if you saw me taking the thing!" She was back to her heavy Gaelic, too numb to care about her speech.

"Perhaps I am—but then, I also know how itchy your fingers have been of late. I knew you'd take the stone given half a chance. And wasn't I pleasantly surprised when you bent over the linen, and I saw my sapphire twinkling between your—"

"Send me to jail then! There at least I won't have to battle you and your bedamned wits!"

"How can I send you to jail for taking something that I want you to have?" He put the huge sapphire to her throat and marveled at its beauty. "I think I should give this to you, Kayleigh. In fact, how can I not when you seem born to wear it?"

"I don't understand. You would give that . . ." She stumbled over her words, wondering if she had heard him correctly. "But I would sell it. You know I wouldn't keep it," she rationalized.

"Yes, that is a perplexing problem. How to give you my little bauble without also giving that cold little heart of yours something to fob off." With an infuriating, mocking little smile, he pocketed the stone. "I'm going to town, love. Until I solve that problem, I suppose I'll have to keep an eye on my little stone. I wouldn't want it to—shall we say, mysteriously disappear?"

"Fine. Keep it with you. I was going to put it back, St. Bride. I know you won't believe this, but I was going to put it back in your casket as soon as you were gone." Frustrated and angry, she shook her head. Och, just once she wanted him to believe her. Just once, she wanted the benefit of doubt given a lady.

"What is it?" he asked, noting her inner turmoil.

"I want you to believe me, St. Bride. Just once, I want you to believe that my actions were pure."

"There will be one time, dark love. I promise." He then nodded and left, his face solemn, his eyes irreverent.

Chapter Fifteen

"Have you got it?" St. Bride looked up from the three-legged tavern table. Laban nodded his head and sat down.

The ale was despicably warm in the hot afternoon, but still men gathered at Le Jeune Cornichon to quench their thirst and discuss their business. Later in the day, the crowd could get rather bawdy, as bawdy as the sign over the door, which portrayed in silhouette a young lad too eagerly chasing a buxom maid. But now the customers were slow and hot, moving only to wipe their sweaty brows with their linen-clad forearms or to leave altogether through a row of double doors that opened to the street.

"I spoke to Thionville's stable master." Laban stretched out his bulky jackbooted legs and accepted the pewter mug St. Bride pushed before him. "The stable master—O'Hurley's his name—is a great talker. Seems to know most of the comte's business."

"Which is?" St. Bride agitatedly rubbed his chest, lightly covered in a brilliant white shirt. His dark chest hair was noticeable below the ties he'd loosened. But it was his eyes, lit with vengeance, that commanded attention.

"Apparently he is what he says, an importer of sorts. Thionville receives merchandise, of late from Glasgow."

"Glasgow! Well, you needn't continue. I know his trade now, and it smells of Erath Straught's nasty little flowers."

"Louis XV has been very fond of the comte," Laban continued. "My guess is that Thionville was rewarded well by his king. With the King behind him, he has control over almost all Louisiana and with it its people." Laban looked at St. Bride, who was stretched back in his crude cypress tavern chair. St. Bride seemed every bit the gentleman at ease, except when one looked closely. Then one could see the muscles of his thighs tighten and bunch beneath the rugged buckskin breeches and that his eyes sparked with too much brilliance.

"So what of Straught? Did this O'Hurley fellow know why he wanted to come here?" St. Bride asked, choosing his words with care.

"Straught claims it's business. What kind of business has been wholly obscure," Laban answered mournfully. But then he added, "However, there does seem to be an indication that this mysterious business of his does not concern Thionville. Duncan disclosed that the comte is not in on all of Straught's personal matters and that the true reason for Straught's visit to New Orleans remains a closely guarded secret."

"Why do you say that?" St. Bride stiffened.

"The stable master told me a story about the night of the comte's party. It seems that Straught was staying at Thionville's house. Malcolm Quinn came running back from town. Then, though in his evening clothes, Straught and Quinn walked hurriedly off toward the Place d'Armes. O'Hurley overhead Malcolm exclaiming, 'I found them! They're down by the river!'"

"'I found them'?" St. Bride repeated the words.

"Yes. Strange, isn't it? Especially since Straught's only previous connection with this place was through Thionville— and even that was through correspondence only."

"There's something odd going on. Let's just hope Erath

Straught proves the fool in this other matter too." St. Bride almost smiled.

"Should I investigate down by the quay? There are lots of things by the river—mostly thieves, I might add—but we could have some luck."

"No, don't bother. Whatever Straught's business was down there, it doesn't help us now. Besides, we've other things on our minds."

"And what are they, my friend? Perchance could one of them be a woman?" Laban smiled wryly.

"Perhaps." St. Bride grinned wolfishly and slammed a coin down on the table. "Either way, it's time for *la belle chasse,* my man. So come along, let's stalk our prey!" Both men laughed and left the cabaret in easy camaraderie.

St. Bride was in high spirits as they walked to the militia stables to retrieve their mounts. Once there, they acquired Canis and a new bay Thoroughbred of well over seventeen hands for Laban. They mounted and traveled leisurely through the center of town, heading for home.

Spying a bundle of stiff red satin sticking out of St. Bride's saddle pouch, Laban questioned him with ribald good humor.

"Have you something there, St. Bride?" He pointed to the rigid fabric.

"It's nothing." St. Bride looked ahead of him on Rue de Conde. They had almost reached the Place d'Armes.

"Nothing, you say? I'm sure that on that wicked black-haired vixen it will be better than nothing!" He laid back his head and laughed, inducing St. Bride into a scowl and a trot. "I say, they look like stays! St. Bride? St. Bride!" Laban only laughed harder at St. Bride's definite lack of interest in pursuing the conversation.

When they reached the Place d'Armes, they ambled by the parish church of St. Louis, hardly noticing the banns and announcements that were nailed to its crudely fashioned door. But squinting his eyes, St. Bride suddenly stopped his prancing horse and dropped the reins.

"What is it?" Laban watched him dismount.

"I don't know," St. Bride mumbled as he dismounted, then walked toward the church with Canis in hand. Glancing over the notices, he found the one that had caught his eye. Reading it, his face, normally bronzed by hours spent in the sun, went noticeably paler. His lips formed into a thin, even line as he read:

MURDERED
Black Bardolph Ogilvie
Originally from Perth, Scotland
By disembowelment

Attacker unknown
The Comte de Cassell
Seeks The Kestrel
A gypsy girl
With black hair and blue eyes
Militia have been notified
YE ALL BEWARE

Even Laban's black visage seemed to whiten as both men read the post. They were quiet for the longest time. St. Bride read and reread the notice as if he were trying to will it away by staring a hole through the parchment to the battened boards.

"You think it's her, St. Bride?"

Slowly St. Bride nodded his head. He spoke as if it pained him. "When she was looking for her clothes that first day, she uttered that name—Kestrel."

"Send her away now, St. Bride."

"Be quiet!" St. Bride snapped at Laban as he tore the announcement from the door.

"St. Bride!"

"I said quiet, man!" Stiffly, sign in hand, St. Bride remounted his steed.

"She will come to no good! Already she has—"

"Silence, I tell you! You cannot give me advice in this matter." St. Bride urged his mount into a trot until they left the outskirts of town.

"I *will* give you advice. You'll keep her around until you've satisfied yourself with her, and by that time it could be too late. Jump her now, I tell you! And then get rid of her!" Laban shouted after him as St. Bride broke into a canter. Cursing, Laban urged his own horse into a canter and followed St. Bride, catching up to him when they were still many miles from Belle Chasse.

"This is dangerous, my friend. She might be worse for your health than Straught could ever be. What do we know about her anyway?" Laban made his angry plea.

"I know enough to give her the benefit of doubt," St. Bride answered, legging his steed on.

"Doubt? *Doubt?* Where is the doubt? The comte has no doubt, or he wouldn't have placed the notice. He is too tightfisted to spend his money on supposition."

"The Comte de Cassell is a fool." St. Bride stared ahead to the watery distance of the road.

"That he is, and a powerful fool at that. If he's looking for her, she must have been the one—"

"We don't know that!" St. Bride snapped in exasperation.

"Why else would they be looking for her?"

"I don't know!"

"You do know." Laban pursued his subject. "Remember the girl's petticoat when we found her? Babet couldn't salvage it for all the blood that had spilled upon it. It couldn't have been your blood alone, my friend. The wound to your hand wasn't bad enough for all that. There was someone else's blood on her petticoat too."

"It's still possible that it was all mine." St. Bride looked at the scar on his hand.

"Then let's ask her, shall we?" Laban moved toward St. Bride. "Let's get the little thief out of her lair and put the question to her: Whose blood was it?"

"Leave her alone. If anyone asks her, it will be me," St. Bride said in a low, commanding voice.

"Methinks you don't want to know, my friend." Laban's words rumbled with melancholy.

St. Bride shrugged his shoulders with apparent indifference, then abruptly left Laban behind, kicking Canis into a full gallop. St. Bride rode like a general on the eve of a battle—one who knew all the maneuvers but who had yet to identify the enemy.

St. Bride seemed furious when he and Laban returned from town. As Kayleigh watched from the gallery, they flung their Thoroughbreds' reins to scarlet-adorned Mathias and stomped up the stairs, not speaking, not smiling. What could have caused such friends to argue? she wondered. Anxiously she watched them enter the house, and then by instinct decided to spend the rest of the evening in her room.

Hearing their harsh words in the salon but not wanting to interrupt them, she stepped softly toward her chamber.

". . . ruin our best-laid plans. One morning she'll slit your throat. . . . Listen to me! . . . she's not worth the risking. . . ." Kayleigh overheard Laban's angry pleading as she slid quietly along the back of the salon near the loggia.

"And I say leave Mary out of this!"

This time she knew it was St. Bride speaking. Her heart leaped to her throat when she heard his next angry words: "I'll have my deal with Straught, and Kayleigh won't interfere."

Suddenly, sensing her presence, both men looked up. But Kayleigh was unable to move—the familiar, awful name sucked away all her strength.

St. Bride grew deadly quiet as Kayleigh stood before him. He refused to meet her eyes at all. But not Laban. He stared at her, and his black, piercing gaze seemed to wrap around her throat until her small hand went up to that very spot in a gesture of self-protection. What was going on? She frowned, unable to move, trapped by their disapproval. They had been fighting about her. And worse, they were fighting about Erath Straught too. Did they know about her after all? Did they know? Her mind spun from the horrid question. But she saw that she would get no answers from St. Bride; he wouldn't even look at her. Instead, he went over to a gilt marble-topped table and poured himself a healthy dose of brandy.

In the ensuing pause, Kayleigh sought refuge in her bed-chamber. The men continued their argument, now whispering harshly to each other as she sat huddled in the walnut fauteuil, wondering what the outcome would be and what it would mean for her dismal future.

Och, how she wanted to run away now! As she paced in her room and listened to the unbearable silence, she turned into a wretched bundle of nerves. The secrecy frightened her. And that name on St. Bride's lips—what did he mean she wouldn't interfere? Would he make sure she didn't interfere? Again the sentence "It will keep Kayleigh in her place" found its way to the surface of her mind. She swallowed and tried desperately to think, but answers wouldn't come.

She wanted to go to the kitchens and sit with Colette as on previous evenings. She wanted to pretend things were what they appeared. In the kitchen they could talk about Colette's new dresses or perhaps about the mischief Venus and Valentine had gotten into that day. Then she would not have to face this terrible problem. How could these ghosts have found her clear across the Atlantic? she fretted.

Opening the doors to the gallery, Kayleigh looked across the rear courtyard and saw Laban enter the kitchens. It was dusk, and in the building's firelight she could see the expectancy on Colette's face as Laban pulled the kitchen door behind them. When she could see only soft darkness once more, Kayleigh bit her full lower lip. It was clear she would not find solace anywhere this evening. What to do? What to do? The question echoed through her mind and grew louder on the rebound.

Pacing in her chamber, she made up her mind to face St.

Bride. It was time she found out what he knew about her. And should he choose to come after her, there would be no hiding from her nemesis in her room. She couldn't even lock him out, for St. Bride was not the kind of man who would let a mere bolt keep him from getting what he wanted. She took a deep breath and opened her door to the salon.

"Come in, Kayleigh," St. Bride growled in the dark, having obviously heard the floorboards creak under her weight.

"St. Bride," she whispered. He stood in the doorway to the gallery, staring distantly off toward the river. Seeing his ominous form, she thought it might be time for a hasty retreat back into her bedchamber. She stood in the middle of the dark salon caught up in a net of fear and indecision, once again unable to move at all.

"Come here," he demanded. His voice sounded surprisingly gentle.

"I—I don't think . . ." she began, but he interrupted her.

"Come here. I have something for you."

Quietly she stepped over to the row of double doors. "I'm here," she uttered, her heart pounding wildly.

"I was in town today," St. Bride stated, clutching something silken in his hands. Tersely, he continued, "Colette told me you wanted a pair of stays, so I . . ." His voice trailed off. She could see telltale lines of stitching on the garment he held, but she couldn't make out its color in the moonlight. She was surprised that he'd thought of such a personal gift for her, but that was just like him, charming one minute, terrifying the next.

"Put them on." He handed them to her rather awkwardly.

"Now?" Her eyes flew open.

"Yes."

"I'm hungry. Why don't we have something to eat first?"

"I want you to put these on." He thrust them into her hands. "Now."

"St. Bride—"

"Put them on now, woman," he said quietly. Then he

turned back to the river, his hawklike masculine profile outlined in the dusky light. He was a man being pursued by some
unknown devil. Now was not the time to test his chivalry.

Once in the safe candlelight of her chamber, Kayleigh
nervously shed her dress. She looked down at the stays in
her shaking hands and saw they were a brilliant scarlet. Hesitantly she pulled the garment to her chest and laced it up.
Had the circumstances been different, she would have reveled
in the nearly forgotten feel of whalebone and silk. The stays
were finely made, and their color was the perfect contrast to
her sweeping raven curls. But these circumstances were dire.
She didn't know what was going on, yet she knew she would
soon find out, for she could hear St. Bride pacing in the other
room, impatient for her return. Slowly, she rehooked her blue
linen dress and opened her doors to the salon.

While she'd been in her room lacing the intricate garment,
St. Bride had lit all the candles in the salon. It was shocking
to have to face him with so much light upon her when before
the room had been so comfortably dim. Trembling, she walked
to the settee where St. Bride sat, noting that every copper
sconce and every silver candelabrum in the entire room had
been set ablaze. When she stepped in front of him, she saw
that he was once again rolling a sassafras root between his
lips. He eyed her with a heavy-lidded gaze that made the
blood shoot to her head.

"Spin around," he said.

She complied and felt a small shiver go down her spine
at the look on his face. He didn't miss one inch of her
appearance, from her narrow, tightly bound waist to the way
the garment controlled her full bosom.

"May I fix you some dinner?" she asked uneasily, trying
to lessen the tension. Perhaps if she played the good servant,
he would tell her what was going on. She smiled although
she wanted to quake. "I do appreciate the gift, St. Bride. It's
been so long since I—well, I do know it's rather an intimate

thing to give a woman, but . . .'' She tangled herself up in her words in an effort to thank him, but he only scowled.

"Go over to the mirror, Kayleigh."

"What?" She paled. The controlled anger in his voice frightened her all over again.

"I said, go over to the mirror." He pointed to the small gilt glass that hung in the pier.

"Why?" She looked at him, her sapphire eyes large and distrustful.

"Do it."

Reluctantly, she made her way to the glass. Her mind turned somersaults trying to figure out what he was going to do. Standing in front of the pier, she turned to him for further directions.

"Don't look at me. Look into the mirror," he commanded.

She complied, staring into the glass at her reflection.

"All right," St. Bride said slowly, taking the root out of his mouth as if in anticipation. "Unhook your dress."

"What?"

"I said, unhook your dress."

"I won't." Kayleigh's voice shook. She looked at his reflection in the glass. He was stretched out on the settee.

"You will. You've always done what you had to do to survive, haven't you?" His tone chilled her.

"No. I won't do this."

"Do it—or I'll do it for you." St. Bride started up from his seat, and her hands flew to the first hook of her bodice. Noting her compliance, he sat back in the settee, but still her hands shook so, it was hard to move fast enough to appease him.

"What have I done?" she asked, hoping for more time. "What happened today in town?"

"Keep unhooking. I want to see my gift."

Her numb fingers undid two more hooks, revealing the high, creamy beginnings of her breasts.

"I must know. Did . . . ?" She began to voice the awful

possibility that perhaps her cousin had something to do with this, but he didn't hear her.

All he said was, "Keep going. Keep quiet."

Turning back to her hooks, she looked down and did what he asked as her mind filled with all sorts of unspoken agonies. With each hook, first the edging of her pristine chemise began to peek through the soft blue of the dress, and then the scarlet of her stays. Each movement of her fingers released more and more of her bodice, and Kayleigh began to feel sick. It wasn't because of the act she was performing, nor was it from the tension in the air that seemed as if it would smother her. Rather, it was because of the colors she saw before her.

The soft blue of her dress was slowly being overwhelmed by the brilliant red of her stays. She'd seen these two colors before like this—not only in her nightmares, but on that day long ago in Scotland. With vivid clarity, she again saw Morna's accident in her mind. She saw herself running down from the knoll to reach Morna. To help Morna. To protect Morna. But instead, Erath Straught was standing over her sister's body. His hands were red, and her sister's sweet harebell dress was . . .

Kayleigh closed her eyes, a small moan escaping her lips. Her dress was completely undone now, and she knew St. Bride was staring at her. Opening her eyes, she fixed them on him. He seemed truly as horrified as she was.

"Your stays—they're the color of blood, aren't they, Kayleigh?" He stood and walked near to her, his turquoise eyes shadowed and unreadable.

"No." She turned her gaze away from him and forced herself to look in the mirror, to deal with the colors before her. She couldn't understand why he was upset by the scarlet of her stays. Could he be remembering too? Did he know about the day Morna had been killed? Had she been a worse fool than she thought?

"No!" she contradicted him again. "The stays are beautiful. They're the color of tulips."

"The color of blood," he whispered to the back of her head. In the mirror, she watched as his hand moved inside the opening of her dress to rest on the scarlet ridges of her stays.

"They're the color of robins," she denied, feeling the warmth and strength of his hand through the silk. He held her to him. He turned her to face him, and he portrayed a terrifying picture as his eyes flashed green and his handsome lips curved downward.

"Whatever you did, Kayleigh, just tell me you were forced to do it, and I'll believe you."

"What has happened? What has changed?" she cried out in fear and confusion.

"Tell *me* what happened. Tell me you did it in self-defense, and I will believe you, my little witch."

"Please . . ." she whispered within his hard embrace.

"Don't lie to me this time, Kayleigh. Don't do it." His voice almost seemed to crack with frustration.

"Lie? I won't lie. But I haven't done anything. Tell me what has happened!"

Suddenly she felt his mouth close over hers as if he thought he could pull the truth from it. His tongue plundered ferociously, leaving no part unexplored. She moaned beneath him when his hands took possession of her waist, ripping the fabric of her dress down the middle as he forcefully pulled on her bound sides. She knew she should fight him, refuse him, run from him. But his was not the kiss of a murderer; his was the kiss of a lover, fiery and questioning, all-consuming and selfish, demanding more from her than was within her grasp to give. So all she could do was meld to his body and accept his touch and his kiss until he pulled away and they could talk once more.

When he was finished kissing her, Kayleigh looked up at him, her cheeks flushed and her black hair mussed from her halfhearted struggle.

"Tell me what has happened," she gasped, wanting to

reassure herself that he was no great friend of the murderer of her sister, that he wasn't involved with Straught at all, except for his wicked poppies. The coincidence of the blue and the red seemed too strong to doubt, but doubt it she did. For some strange reason—which was very much tied to his kiss—she knew she must.

But St. Bride did not dispel her worries. Looking down to where her raven head lay nestled on his chest, he finally asked for answers, answers to the questions that obviously weighed so heavily upon his mind.

"Tell me about Bardolph, Kayleigh," he said as his hands held her head, forcing her to look at him. Softly a moan escaped her lips, and she felt her legs weaken beneath her.

He knows then, she thought, her eyes drawn to his fiery gaze. He knows.

Chapter Sixteen

The silence that followed St. Bride's question was leaden enough to snuff out the candles and calm the winds that blew off the river. But the candles remained lit, and the simpering breezes still wafted through the salon. Kayleigh trembled, her body groping for freedom, her mind groping for an answer.

"Bardolph, Kayleigh," St. Bride prompted her, refusing her hesitation.

"Bardolph." She swallowed and found that the rest of the words wouldn't come to her lips. "W-what do you want to know about Bardolph? I told you, he's dead," she said suddenly, not at all wanting to answer.

St. Bride looked ready to choke her. "I want to know everything! There's a sign posted in New Orleans that claims the Comte de Cassell is looking for a murderess named Kestrel! And I know only two things: you're Kayleigh, and you're also this Kestrel. Kayleigh can pour out tea, read, and speak like a lady, and Kayleigh is everything I want. But today I discovered that there is Kestrel—Kestrel, who lies, steals, and now perhaps . . . murders . . . in a most horrendous fashion."

"Nay, not murders!" she begged, realizing that her cousin had posted the sign. She would never be able to go back to New Orleans now. All kinds of people would be wanting whatever reward was being offered for her return. Though she felt some relief at knowing why St. Bride was so angry, she knew too that there was another threat. Was St. Bride so angry that he would take her to the comte?

"Did you kill Bardolph?" St. Bride shook her, his voice was harsh and rasping.

"I didn't—" Her words began to flow once more.

"Tell me about the blood then. The blood on your petticoat. There was so much of it that night we found you in the swamps." His hold on her grew almost painful.

"It was your blood."

"There was too much of it to be mine," he retorted sharply. "Did you murder him?"

"No!" she cried out, and pushed him away. But he caught her face in his hands. He pulled her head up and forced her to stare into his eyes. They stood for a long moment as St. Bride searched her gaze for truth.

"If you didn't, who did then?" he asked slowly.

"Perhaps Malcolm Quinn did," she whispered, wondering what his reaction would be to the name.

Suddenly a grimace appeared on his face. Again her shoulders were shaken so hard, she felt her head would spin for days afterward. "Give me one reason why he would want Bardolph Ogilvie dead! Give me one reason for that, because I can give you twenty why you would want him dead!"

"I didn't want him dead! I didn't! Someone else killed him! *Not me!*" she protested hysterically.

"Are you spying on me?" he clipped, abruptly changing tack.

"Why would I do that?" She flashed her blue eyes, not able to figure him out.

"Did Quinn tell you to sneak around here, to listen in on my conversations? I know you two are great friends."

The awful realization that St. Bride knew about Quinn hit her full force. Painfully, all she could do was deny all his accusations. "You're mistaken. I wouldn't spy on you. For—for what reason?"

"For Erath Straught, that's why. He's invested his last tuppence in Belle Chasse. Does he not trust me? Has Quinn told you anything?"

"I don't know what you're talking about!" She backed away from his angry stance. "But I had nothing to do with Bardolph's death. I don't know why they posted that sign!"

"But you knew about the sign."

Dreading his reaction, she nodded her head.

"That's what you were running away from in the swamps the night I found you, wasn't it? And that's why you called yourself Colette in front of Thionville." St. Bride's eyes narrowed accusingly.

"No, you're wrong—terribly wrong," she whispered.

"No, I'm right, Kayleigh. And you know it. Your meetings with Quinn and your sneaking around Belle Chasse prove that."

"I've no interest in Belle Chasse."

"Then with your stealing all of Belle Chasse's valuables," he continued, verbally stalking her, "didn't you wonder why I never stopped you?"

"Malcolm Quinn would've—" She tried to finish before he started up again but could not.

"Yes, let's talk about Malcolm Quinn, shall we? You've been robbing me blind to give him trinkets. You didn't think I knew about your meetings, did you?" St. Bride paused, and after an excruciating silence he continued, "Perhaps I've wronged Laban. I thought you were a pathetic bit of lost womanhood, an innocent wrongfully abused. But now I wonder if you're anything but a conspiring little whore."

A loud crack was heard before she realized that her hand had smacked him across the face. It was a split-second reaction, but even St. Bride appeared to have expected it. He had to know that that word offended her. After all they'd been through, he had to know, she told herself. But now, seeing the angry red mark that blemished his cheek, she wondered how she would avoid the rage that surely would follow. Horrified, she noted that he hadn't even flinched from her strike. She shrank back from his fearsome visage, clutching her torn dress and making ready to flee.

But she was not swift enough. He grabbed her up and forced her to face him.

"Malcolm Quinn was blackmailing me! That's why I was forced to meet him!" she cried out. "Please, please believe me—I had to steal those things!"

"And why was he blackmailing you?" St. Bride became furious. "I'll tell you why! Perhaps it wasn't Quinn who killed Bardolph after all. Perhaps you were paying him to keep his mouth shut! He'd come here and seen you and guessed you were the Kestrel!"

"Yes! It's true! He saw me, and I was paying him to be quiet! But not because I killed Bardolph! Please believe me!" She was getting desperate. She could see the vivid green of St. Bride's irises. He was on the brink of murderous rage.

"Believe you? Why, when you've proven to have every imaginable flaw? You steal, you lie, you tease. Tell me, Kayleigh, now that I've cornered you, did you calculate all those interrupted love scenes just to torment me?" Heartlessly he looked to his bedchamber. The emerald-satin curtains gleamed in the candlelight, and Kayleigh knew exactly how he wanted to extract his vengeance.

"I'm innocent. Please—"

"Innocent." He almost laughed. "What an ugly word on your lips. Let's not hear it again." Suddenly, he had her by the hand and was leading her to his room.

"Listen!" Her voice cracked in terror.

"I'm through listening. I've wanted this since the day I met you. Now, after what happened today, I'd say you owe it to me." He pushed her in front of him and into his room.

Backing from the bed, she fled to the corner. She'd seen St. Bride angry before, but never like this. He seemed mad, crazed, and worse, he now thought her a murderess. For that he would be merciless. He would rape her and he would be merciless. She cringed as his shadow moved toward her. Staunchly, she told herself that she had lived through worse and that she would live through this. But still her hands covered her face in cowardice. Coming from St. Bride, the hurt would be unbearable. She would feel it down to the bottom of her soul.

"Kayleigh, prove to me you didn't murder him." She heard St. Bride's voice through the haze of her fear. "Convince me you didn't kill Bardolph. I don't want it like this." He seemed to want to give her every opportunity. After a great pause, he said, "Look at me."

She had to face him. All he wanted was the truth. *The truth.* But how could she give him that? How could she tell him that his friend Erath was involved in killing Bardolph without telling him the entire story? And even if she told him the entire story to convince him of her innocence, would he help her? Or would he hurt her? Suddenly all her doubts about St. Bride came to mind. The note he'd written to Laban and his business dealings with Straught concerning Belle Chasse. She knew without a doubt that whatever she told him would surely threaten his relationship with Straught. Did St. Bride care enough about her to see all his best-laid plans ruined? Kayleigh stared at him, and for the life of her she couldn't come to a decision.

"Tell me now, love. Tell me why you killed Bardolph," he prompted her.

The effort it took not to cry out her cousin's name was enormous. But somehow she squelched the cry. She couldn't be sure she could trust St. Bride, and until she was sure, she knew she had to remain silent.

"Tell me."

"I don't know—"

"I said tell me!" St. Bride squeezed her arms.

"Please . . . you're . . . hurting me. . . ."

"God damn you, tell me!" he shouted, and shook her, his frustration coming to a peak. "You tell me, you black-souled little heathen, or you won't have to go to the hangman—I'll kill you myself!"

Releasing a cry, she was almost pulled off her feet. Her incoherent protests only intensified the dark fury that had gripped St. Bride. She felt no surprise at all when he grabbed her violently and shook her.

Then he roughly flung her aside and turned from her. He took his hand and ran it viciously through the black hair of his crown.

"Get out of my sight," he growled.

"Leave Belle Chasse?"

"No. Go to your room. I don't want to see you anymore. Until I do, you'll remain there."

"St. Bride, I can't—"

"Damn you!" He refused to hear her. Instead, he became ferocious. "Get out of my goddamned sight before I do something I might regret!"

Seeing the grim, tight look on his face, Kayleigh suddenly didn't want him to think her a murderess. But try as she might, she could come up with no plausible answer to who killed Bardolph without telling him the entire truth. Yet St. Bride was in no mood for her deliberations. When she made no move to comply, his arm reached out and violently swept all the articles off his commode. His silver comb clattered to the floor, and the amboyna box cracked open on its hinge, flinging its contents to the far reaches of the room.

He turned on her. "I think perhaps tonight I've become mad!"

With these words, Kayleigh finally did as he asked. She fled the room in horror.

Chapter Seventeen

The storm clacked at the shutters and whipped at the pecan trees outside her room. The noise should have awakened Kayleigh from a sound sleep, but she was already awake—for the third night. She was waiting for St. Bride to make up his mind as to what he was going to do with her now that he thought her a murderess. Her room had become at once a prison and a refuge. Yet she ached to leave it, even if only to wander out to the gallery and feel the sting of the storm's wind on her cheeks.

Lightning jagged across the sky and its flash shot through the crack under the gallery doors. She walked to the doors and swung them open, only to find the shutters locked from the outside. Another bolt of lightning lit up the shutters, and the loud din of thunder followed immediately, but she was undaunted. She opened the slats and let in as much of the fury of the storm as she could.

"Most women cower beneath the covers during a storm like this. But not you. Never you."

The voice startled her more than the resounding thunder that had preceded it. Spinning around in the darkness, Kayleigh made out St. Bride's figure lounging in the salon doorway. In another flash of lightning, she glimpsed an unnatural gleam in his eyes and noted that his stance was a bit less stiff and unyielding than normal. In darkness once more she heard a beaker being set down on her night table, a beaker she suspected was filled with brandy. Then she heard his footsteps come near.

"St. Bride, it's late," she murmured, and tried to ignore him by facing the storm-wracked shutters.

"Yes, it's very late indeed. I've come to the same conclusion."

"What do you want, St. Bride?" she asked, unafraid. Though he had obviously been drinking, he didn't seem hostile at all. In fact, he seemed as if he had found a resolution to his problems this evening and were merely coming to share the good news with her.

"I want to know why you're not afraid of the storms. It's almost as if you enjoy them." He faced her, and although it was dark, she could see his sad smile. "I heard noises in here. I thought perhaps the thunder and wind were frightening you, that you might need comfort. And yet I come in here, and see you clutching at the shutters, begging to be free, to be out there tonight in the midst of it all. What a strange creature you are." He lifted a hand to touch her cheek, but then thought better of it and dropped it to his side.

"Storms have never bothered me," she answered simply.

"Why?"

"I love them. Especially now."

"And why now? What release do you find in them tonight?"

She paused with his question. She thought of everything that had brought her to this moment. "They're so angry."

St. Bride was silent for a moment. Then he touched one windswept curl that had wrapped around her throat and studied her in the darkness. Slowly, his lips parted, and she felt his hot, brandy-kissed breath on her forehead. He leaned against her, not holding her, not capturing her as he usually tried to do, and she felt forced to endure his presence merely because he gave her no real reason to object to it. But when his lips trailed and stroked over her forehead, she gave a start, saying, "Stop, St. Bride. I'll fight you, and as I've done before, I'll win."

"Then you misjudge me." There was a rumble from his chest that seemed like laughter, and his kiss on her forehead became hotter and wetter. Vaguely, she wondered if she was holding him up altogether—his weight was positively oppressive. But nonetheless, she found she couldn't pull back. His touch was too full of practiced seduction, and his words were too soft and arousing.

"What do you want, St. Bride?" She could barely get the question out. His hand was against the doorjamb behind her, but it didn't seem to support him at all. She arched backward, but soon she felt his other hand on her back and then on her bottom as he pulled her up against his hips. Lastly, his palm cupped one of her thinly clad buttocks, and she almost groaned from the spark that shot through her loins. As she was emphatically denying this effect to herself, he stopped kissing her and rested his chin on her head.

"What kind of woman are you, dark love?" he whispered against her. "You spurn my advances and my wealth like a duchess of the realm, and yet you were on the streets stealing for your supper. Now I find you involved in a murder, and I cannot get a straight answer from you about it. Yet through it all, this smooth, guiltless brow seduces me into trusting you. And I do trust you. I trust that you didn't kill Bardolph, and even now I'm convinced that one day you'll explain yourself to me. Why is that? What have you done to me?" His lips came to her forehead once more, and he whispered, "Ah, but how beautiful, exquisite, and blinding your brow is, Kayleigh."

"No," she gasped, rattled by his talk, rattled by his actions.

Softly he asked, "Are you denying it, my witch? My enchantress who's put a spell on me?"

"I'm no witch. I'm the one who's spellbound. Can't you see it?" she taunted bitterly. "Others have."

"Yes, I see it. The spell enchants me too." His hand lifted and tilted her chin upward so that she faced him. Lightning struck outside once more, and his face lit up with an unreal intensity.

"Let me go," she whispered.

"Never." He laughed.

"Laban and his predictions—he may be right."

"Laban and his predictions be damned." He released a slow, sardonic grin. "If you put a knife in my back, I almost think I would take it with pleasure. Whatever it is about you, I've discovered I can't do without it."

"Even if I'm a murderess?" She licked her lips.

"You're not. I don't believe you are. Worse than that, I don't care if you are. I'll take you any way I can." He came down to kiss her. His strength was immense, but suddenly she had no desire to fight him. When his other hand left the jamb and began hiking up her night smock, excitement rose as high in her breast. His palm trailed along her smooth expanse of thigh, and his knuckles were warm and strong against her skin. But she shouldn't want them there, she told herself. She shouldn't want the thrill that went down her spine and made her breath come in short, quick gasps, and mostly she shouldn't want the feeling that she really did want it . . . and more.

"No, St. Bride. I'll fight you."

"Go ahead."

She tried to push his hands away, but already the hem of her night smock was almost up to her bottom. Just when she expected to feel his hands on her naked backside, she felt him touch her where she had never been touched before. Never.

She moaned as his fingers parted her thighs. Her body went rigid and hot, and soon she was sure her flesh was boiling beneath his touch. "Nay, I'll fight you, St. Bride." She clawed at his forearm, but he would not leave.

"Fight then, Kayleigh." He nuzzled her. "Abandon yourself to fury, and soon you'll abandon yourself to me."

"No!" she whispered harshly when his caress grew bolder. Shocked to her very core, she pushed at his arm with all her strength, but he stole her further protests with a kiss. Her moan was muffled as his mouth seemed to devour hers. His kiss came deep and moist and so heady, she found herself drinking of it gladly.

His caress grew bolder still, and her heart thudded wildly in her chest. She writhed against him, feeling herself more and more ensnared in his lovemaking. Then, as if out of Pandora's box, all her passions seemed to be unleashed one by one. A part of her rapturously watched them soar to the heavens, but a bigger part of her wanted them back in the box. That part made her rip her mouth from his. Then, clutching her night smock, she scrambled to the other side of the room.

"Go! Go, I tell you!" she said in a ragged sob, desperately trying to regain her senses. She panted furiously, and the way she felt at that very moment, she wondered if she would stop short of murder.

"I'll not go," he said with a frustrated glint in his eyes. He moved toward her.

"Stay away!" she cried. "Stay away, or I'll hate you forever!"

"Are you sure? Hatred was not in your heart when you were moaning in my arms." He closed in on her, but he stopped short of touching her. He merely stood beside her and watched her, an angry frown to his lips.

A desperate tear slipped down her cheek. She brushed at her tear-spiked lashes with the back of one hand. "I will, St. Bride. I will hate you forever." Despair filled her heart. How she wanted to continue, how her body ached for his touch!

But how wrong it all was—how utterly, heart-wrenchingly wrong.

"Then rest easy, madame," he uttered quietly. "I don't bed women who hate me."

"St. Bride," she cried softly. She didn't hate him—in fact, she was beginning to wonder if her feelings for him weren't as far from hatred as they could be. There was so much she wanted to say, yet no way to form the right words.

As she fought with her raging emotions, a gust of wind snapped all the slats closed with a whack, and the room went into pitch darkness. She felt St. Bride's hand stray upward, and tenderly his knuckles stroked the upper swell of her breast. He released a soft groan, but she was quickly thrust from him. When she spun to face him once more, all she could make out was his silhouette retreating to the door. Finally she heard the door close. And she swore it was the bolt he drove home, not the tingle on her breast, that made her cry out in vexation, "You bloody *rogue!*"

Twice she'd missed her meeting with Quinn. She could hardly help the circumstances, having been locked in her bedchamber for three days, but she knew Quinn would not believe her. There would be hell to pay—of that she had no doubt.

It was the next morning, and although St. Bride had finally freed her from the confines of her chamber, he still kept a close watch on her. All morning she felt his cool turquoise gaze upon her, brooding and watchful. He was trying her soul. She was desperate not to think of him or of last night. But she had cried until the wee hours of the morning, and her entire being ached whenever she thought of how he had touched her, how he had caressed her *there*.

Yet even that thought was now shadowed by a much larger one. She had to meet Quinn. He was waiting for her—she could feel it. He was there right where the giant cattails met the swamps on the edge of the old indigo fields. If she could only chance an escape—just for a few minutes—she could appease him.

But her hopes were dashed. Late that morning, St. Bride came up to her in the laundry and asked her to walk with him at noon. Having no desire to test his mood, she said yes, but when he left, she wondered if her chance to meet Quinn would ever come.

At noon they walked along the dirt road that led to the field slaves' quarters. Kayleigh had never been this way before, and she enjoyed strolling through the allée of baby live oaks that turned toward rows of tiny cypress houses in the foreground. She couldn't help but think that it would have been a pleasant outing if not for the sodden sky that had drizzled all morning and if not for the oppressive thought that she must meet Quinn before it was too late.

"A dreary day for a walk, I'm afraid." Perfunctorily, St. Bride took her hand and helped her over a puddle.

"The rain has cooled things down. I'm quite glad to walk about. I don't like being indoors for so long." She gave him a tentative look.

"Do you like your new stays?"

The question was jarring. It brought back memories of a night they both seemed anxious to forget. "Yes. Very much." She thought of the package that had appeared at her bedroom door that morning. Earlier, the scarlet stays had mysteriously disappeared and now had come another pair, less fine perhaps but of a blessed shade of mauve.

"I thought it best if we got out of the house." St. Bride paused by a tree and glanced at her.

"I'm not fond of being cooped up."

"I know."

"What exactly are we doing here, St. Bride?" she began, but her words dropped off when he scowled.

"I've another gift for you. But I fear it may not please you." He fingered a pouch that was tied to his buckskin breeches. "It has certain implications against which you, no doubt, will rebel."

"What is it?" she asked, warily stepping away from him. She watched breathlessly as he withdrew the pouch's treasure. Her mind whirred with horrible visions of what the gift might be, but in the end all he held out to her was a piece of jewelry.

"A necklace?" she exclaimed softly, allowing the piece to be placed in her hands. It wasn't the necklace that Thionville had given him, but there were a few similarities. The necklace was a plain collar of silver, adorned in the middle with St. Bride's large, unmistakable sapphire. She turned it over and over in her fingers, trying to figure out its meaning.

"Taking your sapphire does not make me your mistress, St. Bride," she finally said to him.

"No, it does not."

"Then why do you offer me something so expensive? You've kept me locked up for three days—now you present me with the means to flee."

"No, you won't flee. I've seen to that."

His words were an enigma. She didn't know how to react. "But I shall if you give me this necklace," she said with utter conviction.

St. Bride studied her, unconvinced. "May I put it on you?" He came closer, his eyes wary, yet full of anticipation.

"You have gone mad, St. Bride."

She allowed him to lift her hair. His fingers were warm and strong on the back of her slender neck. They sent a shiver down her spine that had nothing to do with the weather. Helplessly, she was forced to close her eyes when his lips touched her nape. He kissed her once, gently, then he drew back.

"May I?" He took the necklace from her hands. The collar

felt cold and smooth against her flesh. He hesitated an unusual length of time before clasping it. But finally the necklace was fastened around her neck. He turned her around, then gazed at her, appearing thoroughly enchanted. "Its beauty is only enhanced by yours, dark love. I hope that you will someday forgive me."

"No, it's I who will need forgiveness, St. Bride. You know I'll never keep this." She fingered the silver collar.

But he merely shook his head. "You will. You can't take it off."

"But I will take it off, you must know that. The first chance I get, I'll take it off and I'll sell it."

"You cannot take it off, Kayleigh. It has nothing to do with my desire for you to keep it on. There is a silversmith in town who used to make locks for *les ébénistes* of Louis XIV. His locks are masters of deception. Only he and I know how to take off the necklace."

At his words she lifted her hands to her neck, nervously fingering for the clasp. But there was none! All she could feel was smooth, cold silver. Somehow the silversmith had implanted the lock within the hollows of the collar. Certainly at this angle she would never figure out how it came undone.

"I shall break the clasp." She pulled on it until her neck chafed from the effort and he forced her hands away.

"It cannot be done."

"I shall have it cut off then!" she said, getting desperate.

"Not possible. The collar and the lock are made of a special metal. It's not pure silver. It requires a diamond knife to cut it. I'm sorry, Kayleigh. There's no way to take it off."

"I shall find its lockmaker. He will unclasp it for me." Her voice began to waver.

"He already knows about you. And he knows, too, that I will pay him more than the necklace is worth for him not to take it off."

"Why? Why are you doing this?" Her voice cracked in disbelief.

His words were far harsher than any she'd expected from him.

"Because I want you. Because I'm not going to let you go, and because you'll need me now. You'll need me for the protection I can offer you. For how can you run back to New Orleans or anywhere when thieves will corner you like wolves for that necklace?"

"I'll never need you. Never!" She backed away. She fair wanted to kill him for collaring her as if she were his favorite pet. Now she would be at his mercy to take the thing off, and she would never get away. Unable to sell her only fortune and fearing always that some unsavory beggar would try to force it from her, she would remain within his grasp forever. Futilely, she tugged at the collar again. Again he made her stop. He put his arm around her waist and pulled her to his chest.

"I've got you, Kayleigh. Accept it."

Violently she shook her head. "No," she refused.

"Yes."

"No!" she practically sobbed. "I'll not let you make me your thrall, born to do your bidding!" In despair she turned from him, and in a small, defeated voice she said, "Oh, why are you doing this to me, St. Bride?"

"Prove your trustworthiness, and you'll not have to wear your jewels like a fetter."

"Take off this—this—shackle!" she suddenly demanded, unable to bear more.

"No," he said softly, assuredly.

"You bastard, how I hate you!" she cried out. Och, and she did hate him. She hated his superior wits, but mostly she hated his necklace, which already seemed to weigh her down like a ball and chain. It seemed to close upon her throat until she couldn't breathe. Now all she wanted was to be free of it and his presence. But how would she ever be free of St. Bride as long as his precious sapphire held her captive?

"God, how I despise you for humiliating me like this!" she sobbed.

"I know . . . I know that." He rebuffed her fury, but she refused his solace. She tried to push away from him, but when she couldn't, she lifted her face to his. Her lips were trembling, her eyes reproachful.

"You want me as your mistress, don't you?" she said, although her words shook with emotion.

"I've made that clear enough," he stated, a puzzled look on his face.

"Then kiss me."

His eyebrow shot up.

"I said kiss me, St. Bride. You know how. You've done it before." She looked at him, and her eyes fairly sparked with blue fire.

He slowly moved down to comply. His lips clung to hers for only the briefest of seconds, however, before he lifted his head. He looked upon her. Her face was that of a cold marble Venus, without feeling, without passion.

"Is this how you want it?" she asked him. "Is this how you want our kisses to be? Frigid and perfunctory?"

"No," he answered evenly.

"Then take off the necklace, St. Bride," she begged him for the last time.

"No," he whispered in a harsh, desolate voice.

Without wasting another moment, she pulled from his embrace, yet this time his arms fell easily away. She stumbled backward and took off down the road.

"Kayleigh, come back here!" he called to her. But she didn't listen. She didn't turn to see anger flare up in his eyes, nor to hear the ragged sigh that escaped his lips.

* * *

St. Bride stared down at his drink. The amber liquid swirled about in his glass, just like the gray and white marblizing did around him. It was well past midnight, and he was seated in the marble-painted loggia. Having opened all the louvers, the dark loggia was striped in moonglow. Everything was either black or white or gray except his brandy. Shot with moonlight, its orange depths appeared fiery and potent. But when he gulped it down, its effect fell decidedly short of its appearance.

"What did she say that has you awake at this hour, my friend?" Laban appeared at the top of the stairs.

"Have some spirits, Laban. We should make use of its short supply." St. Bride's words were surprisingly even, and he seemed disappointed at his own sobriety.

"I heard a noise up here, and I was just checking to make sure it was you and not—" Laban bit off his words, sat down, and abruptly accepted the brandy.

"Our little Gaelic witch?" St. Bride smiled into his glass. "She's in quite a fury."

"Yes, she is." St. Bride twisted his mouth into a wry grin. "But then, she never did have a liking for my gifts."

"What are your plans for her?" Laban sipped slowly.

"I've decided I'm going to let her meet her friend Quinn tomorrow. She's been aching to see him, I can tell. Everytime she sets foot outdoors, she looks over to that swamp where they have their little exchanges. He's been there waiting for her, hasn't he?"

"Every day. I've checked on him myself." Laban nodded his head. "He ties his horse in the clearing and then waits, cursing to himself for an hour before he departs. He's getting angry. He's not going to wait forever."

"All right then. Tomorrow we'll see what he's about. Then we'll pay him off and send him packing. I want him out of Kayleigh's life forever." St. Bride refilled his glass from the decanter next to him. Grudgingly, he admitted, "I also don't want Quinn to get any more impatient. He'll run to the authorities if he doesn't get his trinkets." Staring at Laban, St. Bride finished vengefully, "I don't want anyone to know Kayleigh is here."

Laban seemed to labor over his choice of words. He began slowly, "St. Bride, have you even given the possibility a thought? I'm not saying the girl did murder that Bardolph character. But what do we really know of her?"

"Nothing. Everything." St. Bride ran his scarred hand through his hair. The scar caught the moonlight, and both men were aware of it as it reflected, white and shiny. "I don't ask you to understand, Laban. Sometimes I don't understand it myself." He spoke calmly.

"Everything points to the contrary for her."

"I know that!" St. Bride rasped, then checked himself. "It's true. She's as guilty as she could be. Those red stays were her undoing. My God! You should have seen her face! She was seeing blood all right. And Lord knows, it was not her own." He got up and began pacing. "But still, I can't see her disemboweling an old drunkard. Not without a very good reason. If she had a very good reason, then she deserves protection."

"And if she did not have a good reason?" Laban asked quietly.

"If she didn't"—St. Bride smiled a wry, quiet smile— "then I'll never know, will I?"

"Not until you find the same knife in your gut."

"I can handle Kayleigh. She's wild, but I've always been drawn to wild things. Look how much time I've spent in these colonies when I should have been at Scion House doing my duty." He grimaced. "But then, look at how much time I spent doing my duty after my father died, when I should have been looking out for Mary." At this thought he abruptly put down his glass. "Good night, Laban. I don't see the point in debating this issue further."

"No, there's no point when you're in love with her."

"What did you say?" St. Bride asked sharply.

"You heard me."

Suddenly St. Bride began to laugh. "You're wrong, Laban. You can't know how wrong." He stood, but before he left the salon, his gaze involuntarily flickered to Kayleigh's bed-chamber doors, then stayed there until he forced it away and went to bed.

Chapter Eighteen

Kayleigh spent the next morning helping Colette boil lard for candles. The candle rods were ready, hung on the backs of chairs, but the skimming of the tallow would take at least two days. It was hellish work, standing over a boiling caldron all day, and both women were without kerchiefs, their dresses unhooked as far as was decent to keep cool. At noon, unable to endure more of the kitchens' heat, Colette and Kayleigh both took a break. Colette stayed near the kitchens to make sure the lard did not cool, and Kayleigh found the escape she'd been looking for. She scurried to her room for a kerchief.

Her hands fidgeting, she tied a fichu high at her neck. It looked a bit odd, but she couldn't have Malcolm Quinn eyeing St. Bride's necklace—*especially* if the thing wouldn't come off. She shuddered at the thought.

Quickly, she looked about the salon for St. Bride. He was absent—conspicuously so, she thought darkly, but she shrugged off the thought. She was suspicious of this strangely advantageous hour of freedom, but she had to take it. She had to meet Quinn today, no matter what. He would be out of patience by now. With that thought and several coins taken from St. Bride's commode, Kayleigh left for the edge of the swamps.

It wasn't quite raining; rather, a heavy, humid mist hung low over the cattails and palmettos. As Kayleigh walked, she could feel the water bead upon her skin and dampen her rough flaxen dress. Her hand rested upon her kerchief. She glanced back at the house. Brooding and unfashionable, Belle Chasse hung in mystery, appearing almost ungrounded as mist rolled around it like rain-laden clouds. No one was about; only Grand-Louis walked its abandoned courtyards mumbling to those whom no one else could see. The only hint at civilization came from the kitchens, where thin woodsmoke curled up from the chimney.

She picked her way across the edge of the swamps. There was no way of knowing whether Quinn would be there or not. She found their clearing, the one surrounded by bayou and wax myrtle, but Quinn was nowhere to be seen. Resigning herself to wait, she found a cypress stump and sat down, her hand resting warily on her throat.

"Damn you, gel! I'm telling Mr. Straught today your whereabouts!" Malcolm Quinn tethered a swayback mare to a magnolia.

"I've been ill. I couldn't come." Kayleigh knew she looked pale enough to have been. Quinn stood in front of her, and she cursed her hands for trembling.

"Make it up to me, gel." Malcolm smiled, the tip of his tongue wagging at her from the gap in his teeth.

"Here, I've some gold coins for you. It was all I could take. St. Bride has become suspicious of me."

Malcolm threw the coins down viciously and mashed them with his boot. "I needn't this meager wage!" he screeched at her. "You've made me wait here for days, and you bring me this? Mr. Straught will know all about you, and by this evening your pretty white throat will be as red as your sister's back!"

Cringing, Kayleigh forced away the gruesome image. Morna's fate would not be her own. "It was all I could get. I'll bring you something more lucrative next time."

"If that bastard Ferringer is getting suspicious, then your use to me has come to an end. You'll not be able to pay me much longer." Quinn grabbed her chin and pulled it up. Her nose was assaulted with the pungent smell of a wet dog.

She pulled back violently.

"Get away from me, you filthy mongrel!"

"I don't fear Ferringer when Mr. Straught will have the situation well in hand by nightfall."

"I'll pay you to leave me alone! Name your price, and I'll have it by morning, I promise." She tried to fob him off. *Dhé!* She was leaving Belle Chasse tonight! No one and nothing could stop her with Straught riding hot on her trail!

"Where are you going to get . . . ?" Quinn hesitated, and a thought obviously came to his head. "I see—the jewels Mr. Straught gave to Ferringer. Have you a mind for them?"

"Yes. I'll get them for you!" she lied, knowing full well that St. Bride kept those jewels firmly locked away, out of her reach.

"Ha! You little snipe, you couldn't even succeed in taking Ferringer's sapphire when you first met up with him on the docks. How are you going to get all those jewels? What's your plan, miss? I wouldn't want Ferringer and his black ox delivering them to me with a bullet in the gut!" He stepped toward her.

"No. I'll get you whatever you want. Just don't tell Erath," she pleaded. "By morning, I'll have everything, I swear!"

"I don't want an empty promise. You're of no more use to me. Mr. Straught will be notified, but first I'm thinking I'll have a little tumble."

"If you rape me, St. Bride will kill you," she reasoned with him. "I'll tell him everything. He has already vowed to protect me." She trembled. If only he were here now! If only she could trust him enough. . . .

"He won't get the chance then." Malcolm grabbed her with two meaty, odious fists. She tensed from his repugnant touch, and as he struggled to kiss her, she vehemently fought off his advance. Eventually, he half dragged, half carried her to his withering nag, but all the while she tried desperately to wring free. She pushed on Quinn's craggy face to keep it a distance from hers and finally resorted to clawing him, letting his blood with the sharp ends of her nails.

Yet she soon found this was the wrong thing to do. Her struggling disheveled her kerchief. In rapid succession, Malcolm stopped fighting her; then his eyes bugged out of his head like a mackerel's.

"By golly, woman! What have we here?" Quinn's hands went to her neck to uncover the silver collar. The sparkling sapphire at her throat contrasted sharply with the eerie gloom of the swamps. Quinn was mesmerized; Kayleigh, terrified.

"It won't come off—you can't have it, for it won't come off," she told him, trying to be brave.

"Give it up, lass. Perhaps you're of more use than I thought. Ferringer's giving you better trinkets than I could have hoped for." Quinn pulled at the collar.

"I tell you, it won't come off. He found out that you were blackmailing me. He had this especially made so that I couldn't rid myself of it."

"Take it off!" Quinn pulled on it fiercely. Her neck was becoming raw from his brutal grasp, and Kayleigh didn't know who she hated more at that moment, Quinn for being such a worthless, greedy piece of lard, or St. Bride for putting her in this dangerous situation in the first place.

"It won't come off, I tell you! Are you so very slow that you can't understand that whatever?" she cried to him, her eyes beginning to tear from his roughness.

"If it won't come off by normal means, I'll get it off by another." Malcolm pushed her away and grabbed a knife from his boot.

"No, please! I'll get you anything else! Even Straught's own jewels. I'll find a way. I'm clever, Malcolm Quinn. You know this. I've survived because I'm clever."

"You survived because of Bardolph's stupidity. Running

to Louisiana with you did in that old rummy. His soft heart was your escape—cleverness had nothing to do with it.'' Quinn came forward, and the knife reflected the blue of her jewel as if to foreshadow her own death.

"Don't do this! I'll do whatever you want. Just don't!''

"The fine lady, Kayleigh Kerr, down on her back, being my mistress? Are you truly willing to offer me that to spare your life?'' When Kayleigh didn't answer, he continued, ''I never will have you. And don't I know it. You would kill me before I could bed you. I haven't forgotten this.'' Quinn lifted his grimy waistcoat and displayed a brilliant red scar, shining against the white jelly of his stomach.

'' 'Twas an accident.''

"You pulling it out was no accident. The damned knife was more painful coming out than going in.'' Quinn grabbed her hair, which had come undone in her attempts to flee. "No, gel, I'm through with you. I'll be rewarded kindly for putting you to rest—and I'll have Ferringer's notorious little jewel to boot.'' He raised the knife with gruesome finality. Kayleigh ached to scream, but no sound left her lips. She was trapped by her own horror. The world seemed to come to a standstill, and she felt as if she were looking upon the act of murder as a spectator, not as the victim.

But just as Quinn lowered the knife, she heard a loud musket blast from the underbrush behind her. In shock, she watched Quinn fall flat on his back. His forehead was marred by the blackness of gunpowder. Terrified, Kayleigh spun around to see who fired the fatal shot.

Straught! her mind cried out irrationally. He'd followed Quinn and seen them there in the clearing together! Perhaps Malcolm Quinn had set her up for her slaughter and Erath was now taking care of them both—his traitor Quinn and his threat Kayleigh—in one fell motion.

Looking down at Quinn, she saw where the lead ball had neatly run through his brow. *I don't want to look like that—* the words ran through Kayleigh's head. The brush behind her moved, and no doubt Straught was there, reloading his gun for her. She suddenly found the ability to move, and when she did, she ran for her life.

Hands reached for her like the tentacles of moss that hung in her nightmares. She didn't like the swamps, and she had run there once before, only to find danger. But she would take the swamps anytime over those terrible hands that sought her blood and those cold eyes lit with the fires of hell.

"Laban, leave him." A harsh voice called out from behind her. Kayleigh's limbs went weak from relief. The voice was severe and stern, but it was ever so familiar. She turned and faced St. Bride as he emerged from the clearing.

"St. Bride . . . St. Bride . . ." she murmured numbly again and again, not believing that it was he who had shot Quinn. But suddenly, in one split second, all her defenses were shattered. She forgot about her anger toward the man before her, she forgot about his collar and her doubts about his character. By instinct alone, she ran to him. Without pause or invitation, she threw herself into his arms and began to sob.

Her delicate fists clutched at the smooth cambric of his shirt, and her tears dampened his solid front. Like a pauper desperate for bread, she took his embrace. His arms felt like bands of steel protecting her from the world and all its horrors, while a palm gently stroked her hair. St. Bride's voice, deep and soothing, whispered in her ear. "Hush, my love, hush," he comforted, but she hardly heard him. All she knew was that her fragile soul had finally found its fortress.

It was a long time before her sobs subsided. When they did, she stood trembling in his arms, unable to speak or move. She still clutched at his shirt with her cheek upon his chest. His strong, steady heartbeat reassured her; so did his tender caress upon her back.

Eventually, they were forced to break apart. From behind them, Laban gave a discreet cough. St. Bride reluctantly released her.

"Come, love. Let's get back to the house. There's much we need to discuss." He took his thumb and wiped away her last tears.

Stuttering, she said, "He—tried—to—" She couldn't finish. All she could manage was to release a great body-wracking shudder.

"He's dead now. I've seen to that. He'll never hurt you again." St. Bride nodded in the direction of the lifeless mound that was once Malcolm Quinn.

"I'm sorry I've stolen from you," she confessed tearfully. "You've saved my life twice now, and I've proven an ungrateful wretch. But I shall make it up to you, St. Bride. I shall find some way to repay you."

"You should have come to me when Quinn first approached you. You should have looked to me for protection." There was no missing the reprimand in his voice.

"Please, please, believe me, St. Bride. I had no choice." She looked away from him. Guilt stabbed at her. How she wanted to tell him the whole story! How she ached to have his comforting embrace return! But would he despise her for destroying his plans with Straught? Or worse, would he destroy her?

Unable to answer, her gaze wandered to Quinn's body and hovered there in morbid fascination. Laban, who stood over Quinn's form, couldn't seem to look away either. The only one who wasn't staring at the body was St. Bride. He was staring directly at her.

"Tell me why you had no choice," he asked softly.

"He was blackmailing me. I didn't want to steal from you. You've not deserved that," she said evenly.

"I know he was blackmailing you. But I want some other answers. Tell me about Bardolph's death. Who killed him, and why?"

She darted a glance at him—and remained silent.

"Come, Kayleigh, one word of truth. Tell me now, and we can forget the past and start anew."

Her eyelids fluttered down, and she studied her palms. They were chafed from her struggle with Quinn. It was several moments before she gathered the courage to face St. Bride again. But when she finally did, she was astounded by the anger she saw in his gaze.

"Go back to the house. We've got to dress for Thionville's ball." He pointed in the direction of Belle Chasse.

"I can't go to a ball," she gasped, thinking of who she might meet there—her cousin.

But this statement only seemed to make St. Bride angrier. "Admit to me who killed Bardolph Ogilvie, and I'll let you remain at Belle Chasse for the night."

She was silent. She could give him no answer.

"Tell me, Kayleigh. Tell me now, or you'll go with me tonight."

"I didn't murder him. You know that. Isn't that enough?" she pleaded.

"A man's blood is on my hands because of you. I have the right to know why I had to kill him." He looked over at Quinn, then back at her. She remained mute.

"Why did I kill him, Kayleigh?"

This time, she did speak. In a little voice, she said, "I can't tell you why. Not now, not yet."

The anger St. Bride had been holding in check lashed out. "Go to the house! When I get there, be ready to be paraded in front of your executioners!"

"You save my life only to throw me to the wolves? This is Thionville's ball! You know he thinks me a murderess! Why would you do such a thing?"

"Why? Because I want some answers, and if I have to scare you to death to get them, so be it!" He stepped toward her, and that was all it took to send her fleeing toward the house.

Shivering, Kayleigh ran up the loggia stairs and found partial refuge in her room. Whatever had possessed St. Bride? What had caused this irrational anger? He seemed more furious now than he had been after giving her the red stays. She spent the next hour wracking her brain, trying to come up with a reason for his behavior.

She didn't know that the men had overheard only the very last of her conversation with Quinn, and at that very moment, Quinn's words about Bardolph were still echoing through St. Bride's thoughts: *"Running to Louisiana with you did in that old rummy. His soft heart was your escape."*

Chapter Nineteen

The rain fell harder as the day wore on. Kayleigh paced in her room until she thought she would go mad. Her nerves were wound tight as she thought of Malcolm Quinn's death and St. Bride's cold reaction. She wanted desperately to be comforted, but as she had learned in the past, her only comfort would have to come from herself.

She heard St. Bride arrive, but he went straight to his own bedchamber to bathe and change for the evening's social event. It wasn't long after that that Colette scurried into Kayleigh's bedchamber, armed with a hip bath, Venus and Valentine, and a new dress.

In her state of mind, Kayleigh didn't notice the dress until Colette had laid it out on her bedstead like a bridal gown.

The fabric was of snow white silk damask, and the gown was decorated with ruching at the front edges. When Kayleigh dared to look closer, she saw that the gown was overembroidered in a subtle pattern of vines and blossoms. Tossed upon the skirt were various accoutrements accompanying the outfit—a pair of white damask shoes with high French heels, a velvet case containing a pair of silver and marcasite shoe buckles, an ivory *brisé* fan threaded with purple ribbon, and a black satin domino.

Amazed, Kayleigh walked to the bed and took the domino into her hands. She was not going to go to Thionville's ball disguised by only a wee bit of black silk. The thought was almost more than she could bear.

"Dhé, he can't mean to take me with him,'' she whispered under her breath. Suddenly she turned worried eyes to Colette.

"I cannot—'' Kayleigh stopped, noting the harassed look on Colette's face. "I may not return if I go,'' she began again, then helplessly watched as her bath was drawn.

"I may not return . . . ever.'' She felt Colette unhook the back of her dress. Then Kayleigh fell completely silent. There was nothing to be done about it now, she thought to herself. She couldn't get Colette into trouble. Resigning herself at least to bathing, she slipped out of the osnaburg gown and stepped into the hip bath. Venus and Valentine took turns scrubbing her back, and Colette washed her hair. At the end of her bath, Kayleigh donned her shift and stays, and the twins dried her hair by the open shutters. Her tresses were combed until they shimmered with glossy highlights, and then Kayleigh watched Colette get the dress.

"Thank you, Colette. I shall dress myself.''

"Mais, mademoiselle . . .''

"Really, Colette, I know St. Bride sent you up here, but it was unnecessary. I've already taken enough of your time. I know you're still boiling the tallow for candles, and you must need to go down there. Please, I shall dress myself.'' Resolutely, she took the gown from Colette's hands and placed it back on the bed.

"You may go, Colette. She will dress herself.''

The voice spoke from behind them. With a sharp intake of breath, Kayleigh self-consciously put her arms around her chest. Covered in only her shift and stays, she felt little better than naked. When she turned toward her doorway, she was appalled to see St. Bride standing in it.

He was dressed to masculine perfection in black. His hose, his shoes, his breeches, and his coat were all of jet. The only relief to the black was his waistcoat of silver tissue brocaded in multicolored silks. Dressed like that, he looked a scion of power and breeding. When Kayleigh had dreamed of a man courting her, he had looked exactly like St. Bride did at that moment—subtle, yet magnificent.

"Run along, Colette. Laban has already asked for you in the kitchens," he said, entering the bedchamber.

The cloud lifted from Colette's face, and the little mulatto scurried away quickly with the twins, obviously much relieved not to have to be between Kayleigh and St. Bride.

Alone with St. Bride, Kayleigh found herself beneath his penetrating stare. She scrambled for her osnaburg gown and was just about to throw the thing over her head when it was whisked from her hands.

"You've another gown for tonight." St. Bride went to the bed and tossed her the white silk.

"You cannot be serious about this." She clutched the white gown to her bosom to fend off his indecent gaze.

"Is there anything you'd like to tell me?"

"No," she answered timidly.

"Then get dressed." With that, he kicked the walnut fauteuil away from the wall, positioned it carefully in front of her, and then sat stretching his long legs before him. He crossed his arms over his massive chest and waited for her to comply.

"I'm not going," she challenged.

"No?" He raised one jet eyebrow.

"No," she answered bravely.

He laughed. "Well, I suppose not then. For I daresay you'll be ready enough to talk about your relationship with Quinn before we leave this room."

"And why is that?"

"Because I'm not leaving here unless I have either a confession"—he paused grimly—"or you in my gown, ready for tonight."

She frowned and bit her pink lower lip. How he infuriated

her! How like him to put her back to the wall! But she was not going to be forced either into a confession or into his dress, she fumed. This time she would get her way. He would just have to go to Thionville's *bal masqué* without her.

"I think you'd best be off," she said. "New Orleans is far away, and this rain will delay you." Her blue eyes glittered with suppressed animosity.

"You have nothing to tell me then?"

"Nothing."

"Fine." The chair screeched as he stood. Her eyes grew wide when he picked up a pair of white silk hose that was lying near the shoes. Within his strong hands the stockings looked impossibly sheer and delicate.

"What are you doing?" she gasped.

"I'm going to dress you. Somehow I knew you'd not come willingly." He stepped toward her.

"You will not do such an intimate thing!" She clutched the ball gown even closer to her bosom.

He stopped. "Have you something to tell me then?"

"No, but I won't—!"

He took her to him. Unable to catch her breath, she found herself sitting on his lap on the bed. The white gown was somehow out of her grasp in a shimmering pile at their feet. He leaned forward in front of her, clamping her thighs between his lap and his chest. He took one silken calf and in spite of her struggling was able to roll the first silk stocking onto it. She clawed at the massive expanse of his back, but already she could feel him sliding the other stocking onto her other leg. When he was finished, he tied a satin garter to each leg, then rested his hand intimately on her thigh while he reached for her shoes.

"Cease this!" she cried.

"Have you something to tell me?" He paused.

"Never, never, *never!* You cad!" she squealed.

Immediately he reached for her shoes and likewise put them on. He released her, and she tried to make a run for it, but the high heels and the lack of buckles tripped her up. She fell into St. Bride's waiting arms. He dragged her back to the bed, then scooped up the dress.

"You'll never get that on me!" Just as she spoke, his hand took both her wrists in a steely clamp. He held her arms above her head, and the dress fell over her like a billowing white cloud. She moaned in frustration as he pulled the bodice tightly over her bosom and forced each of her arms into the sleeves.

"I'll run away. The minute the coach gets into New Orleans, I'll run from you and you'll never find me again!" she promised as he indecently took his time hooking her bodice. When he reached the hooks at her breasts, his fingers moved with interminable slowness. Unable to take his ministrations anymore, she swatted away his hands and hooked the remaining catches herself.

"Will you comb your hair, or do you want me to tie the domino on now?" He stood over her glowering figure.

"I shall do the rest, if you would but call Colette back here," she requested in a falsely sweet voice.

"If you've had a change of heart, love, why not just tell me all about Quinn and you, and we'll both stay here for the night."

"No, I'd rather go to the ball."

"What?" He gave her a puzzled glance.

"I'd rather go to Thionville's ball." She took the fan from the bed and tapped it on her palm.

"You're mad," he stated.

"You're bluffing." She smiled, and her eyes narrowed.

"Am I then?" His lips thinned in anger.

"Aye, for you've no desire to see me hang. Especially when we've never—"

In exasperation, he cut her off. "You'll not hang, pretty wench. But you will go to this ball."

She gave him a look that would have wilted any other man, but St. Bride merely smiled, his lips seductively turning upward. He pulled several mussed tresses from her cheek and gave her a wickedly hot kiss.

"One thing you should know about me, love," he whispered. "I never bluff."

With that, he strode out of the room, ordering, "Have Colette get you ready in ten minutes." He slammed the doors behind him.

Once Colette returned, Venus and Valentine again in tow, it didn't take long for Kayleigh to finish dressing. Her hair was dressed simply, with one raven curl falling softly to her breast. She removed the marcasite shoe buckles from their case, and the twins eagerly helped attached them. Kayleigh took her first wobbly steps in the high-heeled shoes. Her feet quickly remembered such finery, for she was soon walking gracefully across the room to retrieve a silver-embroidered stomacher from the bed. Her last task was to pin the stomacher on, and she did so skillfully, making sure that not one straight pin could loosen and prick her.

"What have I forgotten?" Kayleigh asked Venus and Valentine, who looked at her as if they were watching a princess emerge from a fairy ring.

"These, mademoiselle." Colette handed her the domino and *brisé* fan.

"Of course." Kayleigh turned to the twins. She made them giggle with the coy fan language she'd spent endless hours practicing with Morna. After all, there had once been a time when she'd had hopes of using it on her beaux. That thought left her a bit sad, but Venus's and Valentine's laughter wouldn't permit her to feel melancholy. She tipped her head back and laughed with them.

"Beautiful. Thank you, Colette." St. Bride entered the bedroom, typically unannounced, and watched Kayleigh with the twins.

"*Avec plaisir,* monsieur. She is beautiful." Colette smiled, silently instructing the twins to pick up any stray toiletries and follow her out the door.

"Colette, wait!" Suddenly Kayleigh rushed to the door. She wasn't sure what she wanted to say, but as Colette, Venus, and Valentine were leaving, she was stricken with a feeling that she would never see them again. She had been sure that St. Bride was bluffing, but now doubt flooded her breast. Something was going to happen tonight. She would either escape from the ball before the carriage took them to it or be discovered by her cousin at Thionville's. Either way, the chances were that she would never again see Belle Chasse.

"Is there something else, mademoiselle?" Colette ceased her awkward steps and looked at her.

"No, it's just that—well, I wanted to say good-bye. I wanted to say thank you."

Colette smiled and took hold of Venus's hand. She turned to leave, and Kayleigh watched her with a lump in her throat. As Valentine followed them into the loggia, she bestowed on Kayleigh a most beguiling little grin and put her small hand up to wave.

"Valentine, I—" Kayleigh stepped forward, unwilling for them to go just yet. But a hand on her waist stopped her.

"You'll see them tomorrow."

"Will I?" she whispered.

"Yes. Wear your domino, and I promise you will." His eyes darkened as he watched her scowl.

"This is cruel of you, St. Bride."

Ignoring her accusation, St. Bride appraised Kayleigh's appearance. As she stood fuming before him, his eyes missed not one detail of her appearance, from the way her skin gleamed like satin against the brilliant damask to the delicate white work of the double ruffles below her elbows. He seemed quite pleased with what he found and did not hesitate to tell her. "You're beautiful, dark love. I knew you would be. But how ironic that white should be your color."

"My mother always wore white." She turned from him, unwilling to offer more.

"She must have been almost as lovely as you then." His voice had dropped to a whisper.

"It's late. If I must meet my executioners, then let's be to it." Uncomfortable at his attention, she started down the loggia stairs, but he stopped her.

"Do you like the gown, Kayleigh? I'd like to see you dressed like this always."

"Whose gown is this?" She'd wondered that ever since she first saw the dress laid out on her mattress. It was impossible that such a costly and elaborate dress could have been conjured up by St. Bride in so short a time. He must have come upon it already made—that had been obvious from the moment she tried it on. The gown fit much too loosely for her nipped-in waist and just a bit too snugly for her generous bosom.

"I'm afraid the gown has a sullied past." He placed his black cloak around her shoulders for the short, rainy trip to the carriage.

"Why do you say that?" She accepted the cloak rather stiffly.

"I would have had a gown made just for you if it were possible. Obviously it was not."

"But how did you come to have such an exquisite dress as this in your possession?"

"The last time I was in town, I bought it rather indiscreetly from one of the river people." He gave her a sideways glance. "The gent—if that's what he can be called—said he thought the dress came from a Spanish galleon that was wrecked off the Florida coast. He speculated that it might have been part of a trousseau that the ship was carrying, along with a healthy dowry of gold."

"But what happened to the ship? How did the man get the dress?" She suddenly felt odd. There was something uncomfortably intimate about wearing another's clothes, especially those that had a past.

"I didn't say a *wrecked galleon,* Kayleigh. I said the galleon *was wrecked.*" St. Bride looked at her to see if she understood.

She did. Wrecking was a common practice on both sides of the Atlantic. Suddenly, wearing the white damask felt traitorous. It had no doubt belonged to a young woman full of dreams on her way to meet her betrothed on the other side of the ocean. But instead, she was reaping the benefits of an act so malicious as to lure a ship aground, ransack its hold, then murder its passengers. The very thought made her fairly want to retch. She wanted to rip the gown off and refuse to go with St. Bride for that reason alone.

"Come, Kayleigh. We can't be late."

Hearing his words, she lowered her eyes and thought hard on rebelling. "I despise this gown, St. Bride."

"As you ought to. It has a bad past, not unlike your own," St. Bride stated dryly, an unreadable expression on his face. He gave her no chance for further thought. Ruthlessly, he led her down the stairs and into his awaiting carriage.

The trip to New Orleans took all of three hours. Kayleigh suspected the trip would have been much shorter without the rain and the boggy roads, but she had to give credit to the four bay horses that pulled them. No doubt they were making the best time they could.

Inside the carriage, Kayleigh watched the rain come down in one golden sheet, lit by the fires of the carriage lanterns. She and St. Bride had hardly spoken two words to each other since they pulled out of Belle Chasse. In the ensuing hours, Kayleigh began to wonder if going to Thionville's ball was such an ill-fated event after all. She would be going back to town at last, and perhaps an escape would be possible before she set foot at the comte's soiree.

Her brow furrowed delicately as she imagined herself fleeing St. Bride's coach just as they approached the streets leading to the quay. Perhaps she would get enough from selling the marcasite shoe buckles to pay for a trip to Edinburgh. While she pondered, St. Bride sat back in a shadowed corner of the carriage, every now and then giving her a perplexed, thought-filled frown.

St. Bride's perusals didn't make Kayleigh relax. As it was, she didn't know how she was going to get along in the rain, even if she did find a way to slip from the carriage. She'd hardly given thought to where she should go that evening. Would it be safe to return to her hut? No, she decided. Unbidden, her hand moved to her throat. She fingered the sapphire collar, and suddenly she was beset by doubts of her ability to protect herself. The people by the river were bloodthirsty, and no doubt St. Bride's collar and Thionville's reward were just what they were looking for. But she would flee the coach anyway. She could not attend this ball! She dropped her hand and resolutely stared at the carriage door. She would have to hide near the docks—that was all. She would spend a night or two on the quay, and then she would get passage out of New Orleans.

They were almost upon the town now, for she could see the rope walk that would eventually be a canal. Discreetly, she turned her eyes to St. Bride's dark figure. How handsome he looked tonight! He was finally clean shaven, which accentuated the well-formed planes of his face. She was presented the silhouette of his strong Apollonian profile when he chanced to turn his head. Even without his fine clothing she would have been drawn to him, especially to his fine lips, which as always held her utterly transfixed.

"How delightfully compliant you've grown this evening, love." The lips suddenly moved, and Kayleigh's eyes opened wide. She chastised herself for letting her thoughts wander through such fruitless territories and turned them again to her escape. She would get out when they neared the quay.

Vaguely, she wondered if St. Bride would go after her. She doubted it, especially in this weather. Yet for the damask dress he might. She didn't doubt that the rare gown had cost him a bundle. Och, but he had a ball to attend, she told herself finally, and she couldn't see him missing that. She would probably be free and clear of him the minute her damask shoes splashed in the first mud puddle. With that dismal thought, she clutched St. Bride's cloak to her and waited for the exact spot to disembark.

The carriage skirted the quay on the way to the Place d'Armes and the Thionville manse beyond. As it went over the well-traveled ruts of the town roads, it rocked most ferociously. Kayleigh was thrown toward St. Bride's quiet figure, and she felt his arm steady her by grasping her shoulders. Disconcerted, she edged back to her place, wondering what it was about him that always left her feeling so contrary. She could still feel the warmth on her shoulder where his hand had lingered, unwilling to let her move away. But his touch seemed only to give her the desire for more. As he had steadied her, she'd suddenly had the urge to press herself into his chest and be enveloped in his arms. She wanted him to comfort her, to protect her. She wanted him to tell her the future was not as bleak as she feared it was because he would see to it that it was not.

But as the last of the quay began to appear through the rainy window, Kayleigh forced herself to shake off this reverie. It would never be. St. Bride was a heartless man who had nothing better to do tonight than torment her with this horrible ball. Thinking this, her hand lightly reached for the carriage door handle. In just a few seconds she would taste freedom. Perhaps that would be balm enough for her flagging spirits.

The ivory door handle felt cool in her palm. The rain pelted against the window, but she closed her eyes to its misery. It would feel good, she reassured herself. It would feel good because she would finally be away. Her hand twisted the handle, and she tensed for flight.

Suddenly, an arm shot out and pulled the cracked door shut. Abruptly, she was shoved back into her seat. Hardly even aware of what had happened, she reached for the door handle again, but St. Bride's hand on her wrist forced her back.

"Thionville's house is not near the quay," he said easily. Then he let her go and sat back on the upholstery.

"I am not going to this ball!" she told him. How was it that he always changed the circumstances so suddenly?

"Ah, but you are," he answered coldly. "You forced my hand."

"I'll not!" She lunged for the door, but St. Bride pulled her back onto the carriage seat.

"Where do you think to go this night, love?" Against her will, he pulled the black-satin domino out from under her. "And where would you go without this? Do you think the comte is the only one looking for you?"

Her silence accused him of all sorts of treachery.

"The sign was posted on the church's clapboards. I know the river people are an uneducated lot, but surely one or two of them can make out the words *murdered* and *beware.*" He shook his head as if the words were distasteful to him.

It was definitely turning out to be a poor evening. First she'd had to endure Malcolm Quinn's attack and St. Bride's questioning after he'd rescued her; then she was forced into going to the comte's ball; and now she'd found out that escape from the carriage was virtually impossible. It all made her nerves absolutely raw. She had no idea how she would get through the rest of the evening, *bal masqué* or not. The thought of seeing her cousin in such close proximity absolutely terrified her.

"Ah, here we are." The carriage rumbled to a halt. Kayleigh's eyes opened wide, and she searched desperately for an escape. But things moved too quickly. St. Bride placed the domino over her face. He tied it beneath its short veil, kissed her lightly on her numb lips, then swung her out of the carriage and onto a veranda before she could even utter a word of protest. She pulled back when he began to escort her through one of the many French doors opening onto the rain-soaked gallery, but he kept a firm hand on her waist and an even firmer grip on her arm.

Once inside, she felt as if she were back at one of Mhor's spring festivals. In front of her, a barely draped Persephone danced with an irreverent Pope Leo X; Henry VIII drank with a group of pink and orange zanies; and a green dragon chased a buxom serving girl, forcing her to hide in the cabinet room. The scene before her was of utter self-indulgent pandemonium, and Kayleigh could only close her eyes to it. But as much as she wanted to run, there was no way out. She was at the Comte de Cassell's ball.

"Erath, St. Bride has arrived," whispered the comte, costumed as Niccolò Machiavelli.

"Where is he? I want a word with him." Straught scanned the room. He spotted St. Bride at the south doors, but he stopped short seeing the masked black-haired girl with him. "Who is his companion?" he demanded.

"Ah, that must be Colette," the comte answered with a lovesick sigh.

"Colette?" Straught's eyes narrowed suspiciously.

"Yes—and how I long for her! My only hope is that St. Bride will grow tired of her. I have seen her without her mask, Erath, and hers is a face no man can tire of. *Elle est angélique*—but not too much like an angel, you understand?"

"Yes, I understand completely," Straught answered ominously, unable to take his worried gaze from the masked girl. "Thionville, have a footman take a note to St. Bride. Tell him I want to speak with him about my man Quinn after the ball."

"What about Malcolm, Erath?" Thionville asked.

"He's disappeared. I've had footmen looking for him all afternoon. I even went personally to his room over the stables, yet the door was locked and there was no answer."

"Perhaps he has met a *jeune fille?*" The comte smiled lasciviously.

"No, something has happened. Quinn knows I'd have his

head for being gone so long. Call your footman now. I want to speak to St. Bride and see if he knows anything about this.''

"Of course. *Garçon!*'' The comte snapped his fingers, and a small footman appeared. He gave him the instructions and pointed out St. Bride, who fairly towered above the crowd. Then the comte turned back to Straught. "Erath, why are you waiting until after the ball to speak to St. Bride? I would have thought—''

"You would have thought! You would have thought!'' Straught snapped contemptuously. "If you've ever thought at all, I'd consider that a miracle!''

"Erath, what has you so angered? What has happened? I do not understand this!'' The comte watched dumbfounded as Straught walked away. *"Mon dieu,"* he finally muttered in exasperation to a passing footman, grabbing another goblet of wine. "He didn't even let me compliment his choice of costume!'' Suddenly, the comte snickered and downed his champagne.

Kayleigh danced to a minuet, stepping nervously to the triple meter. She knew St. Bride was puzzled by her ability to dance, but he kept his questions to himself as if used to them by now. She clasped his hand, then circled. Yet all the while she looked around for her cousin.

But if Erath Kerr Straught was about, he was well hidden in the throng of masked revelers. Was he dressed as a savage from Natchitoches? Was he costumed as a Bourbon king? Suddenly, a drunken Pegasus lurched into her, and she found herself grasping St. Bride's sleeve, silently begging him to leave the dance floor.

"What is this?'' He pulled her from the minuet and took her over to some squab-covered benches that lined one wall.

"St. Bride, please, I don't like this. Can't we go?'' Anxiously, she clasped and reclasped her hands.

"Back to Belle Chasse?" he exclaimed, a sardonic gleam in his eye. "Why, love, the ball has just begun. We certainly can't miss the unmasking at the witching hour."

"The unmasking!" Frightened, she stood and tried to leave him, but he grabbed her hand.

"You want to leave before then? Fine. Give me a reason to want to leave also." His voice turned husky.

"I won't confess to anything I didn't do." In agitation, she swatted open the *brisé* fan and fanned herself.

"A confession isn't the only impetus that would make me want to leave here." He contemptuously scanned the boisterous crowd, then turned his attention back to her. Suddenly, he smiled. "But I must admit, I am reluctant to take you away. After all, every man in this room is wondering who you are and if you're truly as beautiful as they imagine."

"How—how can you say that, St. Bride?" She took her hand from his. Was Straught out there wondering who she was too? She knew her eyes mirrored her worries, but she had no idea that as she looked at St. Bride, her gaze appeared dark and sultry beneath the black satin.

"Do I really need to answer that, or are you playing coy, Kayleigh?" He reached out and ran his forefinger down her smooth cheek. His touch left her quite disconcerted.

"I'm hardly well versed in the art of being a coquette." She closed her eyes as he stroked her cheek once more.

"Ah, but you could be with a little practice. See how beautifully you minuet?"

She opened her mouth to form a denial to this observation, but they were interrupted by a familiar voice.

"Is it the practice in Georgia to take one's bondservant to a ball?"

Startled, she looked up and found Lady Catherine before them. Though the comte's daughter wore an exquisite mask fashioned of tiny baby teal feathers, there was no mistaking the icy green gaze that practically bore holes into Kayleigh.

"Lady Catherine, you give yourself away. I thought you would wait for midnight for that." St. Bride rubbed his jaw, but Kayleigh noted the smile hidden beneath his palm.

"I see you have no fear of divulging your own identity. Why, you aren't even in costume." Lady Catherine pouted.

"Yes. Masks are only for those who have something to hide. What is your secret, Lady Catherine? What is it you don't wish us to see?"

"I shall tell you that, St. Bride, but only when we are alone." Lady Catherine glared at Kayleigh, then gave her full attention to St. Bride. "Speaking of secrets, what does your companion have to hide? I see that she does not flaunt convention. She wears a mask."

"Yes, but even without her mask she is a woman of mystery. For all the good the domino does her, she might as well be without one." St. Bride gave Kayleigh a meaningful look.

Throughout this exchange, Lady Catherine seemed to be seething. She finally stated, "I didn't come to discuss your companion, St. Bride. A footman was about to bring you a message from Erath. I thought it best if I brought it here personally."

"What does he say? I haven't seen him here. How is he costumed?" St. Bride demanded.

"You will find out all that and more when you come with me."

"What is this, Catherine?" He stood angrily. "You may give me the message now." He uttered each word slowly and with emphasis.

"But I choose not to, St. Bride. So what will it be? Will you allow me to deliver the message, or will you stay here with your bondswoman and remain ignorant of it?" Lady Catherine flicked her eyes contemptuously toward Kayleigh once more as if to say she was the cause of St. Bride's inconvenience.

St. Bride was furious, but Kayleigh could see he was anxious to have Straught's message. She prayed he would ignore it, but her heart sank despondently when he turned to her and said, "I've got to go, love. Sit here quietly and talk to no one. I promise I shall be but a minute."

"No, don't go, St. Bride." Shocking even herself, she grasped his hand with both of hers.

Reluctantly, he forced her hands from his. "I won't be long. No harm will come to you this evening."

"No . . . St. Bride, no . . ." Kayleigh's words were useless—he disappeared through the colorful throng with Lady Catherine.

Once alone, she was more anxious than she had ever been before. The crowd, unsavory to begin with, suddenly seemed even more garish and even more drunken. Through the mob she spied Thionville dancing unsteadily with a girl who had to be twenty years his junior. The comte sweated like a swine beneath his Italian velvet.

Kayleigh turned, only to see a crude replica of a jester's face thrust before her. She jumped from the gruesome visage, only to find it was a papier-mâché mask that a man was holding to disguise his face. But she was not comforted by this discovery, nor was she comforted by the nerve-shattering jangling of bells stitched to the man's curled toes.

"What do you want?" she whispered desperately as the gent came closer. She tried to see if he was her cousin, but he was so well disguised, she couldn't be sure. When he spoke, his voice was high pitched and maniacal. Worse, the jester spoke in rhymes that made no sense at all.

> The rain has let, the moon is full;
> Still there was no lusty pull
> At my heart, till I saw you.
> But will she, will she kiss the Fool?

The jester pushed his grotesque mask further into her face until Kayleigh was forced to move away. She didn't know who this man was, but he sent chills down her spine with every syllable.

> No, don't go! We're not through.
> My kind of fun's only had by two.
> I want love, and I want you—
> But will she, will she kiss the Fool?

The jester tried to follow her into the crowd, but she was too swift. She lost him near the dining hall, then sought out some champagne, hoping it would steady her shaking hands. She had the greatest desire to find St. Bride, for his presence would discourage this mad jester from pursuing her. But she knew she couldn't find him, and if she looked for him, she might end up in some deserted part of the house followed by—

Sensing someone behind her, she spun around.

> Life is mad and life is cruel.
> I have her, but I want you.
> I ask myself, what's fair and true?
> Will she, will she kiss the Fool?

"Oh, please, go away. Please, please!" In her fear she dropped her crystal goblet, but it fell noiselessly to the carpet. She watched the jester approach her, closer and closer, until she could see every paper wrinkle on his hand-held mask. She prayed he would lower the thing so she could see his face, but he wouldn't. He came closer and closer, until she was forced to run as if for her very life.

She ran through the dining hall, ignoring the gasps from the servants. Then she found the *grande salle,* where the ball was in high spirits. She dashed through the throng of merrymakers and sought desperate solitude outside on the humid gallery.

It took her several moments to catch her breath. As the jester had said, the rain had stopped and the moon was full. Kayleigh looked around her in the moonlight to make sure the gallery was empty; she was relieved to see that it was.

She put her arm around one of the chamfered posts as if for security and wondered what to do next. She should find St. Bride—he was the answer to this problem. Without even asking herself why she should look to him for protection, and more strangely, without even once doubting that he would give it to her, she went to seek him out.

That was when she heard the bells.

The slight little jingles seemed to sneak up from behind her, but when she turned around, she saw nothing there. No jester with bells on his curling toes, no madmen pursuing her. Shaking, Kayleigh clung to the post and looked in the other direction—there was no one there either. The gallery was empty. *Empty,* she reassured herself. She was alone.

"Will she, will she kiss the Fool?"

Mouthing a silent cry, she turned once more to find the jester right beside her. In the darkness his mask looked more evil than it had in the light. As it pressed forward, her terror rooted her to the floor. Before she could react, the jester pulled at the strings of her domino to uncover her face.

"Kayleigh," he whispered under his breath.

"No, no! Not you—" she replied as the jester lowered his own mask, and she was face to face with her cousin.

"Kayleigh, don't you see? We can't be rid of each other. We're bound together."

"No! Not true!" she cried, and backed away.

"Yes, that's it. You've caught my friend St. Bride, but I'll make him give you up! You're mine! You're destined to be mine! So be mine, Kayleigh. Come. Be mine." He grabbed at her, but she was unwilling to be taken. In horror she skittered back against the columns, then eluded his grasp and ran for the veranda doors. But there were many doors, and she dreaded running into an empty room only to be followed by her cousin. Terrified, she ducked into the ballroom and stumbled through the dancers until she reached the doors that led out onto the street.

There was no use in searching for St. Bride. She didn't have time for that, nor did she know for certain what St. Bride's reactions would be when dealing with her cousin. She made a dash for the door, but it was ill timed. She collided with a tall woman sheathed in a voluminous vermillion cloak.

At the impact, Kayleigh fell to the ground, and the woman barely kept her balance above her. But the cloak slid off her shoulders, and Kayleigh was enveloped in its damp folds. Yards and yards of the shimmering red satin poured over her hands until she felt she was drowning in it.

But she had to get to her feet! By this time the scene had drawn much attention. Kayleigh made haste to stand, looking warily about for her cousin.

"Excuse me," she whispered, and handed the woman back her cloak. In shock, she saw Straught pushing through the crowd to reach her. Suddenly, another fear took hold of her. From out of the crowd a shrill woman's voice suddenly demanded, "Isn't that the Kestrel?"

"The Kestrel!" another voice shot out.

"Of course! I saw that chit once, stealing on the quay!"

"And at the market she cut my purse!"

"Take her! The comte will be most grateful!" Terrified, Kayleigh backed to the door. The crowd turned into a mob, and she feared they would not leave her until she was swinging from a hangman's noose. Her tearful eyes darted from one angry face to another until she saw St. Bride furiously striding into the ballroom from a cabinet room, an ominous look on his face.

"Don't go, Kayleigh."

Straught reached for her, and terror choked her like a noose. She had to flee. Holding her tear-riddled cheeks, she escaped to the front gallery and felt the cool, sobering night air on her face. Although many a voice cried out for her to stop, she paused for no one. For who would help her? Certainly not the murderer of her sister—nor St. Bride, for he had put her in this terrible situation in the first place.

Forcing herself not to think, Kayleigh's feet touched the silt-ridden bricks of the courtyard. Mud splattered her dress, but she ignored it, desperate to get away from the house and from the mob—and from Straught.

Sobbing, she ran blindly into the night. She didn't know where to go, but she knew she couldn't let Straught find her. She ran through the empty Place d'Armes, then past the quay. She became entangled in a clump of river willows in the batture and grasped one for support. But the young tree wouldn't hold her weight, and she broke down completely. Mindless of the mud and the dark, she clutched at the splindly willow and released great shuddering, fearful sobs.

"Kayleigh," St. Bride called as he caught up to her. "Kayleigh," he repeated in a whisper when he approached her.

"Stay away," she cried, and stumbled through the willows.

"Don't be frightened, little one. They won't hurt you. I won't let them." He stepped closer; his own finery was ruined from running in the muddied streets.

"But I am frightened, St. Bride! I am so frightened! Don't make me go back. I beg you—" She clung to another willow for comfort but was soon enveloped in strong arms that comforted her as nothing ever had. Her sobs became even harder, but there was a silk waistcoat to catch her tears, and a memorable scent that spoke of strength and security.

"My God, what a beast I am," she heard St. Bride chastise himself. A hand stroked her hair, and he whispered harshly, as if berating himself, "My love, forgive me. I should have never forced you to come with me tonight. I should have known it would turn out like this."

"I want to be away from this place, St. Bride. I have to get away!" she cried into his chest.

"I'll take you away. Tonight, I promise." He continued to stroke her hair, and his voice turned steely with conviction. He vowed, "I'll protect you. I'll never put you through such torment again, my love. We'll go to Georgia tonight."

PART TWO

Wolf Island, Georgia Colony

Never yet did Gypsy trace
Smoother lines in Hands or Face;
Venus here doth Saturn move
That you should be Queen of love.

Ben Jonson
"The Gypsies Metamorphosed"

Chapter Twenty

St. Bride's power seemed fantastic to Kayleigh. To be able to command a ship out of port at a moment's notice was not a commoner's practice. But then, Kayleigh thought as she gazed numbly at him, St. Bride Ferringer was not a common man. Even when unshaven and unperfumed, he had a mysterious source of power that seemed to be able to awe most any man. Hadn't Thionville the Terror been compliant and grudgingly respectful in his company? Even the coarse-witted Quinn had known to give St. Bride a wide berth.

But how did her cousin, Sweet Erath, view this man? Kayleigh wondered as she shivered on the sodden half-deck of the *Balcraig*. Did Straught look upon St. Bride with admiration? Or with hatred and fear? Seeing St. Bride now, as he turned from his conversation with the ship's captain and gave her a slow, reassuring grin, Kayleigh prayed it was the latter. Straught was a tremendous adversary even on his own, but together with St. Bride, he would be the end of her.

St. Bride was a man of self-control and her cousin was not; even Straught's fury would be impotent against St. Bride's full, unleashed vengeance. Beneath his veneer of civilization, there was a savageness about him that would leave even powerful men with their mouths slack and their eyes wide. Kayleigh knew that that was what Lady Catherine was attracted to, and during her own encounters with St. Bride, it was what worried her the most.

And now they were going to Georgia, to St. Bride's plantation there. Kayleigh stood quietly in the backdrop of the moonlit ship. She watched the torchères along the Place d'Armes dim and mentally bade Mo Chridhe farewell, saddened that she'd had to leave her wicked little kitten behind. But she was not altogether depressed, for she was going to Georgia willingly. There she would be that much closer to Scotland.

Numbed and overwhelmed by all the emotions that still raged within her, Kayleigh watched the lights of New Orleans fade into the Mississippi. Her thoughts returned to the earlier happenings of the night. The *Balcraig* had been moored at the quay when St. Bride's carriage arrived. A well-tended Scottish merchant ship, like many others, it had come to port illegally to pick up bearskins and pitch destined for France. When the carriage had stopped before its gangway, a tremor of nervousness passed through the crew on the decks. When St. Bride embarked, appearing fierce, protective, and rich, the anxiety only increased.

We must make a strange couple, Kayleigh had thought, feeling the captain's stare upon them. Pale, tattered, and muddy, she had ventured up the gangplank, allowing St. Bride's hand to ride her back as he walked behind her.

Although it was midnight, St. Bride had produced some mysterious vellum papers. The high-strung Captain Buckley had relaxed upon seeing that they were not from the magistrate, but he had scowled when St. Bride told him to set sail. He complained bitterly that some of his crew would be left in New Orleans, unforewarned that the ship was making a hasty departure. Yet St. Bride stood firm, informing him that he and his crew would be well compensated for any inconvenience. Despite the protest, the *Balcraig's* captain finally obeyed. Kayleigh had almost come to expect obedience to St. Bride, yet still she turned to him questioningly.

But he refused to comment. Instead, he took off his satin topcoat and enveloped her in it. The summer night was hardly cool, but the moon had come from behind the clouds, and unbeknownst to her, the collar reflected a wealthy gleam. Pulling the coat around her neck, Kayleigh inhaled the familiar scent it emanated, but she also noticed the eyes of the crew following her greedily as she and St. Bride moved about the deck.

However, she was thankful that the crew hadn't time for further appraisal. St. Bride shot them a warning scowl, and the captain yelled orders to unfurl the sails. When stars appeared full in the midnight sky, the *Balcraig* was on its way.

As they pulled away from the moorings, Kayleigh stood at the rail feeling as drained as she had ever felt in her life. But there was a small joy, too, as the ship skimmed through the muddy waters of the Mississippi. She was leaving! And she was determined that wherever her future took her, she would never return.

She was so deep in her thoughts, she hardly felt St. Bride's hand go around her waist. Her mind was too full to seek sleep, and St. Bride seemed content to stand there with her in the quiet of the night. They watched the blackness of the swamps meld with the gray sandiness of the coastline. Not until they passed English Turn did St. Bride speak.

"I've arranged cabins. The trip will take a couple of weeks."

"I see," she said slowly.

She fingered her silver collar, and his eyes took on a shadow of guilt.

"I promised to take you away, love, and so I have. But you must know now that I can't stay in Georgia with you. I'll have to return here right away. The poppies, you understand."

"And Mr. Straught, too, I presume." She couldn't meet his eye and looked away.

"Yes, Straught most of all." His eyes lightened. "But that should be nothing to you. As soon as Straught and I conclude our business in August, I'll return to Wolf Island."

"Wolf Island—is that what your home is called?" She tried to sound lighthearted, but she was too overwrought. Her voice cracked. When St. Bride didn't answer, she continued aloud, "Wolf Island. It sounds quite dangerous. How appropriate."

"Kayleigh, it's near sunrise. You've had a long night. I think we should both retire and get some sleep."

"What cabin do I sleep in?" She bit her trembling lip and looked out onto the black river waters. She was waiting for St. Bride to utter the word, *mine*. But the word never came.

"Every cabin on this ship is yours for the taking. You're free to choose whichever one you desire."

She looked at him. His mouth was set, and his face was grim. As he towered above her, she was engulfed with apprehension. She was indebted to him—this man who looked down upon her with a searching gaze. He'd saved her life, clothed her, fed her, and sheltered her. Now he was taking her away, and if luck were kind, perhaps she would find her way back to Mhor. But still her heart was heavy. In a nervous gesture she fingered the heavy silver collar.

He had every right to take her now, she knew. She was living like his mistress, accepting his charity—and yet he had none of the benefits of such a relationship. If anything, she was a burden to him, chock full of problems and vices. If only she could pay St. Bride back with gold and silver, and not with her flesh.

Self-consciously, her fingers lowered from her neck and she caught her lower lip with her teeth. If she gave herself to St. Bride, would he love her in return? Or would he purchase her cooperation with jewels, silks, and satins as he would a prostitute's?

But she already knew the answer to that question. Without his love, submitting to him would turn her heart brittle and hard.

"Good night, St. Bride," she finally said, handing him back his topcoat. She paused in her ruined white damask and whispered softly, out of his hearing, "Sleep well, my love."

The trip to Wolf Island took many days. It grew hotter as they sailed by the Florida peninsula. But the ship, in contrast to the *Deepwater* which had brought her and Bardolph's passage one year hence, was vastly luxurious.

Kayleigh and St. Bride were the only passengers. During the day, St. Bride pointed out the various ports they passed: Fort Biloxi, St. Augustine, and finally Savannah. At night they dined on silver trenchers with Captain Buckley. But not once did St. Bride approach her for anything other than conversation and companionship. He still seemed remorseful for forcing her to the Thionville ball. And if it were possible, it seemed to Kayleigh almost as if she and St. Bride had started anew. Aboard the *Balcraig* there were no cutpurses, no spies, no worries. There was simply blue water and blue sky. During the days, they watched the porpoises dive alongside the ship. And during the nights, after she'd finally confessed her knowledge of letters, they read to each other, seeking the small print of Captain Buckley's dry religious volumes by the light of one precious candle.

But the *Balcraig* traveled quickly, for the hold was empty and the ship was light. Then—woefully, it seemed to Kayleigh—one day she woke up and found they were in port.

Georgia was not as she'd imagined. Nowhere were there the primitive, old-fashioned houses of New Orleans. Savannah homes were built in the English taste, with center hallways and Palladian windows. Ladies walked about in tiny straw hats and enormous hoops—even their maids wore hoops underneath their flaxen petticoats. Next to them, Kayleigh felt positively shabby in the worn spruce gown that Captain

Buckley had taken from his coffers and sold at a hefty price to St. Bride. But the Savannah ladies were a cheerful sight indeed in their jonquil satins and hyacinth brocades, and Kayleigh watched them avidly.

She noted, too, that Georgia gentlemen, unlike their Louisiana counterparts, strutted the streets, chivalrously showing a leg to the passersby instead of searching for whores all day and all night in drunken stupors. Savannah was a welcome change and Kayleigh renewed her vow that she would never return to Louisiana of her own free will.

"How do you find Savannah, Kayleigh?" St. Bride asked as their carriage rolled through the streets.

"I find it civilized," she replied, taking in every detail of the grand houses.

"Civilized? I once thought it the epitome of primitive living," St. Bride remarked, watching the morning sun rise higher over the spiky palmettos and amber sea grass that grew on the outskirts of town.

"But now?" She turned to him, the salt marshes not capturing her interest as the city hand.

"Now I think New Orleans suits my taste better." There was an odd smile to his eyes. "The wilder, the better."

"Nay, not I. I've had my fill of savage existence," she responded, thinking of Bardolph, Straught, and Quinn.

"Then I shall make sure to play the gentleman"—he smiled, then leaned forward and cupped her chin—"to a point."

Chapter Twenty-one

Their hired carriage took them only as far as the Ogeechee River. There St. Bride procured the pair of matched bays that had been tied to the rear of the hack. It was astride them that they continued the journey. Her mount was a mare called Diana, fitted with a sidesaddle, while St. Bride took the stronger of the pair, an animal astutely named Ganymede. Once they were seated, the driver headed back to Savannah, his pockets pleasantly lined with silver, and Kayleigh and St. Bride were ferried across the river.

"Why didn't the carriage take us the entire way?" Kayleigh asked, once they were on the other bank. She was having a difficult time riding Diana along the soggy road, for she spent most of her energy looking at her surroundings. The fading sun hardly penetrated the murky pools of black water that filled the roadside. She shivered. But then, the huge creepers didn't exactly add lightness and gaiety to the atmosphere as they clung to the roots of enormous cypress trees like a drapery of dying snakes. Since she possessed a healthy Gaelic fear of places as dank and dreary as the Georgia swamps, she prayed they would be out of the place by nightfall.

"The dock has yet to be completed in Darien; otherwise I would have bidden Captain Buckley take us directly there,"

St. Bride explained. "But on the roads ahead, love, you'll see that a carriage would have been more of a torture than a comfort. We hadn't much baggage, so I didn't see the point of making—''

He reined in Ganymede. Kayleigh followed his gaze and saw two men ahead of them on a new road built solely of logs.

To Kayleigh, neither man seemed even remotely human. The first appeared to be an idiot, as big as the cypresses that grew around him. As she looked at him, his misshapen face and split brows skewed into a grin, acknowledging their presence. Her heart beat wildly as she turned to the second man. He was so tall and so excruciatingly thin as to look like a splinter. He acknowledged her not with a smile but with a look that made her freeze in her tracks. She looked to St. Bride and found that he had raised a musket to the two men. When they had changed modes of transport at the Ogeechee, Kayleigh remembered seeing St. Bride load the thing and strap it to the back of his saddle. But never had she imagined he might use it on another human being.

"Who are they?" she whispered, as her heart leaped to her throat and the Splinter turned his shifty eyes to her again.

"Some call them Pinelanders"—St. Bride's eyes turned a startling shade of turquoise—"men who have forsaken civilization to prey upon helpless travelers." His eyes flickered at her collar. He twisted uneasily in his saddle and continued, "They're from the pine barrens south of here. They've wandered farther from home than I would have thought, but perhaps the Pinelanders are here now too. It's almost a year since I've been here."

A year? She would have pondered that incongruous remark had St. Bride not suddenly cocked the musket.

"Move on!" he shouted, looking down the barrel of the gun. "We want no trouble with you."

"We want no trouble with you, sir," the Splinter shouted to them in mild Irish. "We've stopped to admire your pretty wife." He smiled then, showing what teeth he had left. Feeling the man's loathsome stare upon her, Kayleigh backed Diana next to St. Bride. Shivers ran down her spine, and she noticed that the sun was already dimming over the bleak landscape. She certainly didn't want to be caught with these two after sundown.

"Come, Kayleigh, we'll pass them," St. Bride instructed her.

"Aye," she whispered, and nudged Diana closer to Ganymede. St. Bride seemed to have the same worries about the lateness of the day. Their only alternative was to get beyond the two men and make their way out of the swamps.

"We've only a short way to go before we get to Rackrent's inn. Can you handle Diana?" he asked gruffly before they made their first steps forward. Mutely, Kayleigh nodded and followed his lead, wishing she could repel the stare coming from the Splinter.

The Pinelanders let them be, most likely due to the musket aimed at their skulls. They were able to move on, St. Bride assuring her that it was doubtful that they possessed horses with which to follow them.

Taking one last glance back, Kayleigh shuddered at the horrible grin from the idiot. She hoped fervently that they'd have no more meetings with these Pinelanders. When she turned forward again, her hallowed vision of Savannah had been tarnished by the degradation of those individuals.

"Old Rackrent's is coming up!" St. Bride called back to her later. Kayleigh acknowledged him with a nod. She had discovered that his earlier claim of the unworthiness of carriages in the roads ahead was true. Ever since they'd been on what St. Bride called a corduroy road, she'd not even been able to ask him about the Pinelanders. The road appeared to be the only means of traveling through the sodden fareways, and the bumps and slips on Diana's back were as disruptive as they were tiresome. All conversation stopped as soon as they gained ground over the logs. Soon, however, she did believe that her ride on Diana was mild in comparison to how a ride in even the best-sprung of vehicles would have been. That would have been grievous physical tumult indeed, she thought to herself, and she was grudgingly grateful to St. Bride. Although she'd first thought he'd insulted her by forcing her to ride to his island, she could now understand that he had made the far more humane—if less chivalrous—choice of travel.

They arrived at the inn just before the last sunbeams withered in the swamps. As Kayleigh made to dismount Diana, she groaned inwardly. She hadn't been on such a hard ride since she'd left Mhor, and now every muscle from her waist down felt tight and brittle. She took a long time to leave the saddle, although St. Bride helped her down. She let him go on ahead toward the small weathered-clapboard building. With her aching flanks she was not at all disappointed at the inn's apparent lack of comforts. She was too tired to care.

"Rackrent! Rackrent!" St. Bride called out as they entered the small public room of the inn. The crowd inside was sparse—a family of four and three young men who looked so alike, Kayleigh assumed they were brothers. She had little time to further analyze the surroundings, for a man, jolly and rotund, came around a partition in the back, laughing like a banshee.

"Ah, I don't be believing it! It's the noble man, St. Bride! How Georgia's missed you!" Rackrent grabbed St. Bride's hand and shook it vigorously. Then he turn to Kayleigh.

"Have you married, man?" A heavy Irish lilt was present in Rackrent's speech but it was so different from that of the wretched Pinelander's, she couldn't hold the comparison.

"This is Kayleigh." St. Bride nodded to her and though she attributed the vision to fatigue, she almost swore there was a tenderness at the corners of his lips when he smiled. But when St. Bride turned to make the innkeeper's introduction, he became pleasantly sarcastic. "Kayleigh, this is William Rackrent, the tightest coin-pincher this side of Savannah."

"Ah, you wound me, son! And right here, even before I've collected my night's due from the patrons!" Rackrent rolled his eyes, but his amusement shone through.

St. Bride laughed and led Kayleigh to a crude, solid bench, where she sat down very slowly. St. Bride took the seat next to her. His thigh met with her own, and though they were miles away from any kind of civilization, she felt strangely secure.

Ale was poured to all the men, and Kayleigh was given a strong cup of tea. As she relaxed and sipped from her mug, she eyed the other patrons. Soon her gaze fell upon the little family that sat on the other end of the trestle. The man was counting his coins while his wife and two little girls sat in silence.

Sobered, Kayleigh looked down at her rice and bacon that Rackrent was putting before her.

"Their name's Storrowton. They just lost their farm. Heading back up north, heard tell," Rackrent said quietly, reading her thoughts.

"Then they've been blessed with good sense," St. Bride stated, having noticed the family also.

"Why do you say that?" she asked.

"They could have wandered to the Pine Barrens."

"The two men in the swamps today were hardly—"

He interrupted her. "Their ancestors came down here, too, just like the Storrowtons. They had hoped to farm, but, no doubt, found they couldn't since they hadn't the money to own slaves and those few white men they found to hire were, most likely, too proud to do manual work. Some men find it degrading to work with their hands. You see, they equate that with slave labor."

"They themselves could till the fields, like any good farmer," Kayleigh retorted, thinking of how hard the farming families at Mhor had worked.

"The Pinelanders long ago gave up farming, finding squatting and stealing preferable to working their own fields like a black man.''

"But, St. Bride, at Belle Chasse I saw you in the fields, directing the slaves alongside Laban. Why are you not like the rest?'' She shifted her sore bottom and waited for his answer.

"Because people are not always as they seem.'' He took one last gulp of his ale and watched her closely.

But all she could do was agree in a small, distrustful voice, "Aye, how true.''

"You and the wife, are you going to take the loft?'' Rackrent pulled up a place at the board and made a jovial interruption.

"We will have the loft, Rackrent, but I'm afraid Kayleigh is not my wife.'' St. Bride corrected the mistake.

"Not your wife?'' Rackrent seemed truly amazed. "I cannot believe it! We get the gossip from Savannah, St. Bride and we hear of your conquests and all the women you've made so angry. I've heard tell you won't even commit to a mistress, so particular you are. So I just knew Kayleigh had to be your wife—'' Suddenly, realizing how he must sound, he abruptly stopped and turned apologetic eyes to Kayleigh. "Dear me, I am sorry, love!'' He looked around his primitive inn and ended sheepishly, "You know, you live like this for so many years, ma'am, you turn crude on yourself.''

"Your apology is accepted, Mr. Rackrent,'' Kayleigh answered quietly, knowing that her cheeks had to be flame red. In spite of her embarrassment, she did claim some of her blush was due to amazement herself. Particular? St. Bride? That she refused to believe, considering how unruly his behavior was when she was around. She thought of that one night at Belle Chasse when he had seemed drunk on brandy and he had kissed her forehead and lifted her gown and caressed her. . . .

Rackrent's voice intruded upon her thoughts. He was shaking his head and speaking uneasily. "Ah, St. Bride, I've me rules. Though you've your position and all ..." The innkeeper's voice trailed off in indecision.

"I shall stay with Mrs. Storrowton and her girls." Kayleigh suddenly felt nervous. St. Bride had been the perfect gentleman on this trip. Was it here, in this strange, forsaken place that he had reached his boundaries?

"You will stay with me in the loft," St. Bride stated. Though his face looked relaxed, his eyes told her to obey.

"But Mr. Rackrent has rules," she whispered.

"And only for men like St. Bride will they be broken." Rackrent suddenly stood up as if he were more uneasy about causing a rift between her and St. Bride than worried over his rules of the house. "You may have the loft, St. Bride. If you weren't so high and mighty ..." He sighed and turned to Kayleigh with a commiserative grin. "Love, you'd better watch yourself with this one. He could charm that necklace right out from under your nose, and you'd be none the wiser." He then went to fetch more ale for the trappers.

When they were left alone, Kayleigh said under her breath, "St. Bride, I won't stay in the loft with you even if I have to sleep outside. How could you make such a public display? Are you afraid I might run off with the Storrowtons unless you keep me bound to your side?"

"The thought hadn't even occurred to me. Especially seeing the Storrowton clan, I doubt you could get far enough away for me not to catch you." He nonchalantly finished off the ale in his tankard.

"Well, I will not share a room with you." She crossed her arms in front of her chest and scowled. No, she wouldn't share a room with him, she vowed. And if she were to do that, he'd have to come up with a pretty good reason for it.

"It's not safe for you to stay in this tiny inn with just another woman, Kayleigh. There are only two rooms and the loft. How secure do you think that is?"

"Mr. Storrowton has no such qualms."

"Mr. Storrowton didn't run into the Pinelanders today.

And Mrs. Storrowton is not quite so alluring." As he spoke, his eyes swept her face and then paused suggestively at a point below her chin.

The sapphire necklace. Was that her only allure? Suddenly angry, she demanded, "Then take what you value most so tonight I may stay with Mrs. Storrowton." She turned her back to him and presented her neck. She held her hair away from the mysterious clasp and she waited, aching to feel his fingers finally pull the wretched thing off.

But she was granted no such pleasure. When St. Bride refused to comply, she faced him in mute frustration. But he only said, "You're mistaken, love, if you think that necklace is what I value most."

"If you value me more, then take it off anyway," she said softly. "You know how it angers me."

"Take it off just so you may steal it from me in the dead of night? I think not. I'll let it remain, so that I can keep an eye on both you and it."

"Nathrach!" she burst out in Gaelic. Suddenly she stood up, unable to bear his presence for another second. Ignoring the pain that shot through her inner thighs, she walked away.

"Where are you going?" St. Bride demanded gruffly.

"It's of a personal nature!"

"Take Mrs. Storrowton with you, Kayleigh, or you'll be bound to take me." He stood and grabbed her hand.

"St. Bride!" she gasped, blushing to the tips of her toes. She was surely not going to have him around to see her in all her glory doing that!

"I mean it, Kayleigh. This little inn has few luxuries, and Rackrent's only 'convenience' is outside at the end of the path. If Mrs. Storrowton can't accompany you, then I shall—"

"That won't be necessary." Gathering as much dignity as she could, she walked stiffly to the end of the board and sought out Mrs. Storrowton.

Mrs. Storrowton treated her request kindly. Kayleigh had

to fight off her embarrassment to even ask her, but she was soon warming to the young wife.

But before Mrs. Storrowton, her daughters Eugenia and Charlotte, and Kayleigh could begin their little excursion, St. Bride took Kayleigh aside and warned in a hushed voice, "Leave the back door of the inn open. It's a dark night out there." Kayleigh nodded her head and then followed Mrs. Storrowton out the door behind the partition.

"He's a good man, your Mr. Ferringer, is he not?" Mrs. Storrowton held on to her little girl's hands and they made their way down the path. The light from the back door to the inn illuminated their way, but ahead, the rutted path turned, and beyond that Kayleigh could see only darkness. The small candle she held was pitiful against the overwhelming blackness of the night. Suddenly she was glad St. Bride had insisted she take Mrs. Storrowton with her. The night woods were damp and heavy all around them. And she had to fight off the prickle of fear that ran down her scalp. She felt as if she were being watched.

"St. Bride can be quite like quicksilver in his moods." Kayleigh smiled dismally, her frustration showing all too clearly.

"But he cares so greatly for you. Look how cautious he is."

"It's the necklace that causes him to be so overbearing." Kayleigh clutched Eugenia's arm tightly when the little girl stumbled over a thick root in the path.

"Your necklace is truly beautiful. But that's not what he holds dear when he looks at you." Mrs. Storrowton gave her a knowledgeable smile. Kayleigh didn't know what to make of Mrs. Storrowton's answer, but before she could reply, the young wife was already speaking again. "So you're to be mistress of Wolf Island. Mr. and I have heard of it, of course. But never did we imagine we would meet the illustrious master himself. How long have you been married, Kayleigh?"

The question caught Kayleigh offguard and it was her turn

to stumble over the path. "I'm not married, Mrs. Storrowton." Her words came out low and shameful.

"I see." Mrs. Storrowton became very quiet but Kayleigh felt a rush of relief when the pretty young wife continued. "I'm sorry. The necklace and all, I had assumed . . . but this is all my fault. Mr. Rackrent told us that you and Mr. Ferringer had procured your own quarters."

"We're not . . ." *Lovers.* Kayleigh was about to say the word, and then found she couldn't. It was the truth, but she knew the circumstances would make her look like a liar.

"The nobility still has its ways, I suppose. I'm just glad for these colonies, where at least men have become more equal." Mrs. Storrowton stopped by the convenience. It was a weathered shanty hardly worthy of the name *building,* for it looked like it would collapse at any moment. But Kayleigh wasn't looking at the convenience. She was wondering why Mrs. Storrowton thought St. Bride was a nobleman. And hadn't Mr. Rackrent called him such when they first arrived? Kayleigh had thought he had meant a *noble man.* But had he meant *nobleman?*

"Mrs. Storrowton, why—?" Before she could ask the question, she was interrupted.

"Please go first, Kayleigh. Charlotte and Eugenia do take good time, and I wouldn't want the men coming to look for us for their dawdling." Mrs. Storrowton grasped each girl's hand. Looking about the black woods, Kayleigh complied, holding her question for the return trip.

Despite her stiffness, she was through quickly, and she helped the two girls into the small shanty. There wasn't room for the four of them, so Kayleigh stepped out, handing Mrs. Storrowton their lone candle, and shutting the door behind them to give them their privacy.

Dhe! but the woods were ghastly at this time of night. Kayleigh glanced uneasily around her, but she could see nothing without the candle. Not daring to venture from the door, she kept her back to it and tried very hard not to look frightened. This was difficult, however, when all around her the night creatures whispered in the dark. The cicadas shrilled, and owls hooted, and in the background the leaves whispered in the soft night air. "Blue," it seemed to say, and repeated itself again and again.

But soon the whispering grew louder, and Kayleigh began to worry that it was not a product of nature. It came closer and became more articulate. She could hear Mrs. Storrowton fussing with the girls, but she hesitated to call out lest the sounds were in her imagination. Yet, the whispers persisted and she found herself shrinking back against the door.

"Pretty Blue, marry me, marry me, come marry me." A breeze picked up and the branches of a dead juniper tree nearby shook its withered fingers at her. Was she truly hearing these words, or were they only the breeze? Kayleigh was suddenly determined not to find out. She turned and raised her hand to knock on the door. It was better that they return to the inn. But before she could knock she felt spindly fingers on her arm. Fear made her throat constrict. She fought to turn around, hoping that what she felt on her flesh was only the branches of the dead juniper.

But she couldn't move. The whisper came to her ear. "Marry me, Blue, marry me, marry me." Moaning, Kayleigh knew whoever spoke had nothing so honorable as marriage in his mind. She felt herself being pulled back, away from the shanty door, and instinctively her hand went down to reach for her *sgian dhu*. But her garters now held nothing but white silk stockings. Then her voice came back to her and she shrieked through the silence of the woods. At that, the fingers retreated back into the darkness.

She spun around, expecting to see the Pinelander, the thin one she had thought of as "the splinter," gazing down at her with his muddy eyes. But there was nothing there, just the dead branches of the juniper weaving themselves in her clothing and hair until she had to claw herself free. Turning, she found Mrs. Storrowton standing in the open door of the shanty, the candlelight framing her deathly white face.

"My God, what is the matter?" she asked, but Kayleigh refused to explain. She doused the candle flame and then, grabbing Charlotte, for Eugenia was already in the arms of her mother, she gasped, "I don't know! Let's run!"

The women flew along the path and before Kayleigh knew it, they were back at the inn. Mr. Storrowton took Charlotte from her arms and St. Bride tried to still her own shaking hands. Even the trappers were up at arms, all having heard her cry.

"What happened?" St. Bride's eyes fairly blazed at the women.

But Kayleigh couldn't answer him. Instead, she trembled and looked about the common room, desperate to take in all its warmth and security. Mr. Rackrent anxiously pulled at his hair until he looked like an old mangy lion, and Eugenia and Charlotte were being coaxed not to cry while their mother collected her harried wits.

"Kayleigh screamed while we were indisposed," Mrs. Storrowton burst out. "Dear Lord, something surely frightened her!"

"What was it?" St. Bride sat Kayleigh on the bench and stroked her hair where the juniper had snared it.

"I don't know," she answered truthfully. "Something grabbed me. I thought it might have been one of those Pine-landers we saw, but I turned around . . ." She shook her head. "Perhaps it was nothing. Perhaps I've frightened everyone for nothing."

"It's all right, love. Go on up to the loft. I'll join you shortly. I'll bring thread and a needle so you may mend your dress."

"My dress?" She looked down at the huge rent in her shoulder. Had long, cold fingers torn at her clothing, or had it simply been the catch of a juniper branch? She put her hand to her mouth and shuddered.

"Go on, love." St. Bride handed her a candle. He cocked an eyebrow to Rackrent, which the older man acknowledged by nodding his head twice. With this mysterious exchange, Kayleigh apologized to the Storrowtons for frightening them, nodded good night, and stiffly ascended the staircase to the loftroom.

The loft was an old juxtaposition of primitive and civilized living. The overhead beams had not even been stripped of their bark, nor had the boarded walls been whitewashed. But nonetheless there was a clean bed with a mattress stuffed generously with moss. Most surprising was a yellow crewel-worked wing chair that sat near the window. Anxious to ease her aching, saddlesore flanks, Kayleigh claimed the chair immediately, then studied the tear in her shoulder and tried to figure out the best way to mend it.

"Rackrent sent these up to you." St. Bride entered the loft and laid some black thread and a crude steel needle next to the chair. "He wanted to know if you want some laudanum to calm your nerves. I find the stuff vile, but if you think it necessary . . ." His face appeared drawn until Kayleigh resolutely shook her head.

"No, thank you. I just want to forget the entire episode. I'm sure it was all in my imagination." Uneasily, she picked up the sewing implements and paused. She would have to remove her dress to repair it. There was no helping it, so she walked behind the wing chair and allowed the gown to drop to her feet. To retain some modesty, she turned the chair around. Clad only in her shift and stays, she began sewing the dress she'd been given on the *Balcraig,* permitting St. Bride a view only of her profile.

But even her profile seemed to enchant him. He had stripped down to the buckskin breeches he had bought from a sailor on the *Balcraig* and leaned back on the bed, rubbing his naked hair-sprinkled chest. When her gaze flickered over to him, she noted that he'd placed a pistol on the table next to him. She noted, too, that he relaxed in near darkness, for all the available candlelight was on her and her task.

Kayleigh felt his eyes on her, but she tried to keep her mind on her sewing. She had only two gowns, and she didn't want them to look like rags quite yet. Carefully making the tiny embroidery stitches she had learned from her mother, she took great pains to ignore his stare. But that task was more impossible than the one in her hands. St. Bride's eyes took in every aspect of her profile, from the way her thick, dark lashes wavered over each stitch to the way her lips, moist and generous, were parted ever so slightly in concentration. His gaze then moved downward, skimming over her bejeweled alabaster neck to rest on the soft mauve satin of her stays. In the candlelight her legs were visible through the sheerness of her shift. Finally she felt his gaze rove down her rich thighs until they stopped at her stocking-clad ankles, slim yet still bearing the scars of her previous life on the streets.

Unable to bear another perusal, she turned to him and asked, "Why do you stare so? What are you thinking of?"

"You really want to know?" He narrowed his eyes and smiled like a heathen.

"No." She returned to stitching, and her hand shook, although she tried to control it.

"I'll tell you one thing, love, that's more appropriate for your infernal modesty." He propped himself up on his hand. "I was thinking of a girl."

"Lady Catherine?" Kayleigh stabbed the heavy linen with her needle.

"No. This particular girl stole a blue thimble. When I asked her about it, she denied that she'd stolen it, for why would she need a thimble when she could not 'sew whatever,' I think her words were."

Kayleigh dropped her hands over the exacting, damning stitches.

"Yet another puzzle to solve. Would you like to do the

honors this time? Or will you leave it up to me as you have in the past?"

"St. Bride . . ." She took a deep breath. Did she trust him yet? Eyeing him warily, she took in his broad shoulders and the grid of supple muscle that ran along his belly until it disappeared in the waist of his buckskins. No. She turned away. When he looked like that, she didn't trust him at all.

"So you can read and sew and—what else?" He rolled onto his back and laughed. "I can't wait to see the other talents you hide so well . . . my lady."

"You!" She finished her task with a vengeance and pulled her dress back on. Stepping to the washstand, she sloshed water from an earthenware pitcher into a wooden bowl and angrily scrubbed her face with a mean silver of lye soap. Then she took a towel from the stand and wiped the rinse water from her eyes.

Placing the used linen next to the stand, she was suddenly struck by the towel's pristine quality. Any frayed edges had been meticulously mended, and it was as white and clean as the linen at Belle Chasse.

"Is Mr. Rackrent married, St. Bride? I find it odd that we have not met a wife." She held out the used towel. "For surely a wife cares for such things, rather than a bachelor out in the wilds."

"Old Rackrent has a squaw. I believe she's an Orcoquisac." St. Bride watched for her reaction.

"You mean she . . . ?" Kayleigh looked at the towel, so lovingly mended and cleaned. Suddenly she blushed. It was difficult to picture old Rackrent, a man old enough to be her grandfather, with an Indian woman. To cover her bemusement, she added quickly, "How often does she . . . ah . . . work for him?"

"She comes whenever there are no guests. She cleans for him"—he paused for the words—"and gives him companionship. I've met her once or twice, but generally when there are guests Rackrent bids her stay with her family, especially when there are female visitors in the inn. I suppose he's afraid of what they might think.''

"It must be awkward to form such a liaison. Particularly when the two parties are so very different." Suddenly Mrs. Storrowton's talk, alluding to St. Bride's possessing a title, came to Kayleigh's mind. "Mrs. Storrowton said something odd while we were going along the path this evening."

"What is that?" he asked, stiffening imperceptibly.

"First she asked how long we had been married." She colored and shot him an accusatory look. "When I told her she was mistaken, she tossed off the awkward moment by saying something about the ways of the nobility."

"The nobility," he scoffed under his breath. "What would you think if I told you I was a nobleman, Kayleigh? Would that endear me to you, perhaps?"

"Nay, I wouldn't like it by half to find out you have a title."

"And why is that? Most women would prefer one."

"Not I. Men have too much power as it is. They needn't have invented titles to wield it." She could hardly hide the bitterness in her voice.

"Come, let's sleep. It's still a day's ride to Wolf Island," he said tightly.

"Have you a title, St. Bride?"

"I'm a plantation owner. That's all I really am, because that's all I want to be. Now come to bed," he told her.

"I heard Mrs. Storrowton correctly, St. Bride. She knew all about your plantation, and if I recall, even Mr. Rackrent had the same idea in his head. He thinks you quite above anyone else that comes by here."

"You've misinterpreted their talk. I am known in this place, but merely because of Wolf Island. If they've led you to believe otherwise, as I said before, they were mistaken."

"But—"

"Enough. Prying's not healthy, Kayleigh. For anyone."

His voice was as harsh as the roads they had traveled. "Now come to bed. We both need to rest."

But she refused. Instead, she went to the wing chair and stared belligerently at the flickering, dying flame of their candle. Once again she was reminded of the wit and charm that St. Bride wore like a cloak. And like a cloak, it seemed to be used to hide something.

She turned to him and looked into his eyes, which glittered in the shadows. She felt as she had the time she found the note on Laban's door or, worse, as she had that horrible night he'd given her the scarlet stays. She wondered if at times she was too quick to rationalize away whatever menace he presented to her. If so, would it cost her dearly in the end? At this last thought, however, she had the strange realization that she really longed to trust him, that at times she almost ached to run into the circle of his strong arms.

But then, she thought with a darkening brow, it was times like this that kept her from doing just that.

"Kayleigh, come along," he whispered to her.

"I'll be sleeping here." She stood her ground. She couldn't trust him, she daren't trust him. She found it absurd that she had spent weeks in his company yet didn't even know for sure who he really was. It was disconcerting, and she studied him with anxious blue eyes.

But this only exasperated him. "You may sleep in your clothing, you may even sleep on your head if that is what you prefer. But you will not sleep near the open window, nor near the door, which has no lock. Would you have a repeat of this evening? It can happen, you know. Rackrent's inn isn't a fortress."

She frowned as the candle sputtered in its grave of melted wax.

"So come to bed," he beckoned. "I think you'll find it preferable to the floor, and although you may doubt it, I can control myself for one night. Perhaps not forever, I give you fair warning—but for this one night, if you desire to sleep in celibacy, I will grant you that wish.''

Kayleigh watched the flame go out. In near darkness she was reminded of the whispers she had heard near the convenience. Suddenly, even taking St. Bride on in Rackrent's little rope bed seemed preferable to being alone. After several long moments of indecision, she stole over to the bed and slid quietly down next to him. She felt an irrational hope that some miracle had occurred and that St. Bride had been overcome with slumber while she had reckoned with herself in the wing chair. But the chuckling that came from the bedstead belied her fervent wish.

''What spinsterish ways you have, love!'' With his head propped up on one arm, he studied her shadowed form next to him. ''Would it be too much to ask that you at least remove your shoes before retiring?''

Angrily, she sat up and kicked off her heavy shoes. She laid back down and with one stiff, aching motion presented him her back. Her stays poked her ribs, and her heavy gown was unbearably confining. But she refused to even think about undressing until he was fast asleep.

Only when his breaths became deep and regular, after she had lain next to him in rigid self-control for what seemed an eternity, did she gingerly rise to disrobe. She neatly folded her dress, her stockings, and her stays and put them on the plump wing chair, then went back to the bedstead clad only in her sheer batiste shift. With great care she eased herself back into the linens, not permitting the ropes beneath her to creak.

But in spite of her great pains, she suddenly found herself covered with St. Bride's meaty arm. Next to her, he groaned slightly as if in deep slumber, but whether he was truly asleep or not she couldn't tell. Feeling awkward and ridiculous, she was caught, unable to move for fear of waking him—or worse, if he was already awake, of arousing him.

His heavy arm clung tenaciously to her chest, and she was

sure the rapid beating of her heart was loud enough to wake even old Mr. Rackrent. But soon she felt the day's exhaustion wear upon her. Her stiff, aching body beckoned her to relax, and she finally accepted the possessive arm upon her. She closed her eyes and fell asleep at once.

A large hand, sinewed and strong, covered her mouth. In panic, Kayleigh's eyes flew open, and she struggled in the darkness to see who held her so.

"Not a word, my love. Understand?" St. Bride whispered near her, his scent and warmth reassuring her even though she could not yet make out his face.

As she nodded her compliance, his hand freed her. "What is it?" she gasped.

"Do you hear?"

Not daring even to breathe, Kayleigh detected what was causing St. Bride's concern. A slow, methodical stepfall could be heard coming up the steps to their loft. It was scratchy and unshod, and the closer it came, the more her fingers wound around St. Bride's braw arm.

"What is it?" Her lips trembled.

"Stay there. Don't get out of bed." St. Bride rose with the studied calmness of experience. In dead silence his hand took the pistol that lay on the nightstand beside him. Then, like a nocturnal beast, he probed the darkness, taking note of things that she herself could only guess about.

"I'm frightened. Please . . . please, don't go," she whispered to his back. But St. Bride only gave her hand a squeeze, then began stalking the door.

"Oh . . . please . . . St. Bride . . ." Fear thumped in her breast like the beat of a raven's wing. It was an odd, unnatural fear, for this time it was not fear for herself. This time it was for St. Bride.

Watching him, she threw the covers aside and raised herself to her knees. She didn't want to be left alone. She wanted to go with him. She made a start toward the door, but she was stopped by one turn of his head.

"Oh, St. Bride . . ." She put her palms to her lips, almost as if praying. But her lamentations died in her throat as soon as he opened the batten door. A tall figure lurched from the darkness beyond and attacked St. Bride with all the fury of a maelstrom.

Kneeling on the bedstead, Kayleigh was appalled by her own helplessness. She wanted to help St. Bride, but the men moved so quickly, she couldn't discern who was who. She watched as St. Bride and the phantom figure wrestled for the pistol, but soon both men rolled past the door. When Kayleigh could see them no more, she flung herself off the bed with the intention of finally somehow helping St. Bride. Yet she was hardly across the threshold when a shot fired, and a body could be heard tumbling and bumping lifelessly down the crude stairs.

"*Mo chridhe!* St. Bride!" she cried out, running through the door. Her state of undress was of no concern as she rushed down the steps into the public room. She had to get to St. Bride. She had to!

In the darkness she made out a body slumped at the bottom of the stairs. Crying "*Mo chridhe, mo chridhe*" over and over again, she took several horror-filled steps toward it. Her mind went numb as she bent toward the still figure, but before she could even comprehend what had happened, a candle was lit and Mr. Rackrent was before her, blowing the smoke from a freshly fired pistol.

"Correct, St. Bride! He's a Pinelander all right. And a particularly nasty one to boot. He must have gotten in through one of the windows. But what a shot! I haven't made such a noise since a black bear got into the sugar beets." Rackrent kicked at the pale figure.

Looking down in amazement, Kayleigh saw that it was not St. Bride, as she had feared, but the Splinter. The Pinelander lay facedown on the rough floorboards, dead, hardly bleeding from the wound in his chest. His huge idiot companion sat next to him, rocking himself fearfully in the corner. But the most horrifying thing was the fact that the Pinelander's mouth was contorted into a gruesome smile.

"Don't look. Don't look." St. Bride's welcome touch turned her head away into his chest. Kayleigh felt his breathlessness from his skirmish and, too, she felt the cold metal of his pistol, which was still unfired in his hand.

"I thought it was you!" She felt her eyes welling with unwelcome tears of relief.

"More's the pity then, eh?" He pressed her into his naked front, watching with great amusement as Rackrent instructed the half-asleep Babtiste brothers how to remove the body from the public room.

"Don't say that. Don't say it." She shuddered as the youngest and burliest brother hefted the long, skinny Pinelander onto his shoulder.

"So worried then, were you?" St. Bride's attention was now fully upon her. He studied her, and then with an odd expression on his face he touched a teary lid.

"I . . . I . . ." Unable to find the right words, she pulled him to her, kissing him with a ferocity she hardly knew she possessed. Unmindful of their state of dishabille and of the wistful, awestruck stares of the Babtistes, she refused to part with St. Bride until she was sure he understood every aspect of her relief and newborn concern.

There was almost wariness in his eyes when their lips parted, and Kayleigh stood before him with the same mixed emotions. She had proved more to herself with their kiss than she had to him. She knew that if she allowed herself to continue feeling this way, she would become an inextricable part of him and his strange, dangerous games. Yet she suddenly didn't know if she cared. For an entire year she had been forced to put herself first, behind no one, not even Bardolph. She'd played at self-preservation, and for the most part she'd won. But tonight everything had changed. Her own preservation was no longer the only object in this world. Somehow, tonight the rules had been reversed.

"Go back to the loft, Kayleigh. You're drawing stares." He touched her thin shift and whisked his gaze over to the Babtistes.

"When—?"

"Right away. Let me just speak to Rackrent." He dismissed her. But it was not a cold dismissal; rather, it was an anxious one. Kayleigh nodded and went to the stairs with her own feeling of anxiety. She didn't dare look back.

It was still dark in the loft when St. Bride joined her once again. The public room below had quieted, and given the Babtistes' burliness, Kayleigh figured the Pinelander would be buried by dawn. The ropes creaked as St. Bride's weight came down on the bed.

He reached for her, and this time she let him take her in his arms without protest. "Love? *Mo chridhe*—what does it mean?"

"Would you believe 'black cat'?" She laughed softly, selfconsciously.

"I doubt that's what you were saying when you called my name and tripped down the stairs." He touched her cheek with the back of a hand. The hairs on his wrist teased her senses, and she was aware of how small the physical barriers were between them. With a rip of filmy white batiste and another of rough, saddle-worn buckskin, they would finally be together.

"It's of no consequence. A Gaelic expression of no particular note." She felt his hand ride her hip. The intensity about his movements caused her to look down, and in the graying light of predawn, she watched him slide her shift upward, almost to her derriere.

Obviously filled with no small measure of anticipation, St. Bride nipped at her ear, then kissed her throat until she released a moan. She felt the erotic burn of his light beard move all the way down to her chest. His teeth gently grazed the upper swell of her bosom.

"Come along, tell me. What does *mo chridhe* mean?" he teased.

"It means nothing, truly." She gasped when his fingers pulled at the ties of her shift. One full breast was partly exposed, and he found its peak with his tongue.

"St. Bride," she whispered timidly, her throat so constricted with joy that she could hardly speak.

When she fairly flamed with desire, he grinned against her and demanded, "Tell me, *mo chridhe*, tell me. Can you take much more of this?"

She answered with only a secretive nod, then ran her hands down his warm, well-muscled chest.

"Must I then force the answer out of you, wench?"

Her lips turned up in a seductive smile. When he playfully rolled her beneath him, her laugh was more beautiful than the chime of fine crystal. Though she yearned for his large hand on her breast, it stayed where it was, caressing her slim haunch until she begged it to go further. He finally did delve inward, begging and imploring that she part her thighs. Caught in his slow, methodical madness, she willingly moved to comply. But this time when she moaned, it was not a moan of pleasure.

"Tell me, *mo chridhe,*" he whispered, obviously missing her plight.

"Och, St. Bride. No, I can't—" She suddenly put her hands on his chest to keep him away. The muscles fairly burned in her thighs every time she tried to open her legs. Lovemaking would be impossible like this.

"All right, don't tell me what *mo chridhe* means. I'll call you that anyway. I like the sound of it—on your lips, especially." He moved to kiss, her but she shook her head, fearful of the pain lest they continue.

"No need for a play of maidenly shyness now, love." He grinned, obviously thinking she was teasing.

"No, it's not going to work," she moaned.

"But it is, my love." He pressed himself against her playfully, lustily. "I daresay it always has before."

"Och, St. Bride, you don't understand. I'm not going to work." She bit her lip and tried not to moan again. "I'm too sore. The ride, you see?" She gasped when he rested between her legs.

"What?" He snapped his head up in surprise.

"Oh, please move! I'm sore—the ride today—it was so long!"

"This isn't happening!" He looked at her with an angry frown. "Tell me this isn't happening!"

"I cannot! Oh, please move! I am so sore!"

In a gesture of abject frustration his palm hit the crude headboard. The noise of the wood rocking back and forth was enough to wake the dead. Immediately, he rolled off her. After a few seconds she finally got up the nerve to look at him. He lay on his back, mutely staring at the beamed ceiling. It was a long time before she spoke, for he seemed to be wrestling with something inside himself.

"I'm sorry. In fact, I feel quite foolish."

"I've waited for this, Kayleigh. It's almost killed me, but I thought now the time had come." He closed his eyes as if he were in pain even now.

"But it's been so long since I've ridden a horse as I did today. I cannot help the soreness. I wish that I could—" Her voice cracked, proving that she was not immune to the exquisite, unfulfilled torture that he felt.

"I daresay tomorrow's ride won't ease your sore flanks," he stated blackly.

"No—no, I suppose not." Her eyes sought his in the dark, but to no avail. She felt his kiss upon her mouth in one breathless movement, then he left the bed.

"Stay here with me!" she gasped, not understanding what he was about. *"Mo chridhe,* where are you going?"

"Out," St. Bride clipped. He relaced his breeches and made for the door.

"But what have I done? Are you such an unfeeling brute that you cannot see I was willing? For once, I was willing!"

He paused at the door. He refused even to look at her, as if it would cause him all kinds of unnamed agony to do so. "I'm sure you can't understand this, but having you willing and unable is more torture than even *I* can stand." He paused. "Sleep. We leave in two hours." With that, the door closed soundly behind him, and she heard his footfall on the steps.

Scowling, she eased her sore body back onto the pillows. She fretted and fumed over what had just happened, blaming him for everything from her sore flanks to her frustrated heart. But as she settled further into the bed, she realized that she missed the warm comfort of the crook of his arm. To be in his arms seemed foreign to her, yet more natural than all the thistle and tartan of Inverness.

Her next feeling was of amazement: St. Bride had called her *mo chridhe. Mo chridhe!*

She smiled softly. Did he know those Gaelic words meant "my heart?"

Chapter Twenty-two

Traveling the corduroy roads was madness. Kayleigh grimaced, the muscles of her thighs ripping with each cruel motion of Diana's back. Now as they forged ahead through the pine barrens, she wondered if she was crazed to ever have thought the trip to Wolf Island would be to her gain.

Yet there was still St. Bride. Her thoughts drifted to the night before. The pine barrens sprawled around them, and the hot July wind sang in the green canopy overhead. But she was oblivious to the sound. With a furrow between her smooth brows, she was realizing more and more that St. Bride was a force to be reckoned with. Without coercion, he made her lose control. Her soft lips twisted in wry amusement: even in areas where she had never dreamed she had control. Her body was the first thing he seemed destined to lord over. But the more time they spent together, the more he gained ground with her thoughts too. Was her soul next? Her heart? Och, how could that ever be?

She turned velvety eyes to his sweat-ribboned back. St. Bride had been a beast all day, answering her attempts at conversation with only short, clipped phrases. Finally, talk ceased altogether, and they took the excruciatingly painful ride without uttering a word. Heaving a small sigh, she felt

trickles of perspiration well between her breasts. It was hot
and miserable. How she longed to be cooled by something
other than St. Bride's demeanor!

"We'll dismount at Darien. Then we have to be taken
down the Altamaha River to the Sound." St. Bride finally
spoke in full sentences.

"And then?" She squirmed, wishing fervently that she
were a man and didn't have to cope with the back-wrenching
sidesaddle.

"Then we'll be on Wolf Island." Suddenly his eyes lit up.
"Life is much less complicated there, Kayleigh. I've always
found it so."

"May that be true, St. Bride," she answered softly. But
as she met his gaze and felt again the exhilarating, dangerous
swell of emotion that she'd first felt the night before, she
doubted it.

The moon-silvered waters of the Altamaha Sound carried
them to Wolf Island. Because their arrival was unannounced,
they had to travel to the island in what St. Bride termed an
Oconee box. This was a rough, square barge that later in the
season would be piled high with cotton from the neighboring
plantations. Sea Island cotton fluff clung to her gown and to
her hair, but Kayleigh was so grateful to be off Diana's back
that she was completely mindless of her appearance.

Docking at Wolf Island, St. Bride chose to take the path
along the white sandy beach rather than the bricked house
road. Stumbling along the sand in sore, mute exhaustion,
Kayleigh followed, hoping against hope that they would rest
soon.

However, all sensations of misery seeped from her limbs
as they rounded the last sandy bluff. From there they could
make out the dark Atlantic rolling gently onto the Georgia
coast. A thin crescent moon hung in the sky, looking like
half the silver collar that hung about her neck. In its light
she made her way to the water, whose mystical hold over

her increased as she bent and let it run, cool and frothy, through her fingers.

"It's beautiful, isn't it?" St. Bride's voice came from behind her.

"It's more than beautiful," she whispered.

"What are you thinking about right now?" He stepped near, putting her salty fingers to his lips.

"It's the same water, the same ocean that breaks over the coast of Scotland, is it not?" She looked to the black horizon but saw only the line where midnight blue met jet. Out there was Scotland. Overcome by homesickness, she felt that if she'd had the strength, she would have swum there, so much longing was in her heart.

"Let's get to the house."

"Yes, I'm tired, St. Bride," she said numbly.

"Then I'll give you a rest."

Out of the darkness a gentle hand came to her waist. Together they walked along the beach until the house's cupola could be seen rising from the dunes.

Kayleigh looked upon her life as if she were in a dream: days of sea and sand and sky, and nights of silk, satin, and wine. It was too glorious to be true.

Wolf Island proved a delight. More than that, it was the balm her soul had cried out for that last rainy evening in New Orleans. Gone was her fear of her cousin's malevolence, gone was her fear for her own day-to-day survival.

The first night she'd been given a bedchamber with walls of mint green damask. Along with a splendid cherry fourpost bed, there was a mahogany dressing table; from there she could look at herself to her heart's content in the Flemish mirror above it. As she had stood aghast looking at the splendor of the room, a black house servant named Maddie had seen to it that she was bathed, fed, and altogether pampered until she fell asleep.

Kayleigh was treated as if she were the lady of the house.

No task was too small to be performed for her, no trinket too inconsequential to be obtained for her. She'd even been given a slave named Cooper London who was to look out for her anytime she wandered the coast or had a fancy to row along the Altamaha to view the cotton fields. Being on Wolf Island was like being on holiday, Kayleigh had decided.

There were two things, however, that bothered her.

The first was the fact that on the day after their arrival the slaves had made an unheard-of noise celebrating the return of the master. She had asked Maddie why the slaves missed him so much. Maddie had explained to her that St. Bride had been away from Wolf Island for the better part of a year. Her Georgia planter turned out to be no Georgia planter at all. Maddie told her that St. Bride was not even from Georgia originally. But when Kayleigh asked about his true home-place, the maid shut her mouth, advising her in an infuriatingly impertinent way to "speak with the man for yourself."

The other small blight on her landscape had been the arrival of the dresses. They had come in an assortment of willow trunks and violet-lined paper boxes. Maddie had brought them out one at a time, fluffed them, and heaped them onto the bed.

"So this is what it's like," Kayleigh had murmured to herself and picked up a particularly expensive blue-feather headdress, eyeing the mountain of brocaded gowns, roun-deared caps, damask stays, and batiste shifts, "to be a man's mistress."

"Oh, missus, if they ain't beautiful!" Unpacking a particularly fetching gown of silver gauze, Maddie missed Kayleigh's look of distaste.

"Well, if they ain't," Kayleigh echoed in a bitter tone. St. Bride had been the considerate gentleman. But a week had passed, and he was making it known that he expected her to fulfill the promise of the night at Rackrent's. The feeling of yearning for him welled again in her breast, only this time it was tinged with sadness.

She'd thought a lot about St. Bride in the past week, and she had thought a lot about herself, too, and who she really was. She couldn't deny it any longer—she wanted the security of marriage before she could give herself freely to St. Bride. But men never married their mistresses—even she knew that.

Backing out of the room, she ignored Maddie's cry "Missus! Missus! Don't you be likin' the gowns?" Once in the hallway she knew where she wanted to go. Taking the stairs two at a time, she ascended. She reached the third floor, where St. Bride had his chambers; but she was not going to confront him—not yet, at any rate. Instead, she found the dwarfed door to the right of the paned fanlights at the end of the hall. She opened it and took the winding stairs. In haste she fell into the cushioned seats of the cupola.

It was the only place she could truly be alone. It was the only place where she could think. The house at Wolf Island was far grander than she had imagined. Constructed of clapboards with an unusually heavy broken pediment above the main door, it was an odd and beautiful sight, made more so by its location near the beach. The rooms were endless. There was a drawing room, a library, a morning room. There were servants' rooms and dressing rooms, green bedrooms, blue bedrooms, and yellow bedrooms. But nowhere was there a room to just be alone in—except, as she had found out on her first day of exploration, the cupola.

She looked at the beach. It was midday, and the sun reflected brightly off the white sand. Her eyes skimmed the blue waters beyond, but the horizon offered no solution. How to avoid the inevitable was the question—and how to avoid the desire *not* to avoid the inevitable. Her thoughts slowed in the heat and she focused on the sea, where the waves, untouched by her troubles, kept up their mindless pull at the beach.

As she stared, a figure appeared down below. It was St. Bride, of course, making his way to the beach for his daily swim. Kayleigh had watched him before from a distance taking out his energies on the ocean, a worthy competitor. But she usually watched him from the comfort of the window seat of her own room, not from this wickedly advantageous cupola.

As if he sensed he was being watched, St. Bride lifted his hand to his eyes and turned to view the cupola. Kayleigh ducked and knew she hadn't been seen, but still a small tingle went down her spine as she peeked and watched him search for her. Finally, fascinated, she saw him shrug his powerful shoulders, strip naked, then disappear into the sea.

Time stood still for her as she watched him fight his daily battle with the tide. Back and forth he swam, allowing the water to cool his flexing body while the sun bronzed his skin. When he finally walked out of the sea, his physical exhaustion was apparent, yet still his carriage was proud and his height impressive. From his lean, muscular body the Greeks could have modeled their gods. Yet he was forged not out of cold white marble but of supple coppery flesh and warm, passionate blood.

"Missus! Missus! You be up there, missus?" Maddie's deep voice broke the spell.

"I'm here." Kayleigh turned from the beach and looked down the well of the staircase. Maddie was looking up at her, her hands set disapprovingly on her generous hips.

"You don't be likin' the gowns," Maddie stated. "Whew! What that man gonna say to that!"

"Let St. Bride say what he likes. I never asked for them." Kayleigh set her chin.

"You his little darlin'. Now, why you be actin' like such a child?"

Kayleigh refused to answer. It was absolutely none of Maddie's business. She jerked her head back toward the ocean view; then suddenly a solution came to her. It was a rather cowardly solution, she knew, but if it worked in the end, perhaps it would be worth it.

Maddie let out an overly dramatic sigh over her mistress's

silence. "Well, you jus' walk around 'em then. You jus' go on livin' in that ol' gown you got on. It make no matter to me that I be finer dressed than the missus. Make no matter to me at all." She turned to leave.

"Maddie," Kayleigh hid her eyes and made a play at nonchalance, "could you ask Cooper London to take me to Darien?"

"What you be needin' in Darien? You got all that—"

"Please?" Kayleigh tried to look innocent, but she should have known that nothing would get by Maddie's superior perception.

"You be up to no good, child. I can see it in your wicked blue eyes. What you gonna do?"

"I'm going to Darien with Cooper London—that is, if it's all right with you?" In exasperation, Kayleigh lifted a dark brow.

"That's all right with me, missus. But what that man gonna say when you go an' pull tricks on him!" Maddie thumped down the stairs, shaking her head.

When she was gone, Kayleigh ran down to her bedchamber. Taking three of the finest hats, including the blue-feather headdress, she shoved them into a small willow basket and departed her room without even combing her hair.

An hour later Kayleigh sat in the small craft, which the big black youth, Cooper London, was rowing up the Altamaha River to Darien. The willow basket was an object of great curiosity to the slave, and Kayleigh nervously fingered the weaving, hoping she was doing the right thing. She began hesitantly, "Cooper, I know the master might not tell you of such things, but we're friends, aren't we?"

"Yes, missus." Cooper shot her a winning smile that Kayleigh realized she would miss when she was gone.

"Well, if you would just answer my questions, believe me, you won't have to worry what the master will say, for I shall never speak of it to anyone." She coughed and gave him an imploring look before she began. "I would like to know, first, where St. Bride would buy millinery. You know, hats—those he would buy, that is, for the weaker sex. And next''—she coughed again—''I would like to know where one goes to purchase a voyage out of Darien.'' She hoped she was confusing him enough so that he would just spill out the answers and then promptly forget the conversation.

''Missus, you be all wrong. Your Grace don't mind if I know about such things.'' Cooper rowed as fast as he could, which made his huge sinewy arms glisten with sweat.

''Your Grace? I'm talking about your master.'' She bit her lip and wondered if she was confusing him too much. That certainly wouldn't do.

''Your Grace and the master—they's the same.''

''You call St. Bride Your Grace?'' She was incredulous. The thought made her head swim. Good God, what she suspected just couldn't be true—it would be too awful. ''You don't call him Master? He doesn't have you call him Master?''

''No, missus.''

''But he *is* your master. Why don't you call him that?'' she asked in a desperate attempt to clear up the matter. Somehow, she thought, Cooper had gotten confused. He had to have, for although she'd suspected St. Bride of having a title, she'd had no idea it would be this!

''Pardon my sayin' so, missus, but Your Grace ain't *my* master. He's *the* master. They's a difference.'' He slowed the rhythm of the rowing as they neared the small village of Darien.

''I don't understand any of this, Cooper.''

''Let me tell it to you this way. Did you know they's a place called London? Named just for me, 'way over that ocean.'' He pointed past the Sound. ''I could go there, missus. I could go there and see that place anytime I be wantin' to. That be why they's a difference.''

''What you're telling me is that you're free? St. Bride has given you your freedom?''

''Yes, missus. We's all free at Wolf Island. Ain't no place

we can't go.'' He picked up his speed again, and his oars cut the water as if they were merely batting through air.

"If you can go anyplace you want to, Cooper, why don't you? Especially when there are so many wonderful places to be in this world.'' With pain in her heart, she thought of home.

But Cooper gave a fatalistic shrug. "I guess when you free to go to all them places, you also free to stay right where you be.''

"How true,'' she murmured, feeling the silver collar tightening around her neck in the wet heat of the rowboat.

"Now, where you be wantin' to go, missus? I know all there is 'bout town.'' Cooper smiled again. "And Your Grace be wantin' me to take his darlin' wherever she be wantin' me to take his darlin' wherever she be wantin' to go.''

"He's a duke, isn't he, Cooper? St. Bride is a duke, and that's why you call him Your Grace, isn't it?'' she asked hopelessly.

"Yes, missus, that's why. The master is a duke.''

"A duke,'' she echoed. Her entire world crumbled at her feet. How would she ever fare against that?

Chapter Twenty-three

After giving her more speculative looks than Kayleigh cared to receive, the milliner agreed to exchange the feathery creations for a purse. Eva, the stout Bavarian hatmaker, went into her back room and came out, saying, "Of course, anything for Herr St. Bride." She then dropped a heavy silken weight into Kayleigh's hand and smiled a tight farewell.

"Now we go to the new dock, Cooper." Kayleigh exhaled in relief when she had finally left the ribbon-strewn shop.

"We done already, missus?" Cooper asked, keeping an eye out for any ruffian who might cross their path. It was truly endearing, Kayleigh thought as they walked towards Darien's tiny new wharf. Cooper's loyalty was without question. She only hoped St. Bride possessed enough appreciation for the wiry, handsome black youth.

"Would you be so kind as to allow me to speak with the dockmaster, Cooper? I'll be back with you in a few minutes." She smiled, feeling exalted with the rare jangle of coins in her pocket. Kestrel's tough optimism had returned to her in full force.

"I'll be goin' with you, missus."

"Oh, no, Cooper. You ready the boat. It won't take me but a second."

"I'll be goin' with you, if'n tha's all right with you, missus." Cooper hung his head modestly, but the determined jut of his jaw told Kayleigh that he would hold on to St. Bride's instructions like a bulldog.

Disgruntled, she consented. Was it only a moment ago that she had praised that mindless loyalty? Shaking her head, she followed Cooper to the dockmaster.

Farrell Stalwart was his name, and Kayleigh had only to take one look at that sly, shiftless little man to know he would be a problem. Gathering her wits, she approached him with as much confidence she could muster. After all, she said to herself, once her passage was paid for, what could St. Bride do about it? Noting with satisfaction that Stalwart wore breeches no finer than those of the stevedores lounging in the shade outside the dock hut, it seemed a certainty that he would not refuse her gold.

"St. Bride sent ya here, mum?" Stalwart's words had hardly crawled through his lips before Kayleigh's hopes plummeted. How small this Darien was! It seemed everyone knew her and her connection to St. Bride without her ever having left Wolf Island.

"No, I'm not here on behalf of Mr. Ferringer," she began uneasily, and eyed Cooper standing behind her. The black youth was doing his best not to appear interested, but she could almost see his ears prick at her every word. "Actually, I have my own business to attend. Would you be so kind as to inform me when the first ship—Scotland bound, mind you—will be docking in Darien?" She licked her lips and vaguely wondered what she would say to Cooper as they were rowing home. She'd somehow have to keep him quiet about her plan.

"The dock ain't even been used, mum. Ships can't even be coming here until next week." The dockmaster eyed her distrustfully.

"All right then, when the dock is fully operational, when

will the first ship for Scotland arrive?'' She was growing annoyed.

"First ship to Glasgow won't be here till . . .'' Stalwart licked a filthy thumb and sorted through some schedules. "Ah, here 'tis! *Briney Marlin.* Arrives early August.'' Kayleigh felt her heart leap for joy. "Leaves end of September.'' It landed on her stomach with a pathetic thud.

"September! Surely that's too long in port!'' She turned her head and tried to make out the scrawl that was ending her dream.

"Too long in port! Tell that to the miserable bast—ah, miserable men who've been clean up and down the coast for nigh two years. Sorry, mum. The *Briney Marlin* ain't leaving a day before 30 September 1746. And nothing can be done about it neither.''

Calculating swiftly in her head, Kayleigh counted the number of weeks St. Bride would be back at Belle Chasse. September would be cutting it close, but she had no other choice.

"I would like passage on the *Briney Marlin* then.'' She damned the tremor in her voice. Nothing could go wrong now. She might never have so good a chance for passage back to Mhor. And once there, she would be able to prove for all time who she really was. She pushed all her dark thoughts of St. Bride to the back of her mind. She would return from Scotland a different woman. She would return a lady—one that St. Bride would beg to marry, duke or not. All she wanted now was the chance to fulfill her blossoming dream.

To her overwhelming relief, Farrell Stalwart took her money without question. He gave her change from the gold coins, then began inking his ratty quill.

"What will the name be, mum?''

"The name? My name?'' She bit her lower lip and then uttered, "Kayleigh Kerr.''

Och, but it had a beautiful sound.

* * *

She and Cooper London returned to Wolf Island long before evening. After what she prayed had been an impressive speech about the evil of a loose tongue, Kayleigh bid Cooper farewell at the house. Feeling too exuberant to sit inside, she meant to climb to the cupola and watch the sun set over the horizon— the same horizon she vowed to set out for in less than two months. But she never got that far.

"Kayleigh, you haven't thanked me for your gowns." St. Bride sat in an easy chair flanking the drawing-room fireplace. His brilliant gaze wandered through the hall, finally capturing her as she moved to the double-hung staircase. "Come, here, love. We've things to discuss."

Reluctantly, she entered the drawing room. Shutting the cross-and-bible door behind her in accordance with a nod of his head, she went to a wine-colored needlepoint stool and sat down.

"You haven't thanked me for your new—"

"I haven't a desire for them, St. Bride. Truly." She cast her eyes downward and stared at the carpet. It was decidedly French, she told herself, avoiding the inevitable conversation. Her eyes followed the pink-and-green-woven trompe l'oeil flowers.

Her lack of attention obviously angered St. Bride. "Desire them or not, you have them. Wear them." He put his hand under her chin and forced her head up.

"I will not be your pet to dress and play with as you please." She pulled the hand away.

"An ugly image for something that has no ugliness about it." His words came carved in ice.

"I've told you, I shall not be your mistress. I shall not lie with you for the things you can give me. I'll do it for marriage, but not for dresses, jewels, or all the gold in—"

"I know that," he interrupted her.

Taken aback by his swift and unusual acquiescence, she sputtered, "What is this? If the dresses are not payment for my . . ." She fumed and continued, "What do you want from me then, if not . . ." She couldn't bring herself to say the words.

"You know what I want, and I'll get it with or without gifts. But credit me with some intelligence, will you? I've noticed your disdain for my gifts. I'm not such a fool as to think they would impress you now."

"So why give them to me?"

"You need them. You're too beautiful to run around dressed like a scullery chit."

"But you must know that I still won't—"

"You will." St. Bride's handsome lips twisted in a devilish smile. "I told you I would not wait forever."

"And how do you think to convince me?" She was incredulous. The arrogance of the man never ceased to amaze her!

"Why don't you leave that to me, eh, dark love?" His hand swept out to stroke her hair. "Dress for dinner now. Maddie is waiting for you upstairs."

"You're wrong about one thing, St. Bride." She paused before she left the room.

"Correct me then." He rose ominously from his seat.

"You *will* wait forever." She smiled secretly, then left the room.

When she reached her chamber, she flung herself down in front of the dressing table. Leaning against the mahogany-gadrooned edge, she pushed aside all the unused crystal powder pots and enameled rouge pots. She hung her head in her hands and stared wretchedly at herself in the glass.

Any gratitude she might have felt for St. Bride's generosity had been dispelled by his demands. Turning her head to the mountains of silk, satin, and brocade that still lay on her bed, she prickled with anger. Vexed, she had half a mind to paint herself up and go down to dinner with all her new clothes on, regardless of how poorly they matched.

"So we gonna dress you pretty tonight, missus?" Maddie

swayed into her chamber, carrying a batch of extra bayberry candles for the candle box.

"I'll be wearing my own dress, thank you, Maddie." Kayleigh got up and sauntered through to the dressing room, hung with Prussian red damask. She immediately reentered her bedchamber. "Maddie, where is my other gown? I thought you put it in the wardrobe."

"The man told me to throw the thing out." Maddie tightened her lips, obviously waiting for the storm her mistress was going to put forth.

"He tosses out my own possessions, which I've earned in a respectable manner, and without the slightest by-your-leave?" Kayleigh crossed her arms over her heaving chest. Fury sparkled in her eyes. "Fine! Then we'll see just how he likes me in his dresses!"

"What you gonna do, missus?" Maddie tripped toward the Prussian red room, following her mistress.

"Which is the finest, Maddie?" Kayleigh asked a moment later, disappearing into the folds of silk dresses Maddie had already hung in the marquetried armoire.

"The finest?" Maddie echoed.

"Yes." Kayleigh peeked out from the rainbow of satins and brocades. "I want to pick out the finest, most elaborate dress. That's what I'll wear tonight."

"And why is that, missus? Tonight be no special occasion." Maddie definitely looked worried.

"Then we'll have to make it one, won't we?" Kayleigh smiled and pulled out a heavy claret-colored brocade. The dress was appropriate for only the most celebrated of evening occasions.

When Kayleigh was finally ready, she made a sight indeed. She'd even painted her lips with rouge from the pots on her dressing table. Her face was powdered, and her eyes lined with kohl. It was perfectly horrific, she mused with delight as she took one last look at her reflection. She wore the heavy brocade complete with hoops, which laid out the matching petticoat to its fullest splendor. She felt weighed down from all the stiff layers of fabric. But she wanted to make a grand entrance, and she was positive that this was the only way.

She gave Maddie a parting thank you. The servant swallowed convulsively in response; then, before Maddie could protest further, Kayleigh left for dinner with a vengeance.

St. Bride was already seated when she made her appearance. He saw the dress first, his gaze taking in the yards and yards of costly material; then the bodice, where it fit snugly around her waist and dipped generously at the neckline. With a tingle of triumph mixed with fear, Kayleigh watched as he lifted his eyes to her face.

His expression remained implacable. The slightest of glints in his irises told her to beware, but she didn't make overly much of it and walked bravely to the table where he sat.

"How do you like it?" she taunted under her breath.

"The gown? My choice exactly," he stated evenly, rising to assist her.

"I'm so glad you approve. I had nothing of my own to wear since you told Maddie to toss out my dress, and I felt that tonight deserved the best." She picked up her napkin, vowing to be just as cool and collected as he was.

"Yes, I do approve." His eyes flicked downward to the high swell of her neckline. Her skin appeared as pink as sea shells next to the lush claret silk. He seemed pleased at least with her generous display of bosom.

Her painted face was another matter entirely. No sooner had she laid her napkin across her lap than she found his napkin roughly going over her cheeks and lips to take off all the rouge. She jerked back, but his hand held the nape of her neck so that he could get the last smudges of kohl from around her lashes. She was furious; he was complacent. He tossed the soiled napkin to a young black footman and promptly asked for another.

"Savage! You never cease to humiliate me, do you?" she asked angrily while her palms tried to cool her raging cheeks.

"And you never cease to force me into it," he snapped, his eyes going briefly to the collar around her neck.

After that, dinner was a somber affair. They were served Altamaha shad and wild asparagus. Although it was delicious, St. Bride ate in a perfunctory manner without taking the slightest pause to savor his food, and Kayleigh merely pushed the excellent fish around on her *famille rose* plate. She fumed, and her only balm was to think of her passage on the *Briney Marlin*. She would go to Scotland, by God, and she would return like royalty. He would beg her forgiveness! Her eyes glittered as she looked at him.

Before dessert was served, she decided to take a little revenge. Recalling her conversation with Cooper, she met St. Bride's sea-green gaze.

"Cooper tells me that all the blacks here are free. Is that true?" she asked.

He grunted in the affirmative and raised his wineglass to his lips.

"How magnanimous of you"—she paused—"*Your Grace.*"

St. Bride set his glass down hard on the table. With that one gesture he proved his title. Suddenly, Rackrent's and Mrs. Storrowton's enigmatic statements made sense. The commandeering of the *Balcraig* made sense too. Although the thought terrified her, she felt some victory in the fact that she had uncovered a secret of his.

"So you are a duke, aren't you, St. Bride—or should I call you Your Grace?" she asked in a hushed voice.

"You're on dangerous ground, *my love.*" he answered calmly—too calmly.

"But I'm right. I know I am."

"If I'm a duke, I make a pretty sorry one. Why would I be here in Georgia with you and not in England where all dukes belong?" His eyes were hard and unreadable.

"I suppose you usually are. After all, you haven't been here in a year. So where have you been? In England, I'll wager.'' She grasped the wineglass in her hand and took two big, satisfying gulps.

''Kayleigh, get the idea out of your mind.'' He leaned his elbows on the table and rubbed his palms together. All the while he studied her fragile rouge-smeared features.

''I'm right, aren't I? Do you deny it?''

''I'm no duke here. Not in Georgia.''

''Again, we're talking in circles,'' she said with exasperation in her voice.

''You've already told me you'd prefer a colonial plantation-holder. So be happy—you've got one.''

''I prefer a colonial, but I prefer the truth more.''

''The truth!'' He threw his napkin on the table. ''You've never given me the truth about yourself. How dare you think you deserve it from me!'' He looked up at Maddie entered the room. Both their gazes followed her as she made her way to the table.

''There's a visitor to see you, Your Grace.'' Maddie stole a look at Kayleigh, and although she tried to hide it, Kayleigh could see that the servant was truly horrified at the work St. Bride had made of her face paint.

''Where?''

''He's in the library.'' Maddie opened the doors that led into the hall.

When she was gone, St. Bride said, ''Continue your dinner, love. I won't be a moment.''

He rose, but before he could leave, she suddenly burst out, ''You are a duke, St. Bride!''

He laughed and stroked her hair as a reassuring gesture. ''What kind of a duke would this, ah, 'savage'—I think that's what you called me—make?''

She thought hard on her answer. She could reach only one conclusion and whispered, ''I think you would make a fearsome one.''

Hearing this, he turned slightly more grim, but then he shrugged and left for the library, promising to return promptly.

Alone, she decided to forgo the last course, brandied peaches, and chose instead to wait for St. Bride in the drawing room. But there was little to do there, no books to read or tapestry to sew. When St. Bride didn't appear after an hour, she gave up waiting and took the opportunity to retire early to her bedchamber.

Her room was lit by several candles glowing cheerily from their silver stands. She sensed that there was something not quite right about the room, but she quickly shrugged off her premonition, attributing it to the disappearance of the mounds of dresses that were on her bedstead earlier that evening. Tired, she unpinned her stomacher and slipped off her shoes. She then began to undo the lacings of her gown. But something caught her eye and gave her pause. A gold glint came from the bed where Maddie had dutifully turned down the coverlet and laid open the linens for her mistress.

"What?" she exclaimed softly and walked to the bedstead. Looking down, her hand touched a single gold coin that was lying on her pillow. An awful thought occurred to her, and fearfully she flung back the topsheet. To her horror, there lay several more, scattered like buttons on the snowy linen. Turning with dread, she noticed what it was that had seemed odd about the room: the three hats that lay on her dressing table. Not only did they look terribly familiar, but one was definitely the blue-feather headdress that she had sold that afternoon.

"Damn him!" she cried under her breath. "Damn him!" she cried more loudly. With red, impotent rage firing in her bosom, she flung open the door and ran down the stairs.

Confronting St. Bride was the only thing on her mind—confronting him, and for once making him bend to her will, duke or no.

She stalked through the hall with her hands clenched even more tightly than her teeth. The beast would be in his library at this time of the evening, she thought. How, oh, how had he won this time?

Forcing herself into his library, she was determined to find out. She took a mute stance in the large doorframe and stared at him until her eyes positively blazed.

But St. Bride never even moved. He sat in a teal leather armchair and gave her not even the satisfaction of acknowledgment. With an unyielding profile he stared in the direction of a huge mahogany desk-bookcase in the pier. Throughout her whirlwind entrance, he showed not the slightest trace that he even knew she was in his library, except for the soft sound of his fingers tapping on leather.

"How did you know? Was it Cooper?" Kayleigh whispered harshly, forgetting all modesty as she held the front of her unlaced dress together with her hands.

"Farrell." St. Bride studied the knuckles of one hand. "We go way back. He's a low-minded gent, all right. But he likes gold, and like the rest of the townsfolk around here, he knows I'm the best source of that. I'll have you know I had to pay him plenty tonight, along with the coins I gave him for the milliner, who returned the hats." As if he could feel her impotent fury and desired her torture to continue, he picked up a dingy piece of paper and pointed to an illegible name. "But Farrell didn't stop by just for the milliner. No, he stopped by mainly to give me this. It's the *Briney Marlin*'s passenger list. Although I can't make out his measly scrawl, I have it on good authority that this young lass is you." He dropped the parchment on the tea table. "Now, what do you make of that, Kayleigh?"

Unable to take his taunts further, she put her hands on the silver collar at her throat and said, "Take it off. Take it off! If I must be a prisoner here, then at the very least do not shackle me!"

"It was not meant to be a shackle. It was meant to be a gift." He walked near to her. His voice seemed harsher than usual.

"Another unwanted gift," she said bitterly.

He responded with biting sarcasm. "When you take them

to heart as graciously as you do, then aye, I suppose it has been like that.'' He leaned down. His iron caress gripped at her arms, and he shook her. ''Will you ever cease this infernal complicating of our lives? I only want what's good for you.''

''How uncanny that you know me so well! Here I was thinking we're hardly more than strangers . . . Your Grace!'' She flung the title at him as if it were a curse.

''Strangers? By damn, we don't have to be!'' He pulled her roughly to his chest. His gold waistcoat buttons rubbed against her loosely bound bosom. Yet they didn't chafe; they only heightened the tension that was building with every second. Releasing a small gasp, Kayleigh felt her nipples grow hard, as if they yearned on their own for the warmth of St. Bride's implacable chest. Almost sensing her secret desire, his hand wove through her lacings and captured one unbound breast. When she could stand his thumb's caress no longer, she closed her eyes and felt positively ignoble.

''Stop!'' she finally gasped. ''This is not right!''

''No,'' he said evenly, furiously. His hands became less gentle. ''Perhaps this is not right, but I've learned to take my spoils any way I can.''

''Well, you can't take them this way,'' she whispered harshly. Then she shoved him off and ran back up the stairs, all the while fighting the inescapable urge to cry.

Chapter Twenty-four

Maddie helped Kayleigh dress the next morning. The maid had to choose between an appropriate cotton sateen morning gown and a light watered-silk *robe à la française*. In the end, she chose an ice blue linen damask.

With a rebellious arch to one perfect jet eyebrow, Kayleigh allowed Maddie to help her dress. The silk laces were tightened, and Kayleigh held out her hand for the busk. As if passing a foil to a fencer, Maddie handed her the blunt blade. In black amusement, Kayleigh noted it was of bone instead of silver, which was normally used in warm climes. If she couldn't sell her own headdresses, where in Darien did St. Bride think she could fob off a silver busk? Ruthlessly, she shoved it down her stays.

"I can get the rest, Maddie. Thank you." She pulled on two inconsequential bits of pink silk that a cobbler had meant as slippers. She then pinned on her stomacher of plain blue satin.

"It be mighty wet in the air today, missus." Maddie turned her expressive sherry eyes to the window. Beyond, Kayleigh could see the dunes, already white hot in the morning sun. "You'd best come back here later and undress. I'll make the room dark for you."

"Thank you, Maddie. But the heat doesn't bother me," Kayleigh replied coolly, although already she felt telltale beads of perspiration trickling between her breasts. Glancing at herself in the glass, she self-consciously pulled up her bodice and nervously arranged a long curl so that it fell over her bosom. With that, she heaved a warm sigh and departed for breakfast.

His Grace, she thought sarcastically, sat at the end of the walnut butterfly table. At her appearance he looked up from his coffee. Although she could tell he was still angry about her ill-attempted flight on the *Briney Marlin,* his eyes gleamed with healthy appreciation for her charms, and his lips seemed to hide a smile.

"Some would say that that particular robe is overdone for this hour of the morning." His eyes returned to her face. "But in my opinion, love, your choice borders on genius."

"I'm so glad. It shall be my favorite gown. I promise to wear it every day until you positively retch at the sight of it." Her voice was as sweet as the chocolate the footman was pouring for her. She was still angry at him too.

"Touché." He lifted his coffee cup in salute. Clanking it down on the saucer, he allowed her to begin her breakfast.

But she was again wanting in appetite. She stole glances at him across the long table and envied his look of coolness. He wore only fawn breeches, black boots, and a thin, crisp batiste shirt. She nibbled some fresh blackberries, but she had to avoid her chocolate altogether—the steam from her cup almost made her sick in the heat. Even a light damask gown was absolute torture in this weather.

Breakfast seemed interminable. She sat stiffly, feeling the cost of any unnecessary movement in wetness down her chest and arms. Her gratitude could hardly be expressed when St. Bride laid down his napkin, signaling the meal had come to an end.

"Are you going to the rice fields again today?" she asked. She hoped she didn't sound too interested, but she prayed fervently that he would be going. She was stifling. She wanted to go back to her room, after all, and strip down to her shift.

St. Bride offered a noncommittal shrug. Moving to her side of the board, he looked down at her. The day's warmth seemed to increase under his inspection, and she was forced to dab at her forehead and temples with a dampened napkin. He kissed her neck ever so lightly, and she was sure his tongue had tasted the salt of her perspiration.

"Will you miss me?" he asked.

"On the contrary, I shall find respite in your absence." She pulled away, modestly fanning her chest with the napkin.

"Perhaps. Perhaps not." He smirked, then departed.

She left the room in disgust. Hardly surviving the trip to her room, she sat in her window seat and began the tedious process of disrobing. Once down to her shift, she cooled herself with a fan fashioned out of dried palmetto. If only there were a breeze! she thought as she ran a water-soaked linen down the cleft of her bosom. Out the window she eyed the bright, beckoning turquoise waters of the Atlantic with longing. Aye, that would be a sure way of cooling off, she said to herself, damning St. Bride's male privilege of swimming.

But could she? She solemnly shook her head and refused to contemplate the idea further. St. Bride might return early from the rice fields and decide to swim himself. She did not want to have an encounter with him then. There was also the possibility that a servant or a worker bent on cooling himself off in the ocean would intrude. It would hardly do for anyone to see her splashing through the water, wet and nearly naked.

She knew how to swim, of course. There were too many lochs near Mhor for her to have forgone that childhood pleasure. But she hadn't swum in years, not since she'd turned twelve and been proclaimed a lady.

But the heat of the day was unbearable, even in her darkened bedroom. She recalled times as a child when she'd delighted in a swim in a cold loch. Longing for just one dip to cool her burning flesh, she finally shrugged off all caution and threw the damask gown back on. Lacing the bodice through every other hole, she was soon ready for her adventure.

Nervously, she traipsed out to the dunes. Her heart felt naughty, yet light. If she were discovered, it would no doubt bode ill for her. But upon the first glimpse of brilliant blue sea, she knew it would all be worth it.

Soon she was once again undressed down to her shift. She had second thoughts when she realized she would have to go in with the collar on. But perhaps it would serve St. Bride right if she lost the huge sapphire in the ocean. She walked into the waves and peeked behind her, reassuring herself that the only living thing for miles was a blue heron, almost as tall as herself, that rose from the dunes as a phoenix rises from the ashes. She laughed like a water nymph when a chill wave unexpectedly doused her front. Giving in to recklessness, she dove headlong into the cold Atlantic.

Almost an hour passed before she considered going back to the house. She had swum farther out than she'd planned but had spent a wonderful half hour floating on her back and worshiping the sun. Now she knew she'd been gone long enough to be missed. Treading water, she shielded her eyes and looked for her dress on the beach. At first she couldn't find it, and she realized she must have drifted a considerable distance away from the house. She finally found her direction by searching for the cupola—and it was then she spied St. Bride on the deserted beach standing over her dress.

"Mise-an-dhuit!" She coughed out the Gaelic exclamation in her shock, spitting a salty-tasting lock of her hair from her mouth. She kept her head low in the swells and took a moment to decide what to do.

She could just stay in the water until she drowned, she thought wryly. But St. Bride would come after her before that happened—and no doubt drown her himself. Or she could swim back to the beach and take her chances at sneaking to the house undetected. That was her only viable recourse, so she struck out for the beach, directing herself far enough down the coastline that St. Bride wouldn't see her.

She was quite tired by the time her feet found the sand bar. Rising stealthily out of the waist-high water, she scanned the beach for St. Bride but this time, saw no one at all. Had he gone back to the house? Or . . . ? She turned just as he sprung out from underneath the water and lunged for her, his face a mask of absolute, unadulterated rage.

Screaming, she flailed at him as if he were some kind of mythical water horse come to drag her into the depths of the sea. And drag her he did, only out of the water and onto the beach. There he wrapped his arm around her tiny waist and carried her like so much baggage the hundred yards up the beach to where she'd dropped her dress. Only after her feet touched the sand did she realize that St. Bride was stark naked. She stumbled backward and went crimson from her bosom to her temples. The shock at seeing him, so fearsome even with his clothes on, bearing down on her completely nude was more than she could bear. She turned her head and refused to look at him.

"You're supposed to be in the rice fields!" she exclaimed.

"I could kill you for this, I could kill you!" he panted, ignoring her accusation. His eyes blazed. "My God, I saw the dress and knew how long you'd been gone. Do you know what I thought?"

"N-no," she stuttered.

"I thought you'd drowned!" he growled. He shook the water from his head and rubbed his face with his palm.

"I supposed you would be in the rice fields," she repeated dumbly, still unable to turn her head and look at him.

"I'm no longer going to the rice fields. No doubt you were hoping the mosquitoes there would strike me down with fever."

"That's not true!" she retorted, waiting for his heavy breathing to subside.

But while it did, his gaze flickered down to her own state

of dishabille. She was clothed. She still had on the collar. She still had on her shift. However, she was forced to cross her hands over her chest, for the filmy batiste was now almost completely transparent from the water.

"How dare you do such a thing," he finally rasped, still very angry.

"All I've done is taken a swim, as you do every day," she defended.

"Yes, the perfectly bred highborn lady," he spat with biting sarcasm, "cavorting in the waves half naked." His hands whipped out and forced her arms to her sides. His eyes swept down her wet, clinging shift, and he finished hoarsely, saying, "No . . . even better than half naked."

Breathing hard from the tension that fairly crackled through the salt air, she didn't dare look down at her heaving chest. She knew only too well that she would see her mauve nipples straining against the transparent fabric. And she was all to aware of the shameful way her shift stuck to her thighs, more than hinting at the triangle of raven hair between her legs. Her fear-ridden gaze refused to meet St. Bride's. She prayed for the moment when her heart would cease to pound as loudly as the waves on the beach.

"St. Bride—" she began.

"No," he interrupted thickly, "don't talk. Don't say anything." A brilliant gleam appeared in his eye and he demanded, "Look at me."

His meaning was clear. She refused by keeping her head turned. But he demanded again, this time more ferociously, "Look at me, you little witch!"

Startled by his tone, she obediently turned her head to face him. As if by a will of its own, her gaze dropped to his body. All she took in was a blur of bronzed skin, black hair, and taut, rock-hard muscle before she again looked at his face.

"Not enough," he tortured. "Again. Only this time, more slowly." His stare locked with hers, and it coerced her into complying.

Bravely, she started at his neck, tilting her head upward to take in his whole height. After she noted that his neck was strong and well formed, her gaze then moved to his shoulders, which were as she expected—wide, muscular, and bronzed. His chest was liberally sprinkled with crisp black hair—that she already knew. But what she didn't know was that his chest hair, sparkling with droplets of seawater, narrowed at the muscular grid of his belly and then almost disappeared altogether in the region of his slim hips, only to fully reappear again at his . . . Her gaze shot downward to his thighs, also sprinkled with hair and water, and heavily wrapped in muscle. His legs were long and perfectly formed. She realized even with this hasty inspection that St. Bride Ferringer was without flaw.

Her gaze returned to his face. He was grinning madly.

"Am I so repulsive then?" he asked.

"No," she whispered, her eyes darkening with something she didn't quite understand.

He lifted one hand and eased her wet shift off one shoulder, then another. Before he had it down to her breasts, she made one protest: "St. Bride, not here . . . please. Someone will see."

"No one will see. But I daresay you should have thought of that before you took your little swim." He yanked the shift down off her breasts, then, around her waist, used it to pull her to him. He pressed her against his full arousal and looked down at her, allowing her to take in every strong plane of his face. His hair was still in its queue, but now it was wet, dark, and slicked back. He looked younger with it like that, somehow more boyish, yet no less virile. She gazed at the aristocratic straightness of his nose and at the way it crooked ever so imperceptibly at the bridge, as if it had once been broken. Then, before she could stop herself, she touched the rough skin of his cheek, shaved only this morning, no doubt by one of his many servants. With the feel of him beneath her fingertips, her lips parted in unconscious invitation. She dropped her head back and then moaned when she felt his tongue, wet, hot, and salt-ridden, enter her mouth in a ferocious, devouring kiss.

She didn't know how to express the feeling of him crushing against her bare breasts and invading her honeyed mouth with a strong, sure passion. When his hand slid beneath the sheet of her wet hair to stroke the silk of her back, she could hardly utter a moan. But when he cupped her bottom, making an end to all her modesty as her shift dropped to her toes, she released a cry of instinctive joy. Her heart beat against his chest, as if it too were crying out for him. She could only nip hungrily at his mouth when, groaning, he lifted her into his arms and slowly laid her down on her dress, its skirt spread like a silver-and-blue-damask fan on the sand.

"My God, you bewilder me. Am I the seducer or the seduced?" he asked huskily as his mouth left hers to trail down her throat. She shook her head dizzily when his tongue found the hollow at the base of her throat. He lifted the collar to get an even better taste, but her hands wrapped brazenly around his crown and she guided his mouth to the peak of one full breast.

Permitting herself such abandonment was difficult. For Kayleigh, it was disgraceful; for Kestrel, near to impossible. Only for St. Bride would she do such a tempestuous thing. When his strong white teeth grazed her nipple, a current shot through her body and she arched her back for more. It was then that she made a decision to trust him, just this once, just for that dark promise of pleasure that gleamed in his eye.

"What an enchantress you are." He nuzzled her breast and murmured, "You smell sweeter than Carolina jasmine." His tongue licked the tip. "And taste sweeter than a Georgia peach."

"St. Bride," she whispered, holding on to his sinewy forearms as he poised above her, "I want—"

"I know what you want. I know," he reassured her, not

allowing her to finish. Then he grinned and bent over her bosom once more and made each dusky crest tight with hot, aching desire. But when he was finished there, he didn't rise to kiss her mouth. Instead, his mouth burned a trail along her belly until her head tossed back and forth on the damask, fighting the warring urges within her. She was laying herself open to him, and he, like the man he was, was taking full advantage of it. It was not easy for her to allow him to continue, but in the end she permitted it.

Upon her surrender, St. Bride wasted no time. He deliberately parted her smooth thighs and tasted her with scorching precision. The touch of his lips shot a jolt of pleasure through her, the likes of which she'd never experienced before. Gasping from the sensation, her entire body became rigid, and her first instinct was to close her thighs. Yet he anticipated her every move. He kept them open, forcing her to experience the entire onslaught, which ebbed and flowed like the tide beside them. Just before he brought her to the full flowering of her pleasure, he rose to recapture her mouth in a soul-wracking kiss.

He finally rolled her onto him. Facing her, he said with great anticipation and relish, "You wicked girl, I knew you'd like that."

"N-no . . . ," she moaned while sitting on top of him, her eyes black with passion. Not wicked, she'd meant to say, but both his hands had gone to her breasts, and she felt his manhood throbbing against her backside. Could she deny it? She had her doubts, especially when she bent down and put her lips to his, aching for the surge of desire that shot through her every time they kissed.

"I like you that way, Kayleigh—wicked and beautiful," he gasped in her ear when at last they parted. "Don't ever think I'd want an angel. Angels die too young." With that, his hands slid to her hips.

Straddling him between her legs, she thought of the wisdom of his words. Above them the sun blazed; below them the dunes baked; and between them only the mist of seawater and perspiration—and the fragile bastion of innocence soon to be shed—kept them apart.

"You're right. I'm not an angel," she whispered in his ear, and for the first time in her life, she was glad she was not. She wanted him now, here, right by the sea. He'd always reminded her of the sea with his turquoise eyes and his turbulent, persuasive disposition. The entire situation was exquisitely appropriate—yet not one for an innocent.

His grasp on her hips tightened, and he said, "I have you now, don't I, dark love?"

She nodded, and he released a low, animal groan and lifted her to him. He made no effort to hold back in his greed to take her, and with one powerful thrust, he entered her. Completely.

It was as if an Arctic tidal wave had washed over both of them. The unexpected, excruciating pain after so much pleasure made Kayleigh toss back her head and produce a guttural scream. Stunned and confused, she beat on his hands to let her go. She climbed from him and stumbled onto the sand, her only instinct being to get away as quickly as possible from the man who had hurt her.

"Jesus Christ!" St. Bride shot up, his eyes full of horror at the red smear between her thighs. *"Jesus Christ!"* Bewildered, his face drawn and grim, he stood and stepped to her as she knelt in the sand. But she refused to let him get near her. She scrambled to her feet, grabbed her wet, sand-covered shift, and drew back.

"You hurt me!" she cried out to him. "You knew you would hurt me! You meant to hurt me!"

"No!" He tried to come closer, tried to grab her to him, but she scrambled back like a cornered wild bird with terror in its eyes. Hastily, she donned the ruined shift and ran, knowing that he wouldn't stop her. He didn't. He only stared after her as she fled to the house.

He rubbed his temples, searching blindly for his own clothes in the sand. Out of the corner of his eye, he saw the dress, the beautiful, costly dress, also smeared with her blood. Cursing heartily, he kicked out at it and covered the stain with sand.

Chapter Twenty-five

She should have known it would turn out this way. She should have known something so wonderful would have such a horrible conclusion. Curled up on her window seat, Kayleigh watched the last rays of sun pinken the clouds on the horizon. The sea was calm, and already the moon hung in the twilight sky—now only a ghost of its nighttime self. She did not cry.

She found some hollow satisfaction in the fact that her heart was surely turning to stone. She had trusted and been naïve. It had happened before. After she refused Straught, she and Morna had even giggled about his proposal. It had seemed so absurd that Kayleigh, so vibrant and young, would wed someone as abrasive and as old as their father's cousin. Never had they imagined that Straught would be so ruthless in pursuing what he wanted.

A tear slipped slowly down one cheek. She wiped it with her fingertips, then continued to stare out the window. All she had wanted was what Morna had had—someone to love, someone to trust. She had neither in St. Bride.

She'd probably been right about him all along. Another tear slipped down. Then another. She didn't even bother to wipe them away now. She'd been wary to trust him. She'd told herself again and again that he was mixed up with her cousin and could do her no good. She'd avoided him and the way he made her feel. But there on the beach, he'd made her believe she would receive something wonderful. With his every touch, his every kiss, he'd deceived her into thinking that she had actually wanted that last act—and not just wanted it, ached for it.

But she'd been wrong. Her arms wrapped around her chest in a protective hug. She hadn't wanted it. She hadn't known about the pain and about the blood. At Mhor she'd learned hardly anything about went on between men and women. Then she'd left for the New World. On the river-front she'd known prostitutes aplenty. She'd been able to survive with Bardolph by stealing, but she was not ignorant of the duties of a whore. The whores she'd known had men by the dozens, yet they'd given her no indication that their work was anything but tedious at worst—never as painful as what had happened on the beach today. Selling one's body to a man was immoral—but excruciating?

She put a shaky hand to her lips. She needed a new plan. She thought of the *Briney Marlin,* which would now be leaving without her, and she cursed the day she had ever met St. Bride. Fingering her silver collar, she set her thoughts in motion. She would find a way out of this. Somehow, some way, she would get back to Scotland and never set eyes on St. Bride again. Although her heart twisted in her chest at this thought, she scowled and fixed her gaze on the backlighted dunes. He didn't love her. He hadn't believed anything she'd told him about herself. He had taken her like a whore, and he'd given her nothing but pain in return. So she would go, she told herself.

And if her heart gave her trouble? Then she would abandon it right there on the beach at Wolf Island.

"You be needin' somethin', Your Grace?" Maddie asked in the hall as St. Bride passed her. It was late, and all the other servants had gone to their cabins for the night. Maddie, however, slept in the house. She had just been going to her little room when St. Bride, dressed in a rich maroon-brocade dressing robe, stormed up the stairs and strode purposefully down the second-floor passage toward her.

He answered her inquiry with a gruff "Nothing." Yet at that, Maddie's curly brows shot up and her eyes widened. She was unused to seeing her master in any state other than his amiable, relaxed one. Now he looked anything but that. His faced appeared as taut as a drum, and there was anger in his eyes, yet . . . was there also something like contrition? Warily, Maddie pushed back against the wall and allowed him a wide berth. Her eyes grew larger when he stopped at Kayleigh's door. He didn't hesitate to knock.

"Why, Your Grace, that ain't—!" *Your room,* she'd meant to say, but the words died on her lips. St. Bride opened the bedchamber door, ignoring her exclamation entirely. He paused in the threshold; then, as if there were no turning back, he shut the door soundly behind him.

Dreading the intrusion, Kayleigh simply pretended that it wasn't happening. After all, there was no need to look up, no need to see the man who she already knew was there. Without uttering a word, she curled into a tighter, more protective position in the window seat.

"We must talk. Do you hear me, Kayleigh?" St. Bride strode farther into the room. But with every step he took, her vow to ignore him only grew stronger.

"Your appetite is good, I see," he stated when he saw the empty dinner tray beside her on the window seat. There was a note of relief in his voice. But she was determined not to acknowledge it. He'd hurt her, so why should she be glad that he cared about her appetite?

"I sent up a bath. Did you take it? I thought it would soothe you." He reached out to touch her black locks as if he could answer the question himself by gauging their dampness. She could not ignore his hand, and she shrank back like a frightened kitten.

A flash of sorrow crossed St. Bride's face then. But she didn't see it; she was too busy watching his hand, which had dared try to touch her again.

"What am I going to do with you? You have me absolutely baffled. You're a complete mystery now." Again his hand reached to stroke her hair—only this time she lashed back.

"Don't ever touch me again," she said, her eyes midnight blue and reproachful.

"It happened so quickly. God, you must believe me! I wouldn't have—"

"I don't care. It's over now. Leave me alone."

"I can't," he answered, suddenly sounding very tired. "I've thought about it all evening, Kayleigh. And I can't leave you alone. Not now."

"Why not now?" She shrank back even further into the window seat, and her hand itched for the little knife that had come on her dinner tray. Out of the corner of her eye, she saw its silver gleam in the candlelight. She found that very reassuring.

"I was remembering a conversation we had back at Belle Chasse. You talked about the man you would marry. Do you remember that?"

"Is this a further cruelty to be thrust upon me?" she hissed. "You can't mean to ask for my hand in marriage? You? The mighty Duke of . . . Duke of . . ." She fumbled for his title. When she realized she didn't know it, her fury increased. "Look what you've done! You've ruined me for any other man, and I don't even know what your bloody title is!"

"A man would rather take a wife deflowered than never be able to take her at all," he reasoned against her anger.

"What are you saying?" she gasped.

"I'm saying we must try again. Tonight. If we don't, you'll never forgive me for what happened on the beach. Worse, you'll never forgive any man. If you aspire to marriage, you'll have to learn—preferably from me—that men are not so terrible, that being with them is not always going to bring pain.''

"You're mad if you think I'll permit that." Her back rammed against the wainscoting in self-defense.

"You must permit it, love." Again that treacherous hand reached to touch her, but this time she was ready. Her own hand whipped across the seat. In a second the sharp, steel knife was in her grasp, and she held it out like a shield.

"Don't even dare. You've a handsome face, St. Bride," she warned. "I'm sure the ladies will mourn if I cut it."

What she had expected from him, she wasn't sure. Perhaps she had expected surprise, shock; perhaps she was even so smug as to expect a shadow of fear to cross his face. What she hadn't expected was that he'd force all her bravado into an impotent ball and toss it away with one mirthless chuckle: he was laughing at her!

"You threaten my looks! After today, little one, I can't imagine why you're not aiming a few feet lower!"

"That too, damn you!" She couldn't take it any longer. She didn't want to hurt him. If she studied her feelings, she knew she might still find a small, inconsequential fondness for him. But she couldn't let him think she would permit him to bed her again. She struck out, fully expecting to do damage. After all, she'd sliced him before.

But then she'd had the upper hand, the element of surprise. She was amazed at how easily he took her wrist now. Pinning it up behind her against the wainscoting, he lauded her, saying harshly, "Good! Good! I'd rather see you looking like this, with your eyes positively glittering with hatred, than see that still, solemn little creature I found earlier. If I broke your spirit, Kayleigh, I couldn't live with myself."

"Sleep well then! It'll take more than you to break me!"

"I know that. I know that now." He smiled and kissed the inside of her wrist below the knife.

He held her so tightly, she couldn't move the blade even the quarter inch necessary to nick his handsome face. Worse, his warm lips on her sensitive skin sent a tingle of unwanted longing down her spine. Och, had the world gone mad?

"No more," she begged, as his hand brushed aside the sapphire satin folds of dressing gown, exposing one breast. He didn't touch her. Instead, he commanded, "Throw down the knife."

"Never!" she hurled at him. "Laban was right. You'd best not turn your back on me!"

"I don't intend to turn my back on you, but not because I fear you sticking a dagger in it." His grasp on her wrist grew even firmer. He took his other hand to his mouth and licked his forefinger, then slowly brought it to her breast. She had to shut her eyes, unable to bear what he was about to do.

"That's it, close your eyes. Relax. I'm not going to hurt you," he whispered when she released a soft moan. With painful exactness, he circled her nipple again and again with his wet, warm finger, sending scorching shivers of delight right through to her heart.

When he brought his lips close to hers, she cried softly, "No, your kisses lie."

But he wouldn't listen. He reassured her by saying, "Never again." Then his mouth gently pulled on her full lower lip until he finally moved over her in a long, unbroken kiss.

All the feelings she had beaten down and tried to discard came back to haunt her, and she could only assume that she had died and gone to hell. Her punishment for all her wickedness was this—again and again she would be brought to the brink of ecstasy, only to have it end in heart-wrenching agony and pain. Under St. Bride's burning kiss, she was heaved against him, and her breasts—one covered, one bare—crushed against the soft brocade of his maroon robe. As her captured wrist grew numb, her head tossed back and forth against the wainscoting in protest. But he followed her rebellion with lips that asked only for peace and cooperation, that promised only gentleness and pleasure.

Soon his tongue sought entrance, but she refused. Then he filled his free hand with her naked breast and sent her senses raging with desire. Her mouth relented and opened to him, although she told herself that she would stop before the pleasure ceased to be pleasure. She would stop before he demanded a consummation. That she would not give.

His kiss beckoned her own tongue to become more adventurous, but her free hand went to his front, as if she could hold him back with one slender limb. She felt his heart beating triumphantly against the solid mass of muscle, skin, and hair that made up his chest. He was growing warmer, as she was. His breath quickened and his tongue thrust, and unconsciously her reactions began to mirror his. Caught up in the assault on her senses, she groaned when he left her to whisper huskily, "Drop the knife, Kayleigh."

She shook her head, trying desperately to clear it, and she licked her lips, which traitorously ached to be back on his.

"We don't need it, do we?" His other hand grabbed for the hilt before she could protest. She held on to the knife as hard as she could, but she had never been a match for his greater strength. Her only real weapon against him had been her wits, but when her thoughts were dulled and drugged with pleasure, they were not as rapier sharp as his.

"*I* need it!" she sobbed when he took it from her. Stripped of her protection, she lunged for the blade, but it was futile. He held it out of her reach and gave a powerful flick of his wrist. The knife sailed across the air, split the mint green-silk damask that covered the opposite wall, and embedded its tip solidly in the plaster.

Now that she was defenseless, he picked her up in his arms and laid her on the cherry bed. Her dressing gown was parted, and before she could even moan in protest, he was on top of her, kissing her lashes, sucking the tender skin of her throat, and nibbling at her breasts until she possessed not a single lucid thought.

"Kayleigh, I want to know all of you," St. Bride rasped,

his mouth hot on the silken arches of her brows. "I want to make love to you, I want to release that wildness inside you that has me so captivated. And when we're through, I want you to tell me who you are and why you've remained a virgin until now."

"St. Bride . . . no."

"Don't fight—it won't hurt, I promise." He covered her breast with his hand. But seeing the distrust in her eyes, he added, "Your body trusts me, love. See how much it resists?" His palm easily coaxed her nipple into a hard bud. "Mmmmm . . . that's good. See? Not much," he murmured as his teeth closed on the peak.

She flung her head back and groaned with unfulfilled longing. She was spinning out of control. An unbearable emptiness was being created inside her. Her thighs begged to open, and weakly she pulled at his maroon robe with an unspoken wish. He complied instantly, rolling back on his haunches and slipping the offending robe from his body. Then he lifted her out of the sapphire satin that enclosed hers.

When they were finally together, Kayleigh clutched at his strong shoulders, fearful and yet gratified that she had the hard length of his body against her once again.

"My God, I can't think when you're near me." He took her mouth in another soul-blistering kiss. When they parted at last, he panted, "How dangerous you are. You've turned my life upside down. Not even my *belle chasse* has my thoughts when I have you like this."

"Wait, wait . . ." she whispered, her eyes filling with fear. Panicked, she felt his hand between her thighs.

"You trust no one, do you?" He wedged his body between her legs.

"Why should I?" she sobbed, wanting him, hating him.

"You shouldn't. But tonight you'll trust me. Even if it's just to do this one thing." He poised above her and took in her raven locks, scattered wildly against the watered silk counterpane. The sapphire around her neck seemed to reflect in his eyes. His gaze touched her lips, which were ruby with desire, tense with uncertainty; then it flickered to her eyes, as dark as a midnight ocean and just as stormy.

"All I want to see in those eyes, my little enchantress, is wildness and lust"—his arms held off his weight, and he throbbed against her—"but no more sadness." With that, he entered her, and her whole body tightened, waiting for pain to consume her.

But slowly, with every thrust, she realized there was no pain. There was no blood. All there was was St. Bride and his steely, velvety maleness, thundering over her, against her, inside her. She almost swooned from the relief that gushed through her veins, but soon something more potent took its place. Her loins began to quiver as they had when she'd felt his hands and his mouth upon her.

As she arched toward him, he caught his breath. All his muscles tensed, as if he were holding himself back.

But she didn't want him to hold back. Not now. Not this time. So she pressed her hips closer to his, taking him more fully. Her hands moved down the rigid, flexing muscle of his ribs, and in an effort to drive him harder, she pressed her mouth languidly against the pulse beating in his neck.

Kayleigh dimly mused that the only thing missing from the storm of their lovemaking was lightning. But soon a bolt pulsed through her and struck at the place of their joining. She released a muffled cry, and her eyes closed. Her entire body shuddered from the exquisite shock, and she desperately clutched St. Bride to her, knowing that he alone was the source of her pleasure. Only when St. Bride had experienced her full response did he allow himself the same. In the rising heat of his passion, he could take no more. He groaned her name, buried his face in her hair, and lost control.

It was several minutes before either of them could speak. St. Bride lay between her legs, propped up on his elbows. Kayleigh lay beneath him, gladdened that he had yet to make a move to leave.

Suddenly, the relief and happiness she felt surged within her, and she let out an uncontrollable laugh.

"What are you giggling at, baggage?" He gave her a mock scowl.

"You were right. Being with a man is not so terrible." She smiled secretly. "In fact, I think I shall enjoy my husband immensely."

"I'm glad this brings you satisfaction, love. Only don't enjoy it too much."

"Why not?" she asked, her eyes widening as she felt him growing inside her.

"Because I mean to keep you all to myself." His hands cupped her face, and he gave her one fiery kiss after another until she hopelessly begged for more.

Chapter Twenty-six

Kayleigh's bedchamber was shadowed and cool when she awoke. The wooden Venetian blinds clattered in the sea breeze, their slats tilted up to cast the hot sunshine toward the ceiling. Covered with only a linen sheet, Kayleigh brushed the sleep from her eyes and tried to recall the night before.

St. Bride.

She looked beside her in the bed. She was disappointed to see only a depression in the pillow next to her. Leaning back, she inhaled the heady, masculine scent that clung to her body, her hair, the linen. And she recalled with stunning clarity each and every time St. Bride had taken her. As their lovemaking had progressed, he'd become more ferocious more possessive, more demanding. And so had she. Feeling the delicious ache between her legs, she wondered if she would regret her boldness. But then she remembered how spent and utterly at peace she had felt when she had drifted off to sleep entwined in St. Bride's strong embrace. She released a sigh of contentment and knew without a doubt that she had no regret.

Flinging away the sheet, she picked up the sapphire satin robe from the floor and went to dress. Her morning ramblings brought Maddie with her breakfast, and soon the house servant joined her in the Prussian red dressing room to help her choose a gown.

Both women were absorbed in their own thoughts, and they exchanged few words. Kayleigh dressed in a violet toile de Jouy bodice and skirt, pinning a stiff embroidered white muslin stomacher between the ruching of the bodice. Without a word, Maddie handed her the matching muslin apron.

Ignoring the maid's unusually contemplative mood, Kayleigh brushed out her own hair, secretly reveling in its glorious fragrance, which reminded her of her lover. As befitting her mood, she dressed it simply with a violet satin ribbon.

After taking a few bites of the biscuit that Maddie had brought, she was ready to seek out St. Bride. No doubt he was anxious to speak with her, for they had talked very little the night before. Her hands went to her warming cheeks, and she was shocked to find Maddie staring at her as if she could read her thoughts.

"He gonna marry you, child?"

"What?" Kayleigh dropped her hands.

"His Grace—he gonna marry you? What if you get a baby?"

"Maddie!" she exclaimed. "What makes you say these things?"

"I know what goes on in this house," Maddie replied, bobbing her head for emphasis.

"Well, not everything that goes on here is your business," Kayleigh retorted coolly.

"St. Bride Ferringer's child be business of mine, for sure."

"There's not going to be a child. Do I look big bellied to you?"

Maddie crossed her arms over her huge chest. "Tell that to me in nine months, I jus' might see you singin' another tune." She fussed at Kayleigh like a mother hen. "His Grace make things good here, but I ain't always been in this place, child. I know how bad the world can be. And the reason's always because of a man."

"St. Bride has been kind—" Kayleigh didn't finish.

"He also be a man. You get him to a church, child. Reckon with this sin 'fore he can change his mind."

She stared at Maddie for a long time. Marriage? Yes, she'd thought of it—in fact, she truly expected it now. But her brow clouded. Would a duke marry her—even if she had his child?

Kayleigh was struck with doubt. Dukes didn't marry little cutpurses from the street. She furrowed her brow. St. Bride might marry a well-to-do, well-bred Scottish woman. Yet if she were to convince him of who she really was, she would have to either get back to Mhor or confront Straught with his misdeeds. Suddenly, a knot formed in her stomach. She still didn't know why St. Bride was friends with him. How much did she know of their dealings? Worse, how much did she know of St. Bride? Of his feelings for her? There had been passion last night, true, but there had been no words of love.

Kayleigh stared at Maddie for a moment longer. Then her back straightened, and she left to seek out St. Bride with a much heavier heart.

She found him in his study, surrounded by yards of creamy muslin curtains that swayed in the winds off the sea. He was bent over a ledger on his desk-bookcase, looking cool and handsome. She was suddenly overcome by a maidenly shyness. She didn't speak—she couldn't speak; yet he sensed her presence anyway. He looked up at her standing in the open threshold. His eyes softened in appreciation at her new gown. He shoved back his Windsor chair and stood to greet her.

"Your color is quite high this morning, love. I think such nights suit you." He placed a sensual kiss on her lips.

"And do they suit you, Your Grace?" she asked in a slow, even voice.

He grinned wolfishly. She needed no other answer, but he

gave one anyway. "They suit me exquisitely. But you mustn't call me 'Your Grace.' 'My love' will do nicely."

"You prefer not to use your title?" For her peace of mind, she had to have a few of her questions answered. She walked from the circle of his arms and poured herself some tea from a baroque silver teapot set on a nearby satinwood table. Though she desperately wanted to present a calm facade, her hands shook so, she couldn't stir the cream into her cup without rattling the china. Forced to abandon the task, she seated herself on the red tapestried bench and waited for him to answer her.

"Kayleigh, don't you think I'm the one who should be asking the questions?" He stepped in front of her and looked down. His eyes were shadowed with something—anger perhaps. It was obvious he didn't like her air of detachment. "I would like to start with the most pressing question. You'll have to forgive my lack of delicacy, but how is it that I found you . . . intact last night?"

"I'm unwed and hardly nineteen. How else was I supposed to be?"

"That's not what I mean, and you know it." He lifted her chin. "You've obviously been out on the streets for years. Why were there no men? How were there no men?"

"St. Bride," she evaded, "I want to know about Belle Chasse. Those poppies—"

"Belle Chasse has nothing to do with last night. We can talk about that later."

"Tell me anyway."

"Who are you?" As always, he got right to the point.

She stared up at him. Her reply was difficult and long in coming. Finally she said, "Take me back to Scotland, and I'll show you who I am."

He shook his head. "Someday we'll go to Scotland, if you like. But I won't wait until then. Tell me now."

His persistence was difficult to fight. "What do you want to know, St. Bride?" she asked.

"I want to know your secrets. I want to know why you've shunned everything I've given you or wanted to give you, and yet behind my back you've stolen from me, stolen things that aren't worth a fraction of what I would give you gladly. In short, I want to know what your dealings with Quinn were about."

"What else would you like to know?"

"I want to know how it is that you can read and sew and speak so beautifully although I found you on the streets wielding a knife with astounding experience." Tenderness flared in his eyes, and with one finger he gently traced her flawless profile. "Were you orphaned? Is that the explanation?"

She couldn't bear the kindness, the charity in his voice. It melted away all her defenses. After last night, she ached to trust him. She wanted him to care about her. She wanted what her parents had, and this sudden realization gave her the courage to speak.

"My parents are dead, St. Bride. I was orphaned, but a long time ago." She cringed in disbelief that she was telling him these things so close to her heart.

"Have you no brothers or sisters? Or are you completely alone in the world?"

She forced herself to continue. "I had a sister. She was my twin." Her eyes darted to see what his reaction was. Much to her relief, he seemed not to know anything about what she was saying. In his face she saw only pity.

"A twin—yes, that makes sense. It explains why Venus and Valentine so captured your interest." His voice softened. "Did your sister live, Kayleigh? I know that with twins, both babies do not always survive."

"My sister survived her birth." She turned thoughtful. "Still, I was the healthier child, even though I was born after her. You see, that's why I'm named Kayleigh, *Céilidh* in Gaelic. I was born later, on the other side of midnight of the

New Year. My parents named me for the celebrations of Hogmanay.''

"Born just after midnight. Of course." His gaze caressed her face. "The witching hour."

"Yes, the witching hour," she repeated, and thought of her box.

"Where is your sister now? I would like to help her, too, if I can," he said gently.

"She's beyond help." She paused. "She's dead."

St. Bride took the news in silence.

"She was murdered," she choked out.

"Murdered?" His hand tightened on her chin.

"Yes, my sister, my twin was murdered." Suddenly, all the grief and torment that had been building up broke the dam. She had never shared her feelings with anyone since that day at Mhor, and now she spoke so fast, she could hardly keep up with herself, let alone expect St. Bride to.

"My family was very rich. Very rich and powerful. We had a great castle in the Highlands that was so ancient and revered, not even that horrible war with the English could have taken it away from us. But everything changed when my father gave his cousin the hunting lodge. My sister was murdered, and I was brought here to the colonies and forced to survive on the streets—"

"Wait!" He released her chin and held up his hand. "You mean that Bardolph kidnapped you and brought you to Louisiana?"

"He brought me to New Orleans, but I came willingly. If I hadn't gone, I would have been murdered too—or worse." She shuddered.

His next words were quiet and tense. "So you killed Bardolph for murdering your sister."

"For murdering my sister?" The question left her with a momentary blank, but then she found her tongue. "Bardolph didn't kill my sister."

"Then why was he murdered?" St. Bride kept his voice

even, but it was obvious he was getting agitated. Kayleigh jerked her head up and saw that his face had grown taut. A fear that he didn't quite believe her crept into her heart.

"I didn't murder him." She answered his silent accusation, her voice barely above a whisper.

"I don't understand. Why was Bardolph murdered if he didn't kill your sister? And who killed him if you didn't?" Growing angrier and more frustrated, St. Bride persisted. "Who did kill your sister then? Did this cousin do it, the one at the hunting lodge? Where is he now?"

"I . . . I . . ." Suddenly, she burst out, "Yes, my cousin killed my sister!" She had to tell him the truth, but when the next question came, she wasn't prepared to answer.

"And who is this cousin if not Bardolph?"

She looked at St. Bride. The name was on her lips. She wanted to be out with it. She wanted to tell him so that he would make everything all right, so that he would confront Straught with his terrible deed and find her some peace in this world. But she remembered the poppies, and the note to Laban, and the stays.

"Who is this cousin. Kayleigh?" he urged.

She stared at him. Underestimating Straught's passions had ended all her happiness at Mhor. Was she to make the same mistake with St. Bride? "St. Bride, we must be married," she whispered. "We must be married right away. Then I shall be able to tell you everything. Then the past won't matter because I'll know you care."

"What is this?" He straightened. "How can I marry you when I don't even know who you are?"

"You know who I am! Last night proved that! I don't even know what you're the duke of, but I *know* you! Last night is all that matters, St. Bride!"

"Kayleigh!" He grasped her arms and made her stand. Then he shook her. "I ask you to answer me! Tell me who killed Bardolph! Tell me who killed your sister! Tell me that, and I will marry you! Evade me further, and I vow we'll never speak of marriage again!''

"No!" She stumbled backward and fell to the settee. Defeated, she laid her head in her hands. All her hopes and dreams for the future were dying before her. Straught had made sure of that, even this far across the Atlantic.

St. Bride suddenly snapped from frustration. "God! I could almost believe you, you heartless creature! I could almost believe your shabby tale about twin sisters and castles and kidnappings!''

"Those things are true! That's why I was a virgin! I wasn't raised on the streets! I was born to better things!''

"I believe you haven't always lived like I found you," he ground out, "but as to your virginity—I've seen how you protect yourself. As bloodthirsty as you are, I can't blame a fellow for looking elsewhere for companionship, especially when all he gets from you is a knife thrust under his chin!'' He ran an angry hand down his jaw. "How could you dupe me like this? If I didn't already know what you were capable of, I might be surprised that you could make such a mockery of what we shared last night!'' His face went rigid. His eyes flared, and he looked as if he would happily beat her.

"I know this is a difficult story to believe. So take me to Scotland, St. Bride. Or marry me. I'll prove that I am who I say I am—that and ever so much more!''

She rose from the settee, her hands out in supplication, but before she could speak, St. Bride stated wearily, "I am not taking you to Scotland anytime soon, Kayleigh. You must know that the only place you'll be going is back to Belle Chasse.''

Stunned, her mouth dropped open. All she could do was stutter, "But you can't! I can't go back there! The hangman is looking for me. You know that. You promised—''

"I know. But I must go back, and you proved to me the other day that if I leave you here, you'll run the minute I'm gone.'' Stiffly, he went to his desk-bookcase and put a letter in her hand. "Laban's note got here yesterday morning. He must have sent it the day after we left. When I went to find you on the beach yesterday, it was to tell you that I've paid to get the wharf in Darien finished early. I sent for a ship from Savannah, and it's to arrive in two days."

In shocked silence, she read the urgent message, written in a large untutored scrawl. It said:

> St. Bride
>   Straught has been to Belle Chasse. He is disturbed by your absence. You must come back at once. Or there will be *trouble*. I await your ship.
>   Laban

She closed her eyes and placed the note on a nearby card table. Dizzily, she realized how close she had come to telling St. Bride about Straught. Unbeknownst to her, the mighty, mysterious duke, St. Bride Ferringer, was merely her cousin's pawn, to be told where he could go and when he must return. Good God—the power Erath Straught must have to manipulate a man of St. Bride's station! What horrible thing was her cousin holding over St. Bride that he had a duke wrapped around his finger?

She grabbed the corner of the table and grew so pale, she felt as if she would faint. St. Bride moved up behind her, anger furrowing his brow.

"If you hadn't tried that stunt with the *Briney Marlin*, I wouldn't consider placing you in such danger."

"You want to see me hanged, don't you?" She put her hand to her collar.

"Don't be ridiculous. You won't be hanged—I'll see to that."

"I won't go with you, St. Bride," she vowed. "I'm not going back there."

"Do you think I'm going to leave you here with no one but Cooper London to watch over you? Do you think I'd risk letting you out of my grasp after last night? Kayleigh, think again.''

"I'll never forgive you if you make me return there," she said vengefully.

"No, I don't believe you will." His lips kissed the top of her head, nuzzling her silky black tresses. "But you have no choice.''

"No?" she began rebelliously, but he silenced her protests with a long, brutal kiss.

She fought to deny him, but soon her rigid body relaxed against his hard frame. She let out a soft moan. St. Bride's attraction was no more physical force. She longed to summon her contempt for him—he'd proven that he was no more than a puppet dancing to her cousin's commands. But as the kiss grew richer and more intense, she shuddered with unwilling delight, and the only contempt she could find was for herself.

PART THREE

The Belle Chasse

Shall I die? Shall I fly
Lovers' baits and deceits,
sorrow breeding?
Shall I fend? Shall I send?
Shall I shew, and not rue
my proceeding?
In all duty her beauty
Binds me her servant for ever.
If she scorn, I mourn,
I retire to despair, joying never.

Attributed to Shakespeare

Chapter Twenty-seven

When Kayleigh and St. Bride arrived back at Belle Chasse, they were greeted with the news that Colette and Laban had married. The couple had gone to the parish church that overlooked the Place d'Armes and quietly asked the priest to marry them. After they signed the necessary papers, the priest agreed to their joining. Banns were necessary for most marriages, but the priest had chosen to overlook this practice in this case. Kayleigh suspected that it had probably been the look on Laban's face when told how long he would have to wait that had convinced the priest to oblige. She thought it just as well. Except for her parents, and Morna and her fiancé, Kayleigh had never seen any two people happier together.

Her own relationship with St. Bride was another matter. When she'd first greeted Colette in the rear courtyard, all the little mulatto could exclaim was, "Ah, Kayleigh, how terrible you look! So thin! So pale! I think back in Georgia you must have been bitten by another snake!"

She'd been bitten all right, for if unwilling desire were a serpent, it had her by the throat. During the passage from Darien to New Orleans, her usually robust appetite had dwindled to almost nothing. She had been tense and rebellious during the days, and tense and surrendering during the nights.

Their ship had been just as roomy as the *Balcraig,* but she'd not been allowed her own cabin. St. Bride had made it clear that there was now no reason for them to sleep apart. So they'd slept on one bed for the entire voyage. She told herself time and time again that she didn't desire his attentions; yet when she thought of all the nights St. Bride had lain with her, sometimes taking her with frenzied passion, sometimes taking her with a slow burn, she knew that something made her willing—something that her head could not reconcile with her heart.

But now she was back in Louisiana, watching Colette dance about the rooms lighting the sconces for the evening. She had eaten alone with St. Bride spoke with Laban about Straught's visit. When St. Bride failed to appear at bedtime, she suspected it hadn't gone well. Left alone, she ached to steal over to Laban's cabin and listen in on what they were saying. She knew she would get her answers that way, but she also knew that if Laban caught her sneaking around his cabin, he'd have her head on a platter. He had been utterly displeased to see her again—and the feeling couldn't have been more mutual. Suddenly, she laughed out loud. She liked Laban, she realized. They were kindred spirits.

Waiting for St. Bride, she grew sleepy. The voyage had been tedious, and she was anxious for a bed that didn't rock and sway. She arched her back and got up from the bergère.

Walking past St. Bride's room, her eye caught the gleam of parrot green satin. He would want her to sleep in there with him, of that she had no doubt. But she had to get herself under control, she thought sternly, and begin setting boundaries. She'd be leaving him soon. She'd think of a way, now that she was back at Belle Chasse and he had other things to occupy his mind than her escape.

There had been no way to avoid this return to New Orleans. St. Bride had suspected she'd try to run away. He'd watched her the way a wolf watches a doe in the dead of winter, following her almost everywhere she went and never letting her out of his sight for more than a few minutes. So she'd been forced to return.

But she was not going to wait around the plantation until her cousin caught up with her. And she was not going to allow St. Bride to shatter her heart beyond repair. No, she was going to leave the first moment she could, and this time St. Bride wouldn't catch her. She would sneak to the docks and stow away, if necessary.

She took one last look at the satin-draped bed, then went to the bedchamber next to it, stripped down to her sheer batiste shift, and got into her old bed. She thought she would promptly fall asleep, but in the quiet of her room an idea for an escape came to her.

She awoke the next morning beneath a silken tent. She brushed aside the silk gauze, which hung from a hook in the rosette of the canopy, and saw the green satin drapes. Chridhe was a black, furry spot next to her feet and, seeing her mistress, the kitten deigned to open one eye and gaze at her. Kayleigh toed her fondly, glad to see her kitten once more. She then lay back on the pillows chagrined, knowing St. Bride must have carried her to his bed in the middle of the night without even disturbing her dreams. And they had been pleasant dreams at that, she smiled sadly, ignoring the heat that was already prickling at her skin through the linen sheets. The day was going to be brutally hot, but she didn't mind. Her traitorous thoughts turned to St. Bride.

Where was he? she wondered, looking at the rumpled linens beside her. He'd slept there but had risen early, that was clear. Something to do with Sweet Erath, no doubt, she thought darkly.

Frowning, she swung her legs to the side of the bed. Chridhe left the bed, too, and was gone to find her breakfast before Kayleigh had retrieved her shift from a nearby fauteuil. How St. Bride had managed to get her shift off her without awakening her was a mystery. But then, she thought with angry color

coming to her cheeks, if any man could do such a thing, St.
Bride was he. He could charm the pelt from a bear. Why,
she thought hopelessly, he'd probably even made love to her
last night while she slept.

Stumbling over to a blue faience pitcher, she wet a towel
and wiped the perspiration that already clung to her temples
and between her breasts. Och, the day was going to be a hot
one. She sighed and patted the back of her neck.

Dropping her hair, which desperately needed to be combed,
she entertained a few thoughts of going back to her room to
finish her toilet. But she looked out the four open French
doors to the shaded veranda. St. Bride's room was a corner
room. If there was any breeze at all today, it would waft
through here. Since she was already used to sharing their
toiletries during the return voyage, she didn't hesitate to go
to St. Bride's commode and search for his comb.

It was silver, with heavy baroque detailing on the spine.
She knew it well, yet could find it nowhere. It was in none
of the commode's drawers. She was just about to return to
her room to get her own comb when her gaze settled on the
amboyna casket. Of course, that was where he would keep
it. Opening the casket, she retrieved the comb from the top.
She was about to close the lid when a flash of white caught
her eye. She picked it up. It was the note Laban had sent to
Wolf Island, the note that had sent her back to Belle Chasse
to play hide-and-seek with her executioner.

Kayleigh crumpled the note in her hand. Her delicate brow
darkened. No, the note was not the source of her misery.
St. Bride was. He had brought her back here—because his
dealings with Straught were more important than her own
safety.

She trembled. St. Bride was surely deep in Straught's
clutches, but she was as deep, if not deeper, in St. Bride's.
St. Bride held her captive with his touch, but he used her

only as suited his whims. And when he was finished with her? She found herself wiping a lone tear from her cheek. What did all great dukes do with their mistresses then? They discarded them, she told herself numbly. And he would discard her one day, too, if Erath Straught didn't get to her first.

Suddenly, her plan for escape came back to her. She would do it, she told herself desperately. She would flee, if only because she couldn't bear the thought of another night in St. Bride's bed without mention of love.

"Love," she suddenly scoffed aloud, a sob catching in her throat.

"Mmm?" A throaty growl came from behind her. A strong arm hooked around her waist, and she could feel someone nuzzling her neck.

"St. Bride. You frightened me." She kept her voice as even as she could. She didn't move. She didn't breathe.

Shuddering, she took his kiss upon her shoulder and wondered hysterically why even now her body wanted him. He was involved with her cousin up to his forehead, and if she stayed with him, she would be the sacrifice that would keep things that way. She'd known that the very moment Laban's note had arrived at Wolf Island. Yet that knowledge didn't make his kiss any less seductive, nor did it make her body any less responsive.

"I missed having you last night. Can we make up for it now?" His hand slid over her bosom and pulled at the ties of her shift.

"Where have you been?" she gasped.

"I've been to see my flowers, love. They're blooming. Only a few more days now, and we'll be able to leave Belle Chasse." He kissed the lower swell of her breast before bending down to unstrap his jackboots.

"You're very pleased, aren't you?" She watched tensely as he straightened to take off his shirt. When that task was completed, he rubbed his tanned, hair-matted chest and stared at her hungrily.

"The flowers were my sister's favorite." His forehead furrowed and cleared immediately. "Yet Straught will have a particularly good appreciation for them too." He returned his attention to her state of undress and mumbled something about the inconvenience of women's undergarments. Her insides warred between defiance and desire.

"You want to please Straught, don't you?" she whispered. "At all costs you must please him."

"I want to please you." His grin widened, and he grasped the sides of her shift. He tore it apart slowly, maddeningly, revealing her bosom, her belly, her hips, inch by sensuous inch. She gasped a protest, but it was clear just by the glint in his eye that he considered her expensive batiste shift replaceable, but not the passion of the moment.

Before she could will him away, he was kissing her breasts, the curve of her supple belly, and even the silky black triangle between her thighs. He caught her up behind the legs and lifted her to the bed, placing her underneath the white gauze like a delicate treasure. As she knelt on the rumpled sheets, she knew she should be repelling his advances. She tried very hard to think of her sister and all the pain Straught had caused her. Yet at the moment she could not, and guilt weighed heavy on her soul. She wanted so much to be away from St. Bride, yet as she watched him strip off his breeches, she was beset by far greater, far more pleasant images—like a time they had made love in the cupola at Wolf Island.

It had been the day they were to return to New Orleans. They were to leave for Darien soon and she had been frustrated by her botched attempts to avoid going. St. Bride, sensing her mood, had tried to soothe her in the cupola, at first just by holding her, back to chest, and giving her time to accept what he had put before her. They watched the gulls feed along the coast and the sea swirl blue to green under the tempestuous sunshine. She had tried to tell him she didn't want to go back, that there was no need for her to go back. She'd even promised to stay at Wolf Island until his return, and she even thought she might have kept the promise if only she could stay behind. But he wouldn't listen.

His only words were, "You wouldn't miss me?" When she shook her head resolutely, he smiled and dared, "Prove it, and I'll let you stay."

She had meant to prove him wrong if it was the last thing she did. Everything depended upon it. Yet she didn't know where she went astray. She had meant to remain cold and uninvolved, yet she felt herself losing control, slipping once again in the sensuous dream of St. Bride's touch. Soon she realized that he had pulled her gown from her shoulders. He triumphantly caressed her stayless bosom with both hands; then he hiked up her skirts and pulled her on top of him, pleasuring her relentlessly until he had built a trust between them—even if that trust was only between their bodies.

Now she was caught between terror and desire. As St. Bride walked naked to the bed, she flinched that he didn't even bother to close the salon doors. How typical of him to be so assured of his privacy. He knew the servants wouldn't dare interrupt. He possessed a fatal charm to which everyone around him responded, as if it were his birthright to have every one of his needs met, not a luxury. When his weight came down on the bed, she knew with doomed certainty that she was helpless against his charm too. It was something that she couldn't and wouldn't deny, for she craved it too much.

Her chest heaved anxiously for the humid air, but St. Bride took no note of her discomfort. He pulled her beneath him and rested easily, comfortably, between her tense thighs.

"Why were you sleeping in your bed last night? You know I wanted you here with me." He looked down at her, capturing her hands with his own.

"Just because we're lovers doesn't mean we *must* share a bed," she replied warily, hating the feel of his hard body upon hers, hating it simply because she needed it beyond reason.

"The nobility never share rooms with their spouses. Did you know that?" he asked, kissing the pulse behind one ear. "I suppose that's why most men take mistresses."

"Not even a duke may live with his mistress and share her bed every night." She tried to imagine his lips cold and dispassionate upon her skin, but it was impossible. Everywhere they touched her, she was made liquid and glowing.

"Kayleigh, my work with Belle Chasse is almost finished. I want you to go to England with me."

"I only want to go to Scotland."

"What a pair we'll make—we'll set the *ton* on its ear."

"I suspect mistresses don't last long, St. Bride."

"They don't, but you will." She felt his tongue burning the taut softness under her chin. When he looked up at her again, his eyes reflected the light from the white gauze that billowed around them. His eyes were warm yet brilliant. She had never seen them so expressive, nor so tender. She moaned.

"Why must you look at me like that?" she blurted out.

"Why do you look away when I do?" He brought her chin around so that they faced each other once more. "Have you no fondness for me, Kayleigh? None at all?"

"My sorrow, I wish I did not," she practically sobbed.

"Why?" His hand stroked the place on her left breast where her heart drummed against her delicate ribs. "Is it so hard for you to say the words?"

"I'll say the words, but on one condition," she said, her voice trembling despicably.

"Which is?"

Her mind struggled to work despite the motion of his hand. "Take off the necklace. You've everything from me that you've wanted. There's no need for you to force me to wear it now. I'll never be able to leave you—you've already seen to that.''

He thought for a moment. Then he commanded slowly, ''Say the words then.''

It was a lie, she assured herself. She would be lying to gain freedom from the necklace—she'd lied for such reasons before. But doing it now made her feel strange and terrible. ''I love you,'' she whispered in a small, shaky voice.

''Say it again.''

''I love you,'' she repeated.

She would have been all right if he hadn't forced her to say the words twice. But by the second time, tears were welling up in her eyes. Her thick, black lashes were spiked with moisture, and the more she thought on why she cried, the more damp her eyes became. Och, it just couldn't be! She was only spewing meaningless words at him. She didn't love St. Bride. She didn't!

But if St. Bride doubted her sincerity, he didn't show it at all. He kissed each crystalline teardrop as it trailed down her cheeks, and his hands gently went around her neck. There was a twist and pull, and suddenly she was free of the silver collar. He kept his promise, throwing the necklace down to the foot of the bed.

''My beautiful, beautiful girl, all I want is to see you smile.'' He traced the lush pink of her lips and kissed another tear that slipped from her eye. Then he grew pensive. ''Your smile is so breathtaking, Kayleigh, and yet I see it so rarely. How elusive your happiness is!'' He stroked her wet cheek and said with determination, ''But I'm going to make you happy. Forever. I swear.''

He kissed her lips then and began to make love to her as if he hoped that her tears could be replaced by passion. His lips nibbled at the pale ring of skin on her neck left by the collar. It was strange not having the necklace there, and Kayleigh suddenly felt as if part of her were missing. If she hadn't needed it off her so desperately, she might have pulled the collar back on just to feel whole again.

"St. Bride, why ... ? Why ... ? Oh, St. Bride," she moaned as his dark head bent to nip at her breasts. She wasn't even sure of what she wanted to say to him, to ask of him. She needed a single word that expressed her absolute love and her absolute despair, but it was futile to even try to seek one. And when she was sure she would never find it, her fingers laced in the silver at his temples, and she selfishly used all her strength to forget who he was and to concentrate on who she wanted him to be.

She had her coherent thought before his tongue thrust hotly into her mouth, and his hand brushed between her thighs. His chest hair teased at her breasts, and it was clear that he was as impatient for her as she was impatient for him. She gratefully opened to him, and his first exquisite thrust filled her to overflowing. But only when the linen grew wet beneath them, and the white gauze shimmered around them like a billion stars, and the heat of the room reached the boiling point, did she repeat the words once more. But this time, she knew for certain she did not lie.

"I love you, St. Bride," she gasped. Then she laughed blackly through her tears. She clasped her enemy to her breast and sought out her own fiery pleasure to the bitter end. Her betrayal of everything she had loved and held precious was complete, but in her blinding need, she cared not a whit that she had sold herself, heart, body, and soul, to the devil.

Kayleigh had known St. Bride was tired. He'd obviously been up most of the night and had risen early. So after their lovemaking, she was not surprised when he pulled her to him and fell fast asleep. It was not easy extricating herself from his bed. It was difficult to pull her hair from beneath his hand, and it was a task to leave the ropes without making them creak. But mostly it was hard to leave St. Bride.

Her velvet stare caressed him. Through the film of silk gauze, he looked like a fallen Icarus, saved from death in the sea, only to be laid to rest until new wings of wax and feathers could be made for his escape from Crete. He was lying on his stomach with his face turned toward her, his breathing deep and satisfied. She studied his face.

He needed to shave—but then he always did, it seemed. She smiled from the sure, intimate knowledge of how dark and heavy his beard was. He had to use his razor twice a day just to look civilized. Despite that, it never failed to amaze her how boyish his face looked when he slept. Her soft gaze caressed his strong features relaxed in slumber. His hair was still queued, but it hung down his neck tousled and curling. She longed to reach out and grasp a lock and pull on it; to make his beautiful eyes open; to make him smile just for her.

She moved her gaze lower. She studied his bronzed back and his powerful arms, curled above his head. Her eyes moved to his tight, narrow buttocks and then to his long, muscular legs, well sprinkled with black hair. He was a magnificent sight.

But he was also her foe, she told herself, and backed from the bed. He was a man who played not at all by the rules. In the weeks they had spent together, he made no gesture, spoke no word, had no thought for which he didn't have a hidden motive. Hadn't he even said once that he was a man who toyed with his enemies? She trembled at the thought. She had been his enemy all along, for he had toyed with her. He had aroused her affections, and now she wondered if he planned to strangle her with them.

Swallowing a new bout of cold tears, she reached for some clothing. She would leave him. He wouldn't take her again— he would drive her insane if he did.

Her shift was useless. But it was too risky to go back to her room and unpack her trunks from the voyage—she might meet Colette. So she donned the only clothes at hand—St. Bride's. Wearing his clothing was a comfort and yet torture, for every thread of cambric in his shirt smelled of him. When she donned his chamois breeches, she had to keep her mind off the fact that her loins were encased in the same leather that usually encased his. The waist of the breeches were much too big, so she quietly slipped off the straps from inside his jackboots. She buckled them together, then put the entire thing around her waist and buckled it as if it were a belt. This worked fairly well. With St. Bride's sleep-filled breathing in the background, she rolled up the sleeves of his huge shirt; she tucked the silver and sapphire collar onto the waist of her breeches; she gave one last pain-filled look at the man sleeping under the gauze; and then she tiptoed barefoot out of the chamber.

Several minutes later she was rushing through the stable, opening up all the stalls, and spooking the horses with a whip. Free at last, they trotted into the courtyard. Several stallions worked themselves into a frenzy with access to so many mares. From the stable door, Kayleigh panted and watched them run as a group into the old indigo fields. She saw Mathias come bounding across the bricks from the kitchens, where he had obviously been having breakfast. The look of horror on his face was heart-wrenching, and she hoped he'd be able to catch them all safely. But that was not her concern now. As Mathias ran toward her, she ducked into a stall—Canis's stall—and opened the door. St. Bride's stallion was already tacked up and ready to ride. She mounted and was just getting ready to bolt when Mathias threw himself in her path.

"I'm sorry, Mathias. Truly I am. Now get out of my way!" She kept Canis from rearing but not without difficulty. "Please, Mathias. Do as I say!" She brought Canis forward. Her knotted hair was swept over shoulder, and her hand looked very comfortable wrapped around the whip. She knew she looked like every boy's nightmare of an avenging angel, and she used this to her advantage. Her eyes glittered, and she whipped at Canis's flanks. "Get out of my way! All I want to do is leave here. I'm going to take Canis and be off. You have nothing to fear. Just do as I say!''

"But the master! You done killed the master!" Mathias's gaze was riveted on her odd apparel. No doubt the boy had seen St. Bride in these same clothes only hours before.

"He's fine!" she scolded. "Just do as I say!"

"Please have the master be all right!" were Mathias's last words before he stepped aside and let the stallion have its head.

Kayleigh wasted no more time. Fear gave her the strength to stay on Canis's back. She tightened the reins and prayed that all she had learned as a young girl about riding astride on Mhor's nasty Shetland ponies was still with her. She squeezed Canis's flanks and shot out of the stable.

A gathering of house servants, Colette included, watched in dismay as she sped across the courtyard with Canis's steel shoes ringing on every brick.

"Au voleur! Au voleur!"

Startled, Kayleigh spun around and saw that Grand-Louis was behind her, crying "Stop thief!" as loud as his old lungs would permit.

"Hush, you old fool!" she whispered as much to herself as to him, but Grand-Louis rambled on, making his accusations louder. He called out *"Au voleur!"* until she was sure he would even wake St. Bride. But when she looked to the house, she found St. Bride already roused and barely covered by a pair of unbuttoned breeches. He raged down the cypress stairs from the loggia.

Terrified, Kayleigh didn't wait for him to catch her as she galloped Canis—or rather Canis galloped her—down the allée of pecans that led to the River Road. But she did look back, just once, and saw the look of utter betrayal that crossed St. Bride's face as he stopped in the courtyard. He watched her flee, helpless for the moment to do anything about it.

Dhé, she thought as she clutched Canis between her legs and forced him to fly down the hot, rutted road, it was a good thing she was never going to see him again. After the murderous look he had given her retreating figure, she knew that would be best. But still, the anguish of his expression came back to haunt her, and every time it did, she felt wretched indeed.

Chapter Twenty-eight

"Papa, St. Bride has returned. I want you to speak with him."
Lady Catherine followed her father into the *grande salle* and
daintily set herself upon a *pliant*.

"Yes, yes, *ma chère*. But why do you want this particular
man so? St. Bride Ferringer gives me frightful indigestion."

"She wants him because she cannot wrap him around her
little finger, as she has every other weak-kneed imbecile in
this colony," Straught interrupted. He entered the chamber
and regarded Lady Catherine with disgust. She mirrored his
expression entirely. It was obvious they despised each other.

"Mr. Straught, shall I wrap you around my finger along
with the rest of the weak-kneed imbeciles?" Lady Catherine
rose from her *pliant,* bristled, and directed the rest of her bad
humor to her father. "I want to go to Belle Chasse today,
Papa. You know they've returned. I must see St. Bride!"

"Please, Catherine. You must not speak to our house-
guests so!" Thionville turned as red as the burgundy he was
sucking on. He chided nervously, "Erath here is an honored
guest. I can't let him think I have raised a shrew. Apologize,
Catherine."

"Apologize!" She spun in her butter-colored satin gown
and faced Straught. She looked as if she were going to laugh

in his face at the absurdity of the suggestion, but before the first strains of taunting laughter left her mouth, she caught a flash of red in Straught's angry gaze. She was taken aback, as if she finally believed all her father's prattle about the Lowlander's unnatural eyes. She fell down onto a green velvet *pliant* and confined herself to rebelling in silence.

"Catherine!" her father reproved.

"Stop, Thionville. If Catherine has a mind of her own, who are we to rebuke her for it?" Straught looked down at the beautiful girl on the *pliant*. His eyes took in her flawless peach-hued cheeks, her rich, full lips, and her cool, minty gaze. He said nastily, "Let her run her own course. St. Bride knows his own mind, too, and I daresay, he's made his likes painfully clear."

"Ooh!" Lady Catherine swatted away Straught's offending presence and snapped to her father, "Papa, I am leaving right now! St. Bride will have to give up his black-haired *prostituée* and marry me! I give him no choice. I refuse to live in this terrible land and remain a spinster!"

"There, there, daughter! You shall not remain a spinster," Thionville soothed. "When we reap the profits from these poppies, you will return to France in grand style! You will find a better husband than St. Bride—and richer too! I promise!"

"Papa, no! I want St. Bride! I've met the gentlemen of the Court. Those who flock around Louis XV cannot compare." She spat, "I hate that raven-haired witch! Why will he not let her go?"

Her vehemence caught Straught's attention. He said, "You've not the charms to make him let her go." He turned to the comte. "Your man said they both returned last night— St. Bride and the girl?"

"Yes, yes," Thionville answered. "But the girl came none too willingly, if the dockmaster is no liar. He told me St. Bride practically had to throw her into his carriage. I didn't expect them back so soon—not after the way they disappeared from the ball! Why Erath, did I ever tell you that many of the guests thought St. Bride's mistress was this Kestrel you've been looking for? Once she was unmasked, they talked only of her. A most enchanting vixen apparently with the bluest eyes, the blackest hair. She looks like a witch too—she's got the most intriguing brows. Catherine does not exaggerate.''

"She *is* a witch!" Straught spewed ominously. "And she *is* this Kestrel!"

"She *is* the Kestrel!" Thionville sputtered in disbelief. "But Erath, if you knew this, why have we not arrested her? We could have had her weeks ago. We could have taken her last night after they disembarked!"

"Because she's hooked up with Ferringer, that's why. Would you arrest her and risk irritating him? No, we've got to get her without St. Bride knowing you and I were behind it. We've got to do it in such a way that the blame will be put upon another.''

"We're not behind this girl's ruin. She's the one who became a murderess." Thionville looked offended. "If she is the Kestrel, St. Bride cannot blame me. After all, what did I do? I just had the signs posted.''

"Yes, on my instructions," Straught snarled. "What are we to do now?''

"Nothing, I say. The girl is not the one you seek. There is a similarity to the Kestrel, but only in the most superficial way. St. Bride's mistress is no coarse, foul-mouthed street wench. She is the fairest flower in all of Louisiana. Not including Catherine, of course," the comte added hastily, seeing his daughter's boiling expression.

"I don't care what you think of her. She's the one, I tell you! And she's been with Ferringer all the time. My God, he must know all about me!" Straught paled.

"Why must you have this Kestrel? You have never told me," the comte said.

"Perhaps for the same reason you want her," Straught answered snidely.

"Colette is St. Bride's woman, Erath. Perhaps we'd best accept—"

"What did you say?"

"I said, Colette—" the comte tried to repeat.

"Colette—why do you call the Kestrel Colette?"

"Because that is her name. At least, that is the name she gave me when I visited Belle Chasse." Thionville frowned. "What is it, Erath?"

"Of course!" Some of the tension left Straught's face. "She's been using a false name. That's why St. Bride has not come after us. She probably trusts St. Bride no more than she does me! What beautiful luck! He no doubt beat her senseless when he got his hands on her. After all, she put a knife to him when she tried to steal his purse!"

"Erath, you make no sense! The girl is St. Bride's mistress. He even took her with him to Georgia. Colette is no common thief, I tell you! I think, very much, you are mistaken!" Thionville swiped at his brow, which was beaded with perspiration. He didn't like it when his friend got excited. Straught's eyes blazed, and the red spot in his iris glowed like an ember.

"Come, Thionville! We must go to Belle Chasse. I've never gotten a straight answer about my man Quinn from that black Goliath of St. Bride's, so we shall get answers for that—and, if we are lucky, get Kestrel to boot." Straught commanded Thionville off the gilt rococo settee.

"We shall go. Perhaps the flowers are blooming even this day. I shall get the coachman to take us. *Vite!*" The comte was ready to depart, but Catherine delayed him.

"I shall go too, Papa!" she demanded. "I want to be there when the Kestrel is caught. St. Bride may need comforting."

"You are not coming. I'll have no woman interrupting my plans," Straught said with contempt.

"I am coming, Papa!" Catherine looked to her father.

"Now is not a good time, *ma chère*. Perhaps tomorrow, when this nasty business is taken care of."

"Papa! I want to be there—"

Just then the voice of a footman interrupted the argument. "My lord, you have callers."

"Not now!" Thionville dismissed.

"My lord, they say it is urgent," the footman persisted.

"We must go to Belle Chasse immediately," Thionville said. "We've no time for callers, for we've located the notorious Kestrel. Tell them to go away."

"Yes, my lord." The footman was ready to retreat. "However, that is the very matter they've come about."

"They? Who are they?" Thionville questioned.

"They go by the names of Lina and Wolfbane, and the matter they speak of is the Kestrel."

"What do they know of the Kestrel?" Straught asked sharply.

"My lord"—the footman kept his eyes on his master and not on the unwelcome sandy-haired houseguest—"they say they have the Kestrel."

"What?" Lady Catherine, Thionville, and Straught all had the same reply. Suddenly, Thionville found his wits and commanded snappishly, "Then send them in, you fool! *Mon dieu,* why didn't you say so!"

"As you wish, my lord." The footman bowed to hide his displeasure and then departed. Straught's worried eyes followed him until he disappeared around the corner of the gallery.

St. Bride paced his gallery and waited for word on Kayleigh. No word came. So he paced more and watched the sweltering heat shimmer along the eastern bayou. The flowers had bloomed and turned the distant northern fields into the color of a sunset. He watched that, too, but all he could concentrate on was Kayleigh.

He gazed at the road, which lay hot and dormant in the August sun. It had no travelers; no messengers. He cursed under his breath, and his brow grew stormy. He clutched the cigar-shaped cypress pillar of the gallery with both hands.

"The flowers have bloomed, St. Bride. As I said in my note, Straught was highly upset by your absence. We cannot delay calling for him now," Laban said tentatively as he joined St. Bride in the gallery.

"Not until I find Kayleigh."

The statement was expected, and Laban didn't look surprised. He said. "The men we have hired will find her soon enough, my friend. She cannot leave the city, for we have informed the dockmaster of her supposed plan to pay for passage with the necklace. There is nothing we can do but wait—yet the flowers cannot wait. It is time to call in Straught."

"I must find Kayleigh."

"She will be fine. She has lived on the streets most—if not all—of her life. And she left you, remember? She did it of her own free will," Laban admonished gently.

"I must find her, even if it's just to choke the life out of her when I do." St. Bride's hands tightened on the pillar. He grew melancholy and rasped, "She told me she loved me, Laban. And I believed her. I was going to ask her to marry me. Can you believe that? I was going to ask that little cutpurse to be my duchess. And she would have fit in, I tell you! No one would have ever guessed her origins. For all her wickedness, Kayleigh seemed quite gently born at times. My God, how I want her!"

"St. Bride . . ." Laban tried to ease his friend's anxiety, but to no avail. The only thing he could do was rest a hand on the other man's shoulder.

"She was so different from every woman I've ever known." St. Bride continued, "She seemed to want nothing from me. She scoffed at my gifts and ridiculed this shoddy plantation. She was utterly unimpressed with everything I have and everything most women hold so dear. But then, when she finally did want something, the only thing I found to please her was myself." St. Bride's eyes clouded, and he repeated himself as if the words were punishment. "She told me she loved me, Laban. She told me she loved me, and I believed her.''

"The girl is not without guile. You know that. Perhaps she said it for the necklace," Laban rationalized.

"She did say it for the necklace. But she told me she loved me again, after I took the necklace off.'' St. Bride turned to face his friend. "She was a virgin, did you know that? I finally took her in Georgia, and she was as intact as a nun.''

Laban uttered slowly, "Sometimes women have a way of faking the blood, St. Bride—''

"I felt her flesh tear.''

With this irrefutable evidence, Laban fell silent.

St. Bride ran a hand through his hair. "Where is she? I only wanted to help her—to keep her safe—to love her. Why did she do this? What was she afraid of?''

"We will find her, St. Bride. You have the means and the power," Laban reassured him. "But in the meantime you must deal with Straught. The flowers will not be in bloom forever.''

St. Bride released a huge sigh. "All right, we'll finish this *belle chasse*. Send for the bastard, Laban. We'll rid ourselves of him, and if the magistrate gets his claws on the Kestrel in the meantime, we'll do what any good Louisianian would in the situation.''

"And what is that?'' Laban questioned.

"We'll pay him off,'' St. Bride answered simply.

Chapter Twenty-nine

It was her first night of freedom, but she was anything but free. Standing before the Comte de Cassell's doorway, Kayleigh recalled all that had befallen her since her escape from Belle Chasse.

After she'd abandoned Canis to the road, she made for the docks, but her plan to sell the necklace had gone awry. There were no ships bound for Scotland at all. She presented the collar to the captain of a ship out of Le Havre that was ultimately destined for Rotterdam. But the captain took one look at the necklace, proclaimed it stolen, and told her that the hangman wanted her. Frightened, she'd snatched the necklace out of his grasp and fled back to the streets.

That night, she'd tried to sleep in different places, for she dared not sleep in Bardolph's hut. She finally made her bed underneath a raised *colombage* warehouse to the east of the Place d'Armes. She slid between the new floorboards and the clammy earth, and after fashioning a bed of discarded dried palmetto leaves, she lay down.

Then she brought out the necklace and rubbed the silver with St. Bride's shirt-sleeve. A spare amount of moonlight flooded beneath the building, but the silver collar gleamed anyway. In the end she would be saddened to part with it.

The collar was much like the man who had given it to her—smooth and polished on the outside and possessing all sorts of treachery on the inside.

Disgusted that her thoughts had once more turned to St. Bride, she cast the collar beneath her shirt for safekeeping. She didn't put it on, for she hadn't figured out how to release the spring that locked it. So she lay with the cold silver on her breast and cried herself to sleep.

"The Kestrel! The Kestrel! Eaaach! My pockets are lined with gold!" At these words Kayleigh's head shot up from her palmetto bed. She hardly had room to sit—her head met with the floorboards above. Still, she scurried to a kneeling position. She had to keep her wits about her. Someone had found her!

In the darkness beneath the building she saw that the sun had risen and was shining through the uneven boards of the banquettes. Down at the long end of the warehouse she saw a woman, made old from hardship, not age, who peered at her as if she were a new-found coin. Kayleigh knew her instantly.

Her name was Lina. It was short for Angelina, but most of the riverfolk jokingly referred to her as Devilina instead. Yet those who valued their lives were canny enough never to speak the other name in the old witch's face, for Lina was a nasty sort.

"Get away with you, Lina! You have no business with me!" Kayleigh shouted.

"No business with you? The Kestrel!" Lina cackled in amazement. "My pockets are lined with gold just looking at you! Eaaach! What the day has brung me! Come out here, pretty girl! The comte wants a minute with you and some gold for me!"

"I'll not go anywhere with you!" Kayleigh backed away to the other end of the long warehouse. She could outrun the old hag. And she really wasn't that frightened. She tucked her precious collar into the waist of her breeches. She tightened the bootstrap belt even further, then scrambled from beneath the building at the opposite end from Lina. She planned to make her way to the docks, but she didn't get that far.

Devilina had a son, appropriately named Wolfbane, who was posted at this end of the warehouse.

"Wolfbane, you evil-minded son of a dragon! Don't you come near me!" She'd skidded from the lad's reach and backed to the banquette. The many passersby at that time of the morning hardly gave a second look to the filthy girl and the gangly river youth who pursued her. The passersby walked on, and unaided, Kayleigh fought to get away.

"I said let me go! You won't be taking me anywhere! Do you hear?" she screamed at the lad, but Wolfbane remained nonplussed.

Then his mother came up from behind her and knocked her with an old cypress cane. In the end, with no way to fight off her attackers, Kayleigh had to surrender.

She landed on an ancient silk Tabriz carpet. The fall knocked the wind out of her, and she was forced to lie in the middle of the room and lose several precious seconds gasping for breath. When her lungs filled with air, she looked up and saw the person she dreaded most, her cousin, seated on a green-velvet *pliant* in front of her.

He spent a moment examining her soiled and damp appearance. His unnatural gaze didn't miss the fact that she was wearing men's clothing, and his eyes registered that her shirt and breeches were undoubtedly St. Bride's.

"Kayleigh, don't you ever bathe?" he began, with his usual charismatic levity. He looked to Lina and Wolfbane, and his lips curled up in a disgusted smile. "But then, with the company you keep, why should you?"

"Your soul will rot in hell for the things you've done, Erath!" Kayleigh cried out. She scrambled to her feet and made to flee, but the footman's and Wolfbane's presence assured her she would not.

"Is she truly the Kestrel, Erath? Is she truly the girl you've been searching for?" The comte rose from his settee. The sweet smell of Thionville's pomatum was strong in the air, but there was also the faintest scent of lavender. Lady Catherine, too, was already standing before her.

"Whoever she is, Erath, you may have her. She is a filthy *prostituée*, and I want her out of this house. She will give us all a disease! Papa, you cannot let *maman* see this creature in her home!" Lady Catherine looked down at her and smiled in smug satisfaction. Outraged, Kayleigh scowled, but she had a bigger threat to worry about than Lady Catherine's defamation of her character. She turned back to her cousin.

"Erath, dare you murder me in front of all these people?"

"Murder? You speak of murder?" Thionville looked at Kayleigh with softness in his eyes. He didn't seem to mind that she was dirty and damp. All he saw was the girl beneath the filth, the one he had wanted at Belle Chasse, one that he still wanted now. Kayleigh vowed to take advantage of the situation. Thionville's lust for her might save her life.

She threw the comte her most terrified look and whispered desperately, "Erath means to murder me. I didn't kill Bardolph Ogilvie. Erath did!"

"What is the meaning of this?" The comte immediately turned to Straught. "Can it be that you really want her hung? If the girl were old and ugly like that one"—he jerked his bewigged head to Lina—"I could understand ridding the world of one more pestilence. But why Colette? It would be such a waste!"

"Papa!" Lady Catherine cried in outrage.

"Hush!" Thionville quelled her, then waited for Straught's answer.

Straught only laughed. "You think I'm going to kill this girl—Ferringer's whore? Why, you're all fools, the lot of you!"

"We'd like our gold. Me mother and me'd like our gold,'' Wolfbane suddenly came forward.

"Ah, more fools!'' Straught exclaimed, and dug into his waistcoat pocket. He tossed a single brass coin toward Lina and Wolfbane and watched it roll lazily across the pictorial Tabriz. Wolfbane captured it when it came to rest near the door. He seemed quite pleased, but his mother was outraged.

"We've brought you the Kestrel! She's the one you want! Is this our only reward? Is this what the comte has to offer for Bardolph Ogilvie's murderer?'' Lina screeched.

"Get them out!'' Thionville commanded. The footman obeyed.

"The signs! They said reward! Is this all that's to be gotten for the Kestrel?'' Lina could be heard screeching as she was dragged out, Wolfbane following peaceably.

"I did not kill Bardolph, and you know it!'' Kayleigh shouted to Straught through Lina's din.

"But the signs worked—I've got you back!'' Straught leaned forward on his *pliant* and motioned for Thionville to step near. Straught took him aside and said, "I shall lock her up in Quinn's room in the stables.''

"I won't have her harmed, Erath. As I said—''

"Yes, yes, you lecherous old goat. You just want her for yourself. But now we've got to deal with Ferringer. It's becoming clear that we've been duped by him, you ass. For the time being, let me assure you, I want Kayleigh as healthy as possible. She might be our only means of bargaining out of this mess.'' Straught stood.

"I suppose we could use Quinn's room,'' the comte finally stated.

"Yes. Hell will freeze over before we hear from that one again.'' Roughly, Straught pulled Kayleigh to him and led her outside.

They were halfway to the stables before Kayleigh could even register what was happening to her. Her entire being was numb. It had been ever since Straught had uttered the words *"We've been duped"* to the comte. Three small words, and her entire world caved in around her. The worst possibility occurred to her: Had she been wrong about St. Bride?

"Erath. Erath, listen," she burst out hysterically. "I must know, is St. Bride your friend or your foe?"

"What are you mumbling about?" Straught thrust her into an upper room filled with an odd assortment of silver, porcelain, and men's clothing.

"I must know! Is St. Bride a friend or an enemy?" she cried out.

"I suppose that's what I'll be finding out all too soon." His handsome mouth formed into a hard, grim line.

Misery overwhelmed her. Had she been wrong about St. Bride? Had she fled Belle Chasse, only to find she was the betrayer, not the betrayed? With anxious eyes, she studied her cousin. She'd never seen Straught so worried.

Feeling faint, she leaned against the wall for support. If St. Bride *was* duping him, it all fit together so well. In fact, St. Bride was probably the "gent" Quinn had told her about so long ago, the man who was dogging Straught because Straught had dallied with . . . *Mary.*

She closed her eyes. What a fool she was! She had run from her only chance at happiness, only to end up in Straught's clutches. Now she would pay for that foolishness with her life.

"Come along," Straught ordered as he grabbed up her hands. He meant to tie them, but as he pulled her from the wall, he knocked against the collar, which was still tucked in her breeches.

"What have we here?" he exclaimed, extracting the piece from her clothing. The sapphire sparkled like blue fire.

"No!" she cried, and grabbed it from him. She held on to it with both hands and backed into the corner.

"Where did you get that?" A puzzled scowl overrode his fine features. The sapphire seemed to remind him of something. As he studied it, he stepped nearer.

"You cannot have it!" She thrust it behind her, away from his scrutiny.

"Can it be?" he gasped, grabbing the hand that held the collar. He looked at the stone a moment longer, then dropped his hold. Shock seemed to overcome him. He murmured, "Can it be? Is that a *fourth* Lansdowne sapphire? Did that bastard wear it on the *Bonaventure,* all the while laughing at me that I didn't recognize him?"

Suddenly, as if he couldn't bear it any longer, he growled, "My God, I *have* been duped!" Immediately, he turned on her. "Give me that necklace," he demanded.

"No. St. Bride gave it to me," she whispered.

"My beauty . . . of course he did! He was fond of you, wasn't he?" Straught tried to grab it, but this time she was ready for him.

"No, you cannot have it!" she cried before he was upon her. In one smooth motion she pulled the collar around her neck and snapped the lock together. It fastened. She gasped with relief. He'd have to kill her to get it now.

"Take it *off!*" Straught bellowed.

"St. Bride fashioned the necklace not to come off. Only he knows how to unlock it."

"I'll get it off in the end, Kayleigh. You know that," Straught said with false patience.

"Yes, I know," she answered truthfully. "But then, when St. Bride finds out how I was murdered, at least he'll know that I loved him and that I didn't lie to him. Not in the end."

"Love! Can love save your life?" he snarled. Disgusted he grabbed her hands and wrapped a length of rope around them that he had brought with him. She tried to kick him and run, but he shoved her hard against the wall. Her breath knocked out of her, she finally acquiesced. She took heart that her feet were not bound. Somehow she still might get free.

She hadn't counted on one thing, however—the milky translucent vial of liquid that Straught produced from his

waistcoat. He poured some wine from a flask that he had
brought into a dusty silver goblet on Quinn's commode. Then
he tippled several healthy drops from the vial into it. "Laudanum?" he asked.

"I'll not let you poison me," she accused.

"On the contrary, I'm trying to help you. We're going to
meet your lover, Kayleigh, and it wouldn't do for you to act
up while we negotiate. Drink it!" He shoved the loathsome
goblet under her nose. All she could smell was the wine, but
she knew the laudanum was in there. It floated to the top and
swirled through the Bordeaux.

"I will not be put to sleep." She pushed the goblet away
with her bound hands.

"There isn't enough in here to put you to sleep, just enough
to make you docile. If you don't cooperate, love, I promise
you you'll see St. Bride Ferringer's brains blown out the back
of his head. Would you like that?" Straught smiled quite
handsomely.

"He's not involved in this!" she gasped.

"He duped me. Now it's my turn to dupe him. If you care
for him at all, you'd best do as I say. I've a plan of my own
to carry out, and I'll see you cooperate with your end."
Straught shoved the goblet back under her nose. He forced
a sip into her mouth, but she sprayed it out, knocking the
goblet away with her bound hands. It clattered to the floor,
and the red, drug-laced spirits seeped into the floorboards.

"Fine." Straught picked up the goblet and placed it back
on Quinn's crude commode. "I'll see that your lover pays
for your disobedience."

"Why not kill me instead? No doubt you'd take pleasure
in watching me die," she hissed, then sank against the wall.

"You're just like your mother, Kayleigh. She was not one
to be tamed either."

"My mother was nothing like me! She was sweet and kind
and—"

"And she was your father's trial!" Straught looked deep

into Kayleigh's eyes and continued, ''I tried to kiss your mother once, did you know that? No, I suppose not. She never told a soul.'' He laughed. ''I tried to kiss her, and she almost knocked me over the head with one of the claymores chained in the great hall. After that, I let her husband have her. And good riddance, I said!'' He grew pensive. ''But then came you.''

''If you wanted me, why did you kill Morna? I loved Morna.'' Her voice trembled with suppressed sobs.

''I didn't want to kill Morna. I don't want to kill you.'' He looked down at her hunched against the wall. He studied every raven tress on her head, every creamy inch of her complexion, and every curve of her figure. ''But you must go eventually. You'll never marry me.'' He turned morose. ''I promise to be kind, Kayleigh. We're going to the dock and we'll board a ship this evening. I'll put you to sleep while we're at sea, then toss you overboard. It should be quite clean and painless.''

''How gracious!'' she exclaimed slowly.

''I must survive! I'm a Kerr, too, love. That's the Kerr way!''

''That's not the Kerr way! My father was not like that and God help me, though I've had to do things I regret, I've never resorted to murder!'' She raised her bound hands and begged him, ''I want to return to Belle Chasse. I'll never go back to Mhor. I'm no longer a threat to you, Erath, so let me go. Just let me go back to St. Bride.''

''You've got to die, Kayleigh. Just make up your mind whether you want St. Bride to go with you or not.''

''I want him to live'' was all she could utter.

''Then do as I say. Here is my plan.''

After he told her what she was to do, he left Quinn's room. When she heard the door latch, she ran to it, foolishly testing the lock. Then she slumped to the floor.

Slowly, she realized that she was surrounded by the things she had stolen from Belle Chasse. She numbly scanned the silver salt bowls and the Bristol chargers. But when her eyes rested on a gold-buttoned marine blue waistcoat on the floor by the bed, her mind suddenly snapped and she released a moan. It was St. Bride's.

Chapter Thirty

"We've been had," Straught said angrily to Thionville as the carriage rocked and swayed over the uneven terrain.

"We saw the flowers coming up only last week, Erath. What can go wrong? It's true they hadn't bloomed then, but St. Bride cannot take every single plant from the ground just to spite us. Perhaps you've misjudged him," the comte pacified.

"He's Lansdowne, I tell you! He's been after me all along. Kayleigh had his sapphire. That proves there will be no profit from Belle Chasse." Erath straightened in his seat then said "But we do have Kayleigh. I just hope she's worth something to him. I pray she is. If she's got to die, I'd at least like to regain those jewels from Ferringer."

"The Kestrel will not be killed! I will not have it!" Thionville insisted.

"Shut up," Straught said in an ominous tone.

They reached Belle Chasse after traveling at breakneck speed. Anxious to see the blooms in the distant fields, they quickly alighted from the carriage, scuttled through the strangely empty rear courtyard, and heaved up the stairs.

From the loggia, they would be able to survey the nearest fields of poppies. Straught was the first to reach the top of the stairs, and his eyes anxiously scanned the horizon. He searched for the expected red. The fields were ablaze with fiery color, but Straught covered his face with his hands.

"It cannot be!" Thionville croaked behind him in stunned amazement. "It cannot be!"

"It is, you ass!" Straught cried in a murderous rage. "The bloody fields are orange, not red! Goddamn it! He planted black-eyed Susans!"

"But the seeds! Those precious seeds! What did he do with them?"

"Dumped them in the river, for all I know. God, I'll kill that bastard! I'll kill his mistress, and then I'll kill him!" Straught turned to enter the salon. Like the loggia, the courtyard, and the entire plantation, it was eerily vacant. Behind him, there was no giggling of laundresses and house slaves; before him, not a sound came from the shabby, stripped interior. The house was so quiet, it seemed haunted.

"Ferringer! Ferringer!" he shouted, and his words echoed through the vacant rooms. "Where are you, you bastard! You goddamned bastard, I'll kill you!"

"Erath! Wait!" Thionville followed timidly in his wake, looking behind him as if he expected ghosts.

"Where are you, Lansdowne!" Straught screamed as he shot in and out of the huge chambers. He took them one at a time, but when he got to the last room, St. Bride's bedchamber, he stopped. His mouth fell open.

"Ah . . . the Grim Reaper has come for his harvest," St. Bride exclaimed from the interior.

He sat in a walnut chair with his legs slung atop the bed, his feet crossed casually. On his lap were two heavy dueling pistols. And behind him stood his gigantic Negro holding a French musket, obviously bought from one of the infantrymen at the barracks. But neither the guns nor the men were as frightening as the thing that hung over St. Bride's head. From Launier's hook hung a noose, ready for occupancy. In the hot winds off the Mississippi it swung from side to side as if beckoning a visitor.

St. Bride looked up at it, then gave Thionville a contrite smile.

"My apologies, my lord," he said to Thionville. "There would have been a noose for you also, but as you can see, I have only one hook."

"You're Lansdowne!" Straught screamed, his eyes flaming with rage. "By God, I'll kill you!"

"You've figured it out at last!" St. Bride remained deadly calm, lazily inspecting the black walnut handle of one of the pistols. "That's right, I'm the ninth Duke of Lansdowne and Mary Greenling's brother, and I've not even had to change my name to dupe you, Straught."

"Your name should be Greenling!" Straught bellowed.

"Mary Greenling was my half sister. I must say, Straught, I had thought you more intelligent than you've proven to be. You cannot imagine my joy when one of your Highland 'friends' told me you were coming to the Colonies desperate for funds. I found this Belle Chasse, and I knew it would be the way to get you."

St. Bride paused, his eyes flickering to the noose. He then said matter-of-factly, "I've now taken every bit of wealth you had, Straught. Mary's jewels are back in my possession where they'll remain. You must know that the only honorable thing you can do is hang yourself. You've nothing else to live for now."

Thionville whined, "But you've taken my gold too! I had no business in this quarrel between you two, St. Bride!"

"True, my lord." St. Bride looked squarely at Thionville and noted how heavily the man was sweating. He turned back to Straught before adding, "But then, poppies are a nasty business, I think."

At St. Bride's comment, Straught's hand itched for the bulge in his waistcoat, where there was obviously a pistol. But St. Bride didn't seem worried as Straught defended himself saying, "I didn't kill your sister, Lansdowne. You must know that! I have a say in the matter too!"

"I know you didn't kill her," St. Bride said dully. "If you had, you would not be alive right now."

"Then why all this!" Thionville interjected. He continued tearfully, "Why have you gone so far as to dupe Erath out of those jewels, taking me along for the ride!"

"This is all for Mary," St. Bride answered.

"Mary!" Thionville exclaimed. "But Erath did not kill your sister! Even you yourself say he did not! *Mon dieu!* If you must take all my money, at least explain to me why!"

As if it pained him, St. Bride said tightly, "I owe no one an explanation."

"Then I'll explain it!" Straught cried in a nasty voice. "Ferringer's orphaned and neglected half sister was possessed by the devil! She had the Falling Sickness, and no one of the *ton* wanted much to do with her because her fits frightened them. But I was not frightened!"

St. Bride glared at Straught. "Mary was nothing less than an angel. She was vulnerable and lonely. You took advantage of that. Admit it!"

"Yes! You were a poor guardian, Ferringer! You were too busy with your stupid plantation to give Mary the companionship she needed! Now you blame me for doing just that!"

"By God, I do blame you!" St. Bride roared. He lifted his legs from the counterpane and stood, the dueling pistols now tucked in his breeches. "You swept her off her feet in that month I was away. Then you sunk your claws into her. You made her enamored of your good looks and attentiveness, and then you—!"

"Quite true, Ferringer!" Straught shouted. "But you're the one who must live with the guilt! You refuse to, so you use me as a scapegoat! My only wrongdoing was to give Mary the attention she deserved!"

"Yes, and sincere attention it was!" St. Bride bit out sarcastically. "You attended to her only because you thought her the sister of the Duke of Lansdowne! When you began courting her, you no doubt thought the path of marriage would be paved with gold. But when you found out that I controlled her fortune, you threw her off. You broke her heart and''— St. Bride's voice began to shake—''and she killed herself.''

''That's right! She died by her own hand! I didn't force all that laudanum to her lips!'' Straught cried out.

''No. No, you didn't,'' St. Bride said ominously. ''And that's why you're here to speak about it.''

''Mary was very tight-lipped about her great brother, the duke. She didn't want to impress me, but I found out about you anyway.'' Straught backed into the salon. ''You were a prodigal—you misspent your youth, much to your father's dismay—and when your parents died, you overcompensated by devoting yourself to your duty. You left Mary alone much of the time in order to do it!'' he screeched. ''But Mary understood. She thought you were wonderful. What a fool she was!''

''She was sweet and innocent,'' St. Bride countered, then changed his tack. ''But I found out how much she cared for you, Straught. *You!*'' He spat with disgust. ''After it was all over and she was in the ground, I was told that Mary believed you loved her, too, really loved her—in spite of her fits and regardless of her wealth. And you took full advantage of that until you found there was no profit to be had by it. Then you promised to take her to Gretna Green and marry her—with or without my approval, with or without the promise of her fortune.''

St. Bride was stalking Straught now, backing the smaller man into the large baywood armoire that stood against the opposite wall. He growled, ''Mary's maid told me how happy she was that night. If you had come to fetch her, Straught, I would have forced myself to accept your vile presence under my roof, if that was what it took to make Mary happy. But you never showed. She waited up for five nights! For five miserable nights she sat in the hall waiting for your carriage.''

St. Bride's voice caught in his throat. He finished, deadly calm, "And on the sixth night she took enough laudanum to put her to sleep forever."

"She took the laudanum. I didn't give it to her!" Straught's back thumped against the double doors of the armoire. Behind St. Bride, Laban guarded the quaking Thionville.

"She took the laudanum. I take the guilt. But what is your punishment?" St. Bride asked as he towered over Straught. "You've proven time and time again that you've no remorse for what happened. You care not a whit that a sweet young girl died because of your actions." He turned and pointed to the noose in his bedroom. "That's your atonement for what happened to Mary Greenling. You now have nothing to live for either, Straught. You're poor. You have no money. You'll be forced to make your living on the streets, and people will laugh at you and your bad luck. The other beggars will spit on you and hate you because you're used to fine manners and fine clothing. So you see? You have nothing to live for. End it now, Straught—take the easy way out. Just get up on the chair and put your neck through the rope. Laban and I— we'll take care of the rest."

"I have nothing to live for?" Straught let out a shaky laugh. "On the contrary, I have something quite pleasant to live for. Bedding your mistress, Lansdowne!"

Seeing St. Bride give a start, he continued with more assurance, "I have the Kestrel, you know. She goes by the name of Colette here, or so Thionville tells me. She's a comely girl—I'm quite taken with her. She would not object to living on the streets with even a pauper like me, I think. She's not used to better things—or have you spoiled her, Ferringer?"

Watching St. Bride's face turn from vengeful to horrified, Straught released a cocky laugh. "Wonderful! I see you're quite fond of her! Just as I suspected! We'd heard you two got along. So how much is she worth to you? Is she worth, say, ten thousand pounds?"

"Is she with the magistrate?" St. Bride whispered harshly.

Straught smiled. "No—even better. She's with me."

"If you've touched her, I'll kill you," St. Bride said evenly. "I'll take that rope over yonder and wrap it around your neck with my bare hands."

"I haven't harmed her, nor have I any intention of harming her. Rather, just the opposite."

"If you bed her, it's the same as rape. She's mistrustful. She won't allow you to take her willingly."

"But that doesn't apply to you, eh, Ferringer?" Straught smiled again, but this time his mirth was short-lived. He was slammed against the armoire, and St. Bride lifted him off the ground by the cloth of his waistcoat.

"No, it doesn't apply to me," St. Bride growled. "So don't touch her, Straught. Don't you dare. If you do, I'll know by the look on her face that you raped her, and then you'll have breathed your last."

"If you want to see Kayleigh Kerr again, let me down!"

Roping in his fury, St. Bride dropped him to the ground.

Immediately, Straught hastened to the other side of the room. He instructed, "There's a small French frigate named *Détente* docked at the quay. It's leaving tonight for Corsica. I want to be on it with ten thousand in gold." He tossed his head meaningfully toward the trunk. "If you're there by eight o'clock, you can buy your mistress back."

"You'll take me to her now," St. Bride directed to both Straught and the comte.

"You'll see her at eight," Straught answered nervously.

"Now," St. Bride stated, his hands now holding both dueling pistols.

"You think to strong-arm me?" Straught laughed. "Then you'll never see your beautiful lover again, I promise."

"Take me to Kayleigh." Suddenly, St. Bride paused. A speculative, puzzled glint shone in his eye. He crossed swiftly over to Straught. "How do you know Kayleigh's last name?" he demanded.

"She doesn't lie to me, Ferringer." Straught looked at the

anxious expression on St. Bride's face and laughed again. He stepped away. Thionville followed him like a dog. "We'll be going now. Meet us at the *Détente*."

A terrible, furious rage swept over St. Bride's features then. His expression was a lethal mixture of shock, horror, and deadly vengeance as he voiced the realization, "You're her cousin, aren't you, you slimy bastard?"

"What—?" Straught hadn't time to finish. He was again slammed against the wall, yet this time St. Bride held a pistol to his head.

"I said, you're her cousin! It all makes sense! That's why you came here!" St. Bride shouted.

"That's right. I'm sweet Kayleigh's cousin. So what's to be made of it?" Straught struggled against the pistol held to his temple.

"She told me you murdered her twin, that's what." St. Bride jammed the muzzle even harder against Straught's sandy-colored head. "You came here for her, didn't you? When you found her, you murdered old Bardolph Ogilvie, and she escaped into the swamps. Because she knew you were on her trail, I never got a word of truth out of her. How could I, when she thought I was great friends with you!" He suddenly rasped, "By God, you'd better take me to her now, or I'll blow your head off right here and let Thionville lead the way."

"All right, Your Grace," Straught said sarcastically. "I'll take you to her now, but for the jewels. Give me back Mary's jewels."

"Take me to her, and we'll discuss your 'fee' when she's safe."

"Bring the sapphires, or you'll never see her alive again," Straught vowed, fearfully nonetheless.

St. Bride's furious gaze pinned Straught to the wall, but Straught didn't flinch. Finally, St. Bride said, "We'll bring the jewels. Take us now." St. Bride turned to Laban. They exchanged worried looks, then Laban went to gather the jewels.

When Laban returned, Thionville exclaimed from the corner, "But what about me? St. Bride! You must free me from this terrible scheme!"

"Ah, you! That's right. I'll see to it you're repaid." Letting Laban watch Straught, St. Bride strode over to a leather trunk in one corner. He sprang the iron lock and lifted the heavy leather tabs. He took out a silken purse and threw it to the comte.

"You're too kind, Your Grace!" Thionville whispered in amazement.

"I've given you enough and only enough gold to pay for one passage to France. You're ruined, Thionville, but I see no reason why Lady Catherine should suffer. If you're a kind father, see that she returns to Paris and finds a husband." St. Bride stooped and relocked the trunk.

"I see." Thionville looked down at the purse. It was obvious that he enjoyed the heaviness of the bag, but he placed the bag in his waistband and sighed resignedly.

"Shall we be off?" St. Bride asked. He surprised Straught by easily disarming him, taking the pistol from the shorter man's waistcoat. St. Bride then waved his own pair of pistols in the direction of the loggia. Straught and Thionville went first. As the other men followed, St. Bride whispered, "She's in grave trouble, my friend. Are you with me?"

Laban had heard Straught's confession, and his eyes were full of remorse. "I am," he answered with conviction.

Chapter Thirty-one

Somewhere in the night, a bell rang six times. Her attempts to flee Quinn's dark room had been ineffectual, and now Kayleigh merely sat in the corner holding her bound hands in her lap. Just as she was beginning to think no one would ever arrive for her, she heard men's footsteps move along the hallway, then stop at the door. Her heart leaped to her throat.

"St. Bride!" she called out, and started for the door. But her cousin entered first, and he roughly shoved her back down onto Quinn's greasy straw-stuffed pallet.

Her heart shattered into a thousand pieces when St. Bride entered the small cabin. She wanted to shriek from the grief tied up inside her. What a life they could have had together, had their love not been so ill fated! In miserable silence she watched him. He looked tired and grim, but there was a vibrant turquoise sparkle to his eyes that indicated that he was angry.

"Close the door behind you, Ferringer," Straught said, interrupting her speculation.

"The door remains open," St. Bride answered gruffly.

Straught was about to argue when Laban darkened the doorframe, holding a heavy vermilion bag.

"I told him to remain downstairs! Your Negro was not invited!" Straught bellowed.

"I don't take it upon myself to lug about my sister's jewels. You should know that much about my station," St. Bride said stonily. Then he turned to Kayleigh.

He looked at her for a very long time, his eyes not missing any detail of her wretched appearance. He studied her, or rather his, clothing—the soiled breeches and shirt. His gaze slid to her tangled mass of hair, then to the sapphire collar, which he seemed quite pleased to see was back on her neck. His gaze finally rested on her face, and there it seemed to draw out every detail of the past two days. When she raised her eyes to meet his own, they spoke of sorrow and repentance, of hope and joy. But she didn't know if he saw any of this, and her mind became filled with doubt.

"Ferringer is here for you, Kayleigh," Straught said behind them. "But I think you have some rather telling news, don't you, love?" Straught looked pointedly at her.

She slowly wiped the back of her hand across her brow. Now was the time to play Judas. She spoke numbly. "He's right, St. Bride. Now that we've the jewels, I'll be going with Erath back to Scotland."

St. Bride smiled softly. "Ah, so you lied when you told me you loved me?"

"No," she whispered. Then, seeing Straught's expression, she quelled any further rebellion. This was what Straught had told her to do, and she would comply. All she wanted was to keep St. Bride safe, even if it cost her her own life to do it. She hated having St. Bride think the worst of her. She wished he knew about her cousin—and that she despised Erath Straught with her whole being and therefore what she was leading him to believe could not possibly be true. But she kept her mouth closed and gave no more denials.

"Come along, Kayleigh. We must get back to Belle Chasse." St. Bride stood before her, his strong hand out in offering.

"No—no," she said breathlessly. He didn't believe her!
He still believed she loved him! But would it cost them both
their lives? "You must leave without me. Leave, I say. All—
is—settled." She choked down a sob. He had to go! She
wouldn't be able to stand much more of this.

"She told you to leave, Ferringer. Do it. We must be on
the ship by midnight." Straught stepped between them.

"You're not taking her with you." St. Bride easily stepped
around him and brought Kayleigh to his side.

"I am taking her, by God! After all I've been through,
she's mine, I say!" Suddenly, Kayleigh found herself grabbed
by the neck. Taking a knife from the waist of his breeches,
Straught held it to her delicate throat while he forced her
back to the corner. He then reached into Quinn's commode.
Behind several silver bowls he found a small vial. He opened
it with a flick of his thumb and forced half of it between
Kayleigh's lips before she could spit it out.

"Go on, both of you!" Straught shouted to St. Bride and
Laban. "Get back and leave us, or I'll poison her before your
eyes!"

Both men paused. St. Bride's eyes darkened with fury.
"You dare threaten her life in front of me?" he hissed.

"I dare!" Straught watched as St. Bride removed his pistol
from the waist of his breeches. He chuckled and said, "Pull
the trigger, Ferringer! You'll shoot your lover before you'll
ever shoot me! Should you nick me, this will all be down
her throat before I die, I promise you!"

St. Bride hesitated.

"My love, take him! I shan't fall prey to his laudanum!"
Kayleigh exclaimed.

"Quiet!" Roughly, Straught snapped her back into his
wretched embrace. He got several more drops between her
lips in their struggle.

Undaunted, she whispered, "Go ahead, Erath, kill me.
Empty that vial into my mouth or slit my throat. Do it, I say!
Then St. Bride can take his revenge, for I've had enough."

She glared at him defiantly. But just when Straught was ready to do the job, she reached out and slid the figure of Harlequin and Columbine off of Quinn's commode. It shattered, with Harlequin clinging tenaciously to his ruined lover.

With the distraction, St. Bride suddenly lunged for the vial. In a lightning flash the knife was away from her throat, and Kayleigh was flung into the doorway. She landed in Laban's embrace as St. Bride violently struggled with Straught. As he received the onslaught, Straught grunted with surprise, taken completely off guard.

"Dhé! Stop!'' she cried as she watched both men struggle to control the knife. She stumbled forward to help St. Bride, but Laban's steel-wrought embrace held her back and forced her to merely watch the men tumble back and forth. Sometimes St. Bride almost got the upper hand, and sometimes her cousin.

Straught was the smaller of the two, but he was well built and muscular. He held off St. Bride for as long as he could, but it was not long enough. Kayleigh almost fainted with fear when the knife became lost between the bodies of the two fighting men, but her relief was inexpressible when she saw St. Bride fling the weapon across the rough floorboards. Then he bashed her cousin soundly across the jaw.

"You're going to give me the satisfaction of seeing you die for what you've done!" He drew Straught to his feet like a puppet. "I'll see you hang, by God—now I will truly see you hang for the life you've led!"

"I didn't kill Mary!" Straught screamed.

"It's not for Mary now! It's for her!" St. Bride brought Straught before Kayleigh. He snarled, "Look at her, you bastard! Look at her ankles! Look at her hands! Look at the scars you left upon her by forcing her from her home and onto the streets!"

In her confusion, Kayleigh could only watch what was happening. As if in a dream, she began to realize that somehow

St. Bride had found out about her and that he believed her
now.

"How can you know all this? She didn't tell you!" Straught
hissed.

"Kayleigh told me everything—but it's only now that I
understand." St. Bride pushed her cousin closer to her. "Look
deep into her eyes. See the sorrow you put there?" When
Straught forced his gaze away, St. Bride knocked his head
forward again. "Look closely, I say! See the sadness? That
terrible aching sadness in the depths of her eyes? I've tried
to remove it by every means that I know of, and I cannot.
You must pay for that, vermin. I just want you to understand
why." With that, St. Bride lashed out his final accusation,
growling, "You killed her sister, Straught. You murdered a
young girl in cold blood. Kayleigh will attest to that before
the hangman!"

"No! The hangman will never get me!" Stunning St. Bride
with a fierce blow to the head, Straught lunged for freedom.
But St. Bride quickly regained control. He took up his pistol,
aimed it at Straught, and forced him to stand motionless.

"How much will the captain want to take this cur back to
England? Quite a lot, I'll wager." He grinned at Laban, and
his eyes softened when he looked at Kayleigh. "Aye, but we
can afford it! Whatever his price!"

"The hangman will never get me, Ferringer," Straught
stated. Then he calmly turned around and presented his back.
"Go ahead, execute me now. Shoot me as I stand here."

St. Bride paused, and that seemed to be what Straught was
waiting for. Her cousin suddenly laughed.

"You can't, can you? Oh, no!" Straught spat. "Not an
honor-bound nobleman like you! That's your downfall, Ferringer! You have to either let me go or face the dishonorable
task of shooting me in the back. And since you won't shoot
me in the back, I suppose I shall be leaving."

Straught inched across the room. He kept his back to St.
Bride and the pistol at all times. Kayleigh had never seen

Straught look so self-assured. His eyes positively sparkled with self-confidence.

"You need to be put out of your misery, Straught. But I'm not the one to do it. Don't challenge me so." St. Bride loudly cocked the pistol. He looked disturbed as if the task before him were distasteful. But seeing the determination on his face, Kayleigh knew he would do it rather than let Straught go. Her cousin was sorely underestimating him.

"Go ahead, my great duke! Take your best shot at an unarmed man!" Straught chuckled and slid to the doorway out of reach of Laban.

"You won't leave this room alive, Straught!" St. Bride warned.

"Oh, no? All I have to do is walk!"

"But, Straught! You would leave your jewels? The only thing that will keep you alive out there? The only thing you have left to live for?" St. Bride shoved the vermilion bag toward the threshold with his foot.

Straught had always been controlled by his greed. He automatically turned to retrieve the bag. St. Bride gave him a warning glance that said, "Don't move," and a look passed between the two men like devil meeting exorcist. Heedless, Straught gathered the purse. Then he swung it at St. Bride in an attempt to flee out the door.

It was a fatal error. St. Bride dodged the assault of the swinging bag of coins, then did the only thing that would keep Straught in the cabin. He fired and hit Straught neatly between the eyes. The blast sent Straught's body against the far wall. And it landed there, slumped beneath a shower of jewels.

Chapter Thirty-two

Midnight on the quay, and not even the torchères of the Place d'Armes pierced the blackness of the Mississippi. Beyond, the colony of New Orleans was already engulfed in another humid night of pagan excesses, but along the quay all was silent. Only the sloshing of the river cut through the heavy night air, and the harsh, endearing command that seemed to echo along its banks.

"Walk."

"Oh . . . but St. Bride . . . how I must sleep . . . I must sleep!" Kayleigh pleaded with him. "You must tell me all about how you came to be here. But now . . . I must sleep!" she begged.

"Nay, I'll not have you succumb to Straught's vile potion." St. Bride's arm went more tightly around her waist. He pulled her limp body to him; then, when she was sure he was going to kiss her again, he merely bedeviled her once more by saying, "Walk."

"Only if you say the words again. . . ." Her head nodded forward, but he pulled it up and rested it upon his chest.

"And which words do you want to hear again? The ones that ask you to be my duchess, or the ones that tell you how much I love you?"

Her lips turned up, forming a soft, almost innocent grin. "I want to hear all of them, *mo chridhe* . . . but mostly the latter . . . for I should like to hear those all the days of my life." She sighed and slumped into St. Bride's arms. How secure they felt! How sure and trustworthy! All she wanted to do was curl up into them and sleep off the laudanum. She wanted to awaken from the fog she was in and find out that her dreams had come true and that she was not imagining it.

"Ah, I do love you, my dark angel," he whispered against her hair. Spoken in his harsh masculine voice, the words were poignantly tender by contrast. Hearing them, she lifted her face to his.

"And . . . I . . . love . . . you." A smile touched her lips before he kissed them. It was a magic kiss, an enchanting kiss, at once heady and sobering. She clutched him to her, anxious to feel his every muscle and sinew. With him, she lost the ability to be on her own. But this did not frighten her; rather, she delighted in it, for she knew that St. Bride would take care of her. She no longer had to survive on her own. Now she would finally be able to live—with him by her side.

Their kiss deepened, and she felt his tongue slide into her mouth. A shiver that had nothing to do with a chill ran down her spine, and her hands ran down his chest. How she needed him! she thought. She needed his steadfastness, his strength. And he gave them to her: he held her close, he left her breathless. When he was finished, Kayleigh laughed and cried in one joyous gasp.

"Oh, St. Bride, how did you ever know I loved you? I've been so wicked, I can't understand why you just didn' abandon me to my cousin Eráth."

"Laban told me not to," he said, smiling softly.

"Laban? No—not Laban . . . !" she exclaimed drowsily.

He laughed. "Ah, you may find Laban has had a change of heart about you, love. In fact, I truly expect you two to become thicker than thieves in the years to come." He paused then let out a chuckle when her head lolled to his chest once more. "I've killed two men for you, wench," he proclaimed. "No doubt I shall burn in the fires of hell forever. You could at least stay awake to see that my time here on earth is worth that cost!" He gave her a sound whack on her behind and forced her to walk once more.

"I shall burn in hell with you, St. Bride. If heaven is without you, then it is no place for me," she vowed as they slowly made their way back to the docks.

"And what if you really are an angel in disguise and your place is beyond the Pearly Gates? What then?" He looked down at her, and his eyes took on a strange glint.

"Och," she said, trying to hide a sly smile, "then I shall have to do something wicked indeed to make sure that never happens. Have you any ideas?"

St. Bride released a broad grin. "Some" was all he said.

EPILOGUE

What Heaven-entreated heart is this,
Stands trembling at the gate of bliss?

Richard Crashaw
"To the Countess of Denbigh"

The Moray Firth Road was an icy ribbon that wound through the snow-dusted Highland peaks until it ended at Mhor. A ducal-crested carriage made its way cautiously up the heights, its horses stumbling on rocks and packed snow. But the carriage moved on, determined to get to its destination. And when the vehicle creaked to a stop in front of the castle, the carriage door was flung open and the duke disembarked, only to turn and help his duchess descend.

She was home. It had taken almost two years to get here, but now she was finally home. The thought reverberated through Kayleigh's mind with every step to the drawbridge. Anticipation built in her breast as she walked closer and her eyes filled with unshed tears.

Before her, Mhor Castle loomed dark and foreboding in the daylight brilliance of the snow. An abandoned fortress, but she saw only her home. She ran ahead of St. Bride. Her boots crunched on the glazed snow of the courtyard, and she feasted her eyes on the familiar sight of Mhor while St. Bride gave instructions to the carriage driver. She could hardly contain the emotion in her breast when he caught up with her and heaved open the carved, blackened door to the great hall.

Everything was as it had been, yet nothing was the same. A tremor of grief swept through her as she stepped reverently into the hall. Bittersweet memories flooded back as she took in the claymores, battle-axes, and broadswords still mounted along the granite walls beneath the arching Gothic windows. The medieval gold tapestries still hung over the great fireplaces at each end, and even the *banque kas,* with its thick spiral-turned pillars, still brooded in one corner.

Yet everything was gray. Dust was everywhere. Under Straught's supervision, there had been no servants to shake the tapestries, beeswax the *kas,* or shine the armaments. Months of dust had settled like a shroud over the hall, and Kayleigh could hardly bear to see it.

Impulsively, she ran over to the *banque kas* and threw open the door. She was saddened to see that no ugly little troll was living in there after all—but then, none ever had. It had only been in her imagination, and so terribly long ago. She thought of Morna and brushed away a tear.

"Was something valuable once in there, love?" Her husband came up to her and enfolded her in his arms. His chest met with her back; his lips brushed her hair.

"No, nothing of monetary value. I expect all those things Straught sold." She quietly closed the cupboard's doors and turned to him.

"I'll buy them back," he promised.

"I have what I want. I have you, I have Mhor, I have my memories. Straught wasn't able to take those away."

"Come, I'll build a fire." St. Bride held out his hand.

When the hall's fireplace blazed, taking the chill from the air, St. Bride sat down with Kayleigh on a bear rug he'd brought from the carriage. They were silent for a long time, each staring into the flames engrossed with their own thoughts. Kayleigh was the first to speak.

"Thank you for bringing me here, St. Bride," she said quietly. "I've wanted to come back every day I was gone."

"It's a sad homecoming. I didn't realize Straught had

neglected the castle so.'' He pulled her between his thighs and placed his hands on her stays. Then he leaned her into his chest.

''No, it's not sad at all. I'm back at Mhor. The ordeal is over.''

''Yes. It's over, dark love.''

''I want to stay here forever.'' She closed her eyes and sighed.

''The child should be born at Scion, Kayleigh. But I promise I shall have servants come here immediately, and we'll come up to Mhor every summer.'' St. Bride rubbed her thickening waist, and his fingers toyed with the ridges of her stays. Looking at them, he added, ''It's the last days for these, love.''

''Mmm, I do seem to be growing out of my stays earlier than most.'' She took a deep breath and said, ''But then, I suppose with two, that's to be expected.''

''Two?''

''Yes, we're going to have twins.'' She opened one eye and peeked at him.

''And what kind of witchcraft have you been practicing that would tell you that?'' he asked with mock sternness.

''I'm no witch!'' she exclaimed. ''But I think Scion may have one. You see, St. Bride, I've discovered an old woman who lives near the Park. I saw her thatched cottage once when I was taking one of my walks. She invited me inside and made me drink some tea, then she looked at the bottom of the cup. She said I was to have twins, both girls. But after that she would tell me no more.''

''And where was this cottage, Kayleigh?'' he asked, indulging her.

''It's on the east side of Scion Park, near where the hawthorns grow.''

''But there is no cottage there, love.'' Gone was the light tone to St. Bride's voice. He seemed serious now indeed.

''But St. Bride, it *is* there.'' Her blue eyes fairly danced with amusement. "I went into it, I tell you. I saw the old woman. Surely you know what I'm speaking of, for you were born at Scion. No one knows it better than you!"

"But there is no cottage near the hawthorns, Kayleigh. Nor has there ever been one during my lifetime." He studied her, then said, "I'll not have you take any more walks without me. Not even in the Park. There's no telling what kind of mischief you can get into."

"Och, there was a cottage there, St. Bride. It's not mischief. When we return, I'll show you."

"Yes, well, I'm afraid what's been said of you is true."

"And what's that?" she asked playfully.

"Look and see." St. Bride tossed a heavy bag into her lap. He had placed it beneath the seat in the carriage before they left the Mhor village, and she'd meant to ask him about it, but the babies and the trip had made her sleepy, and she'd forgotten about it.

"What is this, St. Bride?"

"Open it and see."

Very carefully, she reached her hand into the silk bag and met with a familiar object. Quickly, she pulled it out. In amazement she held her box in her hands. A flood of bitter-sweet memories came back to her "Oh, thank you, my love! Where did you find it?" she whispered.

"I had my men scout around. They found the captain of the *Deepwater* easily enough, but we had to buy it back from his buyer. An ancient earl living in Glasgow, he was. And quite taken with you. He wouldn't hear of selling it until I told him I was your husband. He then gave it as a wedding gift to the bride." St. Bride urged, "But there's more in the purse. Look further."

She shook the bag and emptied it onto her brocaded skirts.

The breath caught in her throat. She stared down at the object as if she were seeing a ghost. It was Morna's box. Her hand shook as she reached out for it.

"How—how on earth did you find it?"

"I found it in London. No doubt Straught rid himself of it as soon as he pried the jewels off. I hired several men to put advertisements in the London journals stating that I would pay any price for the box. It arrived only a week before we left for Scotland."

"Oh, St. Bride—" She couldn't finish. She looked down at the box, and her eyes once more filled with tears. She had so many feelings tied up in the little object that lay in her lap, she could hardly touch it. But in the end she did. She flipped open the box and looked at her sister's portrait on the lid. There she was as a young girl, fair-haired and naughty, mischief in every sweet curve of her young face. Below she found Morna's name and her inscription.

She placed her box next to her sister's. The difference between them was shocking. One was battered and chipped, and the other was vibrant with garlands of sapphires and diamonds encrusting its rim. Below the portrait of the angelic blond were the words *Morna—The Beloved.* And below the portrait of her raven-haired twin were the words *Kayleigh— The Bewitched.*

"Its true, you know," St. Bride whispered.

"Nay, I don't believe in such things."

"No, it is true. Straught believed it, and I knew it the day I met you. The very moment I looked into your beautiful, luminous eyes, Kayleigh, I knew it to be so."

"Och, St. Bride, you should be a Highlander for all your superstitions." She laughed.

"Does it please you, my love?"

"Very much." She lifted her delicate face to his. Need washed over her like a wave, and she was grateful to find that he felt the same way. He laid her back gently on the bear rug and kissed her with a ravenous, building passion.

"We've only tonight," he whispered. "Tomorrow we return to England. I can give you only one night at Mhor until after the babies are born."

"This is my home, St. Bride. I want to welcome you to

it.'' Kayleigh gazed up at him. The firelight flickered in his eyes, and something else too. She smiled and pulled at his shirt.

''You will not catch a chill?'' he asked, hesitant because of her condition.

''Nay, you will keep me warm.'' Her hand slipped through his shirt, and she parted it. Brazenly, she lifted her head and kissed his chest, letting her tongue ride down to his half-clothed torso. He smiled like winter, fresh and crisp, but there was another scent, too, one that underrode the other. That one was like summer, warm and exotic. She wanted it desperately.

''Will that be enough?'' he asked, his harsh voice softening.

''Everything you've given me has been enough, my love.'' Breathless, Kayleigh looked at her husband. Her feelings for him seemed to overflow the bounds of her body. Words were too limiting to express them fully. Touch was the only way to communicate when she felt like this, so she pulled St. Bride down upon her and kissed him with soul-searing passion.

''My wicked enchantress, do you love me?'' he asked when the kiss was over.

''With all my heart,'' she replied huskily.

And it was true. He had given her a home and soon a family. He had given her all her heart had ever desired. And more than that, he had given her back herself. She released a joyous sigh.

She was Kayleigh again.